oks like
Kenya Taylor."

"Man, if that's Kenya, why don't you want to say hello to her?"
"Let's see. Because she hates me?" Maurice replied.
"You might be right about that," James said, then laughed.
"Still, you should say hello. Look, she's coming this way."

Kenya took an empty seat beside Maurice, but she didn't
look at him as she unwrapped her sarong and spread it across
the pool chair. She dropped her bag on the side of the chair away
from Maurice and pulled out a bottle of sunscreen.

Maurice couldn't tear his eyes away from her as she smoothed
the lotion on her skin. She was Kenya, older, sexier, and right
beside him. He wanted to reach out and touch her and make sure
she was real. Maybe this was his chance to make things right
with her.

Without turning her head, she said, "Sir, please stop ogling
me. I'm sure there is something much more interesting to look
at than me."

Her voice was the same, smooth like honey, thick like molasses, and cool like an unexpected breeze.

"Kenya Taylor."

She turned toward him as if she knew who he was. Snatching
her sunglasses off, Kenya sat up in the chair and focused her gaze
on him, the color draining from her face as if she'd seen a ghost.

"I don't believe this. This is unbelievable," she said, then
began to gather her things.

Maurice rose to his feet and blocked her from leaving. "I
can't believe we just ran into each other like this."

Standing toe to toe with him, Kenya hauled off and slapped
him. The echo of her blow caused everyone in close proximity
to them to look up at them. Maurice held his cheek as it stung.

"Ouch. I guess I deserved that," he said.

Kenya turned on her heels and stomped away.

Also by Cheris Hodges

Just Can't Get Enough

Let's Get It On

CHERIS HODGES

Kensington Publishing Corp.

http://www.kensingtonbooks.com

DAFINA BOOKS are published by

Kensington Publishing Corp.
850 Third Avenue
New York, NY 10022

All Kensington Titles, Imprints, and Distributed Lines are available at special quantity discounts for bulk purchases for sales promotions, premiums, fund-raising, and educational or institutional use. Special book excerpts or customized printings can also be created to fit specific needs. For details, write or phone the office of the Kensington special sales manager: Kensington Publishing Corp., 850 Third Avenue, New York, NY 10022, attn: Special Sales Department, Phone: 1-800-221-2647.

Dafina and the Dafina logo Reg. U.S. Pat. & TM Off.

ISBN-13: 978-0-7582-1976-3
ISBN-10: 0-7582-1976-8

First mass market printing: August 2008

10 9 8 7 6 5 4 3 2 1

Printed in the United States of America

To my sister, Adrienne Hodges-Dease,
Thank you for (mostly) always picking up the phone and
listening to my story ideas
To my parents, Freddie and Doris Hodges,
Thank you for always fostering my love of
reading and writing
And last but certainly not least, to the reader
with this book in her (or his) hands,
Thank you for allowing me into your world

Acknowledgments

To my agent, Sha-Shana Crichton, thanks for having the same enthusiasm about my projects as I do. You're awesome, and I do listen.

To my editor, Selena James, thank you for helping me craft a better and more compelling story.

To the SBS Book Club; Sistah Friend's Book Club; the PWOC Book Club; Jaz Vincent, owner of Real Eyes Book Store; Amesia Brewton, Jewel Pendergrass, Yolanda Cuttino and the Sistah's Unlimited Book Club; the Johnson C. Smith University Alumni Association and the Upsilon Sigma Omega Chapter of Alpha Kappa Alpha Sorority, Inc., thank you doesn't seem strong enough to show my gratitude for your support over the years.

To my friends and family who listen to me go on and on about plots and ideas; Beverly McDuffie; Erica Singleton; Erin Quick; Lauren Kendall; the editorial staff at the *Charlotte Post,* especially Herb White and C. Jemal Horton, who listened to me talk about a romance novel at a football game. You guys rock!

Chapter 1

Nine years ago:
Johnson C. Smith University, Charlotte, North Carolina

Kenya Taylor didn't like surprises, yet she was in for a big one as she walked across the lush green campus of Johnson C. Smith University. Despite the fact that it was late October, the sun beamed brightly, and the temperature had soared to around seventy degrees. She was tempted to pull off her soft leather jacket. But knowing her luck, it would be thirty-five degrees tomorrow, and then she'd be sick with the flu.

With her work-study check in her pocket and another A plus in her political science class, Kenya was ready to celebrate with her boyfriend, Maurice Goings. The high-school sweethearts had come to college together and beat the odds of most couples like them. They were still together. Most of the others had broken up a few months after arriving on campus. Not Maurice and Kenya.

At least, not yet.

She approached his dorm room, with a smile on her lips. Thoughts of the night they'd spent together simply holding each other made her happy, though moments like that were beginning to happen less frequently. She understood he had other things to do and didn't make a big fuss about it.

Maurice was a star football player, and every girl on campus wanted him, but Kenya trusted him and was confident that their love could withstand any temptation. Without knocking, as she'd done on several other occasions, Kenya walked into his dorm room.

"Baby," she said. Then the rest of her words froze in her mouth. The sight before her was indescribable. Maurice wasn't doing this to her. This was a nightmare.

"Oh, yeah, big daddy," Lauryn Michaels screamed as she rode Maurice as if he were a prized stallion.

Grasping the wall, Kenya swallowed the bitter bile rushing up her throat and settling in her mouth. Tears threatened to fall from her eyes. All she wanted to do was slip out of the room and forget what she'd seen. Holding on to the edge of the wall, she spun around to leave the room, but as she made her exit, she knocked over a stack of Maurice's books. The couple turned and looked toward the door. As tempted as she was to pounce on them, she didn't.

"How could you do this to me?" she said, shaking her head.

Maurice and Lauryn untangled their bodies, and he rose from the bed, stumbling to cover his nakedness.

"I didn't mean for you to find out like this, Kenya," he said as he crossed over to her. Kenya shrank away from him as he reached out to touch her arm.

"You, you . . ." Words failed Kenya as she looked at the smirk on Lauryn's face. "She doesn't care about you! She doesn't even know you! It's funny, now that you have NFL scouts looking at you, every skank on campus wants to latch on to you, and you're too blind to even see it."

Maurice ran his hand over his face. "Kenya, I don't

know how to tell you this, but I love Lauryn, and I want to be with her. I'm glad it's out in the open, because this sneaking around hasn't been fair to you, me, or her."

"You love her? How can you even . . ." With closed fists, Kenya pounded his sculpted chest, hoping to reach his heart and break it as he'd broken hers.

"Don't do this," he said as he grabbed her wrists. "You're making a fool of yourself. People grow apart, babe, and that's what happened with us. What we had was high school and—"

"He needed a real woman, not a little, fat girl," Lauryn called out from the bed. "He has me, and you're dismissed."

Maurice turned to Lauryn. "Stay out of this," he said.

Kenya snatched away from him. "You know what? You two can have each other. I hope you're happy with your choice, Mo."

Storming out of the room, Kenya refused to give either of them the satisfaction of seeing her tears. She'd only loved Maurice Goings since she was a freshman in high school. She'd only helped him study for exams that he had to pass so that he would be eligible to play for the Golden Bulls' football team. She'd only given him her heart and her virginity, and all she'd gotten in return was the ultimate betrayal.

Sorrow, anger, hurt, and disappointment flowed through her body like the blood in her veins. *Grown apart? Had we grown apart when I wrote your damned research paper? Had we grown apart when I stayed up all night, helping you grasp the concepts of calculus?* she thought bitterly.

Kenya rushed into her dorm room and flung herself across the bed. Her roommate and best friend, Imani, looked up from her computer.

"What's wrong, *chica?*" Imani asked, noticing her friend's tears.

"Nothing."

"What are you crying about? Failed a quiz?" She laughed, then returned to typing, expecting a quirky comeback from her roommate.

"Leave me alone." Kenya buried her face in her pillow.

Rising to her feet, Imani crossed over to her friend and sat on the edge of the bed. "Kenya, all jokes aside, what's going on? Did something serious happen?"

Kenya focused her teary-eyed gaze on Imani. "Remember when we met freshman year and I told you my boyfriend and I came here together and that we were so in love? I said that we'd probably walk down the aisle to get our degrees and then get married."

Imani nodded. "And I said it wouldn't last past second semester, and look, we're about to graduate, and you two are still together. That wedding is probably going to happen soon."

Kenya shook her head. "Never. It's not going to happen." Her voice was barely above a whisper.

"What?"

Sniffing and wiping her eyes with the back of her hand, Kenya exhaled loudly. "Maurice and I broke up because he's sticking it to that slut Lauryn Michaels."

Imani shook her head and pulled Kenya into a sisterly embrace. "Girl, forget him. You can do so much better than a low-down cheating dog. And if he's sleeping with Lauryn, he'll be in the clinic soon. There aren't too many guys on campus who haven't had the pleasure of her company. If he has a car and money to spend, you can guess who was in love with him."

"But I still love Mo. It's not like I can turn off what I feel for him because he was in bed with *her*. I wish it worked that way. And as wrong as it is, I want to rip the weave right out of that girl's head. Instead, I just stood there, fighting back the tears."

Imani raised her eyebrow, because Kenya wasn't violent. She was always the one who helped her avoid conflict. "Don't do anything crazy. The last thing you need is to get suspended from school at this late juncture."

Kenya groaned loudly. "Everybody's going to know. You know how this campus is. This story is going to grow into something else before it's all said and done."

Imani nodded. "You two did have celebrity status. You were like Will and Jada, Denzel and Pauletta, Russell Simmons and Kimora Lee."

Kenya glared at her. "Aren't you supposed to be comforting me?"

"Hey, I'm just being honest. If the rumors about Lauryn are true, this is going to be all over campus before dinner. She has a mouth like a motor, and if she can make herself look good, then she's going to spread the rumor. You can do better than Maurice, though. He walks around like his crap doesn't stink. Forget him."

Kenya turned away from her friend. "I wish it were that easy."

Imani shook her head and returned to her computer. "It's a shame he doesn't feel the same way. Seems like he's already forgotten you."

Hugging her pillow and leaning against the wall, Kenya closed her eyes and cried silently.

Maurice sat on the edge of his bed, his head buried in his hands and his heart feeling as heavy as a lead brick. Though he'd wanted to end things with Kenya, he hadn't wanted to hurt her. Not after all she'd done for him. Before anything had ever happened romantically between them, Kenya had been his friend. Now she hated him; her eyes had told him that when she'd left the room. She had every right to, though.

"Baby," Lauryn said as she wrapped herself around his torso, "you can't be sitting her thinking about *her* when I'm willing and waiting to do anything you want. I do believe we were in the middle of something before we were so rudely interrupted."

He pushed her away. "I didn't want things to turn out this way," Maurice said, rising to his feet and fishing his boxers out of their pile of discarded clothing. "I've got to find her and make things right."

Lauryn frowned, then stood. "I know she was special to you, but what about me?" She ran her hand down the length of her sculpted body. Her years of cheerleading had given her a figure that was usually reserved for exotic dancers and adult entertainers. She had no qualms about using her perky breasts, small waist, and round bottom to get what she wanted. Right now, she wanted to keep Maurice in this room, and not because she desired him or even wanted to have sex with him. She just wanted to make sure she was in control of him.

So what if he and Kenya had grown up together and were high school sweethearts? This was college, and she wanted Maurice for herself. Why wouldn't any woman want him? He was the star of the Johnson C. Smith football team, and he had NFL written all over his awesome body.

Lauryn wouldn't call herself a gold digger, but she knew a golden opportunity when she saw one. Maurice was her ticket to the good life, and chubby Kenya wasn't going to stand in her way. She couldn't have planned the scene that had happened between them any better herself. Knowing Kenya the way she did, Lauryn knew there was no way she'd take Maurice back. Kenya was one of those "moral majority" chicks or a missionary girl, as Lauryn called it.

Obviously, Kenya hadn't been taking care of home, and that was why it had been so easy to entice Maurice and make him hers. When the NFL money started rolling in, she was going to the one on the receiving end of it, not Kenya.

She had to stop him from going to find Kenya. Leaping into action, Lauryn grabbed Maurice and pushed him down on the bed. Next, she took his manhood into her mouth and tried to suck him until all thoughts of Kenya disappeared from his mind. At first, he tried to push her away, but it didn't take long for Maurice to succumb to the pleasure of her oral sex.

Kenya who? she thought as Maurice moaned in pleasure.

The next morning, Kenya wanted to skip class, but she'd worked too hard to let Maurice and his wayward penis threaten her future.

However, the moment she walked out of her dormitory, she realized that the story of her twisted triangle had not only spread across campus, but it had a life of its own. When she walked by a group of cheerleaders, she heard one of them whisper, "I heard she was in the hospital last night because she slit her wrists."

Ignore them, she thought as she trudged up the hill.

As she passed a group of football players, guys that she knew because of Maurice, she could see laughter in their eyes.

"Damn," one of them called out. "You can cry on my shoulder, boo."

Fighting the urge to flipping him the bird, Kenya continued on and prayed she could make it to the communication arts building without hearing anything else. But as soon as she opened the door to the building, Yvette Mason, the editor of the student paper, cornered her.

"Kenya, my God! I didn't expect to see you today. Are you all right? Will you be suspended? You're the best writer that we have on staff, and we have deadlines coming up. Have you turned in your articles?"

Kenya held her hand up. "What the hell are you talking about?"

Yvette looked around as if she was making sure there were no eavesdroppers around. "Rumor has it that you pulled a knife of Lauryn Michaels after you caught her and Maurice in bed together."

"Get out of my face with that nonsense," Kenya snapped.

"Kenya, I don't want to get all up in your business, but I have a responsibility to the paper, and so do you. If you're going to be suspended or even arrested, we have to get your articles."

Exhaling loudly, Kenya took two steps closer to Yvette. "I didn't pull a knife on anyone, I didn't try to kill myself, and I don't give a damn about Lauryn or Maurice. Now, I'm going to class. As far as my articles go, you'll have them when they are due."

As Kenya turned on her heels to head down to the basement, she saw Maurice walking into the building. She wanted to slap him, push him down the stairs, or break his neck, anything to make him feel the pain that she was feeling inside.

"Kenya, I-I . . ."

"Save it," she barked. "I have nothing to say to you."

"We need to talk."

"Go to hell," she replied as she descended the stairs.

Maurice ran after her and grabbed her arm as she reached the bottom of the stairs. "I didn't want things to go down like this. Can we still be friends?"

"Sure," she said sarcastically. "As soon as hell freezes over, you and I will be the best of friends. Maurice, I hope she gives you a disease and your man parts shrivel up and fall off. Don't ever speak to me again. And tell your whore that if she doesn't stop spreading rumors about me, I'm going to turn her fiction into reality."

Kenya pushed through the double doors leading to the journalism classrooms and promised herself that she wouldn't cry, despite the hot tears stinging her eyes.

When she walked into the classroom, all of the chatter stopped, and eighteen pairs of eyes focused on her. Kenya ran her hand over her face and stared them all down.

This has got to stop, she thought as some people began whispering.

"Listen up, people," she yelled. "I know you've been discussing my personal life. I just have one thing to say. Get your own damned lives. I didn't cut anybody, I didn't cut myself, and I'm sick of the rumors. My boyfriend and I broke up. That's it."

Kenya didn't give anyone time to respond before she ran out of the classroom. The main reason she'd decided to attend JCSU, because it was such a small school, was going to be the same reason she'd have to leave. She wasn't going to be the next Eboni.

Kenya remembered when Eboni Sanders, a popular cheerleader, passed out at a basketball game, and rumors swirled for a year about what had caused her to faint. She'd been rumored to be on drugs, she'd been rumored to be pregnant, and she'd been rumored to have HIV.

As it turned out, she was diabetic, and her blood sugar had been extremely high that day. But the rumors had dogged her until the day she dropped out of school. Kenya wasn't about to allow that to happen to her. Her last few months of college weren't going to be spent dodging rumors and Maurice.

While heading back to her dorm room, Kenya came

face to face with Lauryn and her crew. The smirk on Lauryn's face spoke volumes. She looked as if she'd beaten Kenya. And in a sense, she had. But if Maurice was the prize, Kenya hoped it would rust.

"Hey, Kenya," Lauryn said. "Listen, I'm so sorry about what happened yesterday. But that's life. Men leave women. Don't let it consume you, and please don't try to kill yourself."

"Lauryn, go straight to hell, and take Maurice with you. You guys deserve each other," Kenya replied, then shoved Lauryn as she blew past her. She didn't stick around to watch Lauryn tumble down the hill, but from the laughter that rose from the football players watching them, she knew it was a funny sight. But she didn't take any pleasure in her irrational act. She was acting the way everyone had rumored that she was.

What am I doing? I can't sink to her level, she thought sadly.

When Kenya made it back to her dorm room, she sat down at her computer and logged on to Clark Atlanta University's Web site. She had to laugh as she perused the CAU site. Her mother, Angela, had urged her to go to her alma mater, but Kenya had wanted to attend the same college as her boyfriend.

Mother always knows best, Kenya thought, remembering the conversation she'd had with Angela before applying to Johnson C. Smith.

"Kenya," her mother had said as they looked over college catalogs, "you've always made good decisions, and I want you to choose the college you attend. But following Maurice isn't a good idea."

"Ma, I don't want to go to a school that has an Angela

Taylor Mass Communications scholarship. That's too much pressure to live up to."

Angela had folded her arms across her breasts and had lifted her eyebrows. "No matter where you go, I'm not accepting anything less than a three point zero. I will not hesitate to snatch you out of school and let you work at Wal-Mart if you think you're going to Charlotte to play house with Maurice."

Kenya had frowned and shaken her head. "Ma, I want to get an education. Maurice is going to be playing football, and I'm going to be laying the foundation for my future career as a public-relations executive. I love him, but I'm not a fool. Daddy, please talk to her."

Henry Taylor, who had been reading the newspaper while his wife and daughter argued, had dropped the sports section and had looked at them. "Angela, let the girl make her own decision," he'd said quietly. That was Henry's way, nonconfrontational, until he was pushed. "I just know one thing. This better not be about chasing that knuckleheaded boy.

Kenya had folded her arms across her chest and had shaken her head. "Come on, Daddy. I'm not following Maurice."

"Then explain to me why you want to go to Johns C. Smith," Angela had said.

"Johnson C. Smith," Kenya had corrected. "Well, Charlotte is a growing city, and Smith is a small college, which means less competition for internships and things of that nature. There are a lot of new public-relations companies moving to Charlotte. With all the banks in Charlotte, they are always looking for public-relations folks to tell their stories to the media."

Angela had smiled at her daughter. "Well, I see that you've researched *Johnson* C. Smith and Charlotte. If that's where you want to go to school, then I'll support you."

Kenya had hugged her mother and kissed her on the cheek. "I'm not totally clueless, Ma."

Angela had patted her daughter's shoulder. "I know. Your father and I did a good job."

As Kenya picked up the phone to call her mother, she prayed that Angela had enough clout to get her into CAU without much of a hassle. All she had to do was figure out a good reason for the desire to transfer in her senior year.

"This is Angela," her mother said when she answered the phone.

"Ma, hi," Kenya said.

"Hey, baby. Is everything all right?"

"I can't just call and say hello?"

"Not when you should be in class, and not when I'm at work."

"You're the editor, Ma. You don't get busy until later."

Angela sighed into the phone. "And I know when my daughter has something she wants to ask but is afraid to do so."

"Uh, well, I kinda got into a little trouble."

"Hold on," Angela said.

Kenya heard her mother close the door to her office. She knew this wasn't going to be pretty.

"Kenya Denise Taylor, are you pregnant?"

"No. Ju-just suspended," Kenya said, formulating the lie in her head.

"What! What happened?"

"Uh, I-I got into a fight."

"Kenya, what in the hell is wrong with you? You're a senior about to graduate. Do I need to come up there and talk to the chancellor? I can't believe you did something so stupid as to get into a fight. Tell me that it didn't have anything to do with Maurice."

"Ma, I'm sorry. Okay, I'm not going to lie to you. Maurice and I broke up, and this campus is too small for me to see his face every day, and it was really nasty, and I just want to get away."

For the first time since she'd caught Maurice and Lauryn, Kenya sobbed uncontrollably. She told her mother the entire story about catching Maurice having sex with Lauryn and the rumors.

"You can't run from them, baby," Angela said.

"Ma, you wanted me to go to Clark Atlanta, and now I want to go there. I don't see the problem."

"The problem is, I don't want you to think that you can cut and run when you face some adversity. I know he was your first love, but you will get over it."

"Easy for you to say. You married your first love. Ma, please, I can't stay here and be subjected to seeing him with her and hearing all of the rumors. Please, I'll do anything."

"Let me talk to your father, and we'll get back to you tomorrow. Go to class, and ignore all of the talk."

"Yes, ma'am," Kenya said, all the while thinking, *Easier said than done.*

Maurice rushed to the infirmary when he heard that Lauryn was there. He hoped that the reason behind her being there was another rumor. There was no way Kenya would have pushed her down a hill. That wasn't in her nature. Then again, Kenya was mad as hell, and there was no telling what she was capable of.

God, I hope Lauryn isn't hurt and Kenya doesn't get into trouble for this, he thought as he opened the door to the infirmary. Maurice found Lauryn sitting on a bench, with a sling on her arm.

"Mo, Kenya tried to kill me," Lauryn said.

"What happened?" he asked as he sat down beside her.

"That fat sow pushed me down the hill beside the student union."

Maurice pulled her into his arms. "I'll talk to her."

"No, don't. Just ignore her. I'm going to press charges with campus police."

"Don't do that. Kenya is upset about us, and you really can't blame her."

Lauryn pushed away from him. "Hello! I'm your woman now, and my arm was nearly broken."

"You want her to get kicked out of school? Come on, Lauryn. Your arm isn't broken. Just let it go."

"Okay, who do you want? Me or her fat ass?"

"I'm with you, but you don't have to bad-mouth Kenya."

Lauryn pushed her hair back with her unbandaged hand. "Fine, but you'd better keep her away from me."

"Forget about Kenya. Come on. Let me pamper you until I have to go to practice," he said as he scooped her up into his arms.

Maurice couldn't help but wonder if he'd made a mistake letting Kenya go.

Two weeks later, Kenya got the okay from her parents to come home to Atlanta. Though she'd have to start over at Clark Atlanta as a junior, it was well worth it. Watching the romance of Maurice and Lauryn was sickening. And to add insult to injury, Lauryn now had the entire campus believing Kenya was out to get her. She was happy to go home.

The day she packed her things, Maurice showed up at her dorm room. "Kenya?"

"What do you want?" she said, not looking up at him.

"What are you doing?"

"Minding my business."

"Are you leaving school?"

She slammed her clothes into her suitcase, then looked up at him. "Maurice, get away from me. You gave up the right to know what I'm doing when you put that girl on top of you."

"You fought so hard to come to school here, and I don't want you to leave because of me," he said. Maurice timidly stepped inside the room.

"Aren't you just full of yourself," she snapped. "Who cares what you think?"

"I still care about you, Kenya. Are you going back to Atlanta?" What he wanted to do was reach out to her, but the fiery anger in her eyes pushed that thought out of his head.

"Get out. Don't worry about where I'm going. Just know I won't be around you and your little tramp anymore. You win, Maurice. You and Lauryn drove me away. You broke my heart beyond repair, and I'll never forgive you for that. I hate you as much as I loved you. Now, get out of my way before I do something that I will regret. Enjoy, but regret."

"Kenya—"

"Out!" she said. She knew that she was using anger to mask her pain, and though she wanted to hate him, she couldn't and didn't.

"So, this is how it's going to be? We're not even going to try and be friends?"

She took a deep breath, trying to calm herself down. "Friends? Let me put it like this, if you were on fire, I wouldn't spit on you unless I had gasoline in my mouth. You snuck around behind my back to be with her. Would a *friend* do that? Would a *friend* lie to my face over and over again? Hell no, we're not friends, and we never will be again. Now get out of my face."

A wave of sadness washed across his face. "I still have love for you, Kenya, and if you ever need anything . . ."

She picked up a broken shoe and threw it in his direction. Quickly, Maurice ducked out of the way.

"I need you to get out of my room and out of my life!"

Maurice walked away from the door, and Kenya thought that would be the last time she ever saw him.

Chapter 2

Nine years later:
Bank of America Stadium, Charlotte, North Carolina

"And the Carolina Panthers are headed to the NFC championship for the third time in three years," the television announcer exclaimed happily. "We're standing here with first-year Panther Maurice Goings. What an unbelievable game!"

"I was just catching what Jake threw my way. This was a big game, and we all had to step up and make plays if we wanted to win," Maurice said, with a smile. "Lauryn, baby, this is for you. I love you. Marry me."

"Whoa! Championship run and an engagement," said the announcer. "Lauryn, you're a lucky lady. Thanks, Mo."

Maurice ran into the tunnel. After making sure there were no cameras or reporters around, he dropped his head. Hopefully, she was happy now. Maurice had been a standout wide receiver in the NFL long enough to know that he'd just opened the door for his private life to be put underneath a microscope.

"Damn," he muttered as he walked into the locker room.

Defensive lineman and NFL journeyman Walter Homer popped Maurice on the butt with a towel. "Good game, bro!"

"Thanks."

"I can't believe you just went all Ahmad Rashad out there and asked homegirl to marry you."

"Hell, we've been engaged three months. The damned wedding is planned, but you know how women are. They want a damned show."

"Sounds like the beginning of the end for you, man. Your woman takes high maintenance to another level. Send me an invitation to the reception."

Maurice slapped the back of Homer's bald head. "Whatever. You're going to be a groomsman."

"Damn! I was hoping I'd get a pass on that duty. I'm allergic to weddings. Haven't you noticed that I've avoided holy matrimony?"

Before they could continue their conversation, a crush of reporters entered the locker room, shoving tape recorders and microphones in their faces.

Meanwhile, across town, Lauryn and her girlfriends giggled happily as News 14 showed a replay of Maurice's proposal.

"Girl," Vivian Sanders said, "your man loves you."

Lauryn smiled cockily. "Yes, he does, and I have him wrapped around my finger."

Mya Brown looked at Lauryn and shook her head. "You're really going to marry the money, aren't you?"

"Don't do this," Lauryn warned.

"I mean, I know that you love this lifestyle, but you don't love Maurice," Mya said. "He's always been a means to an end for you."

Vivian observed the two of them talk as if she were

watching a tennis match. Just like with tennis, she had no clue as to what was going on.

"Mya, why don't you mind your business? If you can't be happy for me and Mo, then leave," Lauryn hissed.

"Fine," Mya said as she rose to her feet. "Marrying him will be the biggest mistake of your life."

Lauryn glared at her friend as she left.

"Forget her. She's just jealous. How big is the wedding going to be?" Vivian said.

"*SportsCenter* big. I'm thinking three thousand guests, cameras, and all of that. I want to be the black Princess Diana." Lauryn picked up the phone and called Charlotte's most renowned wedding planner so that the media machine could be pushed into high gear.

But deep inside, Lauryn knew that she was going into this marriage for all the wrong reasons and that Mya was right. She didn't love Maurice. Her heart belonged to another, but there was no way Lauryn could leave the plush life that Maurice had provided for her. She loved their penthouse that overlooked uptown Charlotte. She loved the fact that they always got the best seats at the most exclusive restaurants. They never paid to party in Charlotte, Atlanta, New York, or anywhere else they went. She'd grown accustomed to dressing in the hottest fashions and wearing Jimmy Choo shoes and lots of jewelry—diamonds, rubies, and anything else she wanted. Her jewelry box resembled an upscale jewelry store.

This was what she'd wanted all along. That was why she'd hooked up with Maurice nine years ago. But nine years later, she had to wonder if it was worth it.

I don't care what Mya thinks. I'm marrying Maurice, Lauryn thought. *I've worked way too hard for this.*

* * *

Curled up on her sofa in Atlanta, Georgia, Kenya tossed the latest Dr. Phil book across the room, deeming it a waste of time. One day she'd stop wasting her hard-earned money on self-help books. She was fine; it was the rest of the world that had a problem. Why couldn't people just congratulate her for being a successful contract attorney, one who was licensed in four states and who had finished law school at the top of her class in under three years? No, people always wanted to know why she wasn't married, where her boyfriend was, and why she didn't have children. Kenya refused to be defined by a man or motherhood. It didn't help that her mother and father were dropping hints that they'd like a grandchild or two. Just a hazard of being the only child.

She turned the television on and flipped through the channels, looking for something to occupy her mind. Kenya paused when she came to ESPN.

"Carolina Panthers wide receiver Mo Goings isn't just celebrating his team heading to the NFC Championship game. He's also celebrating his engagement to his high-school sweetheart, Lauryn Michaels."

The camera cut to Maurice asking Lauryn to marry him. Kenya snapped the TV off. "High-school sweetheart?" she said to the walls. "Somebody needs to get their facts straight."

In the silence of the night, when Kenya's bed was really cold and lonely, she'd think of Maurice. What would have been if there had never been a Lauryn? Would she have been on the other end of that proposal? After nine years, she'd hoped to be over him, but every man she met, she compared to Maurice, the good, the bad, and the ugly.

When Maurice was drafted by the Dallas Cowboys a few years back, Kenya had wanted to call and congratulate him. Dallas had always been their favorite team. But she hadn't reached out to him. There was no need for him to know that she still cared.

After he was injured during his fourth game of his rookie season, Kenya had wanted to send flowers or a get-well card, but she didn't. Part of her had hoped his career would be over, because she knew that he loved football more than anything else.

She hated it when her mind was filled with "what-ifs." Kenya knew that she couldn't change the past any more than she could predict the future. Maurice was the past, and according to ESPN, his future was with Lauryn. Why did it bother her so much that the sportscaster had called Lauryn Maurice's high-school sweetheart? That was her title, though it didn't amount to a hill of beans. She was the one who had ended up holding on to her love for him while he'd ridden off into the sunset, with Lauryn Michaels by his side.

Instead of sitting in the house and feeling sorry for herself, Kenya called her best friend and old roommate, Imani, who'd just moved to Atlanta with her husband.

"Imani, it's Kenya."

"What's up, girl?" Imani said.

"Do you feel like heading downtown? Let me introduce you to Atlanta."

Imani laughed. "I wish I could, but Roland and I are going to a jazz concert at the Foxy."

"The Fox, you mean. Sounds like fun," Kenya said, trying to mask her disappointment.

"Want to come with? I'm sure Roland wouldn't mind."

"And be a third wheel? I don't think so."

In the background, she could hear Imani's husband, Roland, ask, "Didn't you go to school with Mo Goings?"

Kenya cringed inwardly at the sound of Maurice's name. "I'd better let you go," she said.

"Kenya," Imani said, "you saw *SportsCenter,* didn't you?"

"Girl, please. So what if I did? That was over years ago. I'm just surprised Maurice didn't trade her in."

"You still have feelings for him, don't you? Don't say you don't, because I can hear it in your voice."

"You and your husband had better get going if you want to find parking downtown," Kenya said. "Maybe we can have lunch tomorrow. Oh shoot, I'm in mediation in the morning."

"I can't believe you, Kenya Taylor. You're still in love with Maurice, and you know that he is a lying, dirty, trifling dog."

"I know who and what he is. Just hearing that those two are still together . . . and they called her his high-school sweetheart. It got to me a little bit."

"Babe, ticktock," Kenya heard Roland say.

"I have to go," Imani said. "But I'll call you when I get back."

"Have fun with your man, and don't worry about me," Kenya replied. "I'll be fine."

After hanging up the phone, Kenya picked up the Dr. Phil book again and started reading. Maybe there was something hidden in the pages of the book that could help her get Maurice out of her heart.

Monday morning, Maurice should have been sleeping in, or if he had to be up, he should've been soaking his sore muscles in a whirlpool. Instead, he was sitting in a television studio, with Lauryn on his arm, pretending that he knew what was going on with his wedding plans.

"And Maurice and I knew we'd get married," Lauryn said as she hammed it up for the camera. "It was magic at Johnson C. Smith."

Maurice nodded like a good lapdog.

"Mo, is the wedding going to be a distraction during the playoffs?" the reporter asked.

"No. I love Lauryn, and she understands that right now I have to concentrate on making it to the Super Bowl," replied Maurice. "I'm going to leave the wedding planning in her capable hands."

"Yes," Lauryn said. "I don't want the fans mad at me. Besides, I want my man to be victorious in February."

"When's the wedding going to be?" the reporter asked.

"When else? Valentine's Day," Lauryn said.

Thanks for telling me, Maurice thought as he smiled for the cameras.

When the interview was over, he turned to Lauryn and shook his head.

"What?" she asked.

"Why are we doing this?"

"Doing what? Getting married?"

"Turning it into a media spectacle? A wedding is supposed to be between a man and woman, not a man, a woman, and the media."

Lauryn stroked his cheek. "But you're famous, and I want all of those women to know that you're mine."

Maurice headed out the door, with Lauryn on his heels. "Baby," she said. "Are you mad?"

He turned around and looked at her. She had a look of innocence on her face, and it melted his heart. "Just tired. This is my day off, remember."

She wrapped her arms around his waist. "I know. I'll make it up to you when we get home. I love you."

"Love you, too," he replied, kissing her on the cheek.

As they drove home, Maurice had to question his sanity. Everyone had told him that Lauryn was a gold digger.

He'd heard those sorts of things about her since they were in college.

College. Kenya. How was Kenya? He hadn't talked to her in nine years, and when he went home to Atlanta for Thanksgiving, he'd driven by her parents' house, hoping to catch a glimpse of her. And if he had seen her, what would he have said to her? She wouldn't accept his apology nine years ago. Would she now?

"Maurice! The light is red!" Lauryn shouted, interrupting his thoughts.

"Sorry." He slowed the car so that he wouldn't blow through the light.

"Maybe I need to run you a bath and let you relax while I hang out with Mya for a while."

"If you want to. I'll probably study some film and sleep. Oh, Homer and his girl want us to have dinner with them tonight at Morton's. Cool?"

"All right," she said flatly. "What's this girl's name?"

"I don't know. Just try to be nice."

"That's all I can do. Try," she said as he pulled into driveway of their home.

Moments after entering the house, Maurice headed for the marble spa tub in his master bathroom, and Lauryn grabbed the phone.

"Mya," she said. "We need to talk. Why don't I come over and we have lunch?"

"Don't you have another news show to do?" asked Mya.

"You can't blame me for what I'm doing. Do you know how long Mo and I have been together?"

"But does he know what you're hiding?"

"I'm not hiding anything."

"There's no need for us to meet for lunch, because I'll see you at dinner," Mya revealed.

"Dinner?"

"Yes, I've decided to go after some NFL money, too. It just so happens that he's Mo's best friend."

"Don't do this, Mya."

"I'm just following your lead. You can't have it both ways, do as I say and not as I do."

The dial tone sounded in Lauryn's ear. How could Mya do this? What was she trying to prove by dating Mo's best friend?

"Lauryn," Maurice called from the bathroom, "you want to join me?"

"I have to run to Mya's, but I'll rub your back when I return," she said as she opened the door to leave.

Moments later, Lauryn found herself sitting in front of a moss-covered apartment complex in the historic Southpark community. Thinking back, she realized that the day she and Mya had met in college, everything had changed for her. Mya had opened her eyes to a new world of pleasure, a world of loving a woman. For the last eight years, they'd kept their affair a secret.

One night, while Mya and Lauryn were in their dorm room, Mya had popped in a videotape of two women kissing and making love. Though it was pornography, Lauryn had never seen sex depicted so tenderly and so erotically. It turned her on, and she wasn't sure what to make of her feelings. Turning to Mya, she had said, "What is this?"

Mya had smiled as she muted the volume. "Ever wonder what it would be like to be touched that way?"

"By a woman?"

Mya closed the space between them. "By me."

Before Lauryn could react, Mya had had her in her arms and had kissed her with an intensity that she'd never felt before.

Shaking her head, Lauryn emerged from the car. She had to do something. No longer could she deny what she felt for Mya, but was that enough to give up what she'd built with Maurice? Could she give up that money? Give up what came along with being an NFL wife?

It wasn't as if Mya didn't reap a reward from Lauryn's relationship with Maurice. As she walked up the steps leading to Mya's place, she resolved to end her relationship with Mya. It had gone on too long. Besides, she wasn't gay. Was she?

No, this is over. I'm ending this, and she can do what she wants to with whomever she pleases, Lauryn thought as she pressed the door chime.

Mya opened the door, dressed in a short silk bathrobe. Temporarily, Lauryn was rendered speechless when she saw her. Emerald was definitely her color.

"We-we need to talk," Lauryn said when she found her voice.

Mya raised her sculpted eyebrows. "I knew you were the one at the my door," she said as she stood aside.

Lauryn walked into the living room and ran her hand across the mantel above the fireplace. "I can't do this anymore, and if you want to date Homer, then go right ahead and do it."

"I don't want him, L. I want you. How do you think I feel watching you with Maurice and knowing that in a few months you'll have this lavish wedding? You can't go through with it."

"You're insane."

"And you love me. Admit it."

"I-I . . ."

Mya dropped her robe, revealing her toned and naked body. "You love me, you need me, and you don't want to marry Maurice."

"I'm not gay."

"Really? What are you then? You love sexing me more than being with Mo, your words, not mine."

"I know what I said. I didn't mean it."

"Then why are you here?" Mya inched closer to her. "You could've told me this over the phone, in an e-mail, or on my BlackBerry."

Their lips were inches apart. Mya wrapped her arms around Lauryn's waist, pulling her closer until she could easily devour her lips.

Though Lauryn should've pushed away, she gave into the kiss, allowing Mya to strip her down and kiss every inch of her body until she felt as if she was going to explode.

"Don't marry him," Mya breathed against Lauryn's ear. "We can be together, make a life together."

"No," Lauryn whispered, holding Mya tightly. "I'm going to marry him."

Mya pushed Lauryn away. "You're never going to be happy with him, and I'm not going to be your little secret anymore."

"What are you saying?"

"It's over. You can live this lie if you want to, but I won't do it anymore."

"Mya, I-I . . ."

Stepping back, Mya pointed toward the door. "Eight years, Lauryn, and that's too long for me to play the background like this. You won't let me move on with my life, and you don't want to be a real part of my life. We're not just friends. That line was crossed a long time ago."

Lauryn dropped her head in her hands. "Please don't do this. Don't ask me to choose when I want you both."

"No more. You can't have both. Go on. Walk out the door, if you can."

Lauryn turned to the door and tried not to look back. But once she grasped the doorknob, she turned around and saw Mya in tears. There was no way she could leave.

Chapter 3

"That's it, that's it. The Carolina Panthers win the Super Bowl on a last-second catch by wide receiver Maurice Goings! For the first time in franchise history, the Panthers are world champions," the announcer yelled excitedly.

Kenya walked away from the bar and back to the table with her coworkers. The firm had rented a ballroom in a downtown hotel for a Super Bowl party. Because she was playing office politics, Kenya was pretending to be enjoying herself. But every time she heard Maurice's name or saw a flash of his fiancée on the screen, she wanted to vomit.

Wallace Norman, one of the lawyers in Kenya's department, took a seat beside her.

"Having fun?" he said as he sucked down a beer.

"Oh yeah," she said flatly.

"Didn't you go to school with Mo Goings?"

"So what if I did? Obviously, we didn't keep in touch," she snapped.

"Hey," he replied, throwing his hands up. "Don't bite my head off." He pushed his beer bottle aside and smiled at Kenya.

Kenya rose to her feet. She'd had enough of this crap. "I'll see you Monday."

Wallace stood, cornering her so that she couldn't get away. "You know what you need, Kenya? A good, long—"

"Can you say 'sexual harassment'?"

"Let me finish. A good massage," he said, obviously backpedaling in terms of what he was going to say. "You walk around the office, looking tense and mad all the time. Do you have a man in your life?"

"Get away from me."

"One date? Dinner, movie, and maybe a nightcap."

Kenya looked at Wallace. He was attractive, about six feet tall, muscular, and the color of milk chocolate. But he was ultra-arrogant. The last thing she needed was to get involved with another man with an ego.

She wasn't about to let another man come into her life and break her heart ever again. *Wallace looks like a heart-breaker,* she thought as she slipped on her coat.

"I'm going to be straight with you, Wallace. Relationships aren't my thing, and dating doesn't rank on my list of priorities. I have way too much work on my plate, and I don't need distractions."

Nodding, Wallace took a step back. "So you're one of those women, Miss Super Career Chick, who doesn't need a man? All right, Miss Kenya. But money can't give you babies, kiss you at night, or hold you when it's cold."

She shook her head and placed her purse on her shoulder. "I can adopt, kiss a dog, and invest in an electric blanket. Good night."

"What are you? A lesbian or something?"

"Do you find it so hard to believe that I don't want you? You're not Mr. Irresistible. I can live without you. I've gotten along just fine this long. I think I'll make it through the night."

"Whatever," Wallace snapped as Kenya turned her back and headed out the door.

As she stepped into the crisp night air, Kenya thought about what Wallace had said about her career. Yes, she'd replaced her longing for love with a drive to succeed. Kenya didn't mind working eighty hours a week, coming in on the weekend, or working though the holidays.

To the firm's partners, Kenya was a shining star. But to her friends and family, she was a train wreck waiting to happen. No one had the guts to tell her, though.

Aside from the occasional business dinner, Kenya didn't go out. Imani was married, so they didn't cruise the bars. The one guy she'd dated briefly couldn't keep her interested. He was handsome, stable, and looking for a relationship. But to Kenya, he was a bottle of Lunesta with legs.

Even now she couldn't remember his name or anything they'd done in the month they'd spent together. She'd broken up with him, using work as her excuse. But the truth was, he wasn't Maurice.

Jubilant. Euphoric. These were the feelings that Maurice should have been experiencing. Instead, he was filled with dread and gloom. Now that the season was over, he was going to have to go through with this wedding. It wasn't the thought of marriage that got to him, because he loved Lauryn. It was the spectacle that she'd turned it into. There were going to be camera crews, a write-up in *Carolina Bride* magazine, and a feature on News 6's *The Carolina Traveler*.

As soon as he walked into the locker room, a spray of champagne hit him in the face. "MVP, MVP," his teammates chanted.

Wiping his face, Maurice joined in the celebration,

snatching a bottle of champagne from Homer and taking a big swig.

"Man, we are the champions. We're on top," Homer said.

"Yeah," Maurice said flatly.

"Wedding bell blues?" asked Homer.

"I wish there was one more game, man. This wedding is a hassle. We could have gotten married on an island somewhere, without all this fanfare."

"You know how women are. They want that Cinderella crap, those Disney weddings, and they think happily ever after, as long as the money doesn't run out."

"Lauryn isn't like that."

Homer popped Maurice with a towel. "Don't be fooled. They're all like that," he said before heading for the shower.

Maurice knew Homer was wrong. He knew one woman who didn't care about money and what he had to offer.

Kenya.

He found it funny that he always thought of Kenya at the strangest of times. Was his subconscious telling him that she was the one that he was supposed to be sharing his success with? After all, she'd helped him lay the foundation, and how had he repaid her? By letting her find out on her own that he was with another woman, without any warning. Nine years ago he'd allowed her to walk out of his life, and he felt so guilty about the way things had ended that he had never tried to contact her and apologize.

His mother, Maryann, had loved Kenya and had not been happy the day Maurice brought Lauryn home for Thanksgiving.

"Maurice, come in the kitchen and help me," Maryann had said when she'd walked in on Lauryn and Maurice kissing again.

"Mrs. Goings, I'll help you," Lauryn had said.

"That's quite all right, Mo, let's go," Maryann had replied.

He'd followed his mother into the kitchen, knowing full well that he was going to be the one needing help.

"I don't like her. What happened to Kenya? She was smart, respectful, and wore clothes that covered her body."

"She had a lot more body to cover," Maurice had mumbled.

Maryann had popped Maurice on the hand with a wooden spoon. "What happened between you two?"

"People just grow apart."

"Or did that one just part her legs?"

"Ma." He wasn't going to talk about his sex life with his mother.

"All I'm saying is you have a future, and she's riding your coattails. What does she really know about you?"

"We're getting to know each other. I really care about Lauryn."

"Don't get her pregnant, and don't make Kenya hate you. Kenya was a good girl, and she really cared about you, not your potential earnings, as if she's a bank about to offer you a loan. I see it in that girl's eyes, Maurice. She out for money."

Why did I take your love for granted? he thought as he stood underneath the hot shower spray.

"Hey, man, you got a crowd of reporters out there waiting on you," one of his teammates called out.

"I'll be out in a minute," Maurice said as he shut the water off.

After toweling off and covering his body with a dry towel, Maurice headed into the locker room to answer the questions from the reporters. It didn't take long for someone to ask him about his pending nuptials.

Forcing a smile, Maurice said, "I can't wait. Not only will I have a Super Bowl ring, but I get a wedding ring, too."

"Which one means the most?" a reporter asked.

"I'm not touching that one," Maurice replied, making everyone laugh. "Guys, I have got to go and meet up with my fiancée. Are there any more questions?"

The reporters shook their heads and congratulated Maurice on his season. As he dressed, his cell phone rang.

"Yeah."

"Brother man! You were on fire out there," James Goings, Maurice's brother, exclaimed. "I hate that I couldn't come to the game. When are you coming back to Charlotte?"

"Probably in the morning. Lauryn and I are going to hang out down here tonight."

"You know, Ma still can't believe that you're marrying her."

"I don't need to hear this tonight," Maurice said. He'd had this conversation with his brother about their mother before.

Maryann had let everyone know that she didn't like Lauryn, and she didn't want her son to marry her.

"When you get back, me and the boys got a bachelor party planned for you," James said.

"Looking forward to it," he said. "I got to go before some more reporters come in here."

When he hung up from his brother, Maurice slipped on his shoes and headed outside to cheers and Lauryn.

"Hey, baby," Lauryn said as he pulled her close and kissed her on the neck. "You were awesome."

"Thanks."

"So, are we going to hit South Beach now?"

"Can we get to the hotel first? I need to relax for a minute."

"Baby, you just won the Super Bowl. You need to party," said Lauryn.

"You weren't out there getting hit by linebackers. If you want to party, go ahead." Maurice stomped away from her and headed for the team bus. Lauryn ran after him.

"What is your problem?" Lauryn snapped.

"Life is more than a party. Okay?"

"Fine. Mya and I will hit the clubs, and you can rest," Lauryn spat before turning on her heels and stomping away.

Maurice wasn't really sad to see her go.

After arriving at the hotel, Maurice sprawled across the king-sized bed, happy for a moment of peace. He turned his cell phone off and kicked his shoes off. He wasn't about to go to a smoky club after the pounding he'd taken on the field. Quarterback Jake Delhomme had kept throwing the ball across the middle, and Maurice had gone for it every time, as had the opposing cornerbacks and safetys. He had nearly been knocked out on a play in the third quarter. Luckily, his teammates had been inspired, and the defense had avenged those hits by sacking the other team's quarterback three times.

When Lauryn walked into the room, she shot a contemptuous look Maurice's way before changing into a micromini skirt and silver halter top. "Sure you don't want to go out with me?" she asked as she strapped on a pair of silver sandals with a four-inch heel.

"Hang out with your girl. It's fine. And look, I'm sorry about before," replied Maurice.

Lauryn walked over to the bed, climbed on top of Maurice, and smiled. "It's okay. Next week we're going to be married, and I know this is a little stressful. You relax. You earned it, MVP."

He kissed her chin. "Your girl and Homer are getting tight, huh?"

"No. She's not that serious about him. They're just kicking it."

"How do you know?" he asked.

"I know Mya. She's not a one-man woman, so tell your boy not to get too attached, or he's going to get his heart broken."

"Sounds like you don't want them together."

Lauryn laughed nervously. "I really don't care what Mya does. But those two don't match."

"Some people say that about us."

"You mean your momma?" She rolled her eyes. "I guess she's not going to like me until I give her a grandchild. Can't she see that I'm the best thing that's ever happened to you?"

Maurice flipped her over so that he was on top of her. "Why don't you stay in with me tonight and let Mya and Homer kick it?"

"How often do we come to Miami? We have the rest of our lives to spend together and only one night here. I'll try to come back early."

Maurice hid his disappointment as he let her up. He knew that she'd felt the throbbing erection between his legs.

"You're sure you don't want to come with us?" she asked as she adjusted her clothes.

"Nah, I'm going to order some room service and call it a night," Maurice said.

Lauryn blew him a kiss as she headed out the door.

Alone in the room, Maurice's thoughts turned back to Kenya. Had the years been kind to her? Was she married? Still in Atlanta?

Maurice sat up, climbed out of bed, and crossed over to the minibar. Pouring himself a drink, he couldn't help but wonder if he'd made a mistake all those years ago. *Why am I thinking like this? I'm about to marry Lauryn, and I haven't heard from Kenya in nearly ten years. Hell, I'm probably the last thing on her mind.*

Kenya leaned back on the sofa, wondering why she was torturing herself. There she sat, watching replay after replay of Maurice Goings. She didn't think it was possible that he could have gotten finer than he was in high school and college, but looking at him as a grown man, she knew that he was.

"Ugh," she exclaimed as she turned the TV off. "I am not going to sit here and ponder what if. Maurice made his choice, and I hope he can live with it."

But when she went to sleep that night, all she could dream about was kissing Maurice.

Chapter 4

Three weeks after the Super Bowl and one wedding-date change later, Lauryn and Maurice were in full wedding mode. The church had been booked. They'd been on every local morning show from radio to TV, and *SportsCenter* had even done a profile of the couple.

Maurice was ready for it all to be over. He'd booked a tropical getaway for him and Lauryn, and she'd promised no interviews on their honeymoon. It was going to be about the two of them starting their life together.

"It's not too late to back out of this," Maryann said as she and Maurice ate lunch at her favorite restaurant in Charlotte, McCormick & Schmick's, a swanky seafood place nestled among the skyscrapers and bank buildings in uptown.

"Ma, when are you going to accept Lauryn? We're getting married."

"And I don't trust her. You men are so blind. You let a pretty face and a nice body take away all of your common sense. Your father, God rest his soul, was the same way. He let pretty women turn his head, and what did it get him?"

"I'm nothing like Daddy," Maurice spat bitterly.

Maryann raised an eyebrow. "Oh no?"

Maurice silently chewed his fish as he thought about the hell his father had put his mother through during their marriage. He remembered one incident in particular.

"Richard, I'm not doing this anymore. You can go out with your whores and flaunt your affairs, but you will not come into my house at five in the morning, making a mockery of our marriage," Maryann had shouted one night long ago, waking James and Maurice.

"I pay the bills in this damned house. I'll come and go as I please," his father had snapped.

Maurice had crept from his bed and had inched toward the stairwell so that he could make sure things didn't get out of hand. Sure he only ten years old, but he was protective of his mother. When he saw his father raise his hand as if he was going to slap his mother, Maurice had sped down the stairs and had jumped between them.

"If you touch my mother, I'm going to kill you," he had exclaimed.

Richard and Maryann had taken a step back, with shock and frowns etched on their faces. The next morning, Richard was gone, and two weeks later a jealous husband had shot and killed him.

Maurice had sworn then that he would never make a woman cry the way Richard had made Maryann cry. Maybe that was why Kenya had stayed on his mind after all of these years. He'd broken his solemn vow.

"Maurice," Maryann said, snapping him out of his thoughts. "I don't trust her, and I don't think you're going to be happy."

"And I love you, but it's my life."

Maryann rose to her feet. "I know that, but I'm not

going to stand by and watch you make the biggest mistake of your life."

"What are you saying?"

"I'm not coming to your wedding, and I'm not welcoming that tramp into my family. I'm going back to Atlanta." Turning on her heels, Maryann stormed out of the restaurant.

Mya ran her finger down the curve of Lauryn's arm. "And you're still getting married tomorrow?"

Lauryn pushed her hand away and groaned. "Don't start this again."

"Start what? You know how I feel, and you know what I think of this wedding. Look me in the eye and say you don't love me, and I'll back off."

"You know I can't choose you." Lauryn couldn't look at her.

"Why do you keep coming here then? You ruined my relationship with Homer by putting that little bug in Mo's ear."

"You didn't care one thing about Homer."

"You won't let me care about anyone else. Every time I try, you find some way to sabotage it."

"That is not true," Lauryn exclaimed indignantly.

"Really? Then what would you call what you do when you see me spending time with someone else?"

"What are you talking about?"

"Anytime you see me with someone else, I become the top priority in your life. Why won't you admit that you want your cake and ice cream, too?"

"I want to be with you, and even if I'm married to Maurice, I can still be with you. Nothing has to change." She reached up and stroked Mya's cheek.

"What happens when you have kids? Will things still be

the same then? Right now, Lauryn, you have to choose me or him."

Lauryn rose to her feet. "I do love you, and if things were different, then I would choose you, but I can't."

Mya rolled over on her stomach and buried her face in a pillow, silently sobbing. Lauryn leaned in to comfort her. "Don't cry," she whispered in her ear.

"I deserve so much better than this," Mya said. "If you walk out that door, don't come back."

"Mya, please," Lauryn pleaded. "Don't do this to me the night before my wedding!"

Mya leapt from the bed. "We've had this argument before, and I'm sick and tired of it. Just go and live your little NFL wife life, and be miserable. When you show up at my door after your honeymoon, don't expect me to open it."

Lauryn pulled Mya into her arms, but Mya pushed her away.

"No," Mya said. "Not again. You're poison to me, Lauryn. I don't know why I thought I could change your mind and make you see that I was the one for you. You're nothing but a gold-digging witch. You're going to break his heart, too. He's just too stupid to see that."

"You did this to me! You made me want you because you thought making the straight girl queer was a game."

"I love you. I've loved you from the day I kissed you. And I didn't make you do anything that you didn't want to do."

Lauryn closed the space between them and pulled Mya into her arms, kissing her until she felt her knees quake. "God, help me. I love you, too," Lauryn whispered into Mya's ear as they fell back into bed.

Kenya leaned back in her desk chair. It was nearly midnight, and she wasn't any closer to leaving work than she had been at five p.m. The case she'd been working on was going to be the feather in her cap when the yearly reviews came up.

She wanted to make managing associate this year. She'd be the youngest lawyer in the firm's history to do so. Besides, this case had come at the best time. Now she didn't have to see the details of Maurice's wedding on all of the entertainment shows and ESPN. Even the local news had run a story on "Atlanta's former high-school standout and Super Bowl champion."

She had to wonder when Maurice had become such a glory hound. Then again, this had Lauryn's dirty fingerprints all over it. Even when they were in college, Lauryn had had a flair for the dramatic.

Why am I even thinking about this? Kenya thought as she cross-referenced a precedent case with her brief. She stood and walked over to the window overlooking the streets of midtown. Everything was quiet, and only a few cars darted down the street. Kenya pressed her hand against the window. Why had she let heartbreak turn her into this? Outside of her job and her family, she didn't have a life. She couldn't spell fun anymore. And love? What was that? So what if she did become the youngest managing associate, which was one step below partner? She would still be alone and lonely.

"I can't keep blaming Maurice for this," she said, thinking aloud. "He probably doesn't even think about me. So why have I wasted nine years thinking about him?"

Walking back to the computer, Kenya decided she'd done enough work, and she was going home.

As she headed down to the parking garage, she decided that she needed to recharge her batteries. Maybe it was time to put the superwoman act on the shelf and do something she hadn't done since she was a freshman in college—take a vacation. She deserved it. How much work was she supposed to squeeze into 365 days, anyway?

The next morning, Kenya awoke with a start, thinking that she was late for court. However, it was only a few minutes after five. Still, she rose from the bed, showered, and fixed herself a pot of Irish creme coffee and a bowl of sugar-free oatmeal.

God, my life is so boring, she thought as she ate her bland hot cereal. She tried to remember the last adventurous thing that she'd done, and she couldn't. She made a mental note to call her mother after court to get the name of her travel agent. Though Georgia winters weren't brutal, Kenya wanted to go somewhere tropical, where her only decision would be whether to wear a one-piece or two-piece bathing suit.

If the thought of a vacation had cheered Kenya up on the drive to work, the decision from the mediator in her land-dispute case put her on cloud nine. The ruling favored her client and gave G&C Industries the right to build housing for low-income families on over one hundred acres of land in Cobb County that had been unused for nearly thirty years. The real estate had originally been zoned for retail use, but the city had changed this to residential use fifteen years ago.

Some adjacent businesses wanted to block the G&C project because they wanted more upscale housing in the area. However, the developer wanted to make sure that people like his grandparents would have someplace to live in the county they'd grown up in.

After months of going back and forth, Kenya had finally won. When she walked in the office, she realized word of her victory had already reached the right people, mainly her manager, Janice Howell.

"Kenya, may I see you in my office?" Janice said, with a smile on her face.

Kenya walked into the corner office that overlooked the capitol building. The huge windows let in the gold reflection of the capitol's dome, bathing the room in a golden glow. Everything looked as if King Midas had touched it. This was the kind of office that Kenya had been working to have. But once she got the office, what would she do then? What professional goal would she set for herself to mask her loneliness?

When Kenya took a seat across from Janice's desk, she had no idea that her life was about to make a 360-degree turn.

"First of all, congratulations on today," said Janice. "I didn't have one doubt about you winning."

"Thank you," Kenya said.

"Your hard work hasn't gone unnoticed here. All of the long nights and your winning percentage are off the charts. That's why we want you to head up our new office."

Yes! Kenya thought excitedly. *This is it.*

"This firm is really trying to put it's footprint on the southeast," Janice said. "We've done that in Atlanta, and we're hoping to do the same in Charlotte. I would love for you to head up our effort."

"Where?" asked Kenya. Her happiness had deflated like a Macy's Thanksgiving Day balloon hooked on a light pole. "You want me to relocate to Charlotte?"

"Yes. You've shown that you're the best person for the job. Your record speaks for itself. There's no way we'd lose with you heading up our North Carolina team."

"Well, uh, I need some time to think about it. My life has been in Atlanta for a long time," Kenya said, stumbling over her words when what she really wanted to say was, "There is no way I'm going to Charlotte and running the risk of running into Mr. and Mrs. Goings."

"I'd like to say take all the time you need, but we want to pull the trigger on this in the next three months," said Janice. "I need an answer sooner rather than later."

"Uh, okay. I can't turn this down," Kenya said. "But if it's all right with you, I'd like to take some time off."

"You've earned it."

Kenya rose to her feet. "Thank you, Janice."

Yes, Kenya needed a vacation, and she certainly planned to enjoy this one. She rushed back to her desk and called her mother to get that travel agent's telephone number.

Chapter 5

Lauryn nervously applied lip liner as time ticked away. It was her wedding day, and she wasn't even sure if she could go through with it. Mya's words echoed in her head. Mya's kiss burned on her lips.

"I don't love her. I'm marrying Maurice," she said to her reflection. Standing, she smoothed her body-hugging Vera Wang gown and placed her veil on her head.

"Knock, knock," Vivian said as she walked into the room.

Lauryn smiled. "Viv, I'm glad you're here. How's my make-up?"

"You look beautiful. Girl, it's time for you to march down the aisle and get that man."

Lauryn stood up and hugged Vivian tightly. "Thank you for standing up for me at the last minute."

"Why didn't Mya do it? You guys are thick as thieves," Vivian said.

"I don't know," Lauryn said. "Let's do this. My man's waiting."

* * *

Mya stood next to her cousin, Lola, as they watched Lauryn march down the aisle. Mya tried desperately to make eye contact with Lauryn. Maybe if Lauryn saw her there, she'd stop this act, this farce of a marriage that would never work. Tears sprang into Mya's eyes as she started for the front of the megachurch, waiting for the pastor to ask the question she had the answer to.

Mya ignored the vows that the couple exchanged, because she knew Lauryn was lying to God and all of these two thousand witnesses. Just last night she'd promised Mya that their relationship wouldn't change and that she loved her. Now she was promising to love Maurice until death. What a crock.

"If anyone here knows why these two shouldn't be joined in holy matrimony, speak now or forever hold your peace."

Mya had made it to the front of the church by now. And when she exclaimed, "You can't do this," all eyes were on her. Mya marched to the altar. "Lauryn, I love you, and I can't let you marry Maurice when I know you love me, too."

Gasps and catcalls rose from the audience. "Damn down low sistas," someone called out.

Maurice looked from Mya to Lauryn, his eyes begging for an explanation. This had to be a joke.

"Maurice," Lauryn said in a whisper as she dropped his hand. "I'm sorry. I thought I could do this."

Maurice looked around for TV cameras or MTV's Ashton Kutcher, because this had to be an episode of *Punk'd*. Smiling, because he knew there was a punch line coming soon, Maurice stood there in silent shock. But when Mya opened her arms to Lauryn, and the two women embraced, then bolted from the church, he knew this wasn't a joke.

Pastor Adams grasped Maurice's shoulder. "Son, I-I'm sorry."

"Was I just punked?" Maurice whispered as he watched the sanctuary empty.

Three weeks had passed, and Maurice hadn't been outside of his uptown penthouse since he'd been humiliated in church. The voice-mail boxes on his home and cell phones were full. Some people were genuinely concerned; others were simply being nosy. For all Maurice cared, they could all go to hell. And if people were making reservations for a trip there, he hoped someone would have the good sense to take Lauryn along for the ride.

Though weeks had passed, Maurice was still hoping that this was a joke, a bad dream, or some pilot for a reality TV show. But realistically, he knew that as sorry and pathetic as this situation was, it was his life. Maybe if there hadn't been so much media attention focused on his wedding, it wouldn't have been so difficult to deal with. But the world had seen his meltdown. Jay Leno and David Letterman had made jokes about it on their late-night shows, and the local media hadn't been any kinder.

He leaned back on the chaise lounge that Lauryn had had to have. The thing wasn't even comfortable, and just like his ex-fiancée, it was confused about what it was—a chair or a sofa. Maurice leapt to his feet, feeling as if he had been burned. Then he pushed the chaise lounge over, jumping back as it wobbled and crashed into the mirrored-glass table in front of it. The sound of the smashing glass drowned out the echo of the front door closing.

"Mo!" James called out as he ran into the living room. "What in the hell?"

"What are you doing here, and how did you get in?" Maurice snapped.

James threw his hands in the air. "Ma gave me her key. Everyone's worried about you."

"I'm fine. Now go."

James shook his head. "Bro, this ain't living. You stink. Your house looks like a bomb went off in it." He pointed to three weeks' worth of empty pizza boxes and Chinese-food containers. "You're going to breed roaches if you don't clean up."

Maurice walked over to the front door, opened it, then said, "You can go and leave me to my breeding."

James folded his arms and stood his ground. "Look, bro. You need to pull yourself out of this funk, get out of the house, and get a life."

Maurice closed the door, then turned to James. "I know people are still talking about it, aren't they?"

"Mo, forget people and what they have to say. You didn't do anything wrong."

Nodding, Maurice let James's words sink in. Then he wondered if this was payback for something he did nine years ago. "Damn, my honeymoon trip was nonrefundable."

"Take the trip, anyway," said James.

"It's for two people."

James held up his arms and spun around like Michael Jackson. "What am I?"

"Oh, that's rich. A honeymoon with my brother? I don't think so."

"So, you're going to waste all of that money. Weren't you guys going to the Bahamas?"

Maurice shook his head. "This is the last week I have to make reservations. Maybe my travel agent can switch us to a singles resort." As Maurice spoke, he began to like the idea even more.

"That's what I'm talking about," James said as he watched his brother's face brighten.

"All right," Maurice said as he picked up the phone. "Let's do the damned thing. When do you want to leave?"

Kenya polished off another glass of chardonnay and shook her head. "Imani, God is laughing at me."

"You're drunk."

"I know. But moving back to Charlotte where Maurice and his new wife are? That's not what I want to do."

Imani moved the bottle out of her friend's reach. "Then don't go."

"And commit career suicide? I have to go, because if I don't, then I won't look like a team player."

"Charlotte is big enough for you to avoid him. I bet you wouldn't even be able to afford a house in their neighborhood," Imani said, trying to calm Kenya's nerves.

"Well, I already said that I was going to take the job," Kenya slurred. "So, the only thing I can do is go."

"It probably won't be as bad as you're thinking."

Kenya stretched against the chair before she stood up. She stumbled a bit as she placed her dinner dishes in the sink. "You think I'm crazy, right? That I should be over Maurice by now, right?"

"Well," Imani said, then shrugged her shoulders.

"And you're right, I should be. But I'm not. My mother was right. I shouldn't have run away, because I-I have some stuff to get off my chest."

"So, you haven't talked to him in nearly ten years?"

Kenya shook her head. "Nope. What would I say to him?"

"Thought you had stuff to get off your chest?"

"Oh yeah, I do."

"Kenya, come sit your drunk butt down." Imani laughed.

Kenya stumbled over to the sofa as Imani started their favorite movie, *The Color Purple.*

"You know," Kenya said, "I'm not going to worry about Maurice. I'm going to focus on my vacation and then my new position."

"And who knows, you might just meet someone on your vacation that will take your mind right off Mr. Goings. I mean, what did that brother put on you that lasted for nine years?"

Kenya couldn't answer, because she had drifted off to sleep.

The next morning, Kenya woke up with a splitting headache and an aching back, because Imani had left her slumbering on the sofa. Drinking was definitely going to be out for her vacation.

The Breezes Sports Club Resort in Nassau was supposed to be a place where singles could go to recharge without the pitter-patter of little feet. There were activities where men and women could socialize and maybe hook up. That was one thing Kenya wasn't going to do. She had no interest in an island fling. Then again, whatever she did in the Bahamas would be between her and the tropical stranger she decided to share whatever with.

Who am I kidding? I'm not going on vacation to be a tramp, she thought.

Kenya's flight to the Bahamas left right on time, and she was sure that her vacation was going to be as smooth as her flight from Hartsfield-Jackson Atlanta International Airport. When she took her seat next to the window, she decided that she was going to throw caution to the wind and let her hair down. Then her seatmate, an elderly woman with an oversized carry-on bag, squeezed in beside her.

Kenya decided to pretend she was asleep until she actually fell into a peaceful slumber.

"Ladies and gentlemen, we are making our descent into Nassau," the captain announced. "Please fasten your seat belts, and return your seats to their upright position. I hope you all enjoy your stay on the island, and thank you for flying Delta Airlines."

Wiping her mouth and opening her eyes, Kenya looked out the window at the crystal blue water and the sparkling sunlight dancing on it. "Wow," she whispered. She could feel her batteries recharging, and the plane hadn't even landed yet.

This is going to be great, she thought as the plane taxied to a stop.

Maurice and James stretched out on a couple of pool chairs, ready for a second day of women watching. It was James idea, because Maurice was content to sit in his hotel room overlooking the ocean and eat. He couldn't help but wonder how Kenya had felt when he'd dumped her for Lauryn.

When James started hooting and hollering, Maurice looked up from his sports magazine to see a group of women walking by who looked as if they'd stepped off the pages of *Sports Illustrated*'s swimsuit edition.

"Hurt me. Hurt me," James called out. "Umm, umm, good."

The women smiled and continued on their way. While Maurice had glanced at the sexy ladies, he had no interest in them, and he couldn't help but wonder if they were all sleeping with each other, while some sap waited for them in colder weather.

"What's that look?" James asked when he noted the

scowl on his brother's face. "A gang of sexy senoritas just walked by, and you're frowning?"

"It's hot, and the sun is in my eyes."

"You're still moping over Ms. Down Low, huh?"

Maurice dropped his magazine over his face. "I'm not thinking about her. But I have to wonder how many other women are doing shit like that." Pushing the magazine down, he looked in the direction of the model squad. "Just like those women over there. How many of them do you think . . ." The sight before him took all of the words out of his mouth.

"Just let me watch," James said, not noticing the look on Maurice's face.

"Oh my God."

James looked in the same direction as his brother. "What?"

"The girl in the red bathing suit. Is that . . . Nah, it can't be."

"Damn, she looks like Kenya Taylor."

The woman in the red bathing suit came closer to where they were sitting. It was undeniably Kenya. But my had she changed. She had a figure that wouldn't quit, shaped just like an hourglass. Her butter-rum skin was smooth and flawless. Her shoulder-length hair framed her face with curly ringlets, a style Maurice had never seen her wear. She pushed her sunglasses up on her forehead and wiped sweat from her face with the back of her hand as she seemingly searched for a chair.

"Hey . . . ," James attempted to yell, but Maurice placed his hand over his brother's mouth.

"Shut up."

James pushed Maurice's hand away. "Man, if that's Kenya, why don't you want to say hello to her?"

"Let's see. Because she hates me?" Maurice replied. "I'm sure I'm the last person she wants to see."

"You might be right about that," James said, then laughed. "Still, you should say hello. That's a fireworks show that I'd love to see."

"Just let her be. That might not even be her." But Maurice knew it was Kenya. She may have slimmed down, but her eyes were the same.

"I know that body isn't hers, because that girl is fine as . . . She's coming this way."

Kenya took an empty seat beside Maurice, but she didn't look at him as she unwrapped her sarong and spread it across the pool chair. Kenya dropped her bag on the side of the chair away from Maurice and pulled out a bottle of sunscreen.

Maurice couldn't tear his eyes away from her as she smoothed the lotion on her skin. She was Kenya, older, sexier, and right beside him. He wanted to reach out and touch her and make sure she was real. Maybe this was his chance to make things right with her. And if he did that, then maybe karma would give him his life back.

Damn, I don't remember her legs being that long, he thought as he watched her stretch out on the lounge chair.

Obviously, she had her eyes closed, because without turning her head, she said, "Sir, please stop ogling me. I'm sure there is something much more interesting to look at than me."

Her voice was the same, smooth like honey, thick like molasses, and cool like an unexpected breeze.

"Kenya Taylor."

She turned toward him as if she knew who he was. Snatching her sunglasses off, Kenya sat up in the chair and focused her gaze on him, the color draining from her face as if she'd seen a ghost.

"I don't believe this. This is unbelievable," she said, then began to gather her things.

Maurice rose to his feet and blocked her from leaving. "This is unbelievable. I can't believe we just ran into each other like this."

Standing toe to toe with him, Kenya hauled off and slapped him. The echo of her blow caused everyone in close proximity to them to look up at them. Maurice held his cheek as it stung.

"Ouch. I guess I deserved that," he said.

Kenya turned on her heels and stomped away.

Chapter 6

Kenya's heart was beating faster than a roaring race car's engine as she stormed into her suite. How in the world did this happen? Why did she end up at the same resort where Maurice and Lauryn were spending their honeymoon? This place was supposed to be for singles, and *they* were here, invading her vacation!

And there he was, leering at her, and he'd just married the same tramp he'd left her for all of those years ago.

I should've pushed him in that damned pool. He has some nerve.

Kenya paced back and forth in her room, kicking off her thong sandals and tossing her sarong on the bed. Though she'd been at her resort for less than three hours, she was ready to go home, because if she saw Lauryn, she was going to push her in the pool.

"No," she said as she stopped pacing and looked at herself in the mirror. "I'm not running from them again. This isn't college, and I spent too much money to come here and relax."

Scooping up her beach bag, shoes, and sarong, Kenya headed outside again. She went back to the pool to look for

Maurice and his new bride. She found Maurice and his brother. That didn't make sense to her. Who would bring a third party on a honeymoon trip?

Kenya hoped in vain that another seat would open up. Fate had brought all of the sunbathers outside, and the only seat was beside Maurice, who was sitting on the edge of his seat, with ice on his cheek.

Did I hit him that hard? she thought as she walked over to the chair.

"Kenya, how are you, girl?" James asked when she approached them.

"Fine," she said, smiling at him. "Look at you."

He hugged her, then held her out. "I'd rather look at you. Atlanta has been good to you. Do they all look like you back home?"

She blushed, not because of his complements, but because she could feel Maurice staring at her as she talked to James.

"You're in Charlotte now, huh?" she asked.

"Yeah, helping my brother out with some community service and running our company," said James.

"Public relations?" she said, drifting back to her goals when she and Maurice had entered Johnson C. Smith together.

"No, real estate. Isn't that what you do? Public relations?" James asked.

"No. I'm a lawyer now."

"Whoa," Maurice and James said in unison.

"I thought you wanted to run your own PR firm," Maurice said.

Kenya turned to him. "There's a lot about me you don't know and never knew. I don't think I was talking to you."

Maurice jumped up. "Kenya, do you have something to say to me?"

"No, I don't," she spat. "Why aren't you with your wife?"

Maurice blanched, and James shook his head. "My wife? You saw all of that?"

"You were all over the news, you and Lauryn. I'm surprised she isn't out here, all over you like cheap cologne."

James cleared his throat. "I'm going to get a drink. You want something, Kenya?"

"No, thank you," replied Kenya.

When James left, she glared at Maurice, tempted to hit him again. "Get out of my face," she said as she attempted to push him aside.

"Lauryn and I didn't get married. It was a mistake."

"Only took you nine years to figure that out?" Kenya said as she took her seat. "I hope you don't expect me to feel sorry for you."

"No, I don't. Why would you? Obviously, you hate me."

"Does that surprise you? You broke my heart, and I don't have to forgive you for that."

"You don't, but I do want to tell you that I'm sorry for what I did. There have been so many times when I wanted to reach out to you and say that. It's really ironic that we ran into each other here."

"Cut the bull, Maurice. You've been living the life of an NFL star with the beautiful fiancée, and part of your perfect life has come crashing down, and you're feeling sorry for yourself. I'm not your salvation, your chance to put karma right."

He stared at her intently, so deeply that she was thrown off kilter. There was something in his eyes that looked familiar. *Ignore it,* she told herself.

"I know that you have every right to hate me, but you have to admit that us meeting like this must mean something."

Kenya placed her sunglasses over her eyes so that she could peer at Maurice without him noticing. He was finer than ever. His skin was the color of dark chocolate; his chest and abs rivaled those of the famed statue *David*. The bead of sweat that ran down his flat stomach made her mouth water, because she wanted to follow the path of that bead with her tongue.

What is wrong with me? This man is toxic, poison, and God, I want to kiss him, touch him, and let him touch me.

"Kenya, are you all right?" Maurice asked.

"Why wouldn't I be?"

"Because I asked you a question about five minutes ago."

"Maybe I just don't want to talk to you," she said, then turned her back to him.

He touched her bare shoulder, and her skin burned with desire. How many nights had she dreamed of his touch? Here he was, standing behind her. But was this a dream or a nightmare?

Turning to face him, Kenya scowled and pushed his hand away. "Don't touch me ever again."

"Do you hate me that much?" he asked. "I know I was wrong, and I've struggled with what happened between us for years."

"Yet, you never reached out to say anything," she said, allowing emotions she'd held in for nine years to bubble to the surface. "Maurice, you're full of it. Whatever happened between you and Lauryn must have really shaken you up for you to stand here and tell these lies."

"I'm not lying. The way things went down between us at Smith was wrong. I never wanted you to be hurt and—"

"Then maybe you shouldn't have cheated on me," Kenya snapped. "You know, the sad thing is that I would have forgiven you, but you claimed that you loved her and that we had grown apart. Though that didn't seem to matter when you needed help with your schoolwork. I mean, you were some piece of work."

He looked at her and stepped back. "Kenya, I—"

"You used me. And when you got what you needed from me, you tossed me aside. Is that what she did to you? With all of the wedding preparation that was broadcasted on the news, she must have left you for a bigger payday."

"It was good seeing you, Kenya. Enjoy your vacation." Maurice turned away from her and headed inside the hotel.

She watched as he walked away, wondering if he'd been the reason for the breakup of his engagement. He had probably cheated on Lauryn, because cheaters didn't change. Kenya didn't feel sorry for Lauryn, though. After all, what goes around comes around.

"Excuse me," a man with a British accent said. "Is anyone sitting here?"

Looking up at the stranger, Kenya smiled, then said no. He was cute. He had obviously spent some time in the gym and in the sun, because his golden brown skin had a slight red hue. He extended his hand to Kenya as he eased into his chair. "Damon Porter. And you are?"

"Kenya Taylor."

"Beautiful."

"Excuse me?"

"You're beautiful, but I'm sure you already knew that. Vacationing alone?"

"You ask a lot of questions."

"I'm sorry, but it's just that I've been here for about a week, and you have to be the most beautiful woman that I've ever seen. How have you slipped past me?"

Kenya blushed as he smiled at her, revealing a set of pearly whites that were blinding. "Thank you," she said.

"You're American, aren't you? A Southerner?"

"Yes."

He gave her the once-over, drinking in her image. Kenya

felt a little uncomfortable under his gaze. But wasn't this the reason why she had chosen to wear a bikini, anyway?

Relax, she thought. *This is why you came on vacation.*

"What American man allowed you to leave the States alone?"

"No man tells me what to do," Kenya replied.

Damon held his hands up and grinned. "Well, I'd love to have dinner with you tonight, Miss Kenya. And I'm asking you, not telling you."

"Okay," she replied. "Where are you taking me?"

"The restaurant here is excellent, and they have ocean-view seating."

"You seem to know your way around this place."

"I've been here before, and I'm certainly glad that I'm here now."

So am I, she thought, smiling.

As they sat by the pool and talked, Damon told Kenya that he was an international stockbroker and spent a lot of time traveling between London and New York. He'd never been married, though he'd come close two years ago. He wasn't opposed to marriage; he just wanted a woman who had her own goals and didn't aspire to be just a housewife.

Kenya revealed that she didn't date a lot, because she was focused on her career as a contract attorney. She told him that this was the first vacation that she'd taken since she was a college student, and that she took it because she'd taken a new job that was going to force her to relocate to another city.

"It could be an adventure," he said. "You don't like to take risks, do you?"

"You figured that out in one conversation?"

He turned on his stomach and looked at her. "That and the fact that you came here alone to unwind and pretend that you're someone else."

"How do you figure that?"

"I can see it in your eyes," he said, staring intently at her. "But we're going to change that. How long are you here for?"

"You are very presumptuous," Kenya said. "Who's to say that I'm going to enjoy dinner with you tonight?"

"I do. And you will."

She shook her head, rendered speechless by his arrogance, but intrigued by his smile and sparkling brown eyes. Then she looked up and saw Maurice and James staring in her direction.

Placing her hand on Damon's shoulder, she laughed throatily, more for Maurice than for her companion. She could feel Maurice's eyes burning into her. Was he jealous? As if he had a right to be. Even if Damon was the most arrogant man in the world, Kenya was going to pretend that he was the most interesting man she'd ever met as long as Maurice kept watching her.

"Look at her," Maurice said to his brother as they sat at the poolside bar. "She's all over that dude."

"That's why I didn't take her the drink I bought her. I didn't want to block her from getting her 'mack' on," James said.

Maurice's anger was unexplainable. He had no right to feel that way, because he was the one who'd tossed Kenya aside. But seeing her with this guy, watching her smile at him, touch his arm, and have a conversation with him, made Maurice jealous. The first thing she did when she saw him was slap him.

"She can do better."

"Kenya was always pretty, but now she is fine, man. You messed up."

"Gee, thanks."

James slapped his brother on the shoulder. "Come on. You ended up with the down low chick when you could have had Kenya and watched her blossom into the diamond that she is now."

"Stop looking at her like that," Maurice said forcefully.

"Can't help it. Those legs, breasts, and the way her face lights up when she smiles. She's fine."

Maurice pushed James from the stool, then stalked over to the pool. He figured if he dove in and made a big enough splash, he could wet Kenya and her newfound friend.

I should've stayed in my room, he thought as he dove into the pool from the edge. The water splashed over the side, gently spraying Kenya and Damon.

"Bloody hell," Damon exclaimed.

Kenya and Maurice locked eyes as he looked at her from the pool. "Sorry," he called out.

Damon looked at him. "Aren't you Maurice Goings of the Carolina Panthers?"

Maurice nodded and smiled. "That's me."

Kenya grabbed a towel from the side of her chair and wiped the water from her legs.

"That was a great catch in the Super Bowl," said Damon.

"Thanks," replied Maurice.

Kenya rose to her feet. "Damon, I'm going to get ready for dinner," she said. "What time are we meeting?"

Turning away from Maurice, Damon smiled at Kenya. "Right at sunset. You have to see it, because it's almost as beautiful as you are."

Maurice dove underneath the water to hide his disgust. So Kenya was going out with this clown. What drew her in? he wondered. His accent? His British mannerisms? Coming up for air, he watched as Kenya walked away, her red bikini bottom clinging to her heart-shaped behind.

"Hey, didn't you get married?" Damon asked, standing in front of Maurice and blocking his view of Kenya.

"Ah, no," Maurice mumbled.

"Oh, sorry. I've never been a huge fan of American football, but that Super Bowl was amazing."

"Uh-huh. So how do you know that lady you were talking to?" asked Maurice.

Damon laughed. "Oh, we just met. You know how these women are when they're on vacation."

"No, I don't," said Maurice.

"Guaranteed panties. I'll have that honey's legs in the air by the time the waitress is serving us dessert."

Maurice leapt out of the pool, and in one swift motion, he had his hands around Damon's neck. "Don't talk about her that way." Water from his biceps dripped down into Damon's glass.

Stumbling backward momentarily, Damon regained his footing and pushed Maurice off him. "What the hell is your problem, man? You can have her when I'm done."

Stopping himself from falling, Maurice grabbed the edge of the table. "I don't like to hear guys disrespect women, especially ones I know. Stay away from her, or you're going to have to deal with me."

"What? Are you her father? She chose me and not you. Bet that just burns your knickers, being that you're the NFL star and I'm just a regular guy. You can have my sloppy seconds."

Figuring that another second talking to this guy would lead to an assault charge, Maurice stomped away from Damon. *I have to find Kenya,* he thought as he dashed to the front desk.

The front-desk clerk, who's back was turned to Maurice, was chatting away with a housekeeper.

"Yo, excuse me," Maurice said, his voice deepened by aggression.

The blond clerk whirled around, hair whipping around her face. "Is there something I can help you with?"

"Yes, I need to find a guest," Maurice said, smiling wide enough to show all of his teeth. "Her name is Kenya Taylor. What room is she in?"

Shaking her head, the clerk replied, "I can't give you that information. Our guests have an expectation of privacy, which I can't violate."

"She might be in danger, and I have to warn her."

Placing her hands on the counter and leaning forward, the clerk smiled a generic smile, then said, "I'll be happy to take a message and deliver it."

Folding his arms across his chest and frowning, Maurice exhaled loudly and took the pen and paper the clerk had extended to him. After looking at the blank piece of paper, he knew it was pointless to leave a note. He knew the moment Kenya saw his name, she wouldn't read it. The clerk turned her back to him and continued her conversation with the housekeeper, and Maurice leaned over the counter, hoping to find something that had a list of the guests.

"Sir," the clerk snapped, catching him in the middle of his snooping. "What are you doing?"

"I, uh, this pen doesn't write," he replied, handing it back to her.

She frowned. "Move away from the desk."

Maurice knew that if he had a few bills to pass to her, she would be happy to give him Kenya's information. Walking away from the desk, he decided that he wasn't above offering a bribe. He headed to his room to retrieve his wallet.

As the door to the elevator opened, Kenya, dressed in a red dress that hugged her body like a second skin, started to walk out. Maurice drank in her image, eyeing her long, toned legs and noticing for the first time the small butterfly tattoo on her calf.

He blocked her exit by grasping her elbow and pushing her back into the elevator.

"What the hell is your problem?" she demanded hotly.

Maurice pressed the button to close the doors. "I need to talk to you," he said as he pressed the button for the twentieth floor.

"Have you lost what's left of your mind? Let me off."

"Where are you going?"

"Are you kidding me? You have the audacity to ask me where I'm going? You don't have the right to even speak to me." Crossing her arms across her chest, she turned her back to him. "If you must know, I have a date."

"With that dude from the pool? Don't do it, Kenya. He's bad news."

"As opposed to you, a liar and a cheater?"

"Kenya, listen to me. That guy's up to no good, and he's out to hurt you, to use you as a sex object."

Kenya's eyes widened to the size of silver dollars, and her mouth dropped open, as if she were about to scream. "What did you just say? Hurt me? No one can ever inflict the pain on me that you did. Now you want to pretend that you're concerned about me. Whatever, Maurice. Get out of my way." Reaching around him, she attempted to press the button for the lobby. Maurice grabbed her hand.

Jerking away, Kenya pushed him against the wall. "Just leave me alone. I don't need you hovering over me like you give a damn."

Circling his arms around her waist, he pulled her against him and could feel her trembling against his chest. He just didn't know if it was from desire or anger.

"Kenya, you can hate me forever, but trust me, this guy is after one thing and one thing only."

"So what?"

He should've let her go. He had only her best interests at heart, and she wanted to act as if he'd done something wrong. But she felt so damned good in his arms. Time had stood still in that elevator. She wasn't angry with him, and he hadn't broken her heart. Before another second passed, Maurice leaned in, seizing the opportunity to kiss her succulent lips.

She was sweeter than he remembered, reminding him of his favorite confection—chocolate-covered strawberries. Slipping his hands underneath her dress, he cupped her perfect ass and pulled her even closer so she could feel his throbbing desire.

For a moment, Kenya was lost in the kiss, allowing him to slip his tongue into her mouth, and she melted against him. But just as quickly as she fell under his spell, she broke away from him and slapped him.

"Don't ever touch me again," she cried.

"You sure about that?" he asked, closing the space between them, their lips were almost touching.

Kenya eased back, bumping into the mirrored wall. Maurice knew he was in her space and she had nowhere to go. He pressed the emergency stop button, and the blaring bells of the alarm went off.

"Are you crazy?" she demanded, pressing her hands against his chest.

He grabbed her wrists and sought out her lips. She turned her head, and his lips landed on her neck—a spot that Maurice knew would get her hot. Kenya was rendered powerless under his kiss, and he knew it. Slowly, he moved down her neck, leaving a trail of kisses as he slipped the straps of her dress down. When her breasts spilled out, he took her chocolate-drop nipple into his mouth. With his hand, he stroked her other breast until her nipple hardened like a diamond.

"No, no," she moaned, attempting to push him away. Her knees buckled as he continued to suck her breasts, alternately kissing each one. "Please. Stop."

Maurice pulled back, running his finger down the center of her chest. "Is that what you really want?"

"No, yes. Yes, I want you to stop." Fixing her dress, Kenya pulled the emergency stop button, and the elevator started moving again. She stood as far away from Maurice as she could, holding on to the rail behind her because her knees were shaking.

As soon as the door opened, she bolted off the elevator, nearly knocking over an elderly couple attempting to enter.

Maurice licked his lips as he watched Kenya run away. Now that he had a taste of her again, he wasn't going to be satisfied until he had all of her. But he was going to have to make sure Damon didn't get his clutches on her.

Chapter 7

By the time she made it down ten flights of stairs, Kenya couldn't breathe. She stopped and held the edge of the wall until her breathing became normal. Turning her eyes upward, she blew an angst-filled sigh. Why had she allowed him to touch her and kiss her? He had stirred feelings inside her that she'd worked so hard to bury in the deepest recesses of her heart. All it had taken was one kiss. One damned kiss that had almost made her forget nine years of pain and all the lies he'd told when he was sneaking around with Lauryn. One kiss had reminded her of the love they'd shared once, the tender moments they'd had sitting in her dorm room, eating pizza and kissing.

He's the one who ruined it all, she thought as she started walking again. *And he had the nerve to tell me not to go out with Damon. Then he gropes me in the elevator, as if he has a right to touch me.*

Sweat dripped from her brow, her hands shook, and her panties were moist as she relived those moments in the elevator. Maurice had every right to touch her, because she wanted him to. She wanted him to make her feel alive, wanted to feel him inside her and taste him again.

At the fifth floor, Kenya used her passkey to open the door to the stairwell. She ran into her room, peeled off her clothes, then jumped in the shower, setting the dial to cold. But she was still on fire. It was as if Maurice's lips had branded her, igniting a desire that burned from the soul and oozed out of every pore. Running her soapy rag over her sensitive breasts, Kenya closed her eyes and fought the urge to hop out of the shower and track Maurice down so that he could cool the fire he'd started inside her.

Am I crazy? That man just left his fiancée at the altar, and he's the same man who cheated on me in college. A few hot kisses aren't going to change the fact that he broke my heart.

Snatching the handle on the shower to stop the spray, she grabbed a towel, wrapped it around her wet body, and headed for her suitcase to find another outfit for her date, for which she was now late. Kenya pulled on a strapless white dress and eased into a pair of sling-back white sandals after smoothing lotion over her body. Dashing out the door, she rushed to the elevator, hoping Damon hadn't left the restaurant.

When the doors of the elevator opened, Kenya saw Damon turning to leave the lobby. "Damon," she called out, jogging slightly to catch up with him. She grabbed his shoulder when she caught up to him. "Sorry I'm late."

Turning around, Damon smiled broadly. "You were worth the wait. We missed the sunset, though."

"There'll be others, I hope," she said.

He clasped her hand with his. "The beach awaits us, princess."

Kenya blushed as they walked toward the beach. Something about the way Damon talked to her made her feel regal. He had manners, which most of the men she'd met in Atlanta and Maurice certainly didn't have.

Glancing over her shoulder, she gave Damon a cool

once-over. He was the color of peanut butter, and his eyes sparkled, as if he held a wicked secret behind them. Maurice's words echoed in her head. *That guy's up to no good.*

"You're quiet," Damon said, slowing his pace once they reached the beach.

"I was just enjoying the view," Kenya lied.

Stopping and standing in front of her, he replied, "So am I. God, you're so beautiful." He pulled Kenya into his arms and kissed her forcefully.

Breaking off the kiss, she took two steps back. "Damon, I didn't come out here with you to—"

"Dressed like that and on a secluded part of the beach with me? What did you think was going to happen?" He pulled her against his body again. "You want me, and I'm going to have you."

Kenya beat her fists against his chest, trying to free herself from Damon's clutches. But he wasn't letting her go and began pulling at her clothes.

"Stop it! Let me go!" she screamed at the top of her lungs. "Get your hands off me!"

Damon threw her down in the sand. "Shut up, bitch," he said as he unbuckled his belt. Kenya kicked him in his groin, temporarily stunning him. She struggled to push him off her. Then, lightning quick, Damon was snatched off her. With her eyes closed, she could hear sounds of a struggle and fists hitting flesh. She was afraid to move, afraid to open her eyes, because she didn't know what she was going to see. Was Damon overpowering her savior? Was she going to be in even more danger?

"Kenya? Kenya, are you okay?" Maurice asked.

She opened her eyes and threw her arms around his neck. "Oh my God."

Maurice lifted her from the sand. "Are you sure he didn't hurt you?"

She shook her head. "But if you hadn't gotten here when you did . . ." Her voice trailed off.

"Let me take you back to the hotel, and we can call the police."

"Just get me out of here." Her lips grazed his ear, and her voice sounded as fragile as a wounded bird's chirp. Trembling against his chest, Kenya held his neck tightly as if she were a vise. She didn't feel the sand that dropped from her dress, because her body was numb. Did she have *victim* tattooed across her forehead in ink, which only men with bad intentions could see?

Why was I so stupid? she thought as Maurice set her down before they entered the hotel. Though her knees were shaking, she wanted to walk.

Maurice wouldn't let go of her hand, and with his other hand, he stroked her back comfortingly. Once they entered the lobby, Kenya realized that she didn't want to be alone right now.

"Don't tell me you're okay, because I know you're not," Maurice said, holding her tightly. He stroked her hair, brushing the sand from it.

Her silence spoke volumes, and without even asking, Maurice led her to his room. Nervously, she chewed on her full bottom lip, torn between her gratitude to him for saving her from sexual assault and her anger with him. In reality, Kenya was no longer angry with Maurice, and if she was honest with herself, she would forgive him. How could she not? She had put her love life on hold, keeping on ice that part of herself that Maurice had hurt. Never had she thought they'd have a second chance, and never had she thought he would save her.

Turning and facing him, she stared thoughtfully into his eyes. "I should've listened. But I was just hoping that you were jealous and trying to stop me from having a good time."

Laughing softly, he placed his hand on her shoulder, which was trembling. "I was jealous. But I had gotten a vibe from him that I didn't like. Nothing happened, did it?"

She ran her hand across her face. "No, but not from his lack of trying. What is it about me that men see and try to take advantage of?" Focusing her stare on him, Kenya really wanted that question answered.

Stroking her cheek, Maurice stared back. His eyes were blank, as if he knew he was one of the men she was talking about. She moved out of the way of his hand, no longer wanting to be touched.

"Maybe I should go back to my room," she said.

"Does that creep know where you're staying?"

"Hell no. I'm not that stupid."

"No one is calling you stupid, but from . . . never mind."

Bristling like a cat that had been rubbed the wrong way, Kenya lashed out at him angrily. "I know you saved me from him, but by no means do you have the right to judge me. I made a mistake. I seem to do that with all the men I chose, including you."

"Can we take this beef between us and grill it? What happened to us happened a long time ago, and I don't know how I can change that."

"You can't, and you can't make up for it, either," she hissed. "Why am I even here with you?"

Wrapping his arms around her waist, he made Kenya face him. "Because I need to make things right, and there are no accidents in this world."

"So what was Lauryn?"

"A mistake."

She pushed his hands away. "But you never said, 'I'm sorry, Kenya.' You never told me what she had that you didn't have in me. I did everything for you. I loved you since we were kids, and the first chance you got to trade me in, you did."

"Kenya, I'm not going to explain away what I did. I can't, because I was wrong, but I was young."

"No excuse, not at all."

Maurice perched himself on the edge of the bed. "I'm not making excuses, Kenya, but are you still holding a grudge after nine years? You know, my life hasn't been a bowl of cherries. I've had my struggles and . . ."

"NFL championship. Wow, what a struggle." Sarcasm dripped from her voice like maple syrup.

"She left me at the altar. That's why I'm here with my brother." His voice dipped low, and for a split second, tears gleamed in his eyes.

Momentarily, Kenya reached out her hand, timidly touching his shoulder. Then she moved her hand as if her skin burned. "What happened?"

"It just didn't work out."

"Took you getting all the way to the altar to figure that out? How do I know you didn't just walk out on her? Your history precedes you," Kenya said as she took two steps toward the door.

"Don't leave." His voice rose like that of a child not wanting a parent to leave him with his grandmother. "I'm sorry, Kenya."

Turning around and seeing the tears glistening in his eyes, she had to believe that his apology was genuine. Then again, he was a master manipulator. At least that was the image of him that she'd developed in her mind over the years.

Don't let him get to you, she thought as she chewed on her lip.

Maurice closed the space between them. "If you walk out that door, I want you to go knowing that I never meant to hurt you. I wanted to reach out to you. I just didn't know how. I figured by now, some dude from back home would have swept you off your feet, and I was out of luck."

Folding her arms across her chest, she frowned and sucked her teeth. "So, Lauryn was the consolation prize?"

"Forget Lauryn. I'm sure she's forgotten about me," he snapped. "Can we talk about us and about this moment?"

"There is no *us*." Kenya opened the door and stormed out of the room. Though her heart was conflicted, she couldn't stay there and listen to him say the words that she'd waited all of these years to hear. Tonight was too emotionally charged. No one was speaking or thinking logically. As she walked to the elevator, her head swam in a sea of confusion. Pressing the button for the doors to open, she wondered if she and Maurice would have another chance.

His words echoed in her head. *There are no accidents in this world.* Maybe their meeting had been fate.

Chapter 8

It took Maurice about two seconds to run after Kenya and reach the elevator just as the doors began to close. Sticking his foot in the small crack, he forced the doors open.

"Kenya," he said, "number one, after what happened to you tonight, I'm not letting you roam around this property alone. Secondly, I let you walk out on me one time and didn't do anything about it, and I won't make that mistake again."

"Don't do this. Just leave me alone," she said in a voice that was as meek as a mouse. Maurice knew Kenya didn't want him to walk away any more than he wanted to leave. Maybe it was because of what had happened on the beach, or maybe she still had a place for him in her heart.

"You shouldn't be alone tonight. It would make me feel better knowing that you're safe." He reached out and pushed a strand of hair back from her face. "I'll sleep on the floor, by the door, if you'd like."

"I don't need you to stay with me. I'll be fine," she said, smacking his hand away. "Maurice, don't you, for one second, think I'm going to let you worm your way back into my life."

"After we leave this island, I'm sure we'll never see each other again."

"I wish that were true," she mumbled as she turned her back to him.

"What did you say?"

The elevator doors opened, and Kenya exited, with Maurice on her heels. "Kenya," he called out.

She didn't turn around; she just slid her electronic key into the lock on her door. "I'm moving to Charlotte to start a new job. I didn't want to take it, because I didn't want to see you and your new bride. I'd seen enough of your impending nuptials on TV. Then the Panthers won the Super Bowl, and you were the hero. But I thought about it and decided that I would no longer let you and that tramp control my life. I left school because of you two. I changed careers because . . . Forget it." She opened the door. "Good night."

Before Maurice could move, the door slammed in his face. He raised his hand to knock on the door. He wanted to tell her everything. He wanted to tell her how he'd been thinking about her for the last nine years, and how that day in her dorm room, he'd wanted to stop her from leaving. He'd never been totally happy with Lauryn, not like when they were together, and he knew that their love had been pure. He wanted to tell her that he'd been blinded by sex, that breaking up with her was the manifestation of his father's legacy.

Momma always said that I was more like him than I wanted to believe. I guess she was right. Then came karma, he thought as he walked away. He heard the creak of a door and turned around quickly. Kenya stood there, cheeks streaked with tears, eyes red and puffy.

"You're right. I don't want to be alone tonight, and even if it's you, I need someone by my side tonight," she whispered.

Crossing over to her, he reached out and touched her shoulder. "I'll sleep on the floor, by the door, if you'd like."

Shaking her head, she said, "You can sleep on the sofa. I think it pulls out into a bed."

Fighting the smile that was tickling his lips, Maurice followed Kenya into her room. Even on vacation she was still meticulous. Everything was in its place. Her clothes hung in the closet, in plastic dry-cleaners covers. Various styles of sexy sandals lined the closet floor. Maurice was digging the red, strappy sandals with the three-inch heels. Her suitcases were stacked neatly in the corner, and her laptop computer was closed on the desk. He was sure that the housekeepers didn't mind cleaning up this room. There wasn't a scrap of paper on the floor.

"Are there any extra sheets or blankets?" he asked as Kenya passed him en route to the bathroom, with her bedclothes in her hands.

"Uh, I don't know," she said. "Check in the bottom drawer. If there aren't any there, we may need to call housekeeping."

"All right," he said as he watched her disappear behind the white oak door. Maurice wanted to be in that bathroom, running her bathwater, slowly stripping her dress from her and massaging her shoulders with bath oil. He'd wash her hair, sensuously stroking her scalp and easing the tension with his touch. Then, in true Maurice fashion, he'd ease into the tub behind her, taking the soap from her hands and run it between her breasts, working up a thick lather. And before he would massage the soap into her skin in a sexual manner, he'd ask her if it was okay. She'd already been nearly violated, and he wouldn't want to add to the trauma. If he was given the green light, he'd play with her nipples until they harden like brown diamonds, waiting for the kiss of his lips.

His eyes were closed, and he was fully engrossed in his

fantasy, when he heard Kenya call his name. His response was, "Yes, baby."

"Maurice!"

Opening his eyes, he saw her standing there, with an over-sized terry-cloth robe wrapped tightly around her body, hiding every inch of what he was dying to see, touch, feel, and taste. "Oh, I, uh . . . What's up?" he asked, his face flushed with embarrassment.

"I don't even want to know what was going on in that head of yours. Did you find the blankets?" she asked, stepping back from him.

"No, I'll be fine, though. It's warm in here." Actually, he was hot, burning with a desire that he'd never felt with Lauryn. The love he'd had for Kenya all of those years ago had been inside of him, like a smoldering ember, and just a few hours in her presence had turned that nugget into a towering inferno. *Why did I let you walk out of my life for Lauryn? Why does it take years and distance for people to see clearly?* he thought as he watched Kenya climb into bed and pull the covers up to her chin.

"Do you want me to turn the air-conditioning down?" he asked as she rolled herself up in the blanket.

"I'm fine," she said. "I can't sleep if I'm not warm."

"Are you sure you want to go to sleep so early? It's not even nine yet. Why don't we—"

"You can do whatever you want as long as you leave me alone," she snapped. "I just need some quiet time."

Maurice walked over to the bed and sat on the edge of it, forcing Kenya to look at him. "Do you want to talk about what happened earlier?"

"Who are you, Dr. Phil? What part of quiet time don't you get?" she said angrily.

"You asked me to stay for a reason, and I don't think it

was because you wanted to ignore me and give me attitude all night."

Kicking out of the covers, she swung her legs over the side of the bed, away from Maurice, and dropped her head in her hands. Though he couldn't see her face, the shaking of her shoulders alerted him to the fact that she was sobbing. Over the years that he'd known her, Maurice had never seen Kenya cry. She was always so strong, so in control of her emotions. To see her this way made his heart lurch. *Did I ever make you cry?* he wondered as he timidly reached out to her, pulling her into his arms.

"I don't want your pity," she whispered. "I've never wanted your pity, and if you're here to ease your guilt about what happened between us, you can leave. I'll be fine."

"I could never pity you, Kenya. I've always admired you, and knowing who you've become, pity is the last thing I feel for you."

Turning and looking at him with puffy red eyes, Kenya went from sad to angry in less than three seconds. "What you feel for me? You're full of it. If you feel anything, it's the embarrassment of getting dumped at the altar. Am I supposed to sympathize with you because you know what it feels like to have your heart trampled on? You got what you deserved."

"Kenya, I-I . . ."

"Sorry. I'm sorry. I don't have the right to lash out at you. I asked you to stay with me, and this isn't right."

"We need to settle this," he said, wiping a tear off her cheek with his thumb. "If we're going to be living in the same city, we could at least be friends. Charlotte's big, but chances are we're going to run into each other."

"Friends?" she asked, her words dripping with sarcasm, like an overturned bottle of honey.

"Are you saying we can't be friends?" he asked, his

heart tingling, thinking that after they returned to the States, they would go back to being adversaries. Would she forget the time that they'd spent together?

"Maurice, we'll be civil, but I doubt we'll ever be friends again." She pushed out of his embrace. "I mean, why would we be? We're adults now, and it doesn't matter if you invite me to your parties or introduce me to your other friends. This isn't high school or college. You have your life. I have mine. No need for them to intersect."

Maurice shook his head, because he wanted their lives to do more than intersect. He wanted her to be a fixture in his life, and he wanted to be a fixture in hers. He wanted to help her pick out a house in Charlotte and drive her to the furniture market in Hickory so that she could find the right furnishings for her house. He wanted her to leave a tooth-brush in his bathroom and argue with him because he never had her favorite brand of juice when she spent the night.

"Kenya." He cupped her face in his hands and brought her lips level with his. He wanted to kiss her, wanted to taste the sweetness of her lips, feel the pinch of her nails on his skin as they made love for the first time in nearly a decade. He thought she would have wiggled away by now. But for what seemed like hours, they sat there, staring into each other's eyes. Her hands were firmly planted on the bed, as if she didn't want to touch him, though he wanted to feel her touch as much as he needed his next breath.

Finally, she pushed his hands away, as if she'd realized who was holding her. "I'm hungry," she said.

"So am I," he said. Unable to control his impulse to kiss her, he captured her lips and devoured them. To his surprise, Kenya melted against his body, and her tongue sought to overpower his.

Immediately, she pulled back, leapt from the bed, and

walked over to the window. "I can't do this. I refuse to fall for you again."

"I'm different."

"You're the same."

"Kenya, trust me. I've seen the error of my ways. I know that I was wrong in college, and that it's going to take time for us to—"

"For us to what? There's no way that anything will ever happen between us again. The most you can ever hope for is that I'll call you my friend, and that's not likely."

Maurice crossed over to her, standing a few inches from her. "Then why do you keep kissing me? The Kenya that I knew and loved didn't do anything that she didn't want to do."

Turning her head to the side, she said, "Kissing is just like a handshake. It means nothing. I thought you wanted something to eat."

"I do." He stroked her hand. "I just don't think it's on the room-service menu."

Pushing him in the chest, Kenya said, "You're disgusting."

He watched her as she walked over to the bed, holding her robe tightly. She reached into the nightstand drawer and pulled out the room-service menu.

"What food do you have a taste for?" she asked, looking up at him.

The only things Maurice had a taste for were her lips, her nipples, and the wetness between her legs. He wanted to pull that bulky robe from her body and see what she had on underneath. "Anything is fine," he replied, never taking his eyes off her.

Maurice listened as Kenya ordered chicken wings, carrot sticks, and rum punch. He didn't know if he'd be able to watch her eat, her lips closing around the chicken and arousing him in ways that only she could. *How am I going to convince her that I'd never do anything to hurt her again? How can I get you back into my life?*

As Kenya spoke to room service, she'd never been more aware of her sexual desire. If Maurice had kissed her one more time, she would have ripped her clothes off and let him make love to her. It seemed as if the incident on the beach was a distant nightmare now that Maurice was in her midst. She'd done what she'd sworn not to do: she'd fallen for him all over again. Tonight he was her knight in shining armor. But what would he be in the morning? If she allowed him to make love to her, would she be inviting trouble into her heart again? What if things weren't over with Lauryn, and what if he cheated again?

Don't do this to yourself, she thought as she hung up the phone. Turning to Maurice, she tried to keep her face expressionless. "The food should be here in about forty-five minutes."

"Okay. Then that gives us time to talk."

Rolling her eyes and stretching out on the bed, she said "What's left to say?"

Shrugging his shoulders, he sat down beside her. "A lot. Nothing. Kenya, if we can only be friends, then I'd be fine with that."

"Good. Then I'd be willing to try and be your friend. But it's going to be hard, because I'm usually friends with people I trust."

Placing his hand over his heart, Maurice impersonated Fred Sanford. "That hurt."

"You want to compare hurt? Or do you want to move on?" She rolled her eyes at him. *If I stay angry, then I won't have to deal with everything else I'm feeling right now,* she thought. *Why does he have to look at me like he can see through me?* Kenya turned away from Maurice's powerful stare.

"We can move on. I'm glad we cleared up some of this stuff between us."

Nothing was clear, except the fact that Kenya knew moving to Charlotte meant moving Maurice back into her life and her heart. Could she handle that?

Chapter 9

The next morning, Kenya woke up in Maurice's arms. His hands were underneath her robe and around her waist. How did this happen? *Rum punch.*

Slowly, she sat up, inching out of his embrace. She still had her panties on, but her pajama pants lay twisted on the floor. The matching tank top still covered her torso, but her bra was missing.

The events of the previous night were fuzzy, to say the least. But what she could remember was the room-service waiter walking in with a pitcher of rum punch. She'd immediately reached for it, needing a drink to take the edge off. Just being around Maurice had her senses frazzled, and add to that the attack on the beach, and the alcohol was welcomed. She'd polished off two cups before Maurice had even opened the plate containing the wings.

"Don't you think you need to eat something?" he'd said as she poured herself a third cup.

"I can handle it," she'd replied as he took off her robe. The temperature in the room had seemed to jump up one hundred degrees when Maurice had taken off his T-shirt.

His rippled chest had looked more delicious than the food before her.

"Not if memory serves me correctly. You've never been much of a drinker." Maurice had poured himself a cup of punch and taken a slow sip. "Strong, but sweet."

She'd watched his lips, and despite herself she'd wanted to taste them again. His kisses were like the drink he'd described, strong and sweet. Had the room been spinning?

"It's hot," she'd said. Then she'd accepted the saucer of wings that Maurice held out to her. The smell of the hot sauce had swirled around her nostrils and made her stomach bubble. Seconds later, she'd been vomiting all over herself.

"Oh, damn," Maurice had exclaimed as he rushed over to her, helping her to her feet. "I thought you could handle it."

"Shut up." Kenya had hobbled into the bathroom, trying to clean the vomit from her pants, but all she did when she turned the faucet on was totally drench herself. Yanking the pants off, Kenya had thrown them over her shoulder, returned to the bed, and flung herself across it. The pants had fallen to the floor in a heap. She'd moaned as the room began to spin again. "Maurice," she'd said. "Hold me."

"You're drunk."

"I know."

He'd wrapped his arms around her, and she'd drifted off to sleep, hadn't she?

Through her foggy eyes, Kenya looked over at Maurice as he lounged in the bed. A smile tugged at the corners of his mouth, making her doubt that all they did last night was sleep. Punching his shoulder, she called out, "Maurice, wake up!"

"Wh-what?" he asked, his voice thick from sleep. "What's wrong?"

"Last night did we?"

Maurice smiled wilily, "Are you telling me that you

don't remember what happened last night? I told you not to drink all of that stuff."

Rolling her eyes and folding her arms across her chest, she replied, "I don't need you telling me what I should've done. Just answer my question."

He laughed, so Kenya kicked him off the bed. After landing on the floor, Maurice looked up at her and said, "Nothing happened. I'd never take advantage of a drunk woman, no matter how much she was begging me to make her feel good."

"You are such a liar!" Kenya leaped from the bed. "There's no way I said anything like that to you. I'm not looking to win an Oscar by acting like I want anything from you."

Standing and adjusting his pants, Maurice laughed uncontrollably. "How do you know? You were drunk."

The icy stare Kenya gave him warned of violence if he didn't straighten up. "Kenya, nothing happened, besides you passing out and proving me right. You couldn't hold your liquor, yet you drank that rum punch like it was non-alcoholic fruit punch. I told you not to do that."

"So you've said already. Give it a rest." Kenya grasped the edge of the dresser as the room began to spin again. The sun flooding though the windows seemed to split her head open and fry her brain. She felt herself swooning, but before she hit the floor, Maurice's arms closed around her. Now her heart was beating overtime, because being this close to him was more intoxicating than the drinks she had consumed the night before. Why was she allowing herself to fall for him again? Who was she fooling? She'd never gotten over Maurice, and as much as she wanted to hate him, she couldn't. He was the man she'd always loved, because he'd branded her his long ago.

"I'm going to put you to bed and order us some breakfast

and a Bloody Mary for you. Then I'm going back to my room to shower and change," he said as he placed her in the bed and pulled the covers up to her chin. "Are you going to be all right?"

"Maurice, you don't need to take care of me. I overdid it last night on my own. Let me suffer alone," she mumbled and turned her back to him.

Placing his hand on her back, Maurice forced her to turn around and look at him. "I know what I need to do, and right now I need to make sure that you're going to be up and ready to have dinner with me tonight."

She raised her eyebrow and shook her head. Dinner with him? Being alone again with Maurice was the last thing she wanted to do. Being alone with him again would allow him to get close to her again. It would allow him to touch her and kiss her, and if the mood was right, then maybe she'd be swayed to make love to him. She'd almost wanted to last night but couldn't. More accurately, she wouldn't. She wouldn't make love to him, because she didn't want to be hurt again.

"I'm in no condition to go anywhere," she replied. Inching away from him, Kenya nearly fell off the bed. Maurice grabbed her to stop her from going over the edge. "See. I'm off balance."

"For now. But call me Dr. Mo, because I'm going to take care of you." Pulling her back to the middle of the bed, Maurice smiled at her. "You're going to let me in when I come back, right?"

"Maybe."

Maurice flashed her a lopsided grin. "You will, because you're looking forward to spending the evening with me as much as I'm looking forward to being with you." He kissed her on the forehead, then bounced out the door.

When she was alone, Kenya sat up in the middle of the

bed, as if she was the princess who'd found the pea. *What have I gotten myself into?*

If he could have floated on air, that was how Maurice would have gotten downstairs to his room. There was just something about being around Kenya—even though the circumstances weren't ideal—that made him happy. How would his life have been better if he'd left things with Lauryn as they should've been, a one-night stand? Thinking back to the night that he'd been seduced by Lauryn, Maurice realized that he'd been duped.

Kenya had had to study the night of a huge fraternity party, so Maurice had gone out with his crew of teammates.

"Your girl's lame," David Thomas, an offensive lineman, had said when he and three other football players had piled into Maurice's SUV. "She don't ever come out and hang with you."

Rico Madison had nodded in agreement as he buckled his seat belt. "I guess she doesn't realize all the honeys that would love to fill her shoes."

Maurice had dismissed what his buddies had said, but he'd been getting tired of Kenya's attitude, her desire always to stay in or just go to dinner and a movie. Sure college was about studying and getting an education, but they were young. And wasn't it time to have fun?

"I'm just trying to get my party on tonight. Kenya can study all she wants," he'd replied. Maurice had just gotten news that an NFL scout was impressed by his play in the CIAA league championship game against North Carolina Central University. It was possible that he could be going to play pro ball, and he was overjoyed. Playing football was all he'd wanted to do since he was a little boy. That dream was close to being realized, and all he'd asked his girlfriend to do was share in his exhilaration. But she'd turned him down again. Just like last week, when he'd wanted to blow off classes, get a room downtown, and spend the day making love to her. She'd had to study for her finals. Maurice had been pretty tired of being denied sex from the woman that had been his girlfriend for nearly seven years. He'd have understood it more if Kenya had been some girl he'd just met and if they'd never had sex before.

He'd been horny the moment he walked in the ballroom at the Omni Hotel, and seeing the half-naked girls shaking what their mommas gave them had aroused him, charging him with sexual energy. Then she'd walked over to him. He'd seen Lauryn around campus and at the games, cheering with the Luv-A-Bulls cheerleading squad. She'd had a body that was BET video-girl quality.

"Hey, Mo," she'd said as she pushed her ample behind into his crotch. If he'd been hard before, he'd become a brick when she gyrated against him.

"What's up, girl?" he'd replied, backing away from her. By the smile on her face, he'd known she'd felt his erection.

"Wanna dance?" she'd asked when a mid-tempo song began to play. Before he'd been able to give her a reply, Lauryn had grabbed his hand and pulled him onto the middle of the floor.

Lauryn had danced so dirty, Maurice had felt as if they'd had sex with their clothes on. Then she'd whispered in his ear that she had a room upstairs and that she'd love to get away from the crowd.

Led by lust, he'd taken her hand in his and left the ballroom. Inside her hotel room, it had seemed as if Lauryn was ready for a guest. She'd had candles surrounding the bed, just waiting to be lit, a bottle of cheap champagne had been resting on ice, and a box of condoms had been on the nightstand.

"Damn," he'd said after taking in the sight. "Thought of everything, didn't you?"

"Well," she'd said as she began to snake out of her clothes. "I was hoping you'd be here, because I've been wanting you for a long time."

Maurice had watched her striptease, with a smile dancing on his lips. Her body had been more amazing than he could have imagined: small waist; round, apple-shaped bottom; and breasts the size of melons. Thoughts of Kenya had floated from his mind the moment Lauryn had pushed him backwards onto the bed and unzipped his oversized jeans with her teeth.

"This is going to be our little secret," she'd said before taking his erection into her mouth.

After that first encounter, Maurice had been hooked and had sought Lauryn out for more sex. Kenya's studying had become a good thing, because the more time she spent in the library, the more time he spent sexing it up with Lauryn. Somehow, he'd confused love and lust, and when Kenya had walked in on the two of them making love in his dorm room, he had thought that his future was with Lauryn.

That was the biggest mistake of my life. If I knew then what I know now, I would've never gone to that party, and I wouldn't have let Kenya walk out of my life, Maurice thought as he unlocked the door to his room.

"Where have you been all night?" James asked as soon as Maurice walked in.

Smiling and pulling his shirt over his head, he replied, "With Kenya."

"No way. I thought she hated you." James walked over to his brother and shook his head. "What are you two doing? Making up for lost time?"

"Not yet. Something happened to her last night, and she needed my help. But she told me that she's moving to

Charlotte." Maurice flung himself on the bed and kicked back. "I'm going to win her back, J."

"Do you really think she's going to take you back? That was a pretty hard slap you got earlier. Hate like that isn't easily overcome. Unless you put something on her last night that erased nine years of . . ."

Maurice threw his hand up. "Don't go there. Nothing really happened between us, but I know and have known for a long time that losing Kenya was the biggest mistake of my life. Besides, it's a thin line between love and hate. I don't believe she hates me as much as she wants me to believe."

"Only took you getting stood up at the altar to figure that one out, huh?" James laughed uncontrollably. "I tried to warn you about that chick, but you didn't listen."

Maurice rolled his eyes. He'd heard this song and dance before from his mother, his friends, and of course, his brother. So, they were right, but he was tired of hearing it. "I get it. Let's move on. Lauryn wasn't right for me, blah, blah, blah. What's good for a hangover?"

"You got a hangover?"

"Kenya does. I told her I was going to take care of her, and that she was going to have dinner with me tonight," Maurice said, his mouth upturned in a smile.

James shook his head. "Taking advantage of a woman recovering from a hangover. That's cold. Get her a Bloody Mary and something greasy. She'll be up and at it in no time."

Maurice sat up; reached for the phone; ordered a breakfast platter of eggs, bacon, and toast; and had it sent to Kenya's room. When he was done, he took a quick shower, dressed, then headed back to Kenya's. Before he left, James called out a warning.

"Don't be surprised if she's planning something to get you back for what you did to her."

Maurice turned around and looked quizzically at his brother. "Is there a woman out there that you trust?"

"Sometimes I trust Ma." James threw a pillow at Maurice as he walked out the door.

Heading down the hall, Maurice tried to dismiss what James had said. Kenya wouldn't try do anything to get revenge on him, whether he deserved it or not. She wasn't that kind of person, was she? He didn't know her as an adult, but Kenya had always had class, even when she'd been pushed to her limit. Maurice knew he and Lauryn had pushed her too far with their relationship, and looking back on things, he didn't blame her for leaving school or for pushing Lauryn down the hill. He blamed himself for allowing her to leave school and for letting Lauryn fool him into thinking hot sex was love. It had taken him awhile to accept responsibility for what had happened between him and Kenya. It was easier for him to blame someone else for his shortcomings when he was younger. Now he had to prove to Kenya that he was a changed man.

When the elevator doors opened, he came face to face with Damon. A heated rage flowed through his veins. "You son of a . . . ," Maurice yelled as he lunged at him, grabbing his collar and jacking him up. "You have some nerve showing your face around here."

Damon pushed Maurice off him, knocking him into the wall. "Touch me again and I will sue you."

"If I were you, I'd check out of this hotel and get off this island, because you're not going to hurt Kenya or any other woman," Maurice growled.

"The bitch wanted me and that—"

With lightning-fast reflexes, Maurice punched Damon in the face, knocking him unconscious. He pushed him out of the elevator and headed up to Kenya's floor. As soon as he stepped off the elevator, two burly security officers were standing there, waiting for him.

"Sir," the tallest officer said, "we need you to come with us."

"Why?" asked Maurice.

"You just assaulted one of our guests, and we're going to have to hold you until the authorities arrive," the other officer said as he pulled out a pair of handcuffs.

Maurice held his hands up. "That guest of yours nearly raped a woman last night, and he's lucky I didn't kill him."

"Are you the victim?" the taller officer asked. "Because if that's the case, then we can—"

"Hell no, I'm not the victim. The man's still breathing, isn't he? This is some BS. He nearly rapes someone, and you want to arrest me?"

The officer with the handcuffs approached Maurice and attempted to put him in the cuffs. It took every ounce of self-control Maurice had not to push the man away. Instead, he allowed the officer to do his job.

"What's going on?" Kenya asked as she opened the door to her suite. "Why are you arresting him?"

"Ma'am," the taller officer said, "please step back into your room."

"No! What are you doing to him?" Kenya demanded. Clad only in her bathrobe, she walked up to the officer. "Why is he in handcuffs?"

"This doesn't have anything to do with you," the officer holding Maurice said.

"Kenya, tell them about last night," Maurice said. "Tell them why I punched that fool."

"Maurice, what did you do?" Kenya asked as she ran her hand over her face.

"I saw Damon when I was coming down here," he said. "Tell them what he did to you."

"Please, let him go," Kenya said. "That man tried to . . . Please, he didn't do anything wrong."

"Ma'am, this is the last time that I'm going to ask you to go in your room and let us handle this."

"If he did anything, he did it for me. He's not the one who should be in handcuffs. What about the man who tried to rape me? Where's he?"

"Possibly on the way to the hospital," replied the security officer holding Maurice as he pushed him toward the elevator.

"Kenya, go get James for me. I'm in room three-four-five," Maurice said as the officers carted him away.

On the ride down to the security office, all Maurice could think about was the scandal that all of this was going to cause in the papers.

Damn, this is not how I want to end up on SportsCenter, he thought as the officers pushed him into a small room to wait for the police.

Chapter 10

Dressed in a terry-cloth skirt and a V-necked T-shirt Kenya dashed into her room. Then she ran down two flights of stairs. After she arrived at Maurice and James's door, she banged on it like a maniac.

"What in the hell?" James snapped as he snatched the door open.

"Maurice has been arrested," Kenya said in one breath. "We got to get to him."

Pulling Kenya in the room, James asked her to slow down. "What do you mean, he's been arrested?"

"Two security officers took him away because he was trying to defend me," Kenya said, jumping up and down. "There's no telling what's going to happen with these foreign cops."

James nodded and slipped on his sneakers. "Do you know where they took him?"

She shook her head furiously. "They're going to have to let me see him because I'm a lawyer," she said.

James raised an eyebrow. "You're sure you want to do this? I thought—"

She cut him off by opening the door. "We can catch up later. Maurice needs us."

Kenya and James dashed downstairs to the lobby, taking the stairs rather than waiting for the elevator. Once they made it to the front desk, Kenya banged on the desk with her fist. "Hello! Somebody!"

A flustered clerk rushed forward. "Yes, ma'am?"

"My client was taken into custody by one of your security officers. Where did they take him, and has the police been contacted?" Kenya demanded in her ultraprofessional tone. Her head was throbbing, but she ignored it.

"Ma'am, I don't know what you're talking about," said the clerk. Then she turned her back to Kenya and James, attempting to ignore them.

Kenya stretched across the desk, snatched the woman's shoulder, and whirled her around. "If you don't find out where those officers took Maurice, there's going to be a problem here."

The woman's face contorted with fear as she gingerly moved Kenya's hand. "I'm going to have to get my manager."

Stepping back, Kenya folded her arms across her chest. "You do that, now."

James turned to Kenya, a smile tugging at his lips. "Remind me not to get on your bad side. You're tough. Maurice is lucky to have you in his corner."

"I'm not in his corner, but what he did was for me, and I have an obligation to do the right thing for him," Kenya snapped. She didn't want James or anyone to think that things had changed. And she definitely didn't want to believe that she and Maurice had a future.

James threw his hands up as if to say he didn't want to get into a shouting match with her.

When the hotel manager arrived in the lobby, Kenya lit

into her, demanding to know where the security officers had taken Maurice.

"Ma'am, you need to calm down," the manager said, smoothing her navy blue skirt. "Mr. Goings and the security officers are with the police in the office. . . ."

"And as his lawyer, I have a right to be in there with them. Either take me in there, or you will be hit with a multimillion-dollar lawsuit, which you will never recover from," Kenya shouted so forcefully that other guests began to look at them.

Quickly, the manager pulled Kenya and James to the side. "Follow me," she said, attempting to stop a scene from developing.

As Kenya and James stepped on the elevator, behind the manager, Kenya watched the woman like a hawk. When she inserted her passkey into the console and pressed the B button, James cried foul.

"Where are we going? To the dungeon?" he remarked.

"The security office isn't a dungeon, sir," the manager spat.

"Where was your security when you had a guest attacking a woman on the beach?" Kenya snapped.

"We can't control what happens outside of the hotel. However, if a guest would've reported that there was a problem, then we would have investigated it fully," said the manager.

Kenya rolled her eyes. What in the hell was she doing? This wasn't the way she'd intended to spend her vacation. She was supposed to be relaxing, unwinding, and getting ready for her move to Charlotte. Yet, here she was, being Maurice's defender. It wasn't as if she was a criminal attorney. Maybe she'd just be able to talk fast and loud to get him out of trouble. The elevator doors opened, and the manager led them to a room no larger than a closet. As soon as they opened the door, the sound of booming laughter met them.

Kenya had expected to find Maurice shackled to a chair, with a blackened eye, a busted lip, and a broken nose. Instead, he, the security officers, and two police officers were laughing it up, drinking what looked to be the infamous rum punch, and taking pictures.

Snarling and curling her lip upward, Kenya said, "What in the hell is going on here? You're having a damn party, and we're—"

"Kenya," Maurice said, jogging over to her and planting a wet kiss on her cheek. She wiped his saliva off and glared at him.

"I thought you'd been arrested," Kenya snapped. "I've been running around this hotel, looking for you, threatening people, and you're here, having a good time."

"Baby doll, you were worried?" Maurice asked, his voice filled with concern. "I didn't mean to worry you."

Kenya slapped his hand forcefully. "Don't you dare call me baby, and if you're not going to jail, then I'm going back to my room." She stormed out of the office, pushing the security officers and the manager out of her way.

Maurice was quick on her heels. "Kenya, look, I didn't mean to worry you, but there aren't any phones down there. When Damon came to, he decided not to press charges, packed his bags, and checked out. One of the officers recognized me from the Super Bowl, and we were just joking around."

"Then don't let me stop you. I'm going back to my room," she said, pushing him in the chest. "Don't bother me anymore."

As Maurice watched her retreat down the hall, he called out, "What about dinner?"

Her answer was to stroll away without looking back.

James placed his arm around his brother's shoulders. "Great job, genius. You might have the strength and the money in the family, but thank God I've got the brains and the good looks." Pushing his brother to the side, James called out to Kenya. "Hey, Kenya, wait up."

She turned around and smiled warmly at James. "Yes."

James ran his hand across his face. "You know Maurice was just being Maurice. He didn't know how worried you were about him. Don't be so hard on him."

Kenya shook her head. "I see nothing has changed with you two. You're still cleaning up his messes."

Shrugging his shoulders, James replied, "That's what brothers do. We look out for each other. Had I been in Charlotte when he needed me, this might be your second honeymoon."

"I don't think so," Kenya said as she jabbed at the elevator button. "There's nothing between me and Maurice. That ship has sailed, sunk, and exploded. Nothing will ever change between us, and that's fine with me."

The elevator doors opened, and James stepped on with Kenya. "I don't think that's true, K. If you didn't feel something for him, you certainly wouldn't have been running around the hotel, looking for him. You don't have to play hard with me. I know you."

Kenya rolled her eyes at him, hating the fact that he was so right in his assessment of her feelings. She shrugged him off. "People change."

"True, and Maurice has. He knows that he messed up with Lauryn. But—"

"I don't want to hear that," she snapped. "So, he and Lauryn broke up, and he thinks that he can go down memory lane with me like we're on some cheesy soap opera? Whatever. Just keep your brother away from me so that I can enjoy the rest of my vacation."

* * *

Maurice made his apologizes to his new friends, then took off in search of Kenya. By the time he reached the elevator, the doors had already closed. He decided to take the stairs. He ran up to the fifth floor, taking two steps at a time. Winded, sweaty, and shaking, he arrived at his destination at the same time Kenya stepped off the elevator.

"Kenya," he called out breathlessly.

Kenya turned and looked at him, and a deep frown darkened her comely face. "What is it, Mo?" she asked.

"I'm sorry. The last thing I wanted was to make you worry. When those guys grabbed me, I thought things were going to get ugly."

Kenya turned her back to him. "Whatever, Maurice. I'm going to try and salvage the rest of my vacation. Why don't you just leave me the hell alone? You've already taken too much of my energy."

He reached out and touched her shoulder, gently turning her around to face him. "I thought we were going to start over. Try to at least be friends."

"Why? You're still the same selfish bastard you were nine years ago, and I'm not going to get . . . Forget it, Maurice. Just leave me alone."

"You still owe me dinner. And I'm going to hound you until we have dinner together."

"No."

He pouted like a child and tugged at her arm. "Come on. If I screw up at dinner or do anything to make you mad, then all bets are off, and I'll leave you alone. Come on. I almost got arrested for you."

"Your point?" she snapped. "If it means getting you off my back, then fine. I'll go to dinner with you tonight. Seven and don't be late." Kenya stomped to her room and slammed the door.

Maurice knew he had to go all out to woo her. Rushing

back to his room, he called the concierge to find out where he could get orchids and the best chocolates money could buy. Just as he was about to book a quiet table at a restaurant recommended by the hotel staff, James walked in and pressed the release button on the phone.

"What the hell are you doing?" Maurice demanded. "I was using the phone."

"We need to talk about Kenya and what *you're* doing," James said.

Maurice picked up the phone and started dialing again. "What do you mean?"

James took the phone from his brother's hand. "I mean, that woman still cares about you, and if this is some rebound, island fling, then you're going to need to leave her alone."

Glaring at his brother, Maurice reached for the phone, but James held it out of his reach. "So, you think you know how I feel? You can see into my mind and tell me what I feel for Kenya?"

"I can tell you this. You should've been with her all along, instead of with that thing you almost married, and I'm not going to sit around and watch you hurt her for a second time. So, what's the deal, baby bro?"

Maurice rose to his feet and stood toe to toe with James and took the phone from his hand. "The only thing I'm trying to do is make Kenya fall in love with me again. That's it."

James leaned back against the wall and jammed his hands in his pockets. "So what happens when you get back to Charlotte and the rumors about your wedding start swirling again? How are you going to handle it? You going to go back into hermit mode and hide from everyone again, including Kenya? And how's a relationship with you going to affect her? She's going to immediately be fodder for the tabloids. Are you going to protect her from all of that?"

Maurice absentmindedly stroked his chin. "Yeah, I can protect her."

James shook his head furiously, "Man, you could barely protect yourself when this all broke down. Do I need to remind you of the state you were in before we got here? Now I'm supposed to believe that you're all healed and ready to move on. How long has it been? The only reason reporters haven't been all up in your face is because no one knows where you are. When Damon goes to tell his story, which I'm sure the weasel will, what are you going to do?"

"Be a man and stand up to them. They're just a bunch of pen pushers with no lives, anyway."

"Uh-huh," James said. "Just know that when you and Kenya leave paradise, there's an ugly world out there, and I don't think you've heard the last of Lauryn."

Dialing the restaurant's number, Maurice pondered what his brother had said. When would Lauryn reappear in his life? *It doesn't matter. I don't want anything to do with her. She's a liar and a cheater, the same thing I was when I was in college.*

Later that evening, armed with a box of Godiva truffles and flowers, Maurice knocked on Kenya's door. When she opened the door, the very sight of her dressed in a simple pair of denim shorts and a pink tank top took his breath away. Maurice had gone all out, putting on a stylish beige linen short set and brown sandals.

"Do I need to change?" Kenya asked as she eyed him. "I thought we were going to have a casual dinner. I had no idea that you were going to be so dressed up."

"Don't you dare change. You look beautiful. I mean, you've always been beautiful. Your clothes don't make you. You make them," Maurice rambled.

Kenya rolled her eyes. "You can stop blowing smoke now."

Maurice laughed and held the flowers and candy out to

her. "It's not blowing smoke when it's the truth. Are orchids still your favorite?"

Kenya smiled as she gently ran her fingers across the flower petals. "I can't believe you remembered that."

Maurice fought the urge to say the clichéd line that she was unforgettable, since he'd already been accused of blowing smoke. Instead, he smiled and offered his elbow to her, as a gentleman should. Kenya ignored him, set the candy on the edge of the dresser, and then closed the door, keeping the orchids with her.

"These are some beautiful flowers," she said. "Thank you."

Maurice dropped his arm, thinking that winning Kenya over was going to be harder than he'd initially thought. Many women that he'd been with would lose their minds over Godiva chocolate and orchids. But those women were groupies, and he couldn't compare those types of women to Kenya.

It wasn't as if he could blame her for being apprehensive about him. He counted himself lucky to even be in her company, because he wouldn't give Lauryn a second chance, no matter what she said or did. Already, Maurice knew he didn't deserve Kenya, because the pain he felt losing someone to another woman had probably hit her ten-fold. They say you never get over your first love, and he'd never really gotten over Kenya. He'd settled for sex and lust, the only things that he and Lauryn had really shared. Since he'd been so focused on his NFL career, Maurice had thought his hot relationship with Lauryn wouldn't amount to anything. Then she'd convinced him that they should marry. Ignoring his family's warnings and the bells going off in his head, Maurice had proposed long before the Super Bowl. Somewhere along the way, Lauryn had gotten the idea to turn their relationship into a media circus. It had only taken a night of the most passionate and freaky sex for Maurice to agree to a public proposal. Lauryn had said that it would prove to his family how much she meant to him. *What a joke,* he thought as he and Kenya waited for a taxi in front of the hotel.

"You're quiet," Kenya said. "Something on your mind?"

Maurice rubbed his throat but didn't reply immediately. He just watched Kenya as she nodded her head.

"Aw, I know that look," she said. "You're either about to tell a lie or I'm going to hear something that I don't want to hear."

"I have to be honest with you about something," Maurice said. "There has been a lot of publicity about Lauryn and me breaking up, and I didn't deal with it well. For about three weeks after everything went down, I closed myself up in my penthouse and didn't talk to anyone, didn't go anywhere, and ignored everything. James said I went into hermit mode. This vacation was really supposed to be about me getting my life back on track. Finding you was an added bonus, which I'm thankful for."

Kenya shifted her flowers from one arm to the other. "And you're telling me this because?"

"I just wanted to be honest with you," he said. He regretted those words because he hadn't been totally honest. His pride wouldn't allow him to say, "Lauryn left me for another woman."

"That's a new approach," she said, then quickly bit her lip.

As the taxicab pulled up, Maurice just opened the door and didn't respond to her dig. He couldn't help but wonder if Kenya would ever let go of the past. Then again, he knew he was asking her to do something that he wasn't willing to do.

I'm just going to have to work that much harder, he thought.

Chapter 11

As they rode to the restaurant, an uncomfortable silence enveloped them, though Maurice wanted to ask Kenya a decade's worth of questions. What had her life been like in Atlanta? What did she do other than work, and how did she really feel about moving back to Charlotte?

Instead, he sat there, watching her, admiring how she'd changed from a cute girl to a beautiful woman. Her face was slimmer, her cheekbones were more defined, and the tropical sun had given her a brown tan, which made her beauty more exotic. She was a candy bar that he wanted to devour, a chocolate treat that he had to taste. She was his addiction, and he hadn't had a chance to feel her lush womanhood or taste the deepest crevices of her body. But he was going to, whether she liked it or not. She was going to love it, because he was going to love every inch of her.

"Do you have something you want to say to me?" she asked. "All of this staring isn't cute."

Maurice's cheeks grew hot. "Can't help it. Are you still a football fan?"

"Yes," she replied as she carefully set the flowers on the

seat between them, creating a boundary that he couldn't cross. Maurice glanced down at the flowers and smiled.

"Favorite team?"

"Still Dallas, even when you were playing for them," she replied. The hint of a smile tugged at her lips.

"Well, you have to support the home team now. I'll even give you my jersey," he said.

Kenya laughed heartily. "I don't think so. I remember when I wore your ratty jersey in high school." She stopped talking, as if the memory pained her. Her eyes went dark. Then she said, "Why did you tell ESPN that Lauryn was your high-school sweetheart? When I heard that, it made me feel some kind of way. I don't know why. I mean, I don't have any kind of feelings for you."

Maurice ran his hand across his face and dropped his head. "I didn't tell anyone that," he said. "Media folk like to say what sounds good and makes the story better. That's what I have to deal with, unfortunately."

Kenya shrugged her shoulders and toyed with an orchid petal. "It doesn't matter. It just bothered me at that moment," she said.

He placed his hand on top of hers. "Tell me something about you. What's life in Atlanta been like for you?"

Inching her hand from underneath his, Kenya turned toward the window. "My life has been and will continue to be work."

"But all work and no play makes Kenya . . ."

"The youngest managing associate in the firm's history," she said proudly.

Maurice studied her profile as she watched the colorful scenery they passed. "Impressive. But you still need a life, Kenya."

"Unfortunately," she snapped as she turned around and

faced him, "my work doesn't mean playing a game. I don't get months and months off, like some people."

"Football is hard work," Maurice said. "My body gets pounded in practice, on the field, and people stay in my business."

Kenya clucked her tongue against her teeth. "That sounds so hard to me. Talk to me when you work eighty hours a week just so someone else can take the credit for what you've worked hard to negotiate. That's work, not tossing a ball around."

"Well, I stand corrected," Maurice replied, not taking his eyes off her. "You take your job very seriously. But being a lawyer wasn't your dream. Why didn't you stick with public relations?"

"People change. Dreams shift," she said. "I love what I do, and I don't think about what could've been."

Maurice read the duality of her words. "I do," he said. "I often think about what would have happened if I wasn't such a fool back then. What if we . . ."

"Mo," Kenya said quietly. "The past is the past. Nothing we can say or do will change that."

"What about the future?" Reaching up, he stroked her cheek. "Can we have a future? A second chance?"

"I don't know," she said, melting against his touch, nearly crushing her orchids. Quickly, as if she'd touched a burning ember, Kenya pulled away from him and inched closer to the door. "I'm not going to let this go to my head. While we're here, with no cameras, no other women, and you nursing a broken heart, I'm what you want. But what happens when you get back to your reality, the groupies, and all of the women who throw themselves at you? You've never been able to turn a pretty girl down, have you?"

"I've changed," he said. "I know it may take you a while to believe it, but I *have* changed."

She rolled her eyes and picked up her flowers, holding them close to her face to cover up her frazzled senses. Being so close to Maurice and inhaling his scent made her remember things that she'd wanted to forget. Prom night. She'd given him her virginity, and he was so tender, gentle. With every thrust, he'd asked, "Are you okay?"

Those memories made it hard to look at him, especially when he looked so good. His arms looked ready to hold her, and as she glanced at his crotch, she thought of dark rooms with candles burning, massage oils, and ecstasy. That was why she had to look away from him when he spoke. Maybe he was trying to seduce her; maybe he wasn't. Whatever he was doing was working, because despite her misgivings about any relationship with him, she knew at the end of the night, he was going to end up in her bed.

Once they made it to the restaurant, Kenya was shaky on her feet, because she was filled with carnal desire for Maurice. How did she get to this place? she wondered as the host led them to a secluded table near a window in the back of the restaurant. The sun was just starting to set, creating a picturesque scene that naturally set the mood for romance.

Setting her flowers on the table, Kenya faced Maurice head-on. *Should I tell him what I'm feeling right now?* she thought. *Who am I fooling, though? If Maurice and I make love, there will be no way that I can walk away from him, because somehow, I still love him. After all of these years, I still carry a torch for this man. Am I pathetic?*

"Everything all right?" Maurice asked. "Is the table okay?"

"It's beautiful. Then again, everything on this island is." Kenya took a deep breath, deciding that it was now or never. "Maybe it's the island or the fact that we're here together, but I want to spend the night with you, in my suite."

Maurice sat back in his chair, not expecting to hear Kenya say those words. "Whoa."

"That way we can have some closure between the two of us, and we can move on with our lives. When we get to Charlotte, we're going to run in different circles, and we're not going to see each other. There will be no need for the two of us to ever speak again," she said.

Another shocker, he thought. "Is that what you really want? You want closure?"

"I didn't get it nine years ago. I want to be able to move on with my life, and I can't do that being stuck in the past," she said. What she didn't tell him was that it had been nine years since she'd made love to a man. She wasn't going to tell him that he was the first and the last man to ever touch her or make her desire sex. That would be admitting that she'd given him power over her life.

"And that's all you want?" Disappointment peppered his tone. "We can't write a new chapter together? Kenya, you may not believe me, but I've never stopped loving you."

She grinned sardonically, then leaned forward. "You don't have to say you love me. We're still going to have sex tonight."

"Not with those strings attached."

It was Kenya's turn to ease back in her chair. Now he wanted to be difficult. "Strings? The only strings attached to this offer is a G-string. Maurice, I'm sure you have women beating your door down. Why do you want to rekindle something that obviously didn't work before?"

Just as he was about to respond, a petite waitress, with a head full of small braids, walked over to take their orders.

"Can we have a few more minutes?" Maurice asked, ready to finish his conversation.

The waitress nodded and smiled. "Honeymoon?" she asked, with a thick accent.

"No," Kenya said a little more forcefully than she should have. "We're not married."

Maurice swallowed hard and smiled at the waitress. "Just a few moments," he said in a voice barely above a whisper. "I guess you want to make sure that everyone knows that we aren't together, huh?"

"It's the truth," she said, fingering her hair nervously. "And you've already made it clear that you're not going to give me what I want."

"Meaningless sex? Not my style." He looked down at the menu so that he didn't have to look into Kenya's eyes. *Who is this woman?* he wondered. Back in the day, Kenya had rarely wanted to have sex. He'd had to tell her repeatedly how much he loved her; he'd had to assure her that he wouldn't have sex with her and leave her for another girl. Now, she was asking him for one night where they could have closure? Not in a million years, because when he made love to her, he wanted it to be the beginning and not the end.

Kenya reached across the table and pushed his menu down. "Tell me something, Maurice. When did you grow some morals? You're sitting here and pretending that you've never had meaningless sex before."

Pushing his menu aside, Maurice stared intently into Kenya's eyes. "So, let's say I agree to what you want to do. Can you handle me walking away?"

Folding her arms across her chest, she raised an eyebrow. "You walked away before. I dealt with it. This time it's on my terms, and I can handle it just fine."

What if I can't? he thought. "Fine. Then let's do it. You want to skip dinner and just go at it?" Maurice asked coldly. "I mean, why should I spend money for dinner when I can get dessert for free?"

Kenya smiled. "Was that supposed to make me change my mind? If it will make you feel better, I'll pay for dinner."

Maurice shook his head. "Sorry. I was out of line, because I don't know if I can handle walking away from you. Why can't we just try our love again?"

"Because I don't want to be hurt again," she blurted out. "If it's not Lauryn, who will it be the next time?"

Maurice grabbed her hands and kissed them gently. "I would never hurt you again."

Closing her eyes, Kenya slipped her hands out of his grasp. "I don't believe you, and I'm not willing to take the risk of having you prove me wrong."

"So, this is it?" he asked. "All we have is one night together?"

"We could've had a lifetime," she whispered, with a far-off look in her eyes. "Listen, if you're going to be weird about this, then maybe we shouldn't do it."

"How many more days are you here?" Maurice asked.

"Three."

"Then give me those three days. After that, we walk away," he said. "Fair?"

Kenya nodded and picked up her menu. "I can handle it if you can," she said.

He smiled only because in the next seventy-two hours, Maurice was going to make sure that she never wanted to walk away from him again.

After dinner, Kenya and Maurice headed down to the beach. The two glasses of wine that Kenya had with dinner had lowered her inhibitions, and she was ready to put her bold plan into action. She couldn't believe that she'd actually said those things to him at dinner. She didn't regret putting her desire for him out there, but was she going to be able to hold up her end of the agreement? When she got on the plane to head back to Charlotte, was she going to be able to forget whatever they were about to share?

"You're quiet," Maurice said. "Changing your mind?"

"No, just thinking about seeing you naked later. I guess you work out a lot these days." She ran her finger down his bicep, following the curve of his muscle.

"I'm not the only one who works out, I see," he said, eyeing her supple body. "I can't wait to peel those clothes off you and see what I've been missing all of these years."

"So, why are we walking around out here?" She wantonly slipped her hand inside his shorts. His pleasure was evident as soon as she touched him.

Breathlessly he said, "All right. Let's catch a cab and get back to the resort. My suite or yours?"

Kenya turned to face him and was about to lean in for a kiss when flash bulbs went off in their faces. "What in the . . ."

Maurice lunged at the photographer. "Get out of here!"

"Mo, is this your new woman?" the photographer asked, shoving a tape recorder in his face. "Have you gotten over—"

"Shut up," Maurice bellowed as he balled up his fists and started to punch the man.

Kenya grabbed his shoulder. "Maurice, stop!" His violence was giving her pause. She understood why he'd pummeled Damon, but all they had to do was walk away from the paparazzo. "Let's just go."

Shrugging her off, Maurice stomped away while the photographer continued to snap shots of him.

Kenya knew that with him in a foul mood like this, they wouldn't be having a romantic romp tonight. By the time she caught up with him at the taxi stand in front of the restaurant, she didn't have two kind words to say to him. So, she kept quiet.

Maurice turned to her; a melancholy smile touched his lips. "I'm sorry. I told you how the media work, and I don't handle it well. Now our private moment is going to be all over some damned tabloid in the morning."

"And violence would've changed that how, Mo? You're lucky that you didn't go to jail earlier today for a fight, and now you get into another one?" Placing her hands on her hips, she shook her head from side to side. "What's with you? I mean, you know that you're famous. You certainly didn't have a problem being on the cover of magazines and on TV when you and Lauryn were together. So, I have to wonder, is it that you don't want to be seen with me?"

Clenching his jaw tightly, Maurice shook his head. "I don't do public-relations events with my life. Hell, all of the publicity surrounding my wedding wasn't my idea. That should've been something between me and Lauryn, but she wanted to make it all about being seen. When I'm on the field and in the locker room, the media can have my time. But when I'm alone with you, I want to be alone with you, without looking over my shoulder to be sure I'm not being filmed. Now, I'm probably going to have to check out of the hotel and find someplace else to finish my vacation."

She turned her back to him, not really buying what he was trying to sell to her. "Maybe that's a good idea, and this can be good-bye," she said, then hopped into the first cab that pulled up. Kenya slammed the door before Maurice had a chance to get into the cab.

Chapter 12

By the time Maurice returned to the hotel, his anger had subsided somewhat. Now he was just disappointed. He'd known that he had blown his chances with Kenya, and not just for tonight, but for forever.

However, he wasn't going to apologize for decking that photographer. Even if he weren't a Super Bowl champion, he deserved some privacy. Besides, he didn't want Kenya hearing from anyone that Lauryn had left him for another woman. He didn't plan on telling her, not right away, anyhow. Especially since she thought he was trying to avoid being seen with her. If Maurice won Kenya's heart again, he'd shout it from every mountain top and put it up on a billboard on the busiest street in Charlotte and in the middle of Times Square. It just wasn't time yet.

Stepping on the elevator, Maurice headed for Kenya's door. Once he got there, he stood there, fist poised to knock, but he didn't. What could he say to her tonight that wouldn't fuel her anger or seem as if he was just trolling for booty? He turned on his heels to leave but stopped when he heard the door open.

"You were just going to walk away?" Kenya asked. "I

saw you through the peephole and wondered, When has Maurice Goings ever been a coward? You can't face me or something?"

She was still dressed in the outfit she'd worn to dinner. Maurice smiled halfheartedly. "I figured you needed your space, tonight, anyway."

"You scare me," she revealed. "Then again, I guess violence is a part of your job and life."

Leaning against the wall, Maurice shook his head. "You make it sound like I'm a contract killer."

Kenya opened the door wider and beckoned him inside. "It isn't like football is ballet. You hit people. You make headlines because you can take linemen out."

"I'd never hit you," he said.

"Supposed to be a selling point or something?" she asked as she took a seat on the bed. "You're not supposed to hit anyone, at least off the field."

"And I don't. I mean, as long as . . . I should just stop," he said when he noticed the suspicious look in her eyes.

"What are we doing?" she asked. "Why are we trying to relive the past when it should just die?" She crossed her legs and stared up at him while he grasped the edge of the dresser. "Maurice, maybe it was the wine. Maybe it was me wanting to live out some sort of fantasy of having sex with you and then leaving, as if you never meant anything to me. But everything I said at dinner was wrong and . . ."

Maurice crossed over to her and sat in front of her, holding her hands down on the bed. "I knew that wasn't you talking, and I know one thing. I can't change the past, but we can build a future, if you give me a chance."

Her eyes misted, and Maurice immediately wanted to pull her into his arms and kiss her tears away. Kenya slid her hands from underneath his and pushed him away.

"Maybe love isn't for me. I mean, I have a lot of work to

do in Charlotte with the new office, and it's all going to fall on my shoulders, success or failure. The last thing I need is to be emotionally entangled with you again," Kenya spat in rapid-fire fashion. Each word stung Maurice like a bullet, that is, until he read between the lines.

Kenya still loved him. Otherwise, she would've been able to ignore what had happened on the beach. She wouldn't be sitting there, with tears in her eyes. That nugget of hope was all he needed to spur him to kiss her, tenderly at first. Then his urgent hunger heated the kiss.

To his delight and surprise, Kenya responded, slipping her tongue inside his mouth as he did the same. Drawing her into his arms, Maurice lifted her shirt and palmed her taut breasts. With his thumbs, he stroked her nipples back and forth until they were as hard as diamonds. Breaking off the kiss, Maurice asked her if she was all right. She gave a silent answer by removing her shirt all the way. He held her out at arm's length and marveled at her body. This was the Kenya he remembered. Despite her new body, she was still a little timid when it came to making love. But Maurice could barely contain his excitement to see the rest of her as he fumbled with the button and zipper of her shorts.

Kenya grabbed his hands and moved them to her hips. "Slow down," she whispered. "I'm not going anywhere."

He kicked out of his shorts as Kenya unbuttoned his shirt. His thick erection nearly sprang out of his boxer shorts when she kissed him down the center of his chest. Leaning forward, Maurice took Kenya's legs and wrapped them around his waist. Her breasts pressed against his chest, making him harder by the moment.

Kenya's lips brushed across his neck as she inched up to his ear, kissing and sucking on his lobe. With one hand, she stroked the back of his neck, and with the other, she stroked his manhood, almost bringing him to a climax. He moaned gutturally, unable to express his desire in words, as Kenya closed her thighs around him, drawing him closer to her burning mound of desire. He reached between her legs, using his finger to touch her wetness, and, boy, was she wet.

"You feel so good," he whispered before kicking out of his boxers. "I don't want to have sex with you, Kenya. I want to make love to you."

Thrusting her pelvis against his, she said, "You don't love me. Don't talk. Just give me what I want, and take what you need." She ground her body against his.

Though he could barely contain his desire to bury himself inside her, Maurice pulled back. "I need your love, and I know you love me, Kenya. Say it."

"I-I . . ." Her voice trailed off; tears pooled in her eyes. "Maurice, please."

"You love me, and I need to hear you say it," he pleaded. "I can't make love to you unless I know that this isn't meaningless sex."

Unfurling herself from him, Kenya stared at him. Her eyes flashed angrily. "Did you love Lauryn when you . . . This isn't what I wanted. Why do you want me to say it?"

"I need to know. Do you love me?"

Turning away from him, she whispered, "I love you, and I hate myself for it." She sat up, easing herself to the edge of the bed. "I should've gotten over you after I left for Atlanta, but I couldn't. I was weak and . . ."

Maurice placed his hand on the small of her back. "You're not weak, because I feel the same way. I've never loved anyone the way I loved you."

She turned and faced him; a deep frown creased her face. "You said you loved Lauryn. You chose her over me and did it so that everybody could see. Do you know how that made me feel?" A single tear fell from her eye, speeding down her cheek before Maurice could wipe it away.

He held her face between his hands. "That was the biggest mistake of my life. You loved me unconditionally, and I took it for granted, allowed my hormones to think for me, but I'm not that guy anymore."

"I don't want to get hurt again, Maurice," she said. "I don't want to have to wonder if another woman, with a better body or a special trick in bed, is going to come by and seduce you again. I won't let you hurt me again." Reaching for the rumpled blanket on the bed, she covered her nudity.

"Kenya," he said, his lips close to hers. "I'm not going to hurt you. I'm not going to let anyone or anything come between us again. All I want to do is love you again."

She melted in his arms and silently sobbed on his shoulder. Her hot tears seemed to seep though his soul. It was as if she was cleansing both of them. They needed this; they needed to get their feelings out in the open. Now that he knew she loved him and she knew he loved her, Maurice couldn't wait to express it physically. Leaning back on the bed, he pulled Kenya on top of him, stripping her blanket away.

He gave her naked body the once-over; she was beautiful all over. With her lying before him, he thought about being on his honeymoon, with Kenya as his bride. Leaning in, he kissed her neck, then used his tongue to blaze a trail down to her breasts. He stopped to kiss and suck her nipples as they hardened at his touch.

He slid his hand down her flat stomach and between her thighs, feeling her wetness on the folds of flesh holding her pleasure. Maurice grew hungry for her, wanting to taste her desire. Easing down the length of her torso with his lips and tongue, Maurice planted his face between her legs and, with his tongue, pushed back the tender skin that held her throbbing clitoris.

Kenya inhaled sharply as he wrapped his tongue around her tender bud. Her legs and her stomach trembled as he deepened his kiss. Intense sensations of pleasure rippled though her body like rain falling into a quiet pond. Clutching the back of his neck, Kenya pressed her body against his mouth, silently urging him to give her more. He responded by kissing her harder, flicking his tongue across her sensitive bud until she came like a tidal wave. Her body burned as the orgasm washed over her. She opened her eyes and looked down at the smile on his face. It was as if her pleasure was bringing him joy.

"Are you all right?" he asked.

Unable to speak, she just nodded, then gripped his shoulders, urging him to continue with his sensual body kiss. It didn't take much prodding for Maurice to continue treating Kenya's body like dinner. Placing her legs on his shoulders, he left a sweet trail of kisses on her inner thighs, and with his finger, he entered her, discovering her to be nearly virgin tight. Maurice couldn't help but wonder when a man had last touched her and made her moan as he was doing.

An unexpected feeling of jealousy blanketed him as he thought about Kenya making love to another. She was his, and tonight, he was going to brand her with his love. With his free hand, he reached for his shorts, grabbed his wallet, then removed the condom.

Turning her head to the side, Kenya watched as he placed the package on the side of the bed. Seeing the shiny gold wrapper made it real. There'd be no turning back. How many nights had she dreamed of feeling the length of him inside her, her legs wrapped around his waist, pulling him deeper into her valley. Kenya reached for the condom, then said, "I want you inside of me." She held it out to him.

Her eyes screamed for him to make love to her immediately, and he was happy to oblige.

Maurice ripped the wrapper open and slid the latex sheath in place as Kenya stared at his dangling erection. As he turned to her, she grabbed his shaft, guiding him to where she needed him most. Her moans were like music to his ears. Kenya ground her body against his as she pulled him deeper and deeper inside. Within minutes, she felt as if she was going to explode. Maurice found her G-spot and the rhythm of her heartbeat, and they began to dance to it.

"I love you," she said in a whisper, which she thought Maurice didn't even hear. Kenya twisted her hips like a Moroccan dancer as Maurice dove deeper and deeper inside her. The heat from her womanly core spread across her body. Even her cheeks became flushed. When Maurice reached up and stroked her nipples with his thumbs, she could no longer contain herself. She climaxed and screamed his name so loudly that she was sure everyone on the floor heard her. But she didn't care. Never had she felt so satisfied, so womanly, so loved.

Wait a minute, she thought. *An orgasm doesn't mean love. This is crazy. I'm professing my love to this man because he made me come?* Part of her wanted to throw his arms from around her and order him out of the room. Instead, Kenya lay in Maurice's arms and accepted the tender kiss he placed on her forehead as he twirled his finger around a tendril of hair above her ear. She didn't want to ruin the afterglow of their lovemaking, but she couldn't help but wonder if he'd held Lauryn this way, kissed her tenderly, and slept against her breasts. How insecure would he think that she was if she asked those questions? But as he lay there, they gnawed at her. Kenya moved his arm from across her chest.

"What's wrong?" Maurice asked.

"I can't breath," she said as she sat up. Kenya pushed her hair back from her forehead and turned her back to him.

"Do I need to call someone? The hotel doctor?" His voice was peppered with concern as he placed his hand on the center of her back.

Kenya recoiled at his touch, as if he'd burned her skin. Quickly, she rose from the bed and stormed into the bathroom.

"Did I do something wrong?" Maurice called out. "Kenya, what's the matter?"

"This was a mistake," she said to the bathroom door. "What the hell was I thinking?" Kenya locked the door just seconds before she heard the springs of the bed move. She figured that Maurice was crossing over to the bathroom door. Seconds later, the doorknob twisted.

"Aw, Kenya, open the door. What's this all about?"

"Me making the biggest mistake of my life. That's what it's about." She slapped her hand against her forehead and silently thanked God that he hadn't heard her when she'd said she loved him the second time. "Maurice, please leave."

"Open the door and face me, or I'm going to break the door down." His tone was serious. "If I did something to hurt you, tell me."

Kenya fought the tears pooling in her eyes. If only she would have closed her mind to the past and just focused on the moment. Then she wouldn't be locked up in the bathroom, analyzing what should've been a beautiful reunion. They wouldn't have needed a reunion if it hadn't been for such an ugly breakup.

"I'm counting to ten," Maurice said.

"You can't threaten me to open the door," Kenya snapped.

"One."

"Maurice, just go. We both got what we wanted."

"You know I wanted more than a roll in the sack with you. I told you that. Two."

"Over the years you've told me a lot of things. Made promises that you didn't keep. So, what makes this time different?"

"Three. I've changed. I'm different. Four."

Knowing that he'd probably make good on his threat to break down the door, Kenya felt that the best thing to do was to open it and face him. Putting on a poker face, she opened the door. "All right. If you're so different, why don't you listen to me for a change and do something that I want you to do and get out of here?"

"Because you don't want me to leave," he said. "What's wrong?"

Kenya pushed past him and got into bed. "I just can't lie here with you, knowing that months or even weeks ago, you were doing this with Lauryn."

Maurice held his chin, closed his eyes, and shook his head. "And what about you? What were you doing before tonight? Everybody has a past, Kenya."

"You're my past. I just don't see you being in my future, especially if I want one without having my heart broken again," she snapped. "I can't kiss you and not think about how you kissed her. I can't sleep with you and not wonder what you and Lauryn did in bed. I will never forget what I walked in on that day."

"That's not how I wanted you to find out about us," he said in a low voice filled with regret. "Lauryn and I are over, and whatever I have to do to prove to you that you're the one I want to be with, I'll do it."

She tried to steel herself and not let go of her emotions, but she broke down. Her shoulders shook as she sobbed. "Why?" she asked. "Why wasn't I enough for you?"

He wrapped his arms around her shoulders. "I let everything go to my head. I was a big star, and I listened to people who told me that I should've been playing the field, and that I was supposed to have all of the girls on campus that wanted to be with me. I wasn't supposed to be with one woman."

"What did you want? Did you want all of that? You still ended up with one girl. So, what did Lauryn do that made you love her?"

"I don't think I really loved her. I was blinded by lust, and she was hanging on to my coattails, just like my family said." Maurice turned Kenya around and made her face him. "We can't stay stuck in the past. We can't let my mistakes stop us from moving forward. Can you let it go and give me another chance, or am I going to have to keep facing this?"

His words angered her. He wasn't the wronged party. Who had given up everything to be rid of him? She had. She hadn't been able to move on, because so much of what she thought about love and men was wrapped up in what Maurice had done to her. Forgive him? Give him another chance? No way in hell.

"You know what? This was a mistake, and it will never happen again. Kindly put your clothes on, and get the hell out of here." She snatched the blanket from the bed to cover her nudity, stormed into the bathroom, and stayed there until she heard the door close, indicating that Maurice had gone.

Chapter 13

When Maurice returned to his room, he paced back and forth like a caged lion hungry to bite something or someone. What was wrong with Kenya? How could she ruin a moment that was so beautiful and so tender? Did she think he didn't hear her when she said she loved him that second time? Maurice chewed on his bottom lip, thinking that he had to do something to ease her insecurities about Lauryn. How could he, though? He knew that if Lauryn tried to worm her way back into his life, he wouldn't take her back, because he'd never be able to trust her again. He'd wonder if a night out with the girls meant that she was planting her face between her friend's legs again or vice versa. He was gaining a greater understanding of what Kenya had been going through.

Maybe it's time to tell her the entire story behind my marriage that never was, he thought. As he turned to head out the door, James walked in, with a deep scowl on his face. Maurice thought for a second that his brother was going to knock his lights out.

"What did you do to her?" James demanded hotly.

"Get out of my way."

James pushed Maurice in the chest, causing him to fall

on the floor. "Kenya's sitting at the hotel bar, eyes red and puffy, and I know you're behind it."

Hopping up like a kicked dog ready to bite his attacker, Maurice grabbed his brother by his collar. "What's your obsession with what's going on between me and Kenya? You act like you want her for yourself."

Pulling away from Maurice, James glared at him. "Kenya is my friend, she always has been, and I saw what you did to her in the past. I won't let it happen again."

"What are you talking about?" Maurice asked. "What do you mean, you saw what I did to Kenya?"

"She was a mess when she came back to Atlanta. She barely wanted to talk to me or anyone associated with you. Kenya didn't care about her appearance or anything. Her mother was so worried about her. One day I was chilling at the Atlanta University Center, and I found her, much like I found her today, crying over you. When she told me that she walked in on you and that girl, I couldn't believe it, because I thought you would have had a little more class than that."

"So, you've been in touch with Kenya all of these years? And let me guess. You fell for her?" Maurice said snidely. "Whatever, James. Is she still at the bar?"

"You're not going down there to mess with her head some more," James snapped. "I don't know what—"

"That's right. You don't know what the hell is going on, so you need to back off." Maurice pushed past his brother and headed downstairs, hoping to find Kenya at the bar.

She was sitting at the darkest end of the bar, head down and her hand wrapped around a half-empty glass of what looked to be whiskey from where Maurice stood. Slowly, he approached her, standing in the shadows and observing the look of sadness on her face. The last thing he'd ever wanted to do was put that look on her face again. He knew that look. That was the same look that he'd seen when she walked in the room that day.

When he reached her, he placed his hand on her shoulder. "Remember what happened the last time you decided to tie one on," he said in a lame attempt to make a joke.

The frown on Kenya's face said she wasn't amused. "What did James do? Run to your room and tell you that I was down here?"

"Believe it or not, his intentions weren't to reunite us," Maurice said. "Can we talk?"

"There's nothing left to say." She picked up her glass and took a sip of her drink.

"I think there is. I have to confess something. I can understand you a lot more than you think," he said as he turned to face her. "I didn't tell you everything about my breakup with Lauryn." Maurice inched closer to Kenya, forcing her to give him her full attention.

"You called my name out during sex, or something corny like that?" She laughed coldly. Her eyes didn't sparkle, as they had when he'd tickled her earlier.

"No," he replied, taking her free hand in his. "Lauryn left me at the altar for her friend Mya Brown."

Kenya cocked her head to the side as if she was deciding if Maurice was telling the truth or not. "Mya Brown? The same Mya who was her roommate in college?"

Maurice nodded. "One and the same. As it turned out, they'd been carrying on an affair for a number of years. Even when we were in college, I'm guessing. While I was shut up in my house, I thought back to all of the nights she had stayed over at Mya's, and to their shopping trips to Vegas, New York, and wherever else they'd gone together. I realized that I had been played for a fool. And she made it so that when she left me, we had a huge audience and a media following. I don't know if she and Mya planned this as some sort of lesbian revolt against men, or if Mya was bewitched by her, like I had been. But now I understand how you felt finding out that I was with another woman. Mya must have given Lauryn something that I couldn't."

The sardonic smile on Kenya's face made him regret his words. Was she mocking him? Had he overestimated how she felt for him?

"Let me get this straight," Kenya began. "Because Lauryn turned gay or whatever, you understand how I felt knowing that you had cheated on me? You're an asshole. Oh, was I supposed to feel sorry for you because she left you for a woman? What was the point of your story? Was that supposed to change something?" Rising to her feet quickly, Kenya knocked her stool over and attempted to storm out of the bar.

Maurice impeded her exit. "Is it possible to love someone and hate them at the same time? How can you run so hot and cold with me when I know you love me?"

"You know no such thing," she snapped.

"I have two ears, Kenya. I can hear and I heard you earlier. You said you loved me twice, and then you kicked me out of bed like I was a gigolo." He held her arm to keep her from bolting. "What is it, sweetheart? Do you love me or hate me? I wish you'd tell me, because I need to know what I have to do to make you see that this is fate. We're supposed to be."

"I'm sorry Lauryn left you for a woman. But I won't be the validation of your manhood. You won't dump your insecurities and shortcomings on me because of what she did. Deal with it. Learn to live with it. I did." Snatching her arm away from him, Kenya stalked out of the bar.

So much for a relaxing vacation, she thought. She was more tired now than she had been when she'd arrived on the island. There was no need to prolong this, she decided.

She was going to Charlotte and back to her old ways of being buried in work.

The move to Charlotte wasn't as taxing as Kenya had expected. Maybe it was because she had seen Maurice already and didn't expect to see him again. The way they'd left things in the Bahamas had given her the closure that she'd needed all of these years. But it had also stirred something inside her, which she refused to acknowledge. At night she dreamed of his touch and smelled his scent when she would inhale deeply, and that made her crave his kiss. Vivid memories of their lovemaking often woke her in the middle of the night or broke into her quiet moments in the office, when she was the only one there, drafting briefs. But there was no way that she was going to seek him out. She had too much work to do, and Maurice was more than a distraction. He was poison.

Kenya might not have seen Maurice in person, but his face haunted her. On the way to work, she saw his half-naked body on a billboard advertising Calvin Klein underwear. Then there was the Carolina Panthers' season tickets billboard with Maurice in his uniform, making his clutch catch in the Super Bowl. Those were all over the city. And the irony of all ironies was the fact that her law office was in a new development across the street from Bank of America Stadium, where the Panthers played. At least football season was over, and she didn't have to see Maurice going over there to practice every day.

Catching herself staring at the stadium, Kenya twisted her chair away from the window and faced her closed office door. *Why can't I just forgive him? Why can't I stop thinking about him? He said he's done with Lauryn, and God help me, I love him. And he knows it.*

"Ms. Taylor," her assistant, Talisha, called over the inter-com. "Your three o'clock is here."

"Thank you," Kenya said as she straightened her coat. It was time for business. According to her calendar, she was meeting with Brothers Reality, a company that was nego-tiating with the city to purchase land in a few of the city's distressed neighborhoods and to create housing for low-income families as well as a community center, which would provide after-school activities for the neighborhood kids and computer training for the adults who needed it. Kenya was excited about the project and couldn't wait to meet the "brothers" behind Brothers Reality.

What she didn't expect was for Maurice to walk into her office. Momentarily, she was rendered speechless. Was she imagining things?

"What do you want?" she asked.

"Is that how you greet all of your clients or just me?" he asked, with a huge smile on his face.

"I have an appointment with—"

"Brothers Reality. That's my company. James runs it, but I lend my name and face when necessary," he said, taking a seat across from her desk without an invitation. "So, how have you been? Are you enjoying Charlotte?"

Did he really walk in here? Is he really talking to me as if we're old friends? Kenya thought as she stared at him in disbelief.

"I've looked over the contracts that were messengered over here," she said, ignoring his attempts at small talk. "The asking price for the land is way too high. Especially when the houses there are scheduled to be condemned by the city. I'm going to recommend that one of our other at-torneys works with you on this contract."

Maurice shook his head, then said, "I want the best, and

from what I know about you, the only person at this firm that I want handling my business is you."

Kenya rose to her feet and smoothed her skirt, wishing that she's worn her Prada pants suit instead of her knee-skimming Donna Karan outfit. "I have nothing but the highest level of confidence in everyone on my staff. If you can't work with someone else, maybe you need to find another firm to assist you."

Crossing his long legs and running his index finger down the crease of his pants, Maurice watched Kenya like a hawk. Her legs looked delectable, and he wanted to reach out and touch them, just to see if she was wearing nylons or not.

She turned and looked at him, catching the lustful look in his eyes. "What?"

"Listen, you know I came here because you work here. I wanted to give you some space between what happened in the—"

"Don't," she said in a whisper. "Don't say anything about what happened in the past, no matter how recent."

He stood and closed the space between them. "I can't stop thinking about you," he said, his lips so close to her ear that his breath sent shivers up and down her spine. "I know you feel the same way. I can see it when you look at me."

Kenya was powerless to move away from him. She didn't have her wits about her, because his lips were just too close to her and his scent of patchouli overwhelmed her. "What about your contracts? This is highly inappro—"

He cut off her protest with a sharp kiss, catching her off guard and causing her knees to buckle. Maurice swooped Kenya off her feet and sat her on the edge of her desk. She didn't resist his kiss. Instead, she plunged her tongue into his mouth, drawing him deeper into hers. Sucking on his tongue, she forgot where she was, what she was supposed to be doing, and the fact that her assistant could walk in the door at any moment with a tray of coffee.

Maurice slipped his hands underneath her skirt, stroking her thighs, and they were just as smooth as they'd looked when he'd seen her standing by the window. She didn't have on any stockings, and that made his manhood harder than he thought it could get. He wanted to rip his pants off and bury himself inside her, because when he fingered the crotch of her silky panties, it was hot and wet. She did want him, and he had to have her.

Before they became too heady with desire, Talisha buzzed Kenya, and they broke off the kiss. "Ms. Taylor, there's a Mr. James Goings here. He said he's a part of the meeting."

"Yes, yes," Kenya said as she wiped her mouth. "Send him in." She dashed behind her desk, straightening her skirt as she sat down.

Maurice licked his lips and raised his eyebrows at Kenya, as if to tell her that they were not finished.

"Sorry, I'm late," James said, looking from Kenya to Maurice. "What did I miss?"

Maurice smiled at his brother. "Kenya was trying to assign us to another attorney."

Shaking his head, James said, "I wonder why. Kenya, how are you, hon?"

She extended her hand to James. "Good, thanks. I was telling Maurice that the city is asking too much for this tract of land that you all want to purchase. I believe condemned property shouldn't cost this much."

"And to think you wanted to just sign," Maurice said to his brother.

"But do we want to get into a bidding war with some larger company? I mean, Maurice is a star and all, but the only thing that matters around these parts is money," James replied.

Kenya folded her hands underneath her chin and crossed her legs, hoping to stop the throbbing in her panties. "Well," she said, gaining her composure, "sounds just like home. But even if you all get into a bidding war, I know that there are minority-business provisions in dealing with the city, which should work to your company's advantage. You all are black owned, correct?"

"I think so," James replied sarcastically. "At least we were this morning."

Kenya pouted, then quickly smiled at him. "I have to ask," she said. "A lot of professional athletes lend their names and likenesses to companies that they have no ownership in. I don't want anything we take to the city to be questioned unduly."

Watching Kenya in her element made Maurice think that she was even sexier. He'd always known that she was smart, but as she explained the law and the potential negotiations that they would need to enter in with the city, he saw that she was brilliant. Still, the dominating thought in his mind was pushing all of those papers off her desk and making love to her. They were on the fifteenth floor. No one would see them, despite the fact that she had huge bare windows in her office.

"Mo, are you listening?" James asked.

"Yeah, I'm listening," Maurice lied. "How long before we take a new offer to the city?"

Kenya smirked at him. "Thought you were listening. I said I'll call the city attorney and set up a meeting next week."

"You're handling it, right?" Maurice asked.

Reluctantly, she agreed. "I'll give you a call, James, when the meeting is set."

James rose to his feet and thumped Maurice on the shoulder. "Thank you, Kenya." He handed her a business card. "I look forward to it."

Slowly, Maurice stood up. "Kenya, it was a pleasure. Why don't you let me buy you dinner tonight as a welcome to the city type of thing?"

"I don't know. I'm going to be working pretty late," replied Kenya. She wasn't going to be alone with this man, not feeling the way she was feeling. They'd never eat, because she would be his main course. "A rain check, maybe."

"I'm going to take you up on that, definitely," said Maurice. With that, he and James headed out the door.

Seconds later, Talisha walked into the office and faced Kenya, with a huge smile on her face. "Was that Mo Goings?"

Kenya shrugged her shoulders. "Yes."

"Oh my God! Is he a client?"

"I don't have to remind you that our client list is confidential," Kenya said sternly.

Talisha nodded and headed out the door, muttering that Maurice was much finer in person than he was on those billboards.

You don't know the half of it, Kenya thought as she dropped her head on her desk.

Chapter 14

When James and Maurice made it outside to the parking lot, James lit into his brother. "I know you're trying to woo Kenya, trying to get her back in your life, bed, or whatever. But this is my business, our business, and that was not cool in there."

"What?" Maurice snapped. "Look, I didn't do anything wrong."

"I'm not blind. I know something was going on before I got there. And what's up with telling me that the meeting was at three thirty?" James said. "I've been heading up this company for years, and now, all of a sudden, you take an interest in it, because Kenya's in town and working with our company. You need to stop it."

"James, I swear to God, you act like a jealous boyfriend when it comes to her. Is there something I should know about you and Kenya?" Maurice started for his car.

James glared at his brother's back. "You know what? I don't have time for you and your BS, Mo. You think that you can have anything you want, and you've been like that since you were a child. The first moment that someone put a football in your hand, you just thought you were all of that.

That's why you played with Kenya's emotions and ended up with that whore, and now you think that because you got embarrassed, you can turn around and suck Kenya into the Mo Show again. When we were on vacation and you were doing your thing, that was one thing, but this is real life and business. We've got too much riding on this deal with the city for you to let your hormones get in the way."

Maurice turned around and looked at James. "All right? You feel better now? Have you been holding that in since we were kids? Listen, I've never acted the way you described. I've never been that cat who thought playing football made me better than other people. You and everybody around me thought that. Everybody except Kenya. You want to tell me that I'm ruining our business? It's really my business, which I allow you to run. I know how important it is for us to build these houses, and I wouldn't do anything to hurt this project, but I'm not going to let you make me feel guilty for wanting Kenya."

"Even though you had her and threw her away? What happens, now that she's our lawyer, when you mess up again?" James snapped.

"Nothing. Because I'm not going to mess up, and that woman is going to be mine. You just stay out of my way," Maurice snapped, then got into his car and sped off.

Kenya sat at her desk, allegedly going over a few case files. But her mind was on Maurice and what had nearly happened on her desk. *What the hell was I thinking?* she thought. *I should've never taken Maurice and James on as clients. Anyone could negotiate their contracts with the city.* She flung her reading glasses off and dropped her head on her desk.

When her cell phone rang, she nearly jumped out of her skin. "Hello?" she said.

"Kenya, it's Imani. How's everything going?" her friend asked.

"I wish I could say great," Kenya said and sighed. "But Maurice was in my office today."

Imani groaned. "Why are you taking up with that jerk again?"

"I didn't say that I was," she said, though the words were hollow. "He's famous here, I'm a contract attorney, and we're going to cross paths."

"How was your vacation?" Imani asked. "I haven't heard from you since you up and left Georgia."

"It was a whirlwind," Kenya said breathlessly. "Maurice was there, too."

"You two are going to get back together, aren't you? You're letting him off the hook, and you don't even know what he did to Lauryn to make her leave him at the altar. Kenya, don't let him hurt you again."

Rising to her feet, Kenya headed for the window and looked out at the twinkling lights of the city. "Maybe he didn't do anything to Lauryn. What if he's changed?"

"Do you believe that he can change?" she asked. "You ran away from him because you found him in bed with Lauryn. Now this man is an NFL star, and women will be throwing themselves at him. What are you going to do when that happens? Run away again? Are you going to nurse a broken heart for the rest of your life?"

"I don't know," Kenya said. "You think I'm crazy, don't you?"

Imani sighed. "It really doesn't matter what I think. It's your life. Just be careful. I'd hate to see you let Maurice ruin your life again."

Kenya fingered her hair. "Did he ruin my life? I mean, look at me. I'm successful, financially stable, and . . ."

"Does he know?" Imani asked ominously.

"Don't go there," Kenya said, pushing the memory to the back of her psyche. "It's been so long ago. There's no need to tell him."

"Why not? He has a right to know, and if you're thinking of starting a future with this man, you're going to have to clear up everything in your past," Imani said wisely.

"And that would accomplish what?"

"Maurice can't be so vain as to think that the only reason you left school was because of him and Lauryn," Imani said.

"It really doesn't matter why I left," Kenya said. "All that matters is that . . . nothing. Imani, I don't want to think about that stuff now."

"How can you not? How can you look at him and not think about what could have been? You two would have a family now if you hadn't—"

"I have to go," Kenya said, abruptly snapping her phone shut.

Walking over to her desk, she fell into her seat and thought back to her first week back in Atlanta nine years ago.

Kenya had moved into her dorm room at Clark Atlanta University. Luckily, she didn't have a roommate, thanks to her mother's string pulling. Sitting on the twin bed, she'd become violently ill. She'd vomited all over the floor before dashing to the bathroom, where she'd continued to vomit. Then she'd felt blood between her legs. The next thing she'd remembered was waking up in the back of an ambulance.

"Ma'am," the technician had said, "you're on your way to Grady Hospital. You're having a miscarriage."

"What?" had been her reply before she'd blacked out again.

Waking up in the hospital had allowed the reality of what had happened to sink in. Kenya had suspected that she was pregnant. That explained her weight gain. But she had been too afraid to take a pregnancy test, knowing that a baby would have complicated her life in ways that she'd never recover from. Then finding out that Maurice had been cheating on her had solidified her resolve not to tell him about her suspicions. Then there was her mother. Angela would have been devastated to know that Kenya had done the very thing that she'd promised she wouldn't do.

The doctor had walked into the room. "Miss Taylor, I'm sorry for you loss," he'd said as he sat on the edge of her bed. "Would you like for me to call your parents or the father?"

"No," she'd said. "I'll be fine."

"You shouldn't go through this alone."

"I didn't even know I was pregnant. You can't miss what you never knew about."

He'd pulled out a pad and had written down the name of a counselor. "I can't make you go see this doctor, but I think you should talk to someone about your loss, if not your parents or the father. Please talk to someone."

Pain had shot through her body as she'd tried to sit up in the bed. Lying back, Kenya had looked at the doctor and told him that she'd be fine.

But she'd never been the same since. She'd never been able to reclaim that lost part of her soul. Losing Maurice's baby and his love had scarred her for life, and hiding those scars had forced her into her life of solitude.

For the rest of her days in college, Kenya had turned down more dates than she could count. When she'd be out and see a young couple with a small child, her heart would lurch. That could have been her and Maurice. And whenever she'd thought of Maurice, she'd wondered what his reaction would have been to her pregnancy. Would he have accused her of trying to trap him and cash in on his potential NFL salary? Would he have left his new relationship to be with Kenya and his child, or would he have harbored resentment toward her for forcing him into something he might not have been ready for?

I wasn't ready for motherhood, and maybe that was God's way of saving my child from a hard life, she thought as she shut down her computer and prepared to go home. *Everything happens for a reason, and I can't question it or wonder what if. Maurice doesn't have to know.*

When Kenya arrived in the lobby, she found Maurice standing at the security desk, signing an autograph for the guard with one hand and holding a bag of Chinese takeout with the other.

"Mo?" she said.

Looking up at her and smiling, Maurice said, "I figured you were still here, so I came to collect on my dinner rain check."

"Not tonight. I have to get home. I still have some unpacking to do, and I stayed here later than I'd expected," Kenya said.

"Maybe I can help," said Maurice.

Oh no, she thought as she looked at him. *You and me alone at my place spells trouble, and you're not going to just eat and leave. I know that much.*

"I got it. I just have to unpack some boxes and set up my entertainment center," she said.

"Have you eaten dinner or even lunch? Basically, I'm

not going to take no for an answer. You can say yes, or I'll just follow you. I can't let this food go to waste. It's already gotten cold," Maurice said, flashing her a smile that made her heart melt.

"If she doesn't want that food, I'll take it," the security guard said. "It sure smells good."

Maurice opened the bag and handed the man an egg roll and a carton of fried rice. "I still have plenty for us," he said, looking at Kenya as if to tell her that they were going to share a meal tonight whether she liked it or not.

"Fine," Kenya said, resigning herself to the fact that she was going to be in his company tonight.

They walked to the parking lot in silence, stealing glances at each other. Kenya wasn't surprised to see Maurice was driving a 1968 cherry red Mustang. When they were younger, that was all he had talked about. As she slid into her Lexus SUV, she thought about the raggedy cars that they'd driven when they were younger, happier, and carefree, and how she'd had their wedding planned and the notes hidden in the trunk of her rusting Camaro.

To be young and stupid all over again, she thought as she started the car. Driving to her condo in the Southpark area, Kenya wondered if she should have allowed him to follow her home. What if Imani was right about him? Could he be faithful when he was in such hot demand?

Why am I worried about him being faithful? she thought as she wheeled into the lot of her complex. *Maurice and I aren't in a relationship, and we're never going to be. He can try all he wants. I've been there and done that. Besides, I'm sure he can have any woman in Charlotte. So why does he want to spend his time with me?*

Kenya hopped out of the SUV and waited for Maurice to park his car. "Nice," she said once he got out. "You always wanted this, didn't you?"

"There are a lot of things I always wanted and don't have." Maurice had a lustful tone in his voice and a dangerous gleam in his eye. It seemed to scream sex and the pleasures that she'd dreamed of since the moment she'd left the island.

"Guess we'd better get inside and have dinner," she said.

"Yeah," he said as he followed her up the steps to her second-story condo. "This area of town is nice. I'm surprised you didn't move uptown."

"I work there. I don't want to live there, too. It's quiet out here, and I love that. From what I hear, the residents of this area fight development tooth and nail to keep things quiet and peaceful." She opened the door and pushed a box of art aside to give them a clear path to the sofa. "It's a mess in here."

Maurice didn't notice, because he was too busy watching Kenya kick her pumps off and remove her jacket, revealing a sleeveless satin tunic that highlighted her toned arms. He marveled at how she'd changed but yet was the same woman that he'd loved all those years ago. She turned around and looked at him.

"You can set the food on that coffee table," she said. "I'll be right back."

As Kenya walked into her bedroom, she prayed that Maurice wouldn't follow her. She needed to breathe in and not smell his masculine aroma. Standing in her crowded living room was too much. She was going to have to eat fast and get him out of her house.

"Where's your entertainment center that you need to put together?" he called out.

"In the corner," she replied. "I don't have any tools, though."

"I have some in the car. I'll be right back."

When Kenya heard the front door close, she felt comfortable enough to take off her clothes and change into velour track pants and a tank top. As she slipped on a pair of socks, she heard Maurice reenter the house.

"Kenya," he called out.

"I'll be right out," she said as she took a deep breath and walked into the living room.

Maurice stood in the middle of the room, with a green toolbox in his hand. She recognized it as his father's toolbox. If Maurice hadn't become a football player, Kenya was sure that he would have been a mechanic. When his father left, Maurice lost visible interest in working on cars and fixing bikes. Memories of their youth flashed in her mind. Days of sitting on the front porch and playing tag seemed like yesterday.

Shaking her head to rid herself of bygone days, Kenya pointed Maurice in the direction of the entertainment center. "I'll heat up the food," she said, watching him as he removed his white oxford shirt. "What are you doing?"

"I don't want to get my shirt dirty," he said. "Problem?"

She looked at his torso, which was hidden behind a tight Under Armour tank top that hugged each rippling muscle, enhanced the look of his six-pack, and made him seem nearly naked. "No," she replied as she bounced into the kitchen. Out of the corner of her eye, she could've sworn she saw Maurice smirking.

Kenya brushed it off as she walked into the kitchen and fished a pair of plates and some mismatched flatware out of her boxes. Then she placed the food in the microwave, ignoring the feelings that were stirring between her legs. "How's it going in there?" she called out.

"Uh, it's coming along. This thing has a lot of pieces. And you were going to put this together with no tools," he replied.

"I would've managed," she said as she pulled the steaming food from the microwave and dumped it on the plates.

When she walked into the living room to survey Maurice's work, she wasn't surprised at how little he had gotten accomplished, because he had tossed the instructions to the side.

Just like a man, she thought. *It would be so simple if he read this.* Kenya reached down and picked up the instructions. "Why don't you read these as we eat? And then you can finish." *And get out of my house, because I can't take being this close to you without touching you, kissing you, and having you inside me,* she added silently.

Maurice nodded, took the instructions from Kenya, and then sat beside her on the sofa.

They ate in silence, commenting only on the taste of a dish. Kenya stole glances at him as he ate, thinking about the last time those lips were on hers and on the most intimate places of her body. Rising to her feet, Kenya had to get away from Maurice before she leaned over and ripped his pants off.

"Would you like something to drink?" she asked as she headed into the kitchen with their empty plates.

Maurice followed her and pressed her against the wall as she dropped the dishes in the sink. "I want something."

Before she could protest, he captured her lips, kissing her fervently. Her knees shook, the room seemed to spin, and she didn't even notice that he was slipping his hands into her pants until she felt his finger at the crotch of her lace panties. Every rational thought in her head was to push him away, but she gave in to the kiss, allowing her hormones and heart to take over. She grabbed the buckle of his pants and pulled him closer to her body. Feeling his every throbbing muscle against her made her melt into a pool of lust.

She allowed him to strip her clothes off and kiss her breasts until her nipples swelled. Then he eased down her torso, kissing and licking her navel as if she held the sweetest nectar there. Kenya held on to the wall as he parted her thighs and kissed the wet folds of skin that hid her desire. She shivered as his tongue grazed her clitoris, nearly causing her to climax. With one hand, she grabbed the back of his neck, pushing her hips into his lips. Moaning from delight, Kenya whispered his name as he alternated using his tongue and his finger to stimulate her.

"I want to be inside you," Maurice declared as he looked up at her. "I'm burning for you. Tell me you want me, too."

"I want you," she replied. "I need you."

Maurice hoisted her up and toted her off to her bedroom. The bed wasn't made, and there were boxes everywhere, but it didn't matter to either of them. They were half naked, hot, and desperate to feel each other.

He gently laid her on the bed and began nibbling on her body again, starting at her neck. Kenya felt as if she was about to explode when he slipped one hand between her legs. Clenching her muscles, she took his finger into her wetness and nearly brought herself to a climax. Maurice spread her legs and fought the urge to enter her without a condom. He had to protect her, though he couldn't help but wonder what it would be like to watch Kenya's belly swell with his child.

My child? he thought as he reached for his discarded pants to retrieve a condom. *I've never wanted any woman to have my baby. But Kenya isn't like any other woman. She should've been the one standing at the altar with me.*

Kenya stroked his face gently. "What are you thinking?" she asked.

"About how good you feel," he replied as he slipped the condom in place. "How I never should've let you go. Kenya, I need you in my life, and not just as someone I sleep with when the feeling hits. I want you to be mine."

She sighed, her breasts heaving as she exhaled. "I'm afraid," she said. "I don't want to be hurt again."

"I won't hurt you," he said as he entered her awaiting body.

Kenya felt a ripple flow through her body as he ground his hips against hers. She met him stroke for stroke, pushing her pelvis into his, making sure he touched every tender spot inside. When he melted into her G-spot, Kenya screamed in delight. How could she keep doing this and not let her real feelings show? This wasn't casual sex, and he'd said he wanted more from her. Was it true, though? Could she risk her heart again when she knew that Maurice had already broken it once?

Grasping his shoulders, she pulled him deeper inside her, unable to think or speak because it felt so good to have him there. He made her juices flow like a river. Kenya tightened her thighs around him, as if she was trying to make him lose himself in her or to weld their souls together.

Maurice shuddered as Kenya bucked and feverishly ground against him, taking her sexual satisfaction into her own hands and making him feel sensations that he'd never felt before.

"Kenya, I love you," he exclaimed. "I love you." Then they climaxed, their hearts beating in sync. As Kenya collapsed in his arms, she didn't think about Lauryn, as she had the first time they'd made love. She felt comfortable this time. Maurice was hers; now she could be his.

Looking up at him, she smiled, then said, "You're going to have to find a new lawyer."

"What?"

"I don't sleep with my clients, and I definitely don't have relationships with them," she replied. "But it's up to you. You can have me or my services."

"Who were some of those other attorneys that you suggested?" he said, without hesitation.

Gently, Kenya pushed Maurice over on his back. Then she straddled his body, immediately reviving his sex organ. She kissed him on his earlobe as she ran her hand down his chest. "I'll make sure you get that list in the morning," she whispered. "But right now, I don't want to talk about business."

Maurice wrapped his arms around her waist. "Let's not talk at all," he said before sinking into her hot, wet valley.

Chapter 15

It had been two weeks since Maurice and Kenya had made it official: they were a couple again. Kenya couldn't have been happier. Maurice was more attentive, more loving, and more caring than he'd been nearly a decade ago. Still, in the back of her mind, she wondered if things were going to be different when football season started and he was on the road with all of the groupies and the other women who would surely be after him. Then there was Lauryn. Kenya figured that she'd resurface at some point. After all, she was going to marry Maurice, and Kenya figured the gold digger would run out of gold sooner or later.

Stop borrowing trouble, she told herself as she headed downstairs to meet Maurice for lunch. *Just be happy.*

Happiness. Could she and Maurice really have true happiness, and had she really forgiven him for what happened all those years ago in that dorm room? And would he forgive her for not telling him about the loss of their child? A frown clouded her comely features as she stepped on the elevator. When Kenya saw her reflection in the steel doors, she plastered a smile on her face and vowed not to ruin their date.

"Hello, beautiful," Maurice said when she stepped off the elevator.

"Hi."

"I made reservations for us at Bentley's on Twenty-seven. It's a beautiful place, with a view of the city that's almost as breathtaking as you are," he gushed. Proudly, he wrapped his arm around her waist and led her out the door. "How's your day been?"

"Normal. Contracts, negotiations, and people wanting stuff yesterday. It's amazing. When I was in Atlanta, I was in court almost every day, but here people love to settle. It's like no one wants bad publicity," she said.

Maurice nodded in agreement. "You see how fast the city came down on the price of that land we wanted once they heard that we had your firm working with us. You all must have some reputation."

"Well, we try. But from what I can tell, no one in Charlotte wants to look bad. This city is all about image, getting a good one and keeping it."

Maurice was strangely silent. His image had taken a hit after his failed attempt at marriage to Lauryn. He wasn't looking forward to training camp, because he was sure that his teammates would have a lot to say about him being left at the altar for a woman. He'd purposely avoided them during the off-season, something that he didn't normally do. He was the guy who organized team-building activities, welcomed the rookies into the organization, and planned the parties for the veterans. He hadn't even spoken to his good friend Homer. They usually played golf and traveled together during the off-season. Maurice tried to pretend that he was busy with his business, but that wasn't the case. He'd left the running of Brothers Reality to James. He could've easily said that wooing Kenya was why he hadn't been in contact with his teammates, but he knew the truth was that he was embarrassed. What did his woman leaving him for another woman say about his manhood?

"What's wrong?" Kenya asked, noting his silence.

"Nothing. Just thinking about the upcoming season," he lied. "We're going to have to work extra hard, because everyone is going to be gunning for us."

"To be the best, you have to beat the champs," she said and grinned. "I'm excited. I may have to come check out a few games."

"You're going to have to check out all the games. You've always been my good luck charm." He leaned in and kissed her on the cheek. "I can put you on my family list, which I'm going to have to update immediately."

"Guess Lauryn is still on it, huh?" Kenya said detachedly. She hated when thoughts of the past entered her head or when she felt jealous and insecure about Lauryn. Maurice was with her now, and their relationship might have been low key compared to the media spectacle that he and Lauryn had shared, but Kenya didn't mind. What went on between the two of them wasn't the business of the city or *SportsCenter*. Then again, maybe Maurice was trying to keep up the illusion of being single so that when the season started, he would have his choice of groupies.

Stop it, Kenya chided herself as she slid into his car. *If you can't trust him, then you need to end this now.*

"Maurice," Kenya said as he peeled out of the parking lot, "have you seen Lauryn since you've been back?"

"Please don't start that."

"I'm not starting anything, I'm just . . . it's just you two were going to be married, and I'm sure . . ."

"She made her choice, and I have nothing to say to her about it or anything else. Why do you keep harping on it?" he snapped.

"Harping? I asked you a simple question, and trust me,

I have a right to wonder about the two of you, considering the past."

"You want to stay stuck in the past, or are we going to move ahead? Really, Kenya, if you're going to keep holding a nine-year-old mistake over my head, maybe I'll go out and make a new one."

"Stop the car."

He slowed down and turned to her. "I didn't mean that."

"Stop the damned car," she yelled.

He did, and she jumped out as if she'd been burned by the seat. Slamming the door, she took off speed walking down the street, into a sea of bankers and construction workers. *How stupid have I been?* she thought. *Maurice is the same arrogant jerk that he was in college, and I am just his mid-season replacement. I won't go through this again.*

Kenya wasn't surprised that when she turned the corner, Maurice—illegally parked—was waiting for her. She ignored him until he got out of the car and jogged to catch up to her.

"Kenya, I'm sorry. I just don't want to think or talk about Lauryn."

"Because you still love her, right? What if she decides that she's straight again? Are you going to go back to her and forgive her? Are you going to ask her to let her ex-lover join you two in a night of sex?" Kenya snapped, rolling her eyes as she spoke.

"Hell no. Lauryn can flip-flop in terms of her sexuality all she wants. I'm done with her. But that whole thing with her hurt me. Maybe it's just my pride that's bruised. Can you imagine what I'm going to hear in the locker room? What defensive linemen from opposing teams are going to say to me on the field?"

Kenya held her arms out as if she were playing an invisible violin. "Karma! I seriously hope you get over yourself. Men kill me. You and your egos. Maybe if you thought with your head and your heart and not with your penis, things like this wouldn't happen to you! Maybe if you would have paid more attention to me in college, you would have known that I didn't want to go to those smoky clubs and sip on liquor, because I was pregnant with your child." She covered her mouth quickly because this wasn't the way she'd wanted to tell him about the baby and the loss of it.

"What did you just say?" he asked, his mouth hanging open like a shocked tourist meeting a drag queen for the first time. "You were pregnant?"

"Yes," she muttered. "But when I got to Clark, I had a miscarriage. I wasn't doing what I was supposed to do to take care of myself and my unborn child. I was too afraid to tell you, because I didn't want you to think I was trying to trap you into a marriage or staying in our relationship when I could feel you pulling away from me. And there was no way in hell I was going to tell my mother that I did what she told me not to do, go to college and get pregnant."

He stood there, soaking in her words. *Pregnant*. He had almost been a father. "Why didn't you tell me?" he demanded.

"Because I was only acting on a strong suspicion that I was pregnant and I was afraid," she said quietly. "When I found out for sure, you were with Lauryn, and I was in the hospital, having a D and C."

"Come on. You had to know. Maybe if you would have told . . ."

"If you had known I was pregnant, you wouldn't have slept with Lauryn? What BS, Mo!" she yelled.

"How do you know? You never gave me a choice. Do you really think I believe you didn't know you were pregnant? How could you not know? Something was growing inside you! My child was inside of you. Miscarriage? Just tell me the truth. You had an abortion, didn't you?"

Before she could answer, a parking enforcement officer walked over to them. "Excuse me," she said. "This car needs to be moved, or I'll ticket you."

"This is not a good time," Maurice snapped.

"And this is not an authorized parking spot," the officer replied. "Move the car, or I'll have it towed. Hey, aren't you Maurice Goings?"

"Yeah, and I'm in the middle of something," he said forcefully.

The officer placed her hands on her hips and pursed her lips. "And I'm not the meter maid who Randy Moss ran over. I'll kick your ass. Move your car."

"Move the car," Kenya said as she began to walk away. Maurice reached out and tried to stop her from walking away. The officer stepped in between them.

"Don't you grab her. She obviously doesn't want to talk to you," the officer said, then pressed a button on her radio.

Maurice tried to sidestep the woman, but their arms got tangled, and the officer fell to the ground.

"Oh, I'm sorry," he said and held his hand out to help her up.

"Don't touch me!" the officer yelled, causing a group of onlookers to gather.

Kenya ran back to them. "He didn't mean it," she said as she tried to help the woman to her feet.

"He was just about to grab you, and now you're defending him?" the officer asked incredulously as she rose to her feet, ignoring Kenya's outstretched hand. Seconds later, two Charlotte-Mecklenburg police cars pulled up, and four officers stepped out.

"Meg, everything all right?" one of the police officers asked.

The parking enforcement officer pointed at Maurice. "He assaulted me."

"Mr. Goings?" said the other police officer. "Maurice Goings, the Panthers' wide receiver?"

"I don't give a damn who he is. He assaulted me, and I want to press charges," the parking enforcement officer exclaimed, waving her hands wildly in the air. "Arrest him, or I will report this to the chief."

The police officers looked at Maurice apologetically. "We have to take you in, sir," said one of the officers.

"Oh my God! This is a misunderstanding that you all are blowing out of proportion," Kenya exclaimed. "This hag is just trying to make the six o'clock news."

"Kenya," Maurice said, "I don't need your help."

Kenya's mouth dropped open, and hot tears of anger sprang into her eyes. Without saying another word, she turned on her heels and headed for the free trolley stop to go back to her office. Maurice could rot in jail for all she cared. *Spoiled brat,* she thought as she waited for the Red Line bus to pick her up. *And to think he had the nerve to accuse me of having an abortion! I wasn't the one caught with my pants down. He can pretend that he would've acted differently if I'd told him that I thought I was pregnant. He's not going to lump me into Lauryn's league. He wanted a way out so he could be single and free. Now he has it.*

By the time Kenya made it back to her office, her stomach was growling, and her feet were throbbing. The Red Line had dropped her off about three blocks from her office, and three-inch heels weren't exactly walking shoes. She kicked her shoes off once she sat at her desk and rubbed her feet.

"Miss Taylor," her assistant said. "Mr. Goings is here to see you."

Thinking it was Maurice, Kenya fought the urge to tell him to go to hell. "Send him in." She bent down to put her shoes on, and when she heard the door close, she said,

"You're such an asshole, and I don't know what you're here for. I guess the police didn't cart you off to jail."

"It's James, not Maurice. Why would he be going to jail?" James asked.

Looking over her desk, she smiled sheepishly at him. "Sorry." She rose to her feet and began explaining what had happened uptown.

James sat down. "So, you guys are arguing already," he said.

"Aren't you going to go check on him?" Kenya asked.

He shrugged his shoulder. "If he needs me, he'll call. I'm concerned about you. I know that you and Maurice are trying this thing again, but I don't want you to be hurt, and I don't want to see my brother get hurt, either."

"It doesn't look like you're going to have to worry about Maurice and me being together anymore." Kenya sighed heavily. "You can't go home again, and you can't relight an old flame."

"I'm sorry," James said. "Then again, maybe I'm not. Maurice blew his chances with you a long time ago, and you can do a lot better."

Crawford Calhoun, one of the firm's associates, burst through the door of Kenya's office. "Turn on the news. Maurice Goings was arrested and charged with assault. They're comparing it to the whole Randy Moss situation from a couple of years ago."

James rose to his feet quickly. "I'm going to head down to the county jail and see what's going on."

Kenya fought the urge to go with him. But Maurice's words rang clearly in her ears. *Kenya, I don't need your help.*

Maurice was treated like a rock star when he was booked at the Mecklenburg County Jail. He signed autographs for jailers and a few of the deputies. He even smiled for his mug shot. Inside, he fumed. Kenya didn't have to blurt out that kind of news on the street. Did she expect him to believe that she had a miscarriage? He remembered her anger when she left JC Smith. She had known that she was pregnant, and she'd wanted him to suffer. So she'd killed his child. Maurice had always wanted to be a father so that he could be a better one than his own father had ever been. He had shared that with Kenya time and time again. When they'd started having sex, he'd always told her that he would take care of her and their child if that time ever came.

I'm sick of lying women. First Lauryn, and now I find out that Kenya has been lying to me for years, he thought as he sat in his holding cell. He couldn't help but wonder what he'd done to deserve this fate. Now he had to worry about the team and the league punishing him for these trumped-up charges, and then there was the possibility of a civil suit. *Second-degree assault,* he thought. *That old hag should be charged with assaulting the concrete with her big butt. The last thing that I need is a reason for the media to bring up my past again.*

"Mr. Goings," a jailer said as he opened the cell door, "you're free to go."

He didn't need to be told twice. Maurice leapt to his feet and headed toward the jailer. "Charges dropped?"

The man nodded. "It seems that you guys were underneath one of the uptown cameras, and the incident was caught on tape. It was clearly an accident, and just between me and you, Meg is an evil witch who needs to get laid."

Maurice nodded and laughed. "I thought it was just me," he said. "Anyone out there?"

"If by *anyone* you mean the media, yeah. But I can show you another way out, if you want me to."

Maurice shook his head. "I'd better deal with it now," he

said as the jailer led him downstairs to pick up his personal belongings.

On the front steps of the jail, every media outlet in Charlotte seemed to be waiting for him. "Mr. Goings, Mr. Goings," the reporters called out.

"Have you been charged with a crime?" one reporter called out.

"No. This was all a misunderstanding and has been cleared up, so there is no story here," said Maurice.

"One of the uptown parking enforcement officers said that you assaulted her. Is that true?" another reporter asked.

"Unfortunately, that meter maid and I got tangled up, and she fell. I tried to help her up, but she didn't want my help. That's what happens in a crowded city," replied Maurice.

"So, what was going on? She said that you were going to assault someone. Was that you ex-fiancée?" asked another reporter.

"I have no comment about anything other than the fact that I wasn't charged with a crime, and I'm sorry that this all happened," Maurice said, then walked down the stairs, refusing to answer another question. He wanted to go home and close himself off from the world, at least for a day. He had to figure out how to deal with Kenya and her revelation. What if she was telling the truth? Her mother would have been very disappointed if she had gotten pregnant. And he wasn't ready for fatherhood back then. *Still, she could have given me a choice,* he thought. *She could have told me. And I guess I could have told her about Lauryn after that first night. We've made so many mistakes. Should we even be trying to do this again?*

"Mo," James called out. "Trying to be the Randy Moss of Carolina?"

"Man." Maurice waved his brother off.

"Kenya told me what happened."

"Oh, did she? Told you everything or just her version of the truth?" His voice was filled with venom. "I'm sick and tired of these women who think they can lie to me over and over again and I'm supposed to take it. Whatever. Kenya wants to throw Lauryn in my face every five minutes, and she's been lying and keeping secrets for years. I'm not going through this again."

"So, you took it out on the meter maid? What kind of secret was Kenya keeping? I mean, she's the most straight-forward woman that I know, and I can't imagine that she'd be lying to you about anything," James said.

Maurice narrowed his eyes. "You don't know every-thing. Again, why do you think Kenya is this paragon of virtue? She's a woman, and by nature, women are evil."

James eyed his brother as if he had sprouted devil's horns and a forked tongue. "What?"

"Even in the Bible, a woman always brings down a man," Maurice said. "Look at what Jezebel did to Samson."

James shook his head. "That was Delilah, and you need to go to church and find out what's wrong with you. What did Kenya lie about? And why do you think you have a right to be so angry? A few months ago you were about to marry another woman. Everyone has a past, and Kenya is . . ."

"Kenya is what? You act as if you want to be with her. If that's the case, then go get her! Maybe she'll keep your child."

"Your child?" James's face wrinkled in confusion. "You got her pregnant already?"

"No," Maurice said. "Before she left school, Kenya was pregnant, and she didn't say a word to me about it."

"How could she? From what I understand—"

"Understand this. I don't buy her brand of bullshit. How could she not know that she was pregnant? I thought a missed period is the first clue. Then she claims that she had a miscarriage. I think she had an abortion."

James didn't believe Kenya had aborted Maurice's child. He understood his brother's attitude, though. Maurice had hated the way their father had treated them as children, and he had vowed to do a better job when he had children of his own. "What if she's telling you the truth?"

"What if she isn't?"

"Mo, you weren't ready for fatherhood back then. Both of you were young, and you'd have just dumped her. Even if she had an abortion . . ."

"Wasn't her decision to make alone. She's being a hypocrite."

"What?"

"I messed up and I hurt her. I can admit that. But she hid this pregnancy from me for all of these years. She keeps throwing Lauryn in my face, but I'm supposed to forgive and forget?" Maurice shook his head. "So, you think she's pure and pious?"

James shrugged his shoulders. "There's always two sides to a story, Mo."

Maurice waved his brother off and started for his car. Then he remembered it had been impounded. Turning around, he looked at James, who had fallen in behind him. "You think I can get a ride?"

"I was wondering when you were going to get around to that," James said, with a laugh. He walked up to his brother and wrapped his arm around his shoulder. "Ever think that maybe you and Kenya aren't meant to be?"

"All I want to think about right now is getting my car, heading to a bar, and getting a drink." Maurice had spent more time in jail than he'd ever wanted to. He deserved a drink and a lot more.

Chapter 16

Kenya sat on the sofa in her apartment, home by seven for the first time in a long while. Part of her wanted to call Maurice and explain everything to him about the baby and her miscarriage. But she was angry. How in the world did he expect her to feel sorry for him? She went through losing the baby alone, she never told her mother, and a year passed before she even shared her loss with Imani.

One evening, Imani and Kenya had been hanging out in her dorm room. Johnson C. Smith's spring break was a few days before Clark Atlanta's, and Imani had come to Atlanta to hang out with her best friend. As they'd sat on Kenya's bed, Imani had commented on her friend's new look.

"I can't believe you cut your hair," she'd said.

"I needed a change," Kenya had replied as she ran her fingers through her Halle Berry type of cut.

"What's wrong, Kenya? And please tell me that you've gotten over Maurice. With all the fine brothers that I've seen around here, I know you can replace his rusty behind."

Closing her eyes to hold back the tears, Kenya had said, "I wish it were that simple. Imani, something happened when I got here."

Imani had reached out and clasped Kenya's hand. "Do you want to talk about it?"

Kenya had begun to sob, her shoulders shaking with each tear that fell. "I was pregnant. I had my suspicions, but I didn't want to know for sure, especially after I found them together."

"You had an abortion?"

Kenya had shaken her head furiously. "No, the decision was made for me. I got sick, and when I woke up, I was in the hospital, and the doctor was telling me that I'd had a miscarriage."

"Does Maurice know?"

"No, and he's not going to. I'm not telling him, and you better not, either. Maurice has made his choice, and he can have that skank," Kenya had replied angrily. "If he had known that I was pregnant, nothing would've changed. He probably would've accused me of trying to trap him. I'm glad he didn't know."

"But you're suffering alone. Did you tell your mother?"

Kenya had laughed through her tears. "No way. Angela would have had a coronary had she known that I did exactly what she said I'd do." She'd wiped her eyes with the back of her hand. "I've decided that I'm never going to find myself in this situation again. I'm going to work on graduating, and I'm not going to let Maurice or any other man get in my way."

"So, you're just going to shut yourself off from the rest of the world?" Imani had asked.

"Yes."

Kenya had done a good job of shutting her heart to love and would've kept it closed if it hadn't been the fact that she'd seen Maurice again. She was weak for him; he was her addiction. This time, though, she was going to go to Mo detox and get over this man once and for all.

"I can do better," she said aloud. She stood and headed

to bed, despite the fact that it was only a little after nine. When she got into bed, Kenya tossed and turned, thinking of Maurice and his situation at the jail and memories of the past. Maybe she should've told him sooner about the miscarriage. Maybe she should've told him the first month that she missed her period that she thought she was pregnant. But what would that have changed? And why couldn't she get past it? Maurice said things were over with Lauryn, but Kenya couldn't help but wonder if he was lying and still harboring feelings for her, despite what had happened on his wedding day.

Sitting up in bed, Kenya decided to call him just to see if he was all right. As she dialed his number, she thought about what she'd say to him if he answered. Should she offer him an explanation about the past, or should she just ask him if he was okay?

"Yeah," Maurice said when he picked up.

"Hi. I was just calling to make sure you were all right," she found the voice to say.

"I'm fine," he said coolly.

"I'm sorry about what happened."

Maurice sighed audibly. "Sorry for what? Me finding out your little secret or me getting arrested? I want to be sure that you're apologizing for something I'd be willing to forgive."

"Go to hell, Maurice. I'm not going to bend over backwards and kiss your ass," Kenya snapped. "You want to act like a child, then fine. But think about this. Had I known that I was pregnant, do you really think I would've had the inclination to tell you after I walked in on you sexing Lauryn? Would you have pulled yourself out of her to play house with me and our child?"

"You know how I feel about children. I've always wanted a child of my own, and you robbed me of that chance."

"I didn't rob you of anything, because I didn't have an abortion! Do you want to see my medical records?" she snapped.

"Swear to me that you didn't abort my child," Maurice slurred.

"Are you drunk?" She'd known that having a child was important to him, but back then there was no way either of them was ready to be a parent.

"I've been drinking," he said. "But you didn't answer me. Swear that you didn't kill my seed."

"Where are you?"

"Swear it."

"Maurice, I swear I didn't have an abortion. I would've never killed my child, no matter what I thought of you. I went through hell for years after the miscarriage, and I had to go through it alone."

"No," he snapped. "No, you didn't. You could've called me and talked to me."

Sighing, she wanted to tell him that she'd called him several times but hung up every time he'd said hello. "Where are you?" she asked.

"At the Blake Hotel's bar."

"You're not driving, are you?"

Maurice laughed. "My car was impounded. Can't go anywhere, and I don't want to."

"Well, I just wanted to check on you," she said, masking her disappointment.

"Are we making a mistake?" he asked. "Can we go back and start over, or should we just scrap it?"

"I don't know," she said. "You tell me."

"I love you, Kenya. I love you with everything in me, but I don't know if I can keep apologizing for what I did. I can't say I'm sorry anymore, and I don't want to have to answer questions about Lauryn every five minutes. Can you truly forgive me and give us another chance?"

Her lip trembled as she pondered her answer. "I can't just forget what happened, Maurice. Do you realize that you're the only man I've ever loved? The only man I've ever made love to?"

"You're kidding!" He'd been sure that when she'd returned to Atlanta, she'd gotten over him by finding a new man. That thought had fueled his jealousy when he first saw her in the Bahamas. Now, knowing that she had truly been branded his, he felt proud. Drunk and aroused, Maurice invited Kenya to the hotel, claiming that he wanted to talk to her.

"You know that 'we're just going to talk' line is about as old as dirt," she said, seeing through his request.

"All right. Then come over in your black lace, and show me that we're all right," he said seductively.

"Oh, we're going to finish talking," she said. "Then we can get to making up."

Maurice realized after hanging up the phone that he hadn't even rented a suite yet. Slowly, so as not to lose his balance, he rose from the bar stool, then headed to the lobby to secure a room.

As soon as he stepped into the hallway, he ran into a woman he never wanted to see again.

Lauryn.

"Hello, Mo," she said.

Rolling his eyes, he sidestepped her. Despite himself, he turned around and looked at her. She was still sexy and still wore clothes that were short and tight enough to show off her lithe body. She watched him as he gave her the once over and mistook his stare for a come-on. Walking over to him, she twisted her hips a little more than she had to.

"You can't speak, but you're going to stand there and stare at me?" she said, with a smile on her plum-tinted lips.

"Where's your woman?" he asked bitterly.

"We're not joined at the hip. Seriously, though, how have you been?"

Maurice shook his head. "Do you really think I'm going to have a conversation with you? You can go to hell."

"Would you like to join us one night and see how much fun we can have together?" she asked, biting her lip and raising an eyebrow seductively.

Most men would have loved the chance to be with two sexy women at one time, but Maurice would never succumb to what Lauryn was proposing. It would be like saying that what she had done was all right and he approved of it. Besides, seeing her now and watching her pimp her girlfriend turned his stomach. "I wouldn't touch you or Mya with a dildo," Maurice snapped. "Excuse me."

She looked at him longingly as he walked into the bar. Lauryn had to admit that she missed Maurice, or at least his money. She'd hoped that he wasn't still in a funk about their wedding and that he would beg her to come back. She loved Mya, but love couldn't buy Prada. And Mya had changed. She wanted the two of them to be the poster children for gay rights, and Lauryn still wasn't sure she was gay. Men still turned her on, especially if they had money. She definitely didn't want to be known as "that lesbian Lauryn."

Mya, on the other hand, had joined the gay and lesbian community center's board of directors, and she was working on the black gay pride event that was coming to Charlotte in the summer. Lauryn had had to get away from her activist girlfriend for at least a night, and that was why she'd checked into the Blake Hotel. Seeing Maurice was an added bonus that she hadn't expected. Maybe if she could remind him of the good time they'd had she could work her way into his bed. It was obvious that he was alone here tonight, and after what she'd seen on the news, she imagined that he needed to release some tension, and she had the remedy for him.

Just as she started for the bar, she looked up and saw Kenya walking through the front door. *No, he didn't dig her up to heal his heart,* she thought as she stood in the shadows and watched Kenya walk into the bar where Maurice was.

She grudgingly admitted to herself that Kenya looked a lot better now than she had when they were in college. She was slimmer, more stylish, and more confident. But she was still Kenya, and Lauryn wasn't going to lose to her. She fumed as she watched Maurice kiss her and hold her tightly. *I worked way too hard to let her come back and get all the money,* she thought. *If he doesn't want me, fine, but she's not going to get him.*

Kenya sat close to Maurice, smiling at him as he ordered himself a cup of coffee. "I was really surprised to find you in the bar," she said. "I figured you'd had enough."

"Just came for the coffee," he replied, then slipped his hand between her thighs. "I want to be alert and attentive when we get up to my suite."

Leaning in, she kissed his lips gently. "Maurice, should we really be doing this?"

"I don't see why not. Listen, I know that I was harsh earlier, but I thought that you had aborted my child, and you know how I feel about being a father. As I thought about it, I figured that you were young and in denial. Remember when we got to college and your mother sat us down and said she wasn't ready to be a grandmother?"

Kenya nodded. "She told me not to run from you and

Lauryn. But when I told her that I wasn't leaving because of that, she was happy to get me into Clark."

"What happened to you wanting to go into PR? Not that you're not a great lawyer, but you said you wanted to own your own business and . . ." He stopped talking, remembering that the public-relations firm Kenya had planned to start was going to be half his as well.

"Well," she said, as if she was reading his mind, "my partner was otherwise occupied."

"Do you love what you do now?"

Shrugging her shoulders, she replied, "It's a living. I can't complain, because I'm very successful at what I do."

"Doesn't mean you're happy."

She looked deeply into his eyes and smiled, but her smile didn't conceal the wave of sadness that had washed over her. "What's more important? I know plenty of people who are happy and struggling. Really, I'm fine. But who can be happy working nearly ninety hours a week?"

"Slight workaholic?" he teased.

Kenya wanted to tell him why she worked all the time. It was to keep her mind off him and what could've been. What if she had paid more attention to her body? Would she be a mother now, with a little girl or boy that had his eyes? Would she have fought harder for their relationship, or would she be bitter and hating him? Maybe she didn't need the answers to those questions, because they were poised to write new chapters in the book of their lives.

"You want to get out of here and take my clothes off?" she asked boldly.

Maurice smiled devilishly because he had been ready to make the same suggestion.

"You don't have to ask me twice." He waved for the bartender so that he could pay for his coffee.

Like two teenagers sneaking to a motel, they laughed

and giggled as they headed for the front desk to rent a room, but the laughter died on Kenya's lips when she saw Lauryn heading in their direction. *What's she doing here?* Kenya thought. Her mind immediately flashed back nine years. *It could just be a coincidence. Just because she's here doesn't mean she's here to be with Maurice. Maybe there's a gay convention being held here.*

Looking at Lauryn, Kenya wondered why Maurice had ever wanted her in the first place. Lust could only take you so far, and Lauryn didn't have a soul. She could tell by looking into Lauryn's cold eyes.

"Hello again, Maurice," Lauryn said. "Is this Kenya? Wow, was it Weight Watchers or lipo?"

"Excuse me?" Kenya snapped.

"Your dramatic weight loss," said Lauryn. "I thought by now you'd be at least three hundred pounds. You actually look all right."

Kenya inhaled deeply to calm herself. She wasn't about to get into a childish shouting match with Lauryn. But what had Lauryn meant by "hello again"? So Maurice had seen her recently? Had he turned to her for some reason?

"Excuse us, Lauryn. We're leaving," Maurice said as he and Kenya walked away from the desk clerk.

Lauryn watched as they got on the elevator and Maurice pressed the button for the twentieth floor. Quickly, she hopped on. "I'm going up, too," she said, smiling brightly. She turned to Kenya, who had linked her arm with Maurice's, and said, "So, how much weight did you lose? How did you do it?"

"Lauryn, why don't you give it a rest?" Maurice said.

Batting her eyelashes, Lauryn turned to him and said, "You never did. That's one of the things that you loved about me. The fact that I wasn't fat and took care of my body. Remember how I used to—"

"How's your girlfriend?" Kenya asked. "You're a lesbian now, right?"

Lauryn looked from Maurice to Kenya. "You-you told her that?"

"Oh, he told me a lot of stuff. Mya was your college roommate, right? How long have you and she been doing this sort of thing?" Kenya asked.

When the elevator stopped on the tenth floor, Lauryn hopped off. Before the doors closed, she hissed, "Even if I'm a lesbian, I was more than woman enough to take Maurice from you before, and if I want to, I'll do it again."

The doors closed before Kenya could reply. Maurice rubbed her back gently in an attempt to calm her down, but inside she fumed. Turning to him, she said, "Do you believe her? And just what did she mean by 'hello again'? Were you two together?"

"Don't start with that," Maurice said. "I ran into her while I was in the bar, waiting for you. I don't want anything to do with Lauryn."

Where have I heard that before? she thought bitterly. Kenya had figured out that Maurice was in Lauryn's sights when she saw how Lauryn would cheer every time he made a touchdown and how she'd scream his name across campus when he walked by. He'd said he didn't want anything to do with her then, but lo and behold, he'd ended up in bed with her.

"Maurice, I think I'm going to go home," Kenya said. "This is too much, and I'm not going to be the same fool twice."

"What are you talking about? If you think that I'm still involved or want to have something to do with that woman, then you're wrong. When are you going to realize that you're the woman I want?"

She wished that she had the answer, wished that there was

a magic word that he could say that would make her memories of being hurt and finding them in bed together disappear.

"Kenya, what more can I do?" he said. "What more can I say to make you understand that I don't want Lauryn or anyone else but you." He drew her into his arms. "The biggest mistake I've ever made was letting you walk out of my life, because I was blinded by sex."

She wanted to believe him; everything inside her told her that she could trust Maurice and his love. But there was that nagging voice that said she'd be hurt again.

"Mo," she whispered, "I'm afraid."

"You don't have to be, because I love you. I need you more than I need my next breath." Stroking her cheek, he wanted to make love to her right there in the elevator, for the security cameras and everybody to see. He wanted to prove to her that the past was dead and their future was right there, and that all they had to do was step into it. "Kenya, this is real."

Her body quivered as he held her and touched her gently. "All right," Kenya said. "I believe you."

"Then you're going to stay with me tonight and forever?" he asked. His voice seemed desperate.

"Yes," she moaned. "I'm yours."

The elevator doors opened on the twentieth floor, and Maurice swooped Kenya off her feet as if she were his bride on their wedding night. With great skill, he unlocked the door to his suite, with Kenya in his arms, and kicked the door wide open. Then he laid Kenya on the bed. She looked up at him, smiling at him. Her innocent look sent a shock wave though his body, filling him with a hot yearning that nearly caused an explosion in his trousers.

"I want to taste every inch of you," he moaned as he began to peel her clothes from her body. He unbuttoned her blouse and lifted her bra until her breasts slipped out.

He salivated at the sight of her nipples and took them into his mouth as she moaned in delight. Tonight, he was going to make love to her body, soul, and mind. He blazed a path of kisses down her stomach to the waistband of her pants. With his teeth, he unbuttoned them and was surprised to see that she wasn't wearing any panties. That brought a smile to his face. Kenya used to be so reserved, so timid, when it came to lovemaking. Now, she was different, more passionate and willing. He loved it. Needed it. Hungered for it.

Slipping her pants off, he spread her thighs and felt the heat radiating from her womanly core. Seductively, he licked her inner thighs, causing her to arch her back and silently urge him to taste her. He was happy to oblige. Burying his face between her thighs, he sought her sensitive bud with his tongue, reveling in the taste of her juices and going deeper and deeper into her as she clasped her hands around his neck.

Kenya's body shuddered as the waves of an orgasm began to wash over her underneath Maurice's tongue lashing. Her body responded to his touch as he reached up and squeezed her breasts while continuing his kiss. She was wetter than she'd ever been, and Maurice got off on it. She felt him grow harder and harder as she let go and gave in to ecstasy. "Maurice," she moaned. "Oh God!" He blew gently on her hot core, making her shudder and shiver.

He looked up at her and said, "Delicious."

"Make love to me," she demanded wantonly. "Now. I want you now."

He shook his head. "I'm not done yet." Sliding down her thigh, blazing a trail with his tongue, Maurice took her immaculate toes into his mouth, one by one. Her body was on fire as he sucked her toes as if they were covered in Godiva chocolate. She sank into the bed, holding on to the bedspread so that she wouldn't fall off the edge. Her breathing was shallow as Maurice reversed his position and ended up between her thighs again, kissing her throbbing core, then her navel and her tender breasts. Kenya's nipples were harder than mountaintops. Clenching her legs around his waist, she made her desires clear: she was primed and ready to feel his manhood inside her. Maurice slipped inside her, momentarily forgetting that he hadn't protected her. Despite how good it felt, and how she gasped and called his name, he pulled out.

"I have to protect you," he said as he reached into his wallet and grabbed a condom.

Kenya's insecure side wondered why he had brought condoms to the hotel. Had he done so because he and Lauryn were planning to have sex? Closing her eyes, she silently chided herself for entertaining those thoughts. He'd just confessed his love to her, and she was still second-guessing him. Maurice seemed to sense her apprehension.

"I got these after I talked to you."

"And suppose I had decided not to come up here with you?" she asked as he slid the condom in place.

Turning to her, with a sly smile on his face, he said, "I probably would have gotten drunker, made water balloons with them, and dropped them off the balcony." He dove in between her legs, swimming in her hot ocean of love. Kenya closed her legs around him, pulling him in deeper and deeper. She pressed her pelvis into his, meeting his passion with her own heated desire. Kenya had never felt this way, had never felt so alive and desirable. Her inhibitions were gone when she was with him. Maurice rolled over, allowing Kenya to mount him and take control of her pleasure.

Once she was on top, she arched her back and bucked like a rodeo star. Maurice moaned in delight as she grabbed his ankles. He sat up so that he could suck her breasts and hold back the explosion that was building inside him. Kenya made it impossible to do so as she tightened her grip on his penis. Kenya collapsed on his chest, and he held her tightly. Sweat poured from their bodies as they basked in the afterglow of their lovemaking. Kenya drew circles in the sweat on his chest. "Do you think that we can be like this forever?" she asked.

"I like the sound of that." He kissed her on the chin, then cupped her bottom. "My brother thinks that we're making a mistake."

"He's wrong. The only mistake that we could make is to let the past come between us again," she said.

"Ah, she finally gets it," Maurice said. "I love you."

"I love you, too." Kenya could feel him growing against her thighs, and she reached for another condom. "Round two?"

Chapter 17

The next morning, Kenya woke up in Maurice's arms, feeling more secure in his love than she'd ever thought that she could. For once, she didn't have the nagging questions about Lauryn tormenting her. She wanted to plan their future; she wanted to plan their life together. She snuggled closer to him and brushed her lips against his, causing him to stir in the bed.

His eyes fluttered open, and he saw Kenya's smiling face.

"Good morning," she said warmly.

Stroking her thighs, he replied, "It certainly is. You feel good. Like silk."

A flutter started in the pit of her stomach, and heat spread through her body. It was so easy for Maurice to turn her on. It took just the touch of his hand, the sound of his voice, and the feel of his lips against her skin.

"Don't you have to work?" he asked.

"I'm going to head in late," she replied. "I think I deserve it."

"And so do I." Maurice greedily kissed her, causing her to melt against his body. She felt his manhood grow against her thighs, and she got as wet as a marsh during a summer rain. Kenya spread her legs and guided his erection to her awaiting valley. Neither of them had thought about a condom, because passion had taken ahold of them, at least momentarily. Maurice quickly pulled out before he nearly climaxed inside her.

"I can't believe we did this," he said as he sprang from the bed and dashed in the bathroom. "The last thing either of us needs right now is something unexpected happening."

Wrapping herself in a sheet, Kenya rose to her feet and said, "You're right."

Maurice walked out of the bathroom, with a towel wrapped around his waist. "Not that I wouldn't want you to have my baby," he said. "I'd love to see your belly swollen with my son, Mo Jr."

"And why do you think I'd name my son after you?" she ribbed. "What if I want to give him his own identity?"

"I guess it would be a lot for him to live up to, being Maurice Jr. After all, Michael Jordan didn't name his first-born after himself, or did he?"

"Are you comparing yourself to the greatest basketball player of all times? Dude, you have one ring. He has six," Kenya joked as she tugged at his towel.

"I'm working on it, which reminds me. I'd better hit the gym today, or training camp is going to be a killer. I can't have some rookie come in and steal my spot."

She wrapped her arms around his neck and kissed him on the cheek. "Then I'd better get out of here and get ready for work." She glanced over at the clock. It was nearly ten thirty. "I have a lunch meeting I need to prepare for."

"Tonight, you and I will have a date, dinner, and then a dip in my hot tub. Clothing optional," he said, with a wink.

"Sounds good to me," Kenya said as she let him go.

Maurice ordered a pot of coffee and danishes for breakfast as Kenya checked in with the office on her cell phone.

Watching her, he felt his heart swell with pride and love. She was such a professional and was sexy as hell when she chewed her bottom lip and crossed her legs. He liked seeing her in control and so sure of herself. Just like the girl he'd fallen in love with when she'd bossed the other kids around on the playground. He hated that he'd taken part of that from her when he made the mistake of choosing lust over true love. He'd never make that mistake again, and he'd never hurt her as long as he lived, because she was the most important thing in his life. Maurice knew that if the fame and fortune went away, Kenya would be there with him through thick and thin.

Lauryn would've left as soon as the money went south. How could he have been so blinded by the tricks she'd pulled in the bedroom? That was a trait that was passed on to him by his womanizing father. Maurice swore that he'd never let another woman blind him with a tight waist and big breasts. Then he looked over at Kenya and realized that he had all he needed in her. She was sexy and sexually pleasing, and more than anything else, he loved her with all of his heart and soul. Why couldn't he see that all those years ago?

She looked up as she snapped her silver phone shut. "What?" she asked when their eyes locked.

"I was just thinking," he said. "Why does it take time and distance for us to realize that everything we've ever wanted was right in front of us?"

She shook her head. "Been watching the *Wizard of Oz* and *Rent,* huh?"

Maurice stood up and closed the space between them. "I'm serious. Marry me, Kenya."

Slowly, she rose to her feet and looked him in the eye. "What?"

"We should be celebrating our fifth anniversary, anyway.

I have wasted too much time, and I nearly lost you. I don't want that to happen again."

"This is too sudden," she said. "I mean, we've only been back together a short while, and there are a lot of things we need to do before we can entertain the thought of being married."

"You love me, right?" he asked as he closed his arms around her waist. "That's all we need."

"Love isn't all we need," she replied. "Can we talk about this later? I have to go." She pushed out of his embrace and dashed out of the room, leaving him standing there, dazed and confused.

After leaving the hotel, Kenya could think of nothing but Maurice's proposal. Was he crazy? Or was this the real thing? The moment she entered her office, she told her assistant, Talisha, to hold all her calls. She headed for her private bathroom, showered, and changed into her spare business suit, which she kept in her office, and called Imani's cell phone. When she didn't get an answer, she called her mother.

"Angela Taylor," her mother said in a clipped tone.

"Ma, it's me. Did I interrupt your editorial meeting?"

"Ah, the prodigal daughter phones. I haven't heard from you since you went on vacation. How's Charlotte?"

"Great. Business is good. Since there's so much development here, everyone needs a lawyer."

"And you're okay? Any Maurice Goings sightings?"

"Well," Kenya began, "Maurice and I have been seeing each other since we linked up in the Bahamas."

She heard Angela's office door slam shut. "You want to repeat that?"

Kenya recounted how she and Maurice had ended up at

the same resort, leaving out her near sexual assault and her night of overindulgence. "And this morning he asked me to marry him," she concluded.

Angela sighed heavily into the phone. "I hope you said no and will get over this thing you have for that boy. I thought that he'd gotten married, anyway."

"She left him at the altar."

"Did he cheat on her, too?" Angela asked coolly. "You can't be considering marrying that fool, can you?"

"I love him and he loves me, but for the record, I didn't say yes."

"Thank God. Your father still hates Maurice, and you can best believe that he would hit him harder than any offensive lineman."

"Defensive lineman, Ma. Maurice is a wide receiver," Kenya said.

"What's offensive to me is the fact that you have allowed this man back into your life, as if you've forgotten what he did to you. You left school because you caught him in bed with that tart. Wait a minute. Was that the woman that he was going to marry?"

"Yes," Kenya said, starting to regret calling her mother in the first place.

"Please tell me that you're not going to seriously entertain his proposal, because I don't want to see you crawling back to Atlanta, crying again," Angela said.

Kenya took a slow breath. "I don't mean any disrespect, but I'm an adult. If I want to be with him, why would I let you stop me?"

"Oh, so you want to play grown-up now? If you were so sure about Maurice and being his wife, then you'd be calling me to tell me that you two are getting married. You're no fool, Kenya. I hope to God that you don't think that because he has money now, he has changed."

This call is definitely a mistake. I don't need to hear a lecture right now, Kenya thought. She should've known that Angela wasn't going to be happy, because she still hated Maurice. Obviously, Kenya didn't think that marrying him was a good idea, but she definitely didn't want her mother judging her because she and Maurice were seeing each other again. She made an excuse to hang up with her mother and stared blankly at the wall, thinking about their conversation. Angela had done a good job of stirring up old doubts that Kenya was desperately trying to put behind her.

Yes, she still loved Maurice, but marriage? There was so much about him and his life that she was still in the dark about. Was her mother right about him? Maybe he was the same selfish jerk that he'd been in college, and maybe she was asking for more heartbreak. Then again, he could've changed. He could really be in love with her. *Yeah right.* Her mother's voice echoed in her head. *Maurice loves himself, and if he wants to marry you, it's probably because he wants to repair his reputation from being left at the altar. What happens when he goes on the road and another woman offers her body to him? Do you think that he's going to turn it down because you're sitting at home, waiting for him?*

Twisting in her seat, Kenya turned toward the window and looked out over the city.

"Miss Taylor, you have a delivery," Talisha said over the intercom.

"Please send it in," she said. Kenya straightened her jacket and turned her seat around and watched the door.

The first thing she saw was a huge bouquet of roses. She looked down at the delivery man's linen pants and wondered which florist had such luxurious uniforms. When he lowered the flowers, Kenya shook her head. "Maurice, what are you doing here?"

"Isn't it obvious?" He held the flowers out to her. "I wasn't sure if you'd left me, considering the way you ran out of the hotel this morning."

Kenya stood and accepted the flowers. "They're beautiful, but I have a meeting in a few minutes."

"I know, but you didn't answer my question this morning." Maurice reached into his pocket and removed a black velvet box.

Kenya looked away, knowing what was inside. Why was he doing this when she had just told him that she had work to do?

"Maurice, I can't do this right now. Damn it, you know I have a meeting, and yet you come in here with your roses and your . . ." He was standing in her face now and holding the sparkling three-and-a-half-carat diamond and emerald ring underneath her nose so that she had to face it. Kenya couldn't deny that it was beautiful, because it was the same ring she'd picked out when they'd been daydreaming in high school.

"Maurice," she said, her voice barely audible.

"I want you in my life forever. Marry me, and I'm not taking no for an answer, and I'm not leaving until you say yes."

Before Kenya could answer, Talisha called her on the intercom. "Mr. Peterson is here for your meeting."

"Just a minute," she told her assistant. "Please apologize for my tardiness." She pressed the button to turn the intercom speaker off, then turned to Maurice. "You have to leave."

Folding his arms across his chest, he simply shook his head and sat down in the chair across from her desk. "Why won't you answer my question?"

"Out," she snapped. "If this is some kind of game to you, then you can just find another playmate."

"This isn't a game. It's real, and I'm speaking from my

heart. I love you, and I want to spend the rest of my life with you."

Kenya walked over to the door and placed her hand on the knob. "Please leave," she said. "This is an important meeting for me."

"Fine. I'll wait out front until your meeting is over," he said as she opened the door. "Then I want an answer."

Mr. Peterson immediately recognized Maurice and extended his hand to him. "Mo Goings! How are you? That was a great catch in the Super Bowl."

Maurice shook the man's hand and smiled brightly. "Thank you," he said. But his eyes never left Kenya's face.

"Do you think that we're going to make it back to the big game this year?" Mr. Peterson asked.

"We'll see," Maurice replied as he took a seat on the leather chair in the waiting area. "Don't let me interrupt your meeting with Miss Taylor."

Mr. Peterson turned to Kenya and smiled. "You must be some lawyer if you have Mo Goings as a client."

She smiled tersely and ushered Mr. Peterson inside her office. As she closed the door behind him, Kenya turned around and glared at Maurice. In return, he blew her a kiss.

Maurice had been waiting for two hours before Kenya emerged from her office. Mr. Peterson walked out first and gave Maurice a thumbs-up before heading for the elevator. Kenya stood in the doorway, looking at Maurice and shaking her head. "Why are you still here? And where is Talisha?"

"She went to lunch. I told her that I'd listen for the phones for her."

"I have a lot of work to do this evening, and I don't have time to deal with you, all right, so if you don't mind, leave."

Rising to his feet, Maurice stood inches from her. "You don't listen, do you? I said I'm not leaving until you give me an answer." Maurice pulled the ring from his pocket and held it out to Kenya. "This is your ring, and I want to be your husband."

"This is crazy," Kenya said. "What do we really know about each other?"

Maurice shook his head. "All we need to know is that we love each other. Hell, Kenya, we've known each other since we were little kids. The question is, What don't we know about each other?"

"We've changed, grown up. What about your lifestyle? Really, how do I fit into it? You're on the road for months. Then there are the women, the groupies. You can have any woman you want. Why me?"

Furrowing his brows, Maurice grabbed her hand and dropped the ring in it. "This is how you fit into my lifestyle."

Kenya looked down at the ring, but much to Maurice's dismay, she didn't put it on. "Is this about getting left at the altar? Proving your manhood?"

"No, this is about me loving you and righting a wrong. Give me one reason why we shouldn't get married. We'd planned to get married, and I messed up. I want to make it right."

Shaking her head, she stepped into her office, with Maurice on her heels. He closed the door and locked it. "I don't have to prove anything to anybody but myself, and I know nine years ago, I made the biggest mistake of my life by letting you walk away."

Kenya grabbed the edge of her desk. "And in nine years, you've become a multimillionaire who has his pick of women. I'm sure you have to beat them off with a stick. What happens when you're on the road, groupies come after you, and you decide that a little romp won't hurt?"

Maurice laughed. "I'm not going to lie to you. Early in my career, I slept with a few groupies. I was happy about being able to pull any woman that I wanted. But guess what? It got old. I don't want someone who's with me only because I have money and they've seen my face on TV and in magazines. I want something real, you know. I want you."

She sighed and folded her arms across her chest. "You had all of that, and you threw it away. How do I know you won't do it again?"

Maurice threw his hands up and released a slow, long sigh. "Because I just told you, and if you don't trust me, why have we been spending this time together, and why have we been sleeping together? What's your angle, Kenya?"

Slamming her hand against the desk, she said, "This is a waste of my time, and I don't feel like talking about this anymore. I can't do this, Maurice. I'm not going to rush into an engagement and a marriage because of nostalgia."

Closing the space between them, he pulled her into his arms and captured her lips, kissing her until her knees buckled and she shivered. Maurice could feel her trying to resist him, but he continued to kiss her until her resistance crumbled and she kissed him back with the same passion and fervor that he possessed. She shuddered as Maurice toyed with the button on her slacks. Slipping his fingers inside her slacks, he could feel the heat radiating from her core. Maurice wanted to take her right there on the desk and make her moan in delight as he wrapped her legs around his waist and found her G-spot.

Kenya pulled away like she'd gained control over her senses. "I can't keep doing this," she said. "We argue, we disagree, and then we have sex. But what changes?"

Exasperated, Maurice walked over to the window. "You're the one who won't change. You keep holding on to all the mistakes I've made and the ones that you think I'm going to make." Turning and looking at her, he added, "I'm not the only one who's made mistakes in the past."

His words seemed to punch her in the stomach. "Get out," she snapped. "I'm not the one who . . . Just get out."

"Fine. But when I walk out this door, don't expect me to come back," he said.

Kenya dashed over to the door and opened it. "I don't give a damn what you do. If you don't want to come back, then don't."

Maurice walked over to the door and closed it. "All right. I don't want to fight. I don't want to leave. I'm not going to let you run me away, and I'm not going to let you run away again. Why don't we go somewhere and talk? You can ask me anything you want."

She rolled her eyes and shook her head. "This is insanity. I don't want to fight with you, but I can't help what I feel."

"What do you want from me?" he asked. "I don't want to feel like I'm forcing you into something."

"Meet me tonight at Blue around seven," she said.

"All right," he said. "Bring an open mind, and I still want you to keep the ring, whether you say yes tonight or not."

Watching him walk out of the office, Kenya wondered if she was making a mistake by pushing him away. She slipped the ring on her finger, even though she wasn't sure what her answer would be.

Chapter 18

Maurice walked into the trendy uptown restaurant at seven on the dot. Tonight he was going to prove to Kenya that she would be safe in his love. In his arms were more roses. He'd tried for about three hours to find some orchids, but he couldn't. Taking a seat at the bar so that he could see Kenya when she walked in, Maurice prepared to open up about everything in his past. He was going to tell her how he'd thought about her often, even when he was with Lauryn, sometimes when they were in bed together. He'd tell her how in quiet moments, when a song that they'd listened to while they were together would come on the radio, she'd pop into his mind, and he'd want to call her. He'd tell her how, when he went home to Atlanta for the holidays, he would fight the urge to drive to her house just to see her walking in the front door.

"Well, Maurice, we meet again," Lauryn said, slipping onto the stool beside him.

"Go away."

"Roses? You must have a date."

"Again, go away."

Licking her lips, she said, "Why can't we be friends?"

"Because I don't want to be your friend or anything else. Will you get lost before Kenya gets here?" His voice was peppered with irritation.

"Are you and Kenya together now? Trying to relive the past?"

"Where's Mya?"

Lauryn shrugged her shoulders. "I don't know. She's on some human-rights committee thing. I messed up. What I was doing with Mya was a mistake. I miss you."

Maurice looked at her outfit, which consisted of last season's Gucci, two-year-old Prada shoes, and a three-year-old Coach bag, all things that he'd purchased for her. "You miss me or my black card?"

"It was never about the money," she lied.

"Right."

"Can we have just one night together? One night to rekindle our past? It's been so long since I've felt a man's arms around me, lips kissing me, d—"

"Isn't this cozy," Kenya said as she walked over to Maurice and Lauryn. "Just like being in college all over again."

Maurice rose to his feet quickly and kissed Kenya. "Lauryn was just leaving."

"Actually," Lauryn said, "Maurice and I were talking about the past and how good we were together."

Glaring at her, Kenya didn't say anything. Maurice knew that she was fuming on the inside, and that Lauryn was playing on all of her insecurities, insecurities that his reckless actions had caused.

"No," Maurice said. "You were talking about how you're trying to switch teams again. Lauryn, you know that we're done, and you can try and come between me and Kenya, but I've learned my lesson. I have a real woman who knows that she wants to be with a man." He wrapped his arm around Kenya's waist, and they headed to the hostess to be seated.

"I tell you what," Lauryn said to herself. "She's not going to have you when I'm done."

Kenya turned to Maurice when she was sure Lauryn was out of earshot. "So, she wants you back?"

"I don't give a damn what Lauryn wants. She's confused, and she's no longer my concern."

Believe him, Kenya thought. *It's not like you walked in and saw them kissing. You didn't catch them having sex.*

Maurice held her chin in his hand. "Don't let her get to you. Lauryn, I finally see, is a gold digger. She misses my money, and that's it. She never loved me. She wasn't real, like you."

"Huh. Only took you nine years to figure that out?"

He kissed her nose gently. "What can I say. I was a few test scores short of riding the short bus to school."

The hostess walked over to them, letting the couple know that their table was ready. As they walked to the table, Maurice looked down at Kenya's left hand. She was wearing his ring. It was a positive sign that he was happy to see.

Once they were seated and their drinks ordered, Maurice took Kenya's hand in his. "So, you're wearing it. What does this mean?"

"That I've always loved diamonds and emeralds. This ring is beautiful, but I don't know if I'm going to keep it."

"Yes, you are, because it's yours. The jeweler who designed it for me actually named it the Kenya cluster. I have a certificate to prove it."

She beamed and shook her head. "Maurice, you know I can't be bought, right? I'm not one of your groupies or

Lauryn. I have to know that I'm the only woman that will be sharing your life and your bed."

"You are and you will be. Kenya, I don't want anyone but you."

"Since tonight is about honesty, it's time for me to come clean. I've never stopped loving you. Not even when I tried to hate you. I've been hiding behind my work, avoiding dating, because no one compares to you," she said.

Maurice listened intently as she spoke, watching the pain in her eyes. He hated himself for hurting her and leaving such a deep scar. He was truly no better than his father. He could understand why James didn't want to see him and Kenya together again. His brother saw their father in Maurice.

"I still don't trust you completely," Kenya said. "And when I saw you and Lauryn at the bar, I started to turn around and leave. But I'm not running anymore. We didn't meet up in the Bahamas for no reason. I didn't get transferred to Charlotte for no reason. This is it, Maurice. This is our last chance, and I swear, if you blow it this time, there will be no going back."

Reaching across the table, he kissed her tenderly. "So, is that a yes?" he said when they broke off the kiss.

"Yes. I'll marry you."

Leaping from his seat, Maurice crossed over to Kenya, lifted her from her chair, and spun her around. "Woman, I love you more than you'll ever know."

"Uh, excuse me," the waiter said. "Do I need to come back?"

Maurice turned to the man and smiled. "We're getting married!"

"Congratulations," said the waiter. "Do you want to hear tonight's specials?"

Kenya laughed as Maurice let her go. "Sure."

They settled into their seats, and the waiter rattled off the specials of the evening, but Maurice was too excited to listen. He couldn't believe that Kenya had agreed to be his wife, and he knew this time around there'd be no surprises at the altar and no media blitz, either. But whatever Kenya wanted was what she was going to get. Looking into her eyes, all he could see was their future. A few children, a house out in the exclusive Ballantyne community, and a vacation home in Miami.

"Maurice," Kenya said. "Have you decided on what you want to eat?"

Smiling sassily, Maurice said, "It's not on the menu." The blush on Kenya's cheeks made his blood run hot. "But I'll take the first special you talked about."

"Thank you. A good choice," the waiter said as he walked away.

Maurice turned to Kenya, with a broad smile on his lips. "Why don't we take this food to go and celebrate our engagement?" he said in a sultry whisper.

"You're so bad," she said. "But let's do it."

Maurice waved at the waiter and motioned for him to wrap up the food. "We'll meet you at the door," he mouthed as he rose to his feet.

He and Kenya headed for the door. Maurice stuffed a wad of cash in the waiter's hand and took the boxes that he held out to him. It didn't matter that he had paid two hundred dollars for a dinner that cost fifty. All Maurice could think about was getting Kenya back to his place and stripping her clothes off piece by piece.

Lauryn watched Maurice and Kenya leave, and she saw the money that changed hands. She chalked it up to Maurice showing off again. He used to do that whenever she asked him for money to shop when she was around her girlfriends. That was why she'd only ask for money when they were around. It wasn't like Maurice was cheap, but he loved to put on a show. Kenya was getting the benefit of the life that should've been hers.

"I refuse to let her win," Lauryn muttered. "I took him once, and I can take him back, and this time I'm going to stay married to him long enough to get a hefty settlement."

The bartender leaned over and looked at Lauryn. "You all right, honey? Sitting here, talking to yourself, isn't a good look, no matter how pretty you are."

Lauryn rose to her feet and stormed out of the bar, leaving her unpaid bill on the counter. As soon as she got outside, she saw Maurice and Kenya getting into his car. She'd talked him into buying that sports car, because he'd wanted a bland SUV.

I deserve all of this, the fancy dinners and the cars, she told herself. *Why did I listen to Mya and turn my back on this life? I was fine having the best of both worlds, and listening to her has left me with nothing but an apartment that she's crowding. She can have this bohemian lifestyle and live like the characters in* Rent, *but I'm not happy.*

Lauryn stomped off to the bus stop and waited for the one that headed to east Charlotte. All the while, her eyes were focused on the car speeding by her.

By the time Maurice and Kenya arrived at his place, dinner was the last thing on their minds. The only thing they could think about was getting in the door, ripping each other's clothes off, and feasting on the other's body.

After Maurice hopped out of the car, he walked over to the passenger side, scooped Kenya up in his arms, headed up to the doorman, and slipped him a tip just for being there.

"Mr. Goings, Ms. Michaels is inside, waiting for you."

He wanted to take the money back from the doorman as he lowered Kenya to the ground. "I thought I told you that she wasn't welcomed here."

"She was very insistent," the man said, casting his eyes downward. "I figured since the two of you were living here together at one time and . . ."

Maurice threw his hand up and glanced at Kenya sideways; her body language told how uncomfortable she was about hearing that he and Lauryn had lived together. "I'll take care of it, but from now on she's not welcomed here anymore," he said, grabbing Kenya's hand. "This is the future Mrs. Maurice Goings and the only woman who has carte blanche to my place."

"Yes, sir," the doorman said.

Kenya walked in behind Maurice and held her hand out for his key. "You deal with your garbage, and I'll meet you upstairs."

Lauryn glared at Kenya as she stepped on the elevator. Then she turned to Maurice. "That's what you want?" she asked.

"Lauryn, why are you here?" Maurice said. Folding his arms across his chest, he leaned back on the wall. "You left me at the altar, remember? How does Mya feel about you stalking me?"

"Maurice, I made a mistake, and I want you back. I want our life back." Lauryn closed the space between them and stroked Maurice's cheek. He slapped her hand away.

"Woman, have you lost your mind? Kenya and I are getting married, because she knows what she wants. You, on the other hand, don't. One day you're a lesbian, and the next you miss our life? Or is it that you miss the money, the gifts, the trips, and the attention? You wanted to be an NFL wife and a closet lesbian. You wanted me to be your bankroll, and to be honest, that's all you've wanted from the first time you spread your legs in that hotel room."

Lauryn turned her head away from Maurice's intense stare. "That's unfair."

"Unfair, but true. I was a fool. I let what's between your legs cloud my brain, make me think that you were better than that woman waiting for me upstairs. I wasted so much of my life with you. I wasted so much money on you, trying to keep you happy and trying to make you a housewife when you were nothing but a common—"

Lauryn slapped Maurice before he could finish his statement. "You son of a bitch. I wasn't all of that when you were screwing me any way you wanted to. Your problem is that you don't think you're man enough to satisfy anyone except Kenya, who probably hasn't had another man look her way since you dropped her for me. You're embarrassed because I left you standing at the altar. I was the best thing that ever happened to you, and if you don't see that, then you're a fool."

Maurice pushed Lauryn away from him and headed for the elevators. He turned and looked at her. "You're right. I'm embarrassed, embarrassed that I fell for a tramp like you. But I have a real woman upstairs, waiting on me. Don't you have a woman at home that you need to go tend to?"

Kenya tried not to let her mind wander, but she couldn't help herself. What if Lauryn had seduced him again? *This isn't college. You have to trust him,* she thought while she paced from the window to the sofa. *What are they going to do? Have sex in the lobby?* She was sure that she'd walked a groove in the carpet with all of her pacing.

Looking around the room, Kenya took stock of the fact that she'd never noticed the décor of Maurice's place until now. Sure, she'd known that Lauryn had lived there, but she hadn't thought about the fact that Lauryn had left her touches all over the place. The living room reeked of her style, eighteenth-century French inspired, except for the solid oak coffee table and a round sectional leather sofa, which only now seemed out of place.

Kenya marched into the bedroom and surveyed the stainless-steel bed and its mattress.

I hope he bought new sheets, she thought as she looked at the slightly worn mattress. The mattress and box spring were obviously new, because the plastic was still on the box spring. It was obvious that the sheets weren't new. Snatching them off the bed, she threw them across the room. Were those the sheets that he and Lauryn had made love on before they broke up? Were these their favorite sheets, sheets that had been on their bed every time the mood struck them?

She wanted to burn those sheets and anything else that Lauryn had left in the house. Stalking into the bathroom, she opened all of the cabinets, looking for old make-up, old hair spray, and the like. Her head was spinning; the temperature in the room seemed to have jumped up a hundred degrees. Leaning back on the oversized tub, she caught a glimpse of herself in the mirror. Sweat had beaded on her forehead, and make-up ran down her cheeks. She felt as mad as she looked.

"What's going on?" Maurice asked as he entered the bathroom.

Looking up, she gave Maurice an intense stare. "When's the last time you bought new sheets? How much of this furniture did Lauryn pick out?" she ranted. "I'm not going to play house with you while living with another woman's relics. As a matter of fact, I don't even want to be here in this place, knowing that she lived here and made this place your home."

Maurice grabbed her shoulders. "Kenya, calm down.

Lauryn is trying to push our buttons, trying to come between us, and I'm not going to let it happen."

"Like before, right?" she snapped, then immediately regretted the words.

Dropping his hands to his sides, Maurice shook his head from side to side. "Why do we have to keep going back to the past?"

"Because she keeps showing up," Kenya said, her voice low and angry. "Why is that, Mo? What kind of signals are you giving her?"

Taking a step back, Maurice grabbed the edge of the sink. "I can't keep defending myself every time Lauryn shows up. She's going to be around. Charlotte isn't that big. What do you want me to do? Ask to be traded? Then are you going to quit your job and join me wherever I land? I can't control what she does. But you have to trust me when I say that I'm finished with her."

She dropped her head in her hands and exhaled slowly. "I can't help that I feel insecure about you and Lauryn. I can't get that image out of my head. I see you with her. I see all of the media reports about your marriage and—"

Maurice reached out and pulled Kenya into his arms. "She's nothing, she means nothing to me, and I want nothing to do with her. She chose someone else, another life, and I have you. We have each other, and that's all that we need," he said, his lips close to her ear.

Closing her eyes, Kenya prayed for trust and forgiveness. She prayed that when she went to sleep tonight, she would see the future that she and Maurice deserved, and not the past that she couldn't leave behind.

But she wasn't going to sleep until they bought new sheets.

Casting her eyes upward at him, Kenya made one request. "We need to go to Target."

Chapter 19

Lauryn smiled as the videographer handed her a DVD and a VHS tape.

"This is some hot stuff," he said. "You're quite the performer."

Licking her lips, she replied, "You think so, huh?"

Practically salivating, he nodded like a hound dog. "You know there's a bed in the back."

"Then you should get in it," she said, slipping her items in her purse. "Alone." Lauryn flounced out of the store, smiling broadly as her plan took form in her head.

As soon as she stepped on the sidewalk, Mya stood in front of her. "What the hell is going on, Lauryn?"

"Nothing."

"Bull. You haven't been home in two days. If this isn't what you want, let me know. I thought you chose me when you left Mo at the altar, but obviously, you're looking for something I can't give you."

"I'm not a lesbian, Mya, and you've become someone I don't recognized. What happened to you?"

"I'm myself. I'm a same gender–loving woman who's out

of the closet. I thought we were going to be on this journey together. If that's not the case, then why did you leave him?"

"Mya, I'm sorry, but this isn't what I want anymore," Lauryn said.

Running her fingers though her wavy hair, Mya blinked back the tears. "You're such a selfish bitch. I don't know how I allowed myself to fall in love with you."

Lauryn smiled. "You seduced me because you couldn't resist me. But I'm not a possession and I can't be contained by one person and I won't let you define me by your dictionary."

"You can't keep doing this to people," Mya called out after Lauryn as she walked away. "You can't play with people's hearts like it's a poker game."

Lauryn waved her hand in the air as she walked away. She could care less what Mya had to say, because she was going to make sure that Maurice and Kenya weren't happy and that they wouldn't make it to the altar. Though Lauryn didn't know if they were getting married or not, her goal was to make sure that it didn't happen.

Maurice and Kenya had been in Hickory, North Carolina, looking for furniture, and he was tired. Though he was willing to let Kenya redecorate what was going to be their house, he couldn't wait to get home, get something to eat, and go to sleep.

Why do women spend all of this time shopping and only end up buying one thing? he asked himself. In the four hours that they had been shopping at the furniture mall, the only thing Kenya had picked out was a leather sofa and matching love seat. Maurice had to admit, her taste was better than Lauryn's. She wasn't as pretentious as Lauryn was, and she asked Maurice's opinion on how he wanted things to look. Now his place was going to feel like his home and not Lauryn's version of what their house should look like. Lauryn had wanted to turn their house into something that she'd seen on *MTV Cribs*. Hell, she probably had wanted to be on that show once they were married. If she'd really paid attention to Maurice, she would've known that he wasn't much for the media spotlight. And if he had paid attention to her, he would've known that she was only with him for the media attention and the money.

I was such a fool, he thought. *I could be celebrating my anniversary with Kenya, instead of starting all over again.*

"Are you bored with all this?" Kenya asked, mistaking his silence for indifference. "I promise this is the last stop."

"All right," he said, then kissed her on the cheek. "I'm fine. We just need to go get something to eat."

"That's fine," she said as they walked into the Ashley Furniture outlet. "I'll even treat."

"Now that's what's up," he said. "What are we looking for in here?"

"Something to brighten up the living room," she said. "I know you like black, but maybe we should add a little splash of color?"

"As long as that color isn't pink," he said, ready to take a seat and let Kenya do her thing.

"I'll take that into consideration," she said as she headed for the accessories section.

Maurice sat down on one of the display sofas and watched her walk away, her hips swaying underneath her A-line cotton skirt. He couldn't wait to peel that skirt off her, spread her legs, and dive for her buried treasure.

"Hey," said a boy about twelve years old. "Aren't you Mo Goings from the Carolina Panthers? What are you doing here?"

Maurice pointed to Kenya. "Whatever she wants."

"Man, my friends aren't going to believe this. Can you sign my T-shirt or something?" the boy asked excitedly.

"Sure, kid," Maurice said. "You got a pen?"

The boy produced a Sharpie marker from his jeans pocket and handed it to Maurice. Then he lifted his sweatshirt, revealing a Carolina Panthers T-shirt. "I'm glad you're not a jerk, like some other players."

Maurice shook the boy's hand and smiled. His mind flashed to Kenya's confession of her miscarriage. He wondered what their son would've been like. He didn't even consider the fact that the lost child could have been a girl. He wanted a son, someone he could toss a football with and teach the rules of the game that he loved. Kenya would watch them from the porch and maybe even bring them some snacks. A family had never been something Maurice had daydreamed about when he and Lauryn were together, but he wanted that with Kenya more than he imagined.

Rising to his feet after signing the boy's shirt and watching him happily run away, Maurice walked up to Kenya, who was standing in the lamps section of the store, and wrapped his arms around her waist.

"Hey, babe," she said, then pointed to a pair of Tiffany floor lamps. "What do you think?"

Shrugging his shoulders, he said, "Didn't your grandmother have some lamps like these when she used to baby-sit us?"

Kenya laughed. "And as I recall, you and James broke one while playing football in the house, after she told you not to."

Sharing the memory, Maurice chuckled and kissed her neck gently. "She whooped me good, too," he said. "And it wasn't even my fault. James couldn't throw a football to save his life."

"I guess it's good that you're the star in the family," Kenya said.

"Maybe we need to have a little star of our own?" he whispered.

Whirling around, she raised her eyebrows and asked, "What?"

"I want to start a family with you. I want us to have the life that we should've had all those years ago. We should get married immediately. What's the point in waiting?"

Kenya smiled broadly and shook her head. "Maurice, this is too much too fast. How are we going plan a wedding with my schedule and you getting ready for training camp?"

"We can fly to Vegas tonight and get started on making Junior tomorrow," he said gleefully.

"Why are you in such a hurry?" she inquired. "I mean, I'm not doing some tawdry Vegas chapel for my wedding. And that's not to say that I want the Princess Di treatment, but I want my mother and my friends around when I get married."

He respected her wishes, but he didn't want to wait much longer. "How do you think the family's going to react to the news? The last time I saw your dad in Atlanta, he tried to kill me with his eyes."

Kenya laughed nervously, telling Maurice that he still was persona non grata in the Taylor family.

"Have you even told them about us?" he said.

"My mother knows."

"What did she say?"

Exhaling exasperatedly, Kenya said, "I'm an adult, and I can make my own decisions, without my parents' approval."

"So, she's not happy about us being together, huh?" he said.

"That's putting it mildly," Kenya said. "But my mother,

father, and others are going to have their opinions about you. I know the truth, though."

"And what would that be?" he asked, hugging her tightly.

"That you love me, and I love you back. It's you and me, boo."

"You're not just saying that so I'll buy these ugly lamps, are you?" he teased, kissing her on the bridge of her nose.

After purchasing the lamps, a new king-sized bed, a softer sofa and love seat, and a host of other household items, Kenya and Maurice headed back to his place for a dinner of Chinese takeout and a bottle of merlot.

"Want to watch a movie?" Maurice said as he picked up his mail. "These just came from Netflix." He held up a brown package that looked like it had come from the Internet movie-rental company.

Kenya shrugged her shoulders as she set the food on the coffee table. "Right now I just want to eat. I'm starving. I'm going to get some plates. What do you have to drink in here?"

"I have some tea, water, and juice," he called out as he opened the DVDs.

Kenya grabbed the plates and flatware and asked Maurice what movies had been delivered. "And please don't say action and adventure. I don't want to see anything blow up tonight."

"I have no idea what these movies are, because they aren't labeled," he said, watching Kenya walk into the living room.

"Huh," she said as she set the plates on the oak coffee table. "What kind of bootleg company are you dealing with?"

Maurice shrugged. "James signed me up with this mess. There's no telling what kind of company this is." He popped the unlabeled disk in the player and sat down next to Kenya after pressing PLAY.

She handed him a plate filled with sweet and sour chicken and fried rice. "Is this a mystery or something?" she said, glancing at the black screen.

"I don't know," he said.

An image of Maurice's bedroom appeared on the screen along with the headline from yesterday's paper.

"What the hell?" Maurice muttered, inching to the edge of the sofa. "Is this some kind of joke?"

The screen faded to black, and then Lauryn's image appeared. "See," she said, "some things never change. Kenya, you will always come in second to me."

Kenya turned to Maurice. "What the hell is this?"

They both looked at the screen and saw what seemed to be Maurice and Lauryn having sex.

"What is this?" Kenya demanded again.

"This is a fake. She wasn't here yesterday. I was with you nearly all day," he said. Maurice shut the DVD player off. "This is—"

Kenya quickly rose to her feet. "You slimy bastard. I knew Lauryn wasn't showing up just because she was trying to get back with you. You've been with her behind my back all this time. How could you do this to me again?"

Grabbing a pint of rice, Kenya tossed it in Maurice's face. He screamed as the hot rice hit his skin.

"Are you crazy?" he yelled.

"Yes, I am, for getting involved with you again. I must be insane. Did you have fun sleeping with me and Lauryn, comparing notes, and videotaping it?"

Maurice grabbed a napkin and wiped his face, then quickly rose to his feet. "I didn't sleep with Lauryn. That DVD is a fake."

Kenya glared at him as she grabbed her purse and keys

from the end of the sofa. "Go straight to hell!" she shouted then snatched her engagement ring off her finger and flung it across the room. Kenya ran out of the apartment, and slammed the door behind her just as hot tears welled in her eyes.

As she waited for the elevator, Maurice ran out into the hallway. "Can we talk about this?"

"There's nothing to talk about, Maurice. The DVD didn't lie. Lauryn can have your sorry ass, because I'm done."

"That DVD is a lie, and if you won't take my word for it, then let's have it analyzed."

The doors to the elevator opened, and Kenya stepped in, ignoring Maurice's pleas to talk to him about the DVD.

By the time Kenya reached the lobby, she was a bucket of tears. She pulled it together long enough to ask the doorman to call her a taxi. She'd rode with Maurice all day, and her car was in South Charlotte.

"Miss, are you all right?" the doorman asked when he hung up the phone.

Wiping her eyes with the back of her hand, she nodded but continued to cry. "I'll be fine," she said, then headed out to the sidewalk. Tears blurred her vision, and she wasn't paying attention to the person walking in the door. It was James.

"Kenya, what's wrong?" James asked, noting her tears and shaky demeanor.She flung herself into his arms. "I was such a fool. I made a mistake giving him a second chance, and he did it to me again."

Pushing her chin upward, James looked into her eyes. "What did he do?"

"Lauryn."

"Come on. Let me take you home," James said.

Kenya allowed James to lead her to his car and drive her across town. On the ride to her place, she stared out the window, wishing that she could hurt Maurice the way he'd hurt her. Then again, what would that solve? However, Kenya wasn't thinking rationally. Her first thought was to drive over to his place with a baseball bat and smash his car until it was unrecognizable. Then she thought about entering his apartment and lighting his bed on fire, with him in it. Turning to James, she thought that he might somehow be the key to her revenge. But if she did what she was thinking, there would be no turning back, and Maurice would never forgive her. That was fine with her, because she was never going to forgive him for what he'd done to her, again.

Chapter 20

Maurice watched as his brother drove off with Kenya in the front seat. Figuring that she was in good hands with James, he decided to go find Lauryn and get to the bottom of that DVD. Running back upstairs, he grabbed the package, then his keys, and headed for the garage. He headed to Mya's place, hoping to catch Lauryn there.

The trip to Mya's stirred confusing thoughts in him. He remembered all of the times that Mya had gone out to dinner with him and Lauryn, the trips, the Super Bowl, and all the times he'd tried to set her up with his single friends. *A damned smoke screen,* he thought. *All along she wanted what I had. I wonder how she feels now that she has it?*

Maurice pulled into the driveway of the apartment complex and parked his car. Looking up at the building, he thought about the nights that he'd dropped Lauryn off to have girl time with Mya. How many times did they end up having sex? Though questions like that nagged at him at times, Maurice didn't care about what Mya and Lauryn had. It was his pride that had his head spinning at the moment. Maurice walked up to Mya's door and banged on it as if he were a police officer about to serve a warrant.

"What the . . . Mo?" Mya said when she opened the door.

"Where's Lauryn?" he demanded.

"Don't know. Don't really care," she replied and started to close the door. Maurice shoved his foot in the doorway.

"Mya, if you know where she is, you need to tell me, because I'm not letting her get away with this." He shoved the DVD under her nose. "What do you know about this?"

She pushed the door open. "My neighbors might call the cops. Come in."

Maurice stepped inside and stayed in the foyer. "Where is Lauryn? I don't know how she did it, but I'm going to find out."

"What is this?" Mya asked as she took the DVD from his hands.

"It's your girlfriend pretending to have sex with me yesterday. This DVD is obviously altered, and I don't know what she's trying to prove."

Mya smiled sardonically. "So that's what she was doing."

"What?"

She sighed and walked into the kitchen. "Want something to drink? You probably need one."

"I need to find Lauryn."

"Cut your losses and move on. I have. Lauryn is too selfish for words, and I can't deal with her anymore. She's toxic."

"How long had you two been doing this?" Maurice asked. Curiosity had gotten the best of him.

"Doing what?" she asked as she poured herself a glass of wine. "Oh, *this* as in a relationship? Lauryn and I have been 'doing this' since college. We were roommates, and I thought at first that Lauryn was a lesbian. At that time I was confused about my sexuality. I knew I was attracted to women, but I didn't think that I would ever act on it. Then Lauryn moved into my room. The way she used to flaunt her body and walk around the room in skimpy little outfits made me realize that I wasn't just going through some phase in my life. I wanted this woman, and I had to have her."

"But you knew that she was straight," Maurice said.

"So? I knew I wanted her, and I could tell that she was curious. I fell in love with her, Mo, just like you did."

"I wasn't in love with her. It was more like lust," he snapped. "But that's neither here nor there. Where has Lauryn been spending her time lately?"

Taking a swig of wine, Mya shrugged her shoulders. "I haven't a clue. She hasn't been here, and I thought maybe she'd taken up with some other rich man."

Maurice turned and headed for the door. He grabbed the knob and turned around. "So every time you two were together, did you just laugh at what a fool I was?"

Mya snorted. "This was never about you, Maurice. Lauryn was selfish, and she played both of us. Just let it go."

"Where did you say she had this DVD made?"

Mya rattled off the address of the videographer.

Maurice dashed out the door, ready to give Kenya the proof that she needed to see Lauryn was a liar.

Kenya crossed her legs and leaned closer to James as they sat on the sofa, watching the news. She'd told him that she didn't want to be alone after finding out that Maurice had cut her so deeply for a second time and that she really wanted him to stay. The truth was, he'd be the knife she planned to cut Maurice with. When Maurice got wind of what happened with her and his brother, he would feel the same pain that she had felt when she pressed PLAY on that DVD player.

Two wrongs don't make a right, her voice of reason said to her. Kenya ignored that voice and looked over at James. Sleeping with Maurice's brother wasn't going to change the fact that her heart was broken again. Inching closer to James, she made up her mind that it didn't matter what the consequences would be: she was going to make her move. After all, James was there for her all of those years ago. Maybe he had feelings for her that she could squeeze out of him.

James had stayed with Kenya because he felt as if he owed her something. It was déjà vu. They could just as easily have been in Atlanta nine years ago, sitting on her mother's porch, with her head buried in his arms.

He'd promised himself that he wouldn't let Maurice hurt Kenya again. Yet that was exactly what had happened. How could Maurice be so stupid as to take up with Lauryn again? Hadn't she embarrassed him enough by leaving him at the altar after turning their wedding into a media circus? His heart broke for Kenya as he put his arm around her shoulder in what he meant to be a brotherly show of affection.

Kenya turned her head slightly. Their lips were inches apart. Feeling that she'd lose her nerve if she didn't do it now, she leaned in and kissed him. However, as she slipped her tongue in his mouth, she imagined that she was kissing Maurice. When she eased her hands between his legs, she thought about all the times she'd made love to Maurice. James's body wasn't as muscular as Maurice's or as lean, but that didn't matter to her as she unbuckled his belt.

James pulled back from the kiss, eying Kenya as if she were a stranger. "What are we doing?" he said, running his hand across his face.

"I need you," she said. "I just want to forget." Kenya cupped her hands around his face, trying to coax him into kissing her again. She could tell that he was weak when he closed his eyes and leaned into her.

She closed her eyes, too, imagining that Maurice was sitting beside her, getting ready to make love to her.

James pulled Kenya's hands from his face. "This is wrong. You're hurt and angry and . . ."

Rising to her feet, Kenya wiped her hands on her thighs. "Maybe when I got back to Atlanta, I should've looked at you as more than just a friend. Maybe you and I should've been together, and this wouldn't have happened again."

James crossed over to Kenya and wrapped his arms around her waist. "You don't mean that. I know you're hurt, and you're not thinking clearly right now. Anything that we do right now, we're going to regret when it's over."

Turning around to face him, Kenya knew James was right. Having sex with him wasn't going to make her any happier. She'd still be hurting over the fact that Maurice had betrayed her again.

"I don't know what I'm doing right now," she whispered. "I shouldn't try to pull you into my mess. Maybe you should go."

He nodded, then kissed her on the forehead. "And just so you know, if things were different, if I knew you wanted me for me and not as a means to get him back, nothing would stop me from making love to you. But you and Maurice have to work this thing out. Put some closure on your relationship or something. I don't want to stand by and watch him hurt you again, and I don't want you to do something that you're sure to regret."

When James left, Kenya buried her face in one of the pillows on her sofa and sobbed until she drifted off to sleep.

It must have been after midnight when she heard the banging on her door. Initially, she wanted to ignore it. But as it continued, Kenya knew whoever was at her door wasn't going away. Pulling herself up off the sofa, she ambled to the door, looked through the peephole, and saw Maurice's face.

"Kenya, I know you're there. Please open up," he said as if he could see through the door.

"Go away."

"Not until you hear what I have to say." He placed his hand on the knob and turned it.

Kenya sucked her teeth. "Do you think you're getting in here tonight after what you've done?" she hissed. "Why aren't you with Lauryn?"

"Because I don't want to be with her," he said. "Kenya, do you really want all of your neighbors to hear this?"

"Go away."

"Open the door."

She started to walk away from the door, and Maurice called out, "I'll wait here all night if I have to."

"Then have a good night, jerk," she snapped but didn't walk away from the door. Peering at him, she saw that he had what seemed to be the infamous DVD in his hand. *This man's insane. Or I am because I am still in love with him, and it's so obvious that he can't get Lauryn out of his system.*

Maurice banged on the door again. "I'm not leaving, Kenya. And you got people opening their doors, wondering why I'm out here begging you to open this door."

She could imagine the spectacle of Maurice banging on her door and waking her neighbors. It wouldn't be long before someone called the police, and then this would be another media event. Kenya opened the door.

"You have five minutes," she hissed.

Maurice walked in and handed her a DVD. "Watch this."

She threw the disk in his face. "You think I want to see you and Lauryn having sex?"

"I can tell you all day that I'm not the one on this DVD, but until you see the truth, you're not going to take my word for it."

Turning her back to him, she glanced up at the purple clock on the wall. "You have two and a half minutes left."

"Damn it, Kenya, if I wanted Lauryn, I would've forgiven her when she left me for that woman and married her. But I didn't. I got another chance to be with you, and that's what I want. This DVD is a lie. She had it made by a videographer on Central Avenue. Mya saw her leaving that shop this morning. She's been stalking us since she saw us in the Blake Hotel, and she knew how you'd react if you thought that we were sleeping together behind your back." Maurice dropped to his knees and grabbed Kenya around her waist, forcing her to look at him.

"I don't believe you. I don't trust you, and I want you out of my house," Kenya said coldly.

Standing, Maurice grabbed her hand. "If you think I'm going to let you run from me again, you're wrong."

Yanking her hand away from him, she shot him an icy glare. "The only thing that I was wrong about was thinking that you'd changed. Everybody was right about you. He has more money, but Mo is just the same ass that he's always been. Why don't you, Lauryn, and her lesbian lover go somewhere and make another DVD?"

Maurice walked over to the television, ignoring the angry look that Kenya shot at him. "This DVD was faked. Lauryn had my bedroom superimposed as she and some man had sex. Then my face was put on his body so that you would think this was me."

"Do I look like I was born yesterday?" Kenya snapped. "For all I know, you could have taken this in and had it doctored yourself. Maurice, why don't you just go out and find one of those mindless groupies and marry her? We're done. Now get the hell out of my house."

He grabbed Kenya, roughly pulling her against his body.

"If you want more proof, then come with me to the videographer. He'll tell you everything he did for Lauryn."

She pushed against his chest, but Maurice didn't release her. "Like you didn't pay him to say what you want. I'm not falling for your lies again!"

"I've never lied to you. And I haven't lied to you about this DVD or being with Lauryn. When did I have time to do that? Kenya, can't you see that I love you and I want to be with you and only you?"

"Well, seeing you having sex on DVD isn't really convincing me that I'm the only woman in your life." She punched him in the chest until he dropped his arms. "I want to hurt you, make you feel the pain that you've caused me. But I'm not that kind of person."

"I didn't do anything," he said.

"So you say."

Maurice closed his eyes and dropped his head. "What do you want to do? Do you really want things to be over between us?"

"Yes," she said in a voice barely above a whisper. "I want you out of my life, out of my head, and out of my heart."

Pointing his finger in her face and shaking his head, Maurice said, "I know that you don't mean it, because if you wanted me out of your life, I wouldn't be in your head and heart. You wouldn't be trembling like a leaf." Stroking her cheek, he brought her mouth level with his. "Kenya, this isn't right. We can't give Lauryn what she wants."

"If she wants you, she can have you." Kenya didn't step away from him, because everything that he was saying was true. She loved him, and she wanted to be with him more than anything, but the DVD and the past, coupled with all of her insecurities, were keeping her from totally committing her heart and soul to him. How could she when the days changed but the questions remained the same? The pain never seemed to go away. Her mother was right, Imani was right, and her heart was wrong.

"Get out," she found the voice to say. "I don't want this anymore."

He nodded. "I'll leave now, but I'll be back." Maurice opened the door and found James standing on the other side. "What are you doing here?"

"The bigger question is what are you doing here? Haven't you hurt her enough?" James said angrily.

"So is this what you're doing? Swooping in to pick up my leftovers?" Maurice pushed his brother against the wall.

Kenya stepped in between them. "Stop it!" she exclaimed. "Maurice, leave."

"Is there something going on with you two? From the moment we saw you at the resort, James has had some sort of fixation on you. What the hell is going on?"

James snorted. "You have the nerve to question her when you've been sleeping with Lauryn again?"

Shaking his head, Maurice turned to go down the stairs, convinced that James was trying to make a move on Kenya. Why else would he be there after midnight? Maurice vowed to get to the bottom of things, but not tonight. In the morning, when cooler heads would prevail, he, Kenya, and James were going to have it out. *I can't believe my brother is trying to do this to me,* he thought. *I'm pretty sure he's trying to comfort Kenya, but I can't help but feel like there's something else going on here.*

Kenya shook her head as she closed the door behind James. "What are you doing back here?" she asked him.

"I didn't like the way we left things," James said. "What does Maurice being here mean for the two of you now?"

"Nothing," she said. "He was just telling more lies."

Kenya led James to the sofa. "Will you stay here tonight, on the sofa?"

"I guess I can. I don't want what happened earlier today to hurt our friendship."

Throwing her arms around his neck and hugging him tenderly, she said, "I'm sorry that I tried to put you in the middle of this thing with me and Mo."

"You don't need to apologize," he said. "Maybe it's time for me to stop trying to clean up Maurice's messes. He's a grown man, and it's time for him to take responsibility for his own actions."

She nodded. "And I need to do the same," she said. "Maurice and I don't belong together, and I've been trying to force this relationship, despite knowing that I didn't trust him. You can't have love without trust. And there was no way I could've married him."

"Married?" James said incredulously. "When did this happen? Maybe you two need to talk, Kenya. If you loved him enough to accept his marriage proposal, then maybe it isn't over."

She rose to her feet quickly. "And I thought you were going to stop trying to clean up your brother's messes."

"I'm just being a friend, Kenya. You and Maurice can't seem to get enough of each other. After all that time had passed, the two of you found your way back to each other. Maybe it's destiny."

She folded her arms across her chest and pursed her lips.

James continued speaking. "You love him. If you didn't, you wouldn't be in such pain, and he wouldn't be trying to convince you that the DVD isn't real if he didn't love you just as much."

"Sometimes love isn't enough," she mumbled.

"Then what is? If you and Maurice love each other, then

you owe it to yourself to give it a chance or at least hear him out about this whole mess. What if Lauryn is just making trouble for you two because she's trying to worm her way into Maurice's pocket again?"

Rolling her eyes, Kenya said, "It's funny that Lauryn's trouble always ends up with Maurice between her legs. I can't think about this anymore tonight. I'm going to bed." She headed for her bedroom, trying to push James's words out of her head. He was right, and she didn't want to admit it.

As she eased into bed, she decided to call Maurice in the morning to see if there was anything left to work out.

Chapter 21

Maurice's first instinct when he woke up at six in the morning was to head over to Kenya's house and try to talk to her about everything that was going on. Instead, he picked up the engagement ring that he'd given her and stared at it. He thought that he'd done everything right this time. He'd remained faithful to Kenya, he'd put her first, and he'd been honest about his feelings. But in the end he was still alone.

Sitting up in bed, still holding the ring, Maurice stared into the stone, wishing it were a magic ball that could show him the future he'd dreamed he and Kenya would have. He thought their meeting at the Bahamian resort had been destiny giving them another chance. *Maybe this isn't destiny,* he thought. *Kenya doesn't trust me, and there's nothing I can do to change that. But I'm not going to let her think that I betrayed her again with Lauryn. She has to know that I won't be the same fool twice.*

Maurice hopped out of bed and took a quick shower. All the while he thought about how he was going to make Lauryn pay for interfering in his life. After dressing, Maurice headed to Kenya's place. He wanted her to be with him when he confronted Lauryn with the evidence proving she'd faked the DVD. Maurice couldn't help but smile sarcastically as he thought about Lauryn. She had had him all to herself, but she'd chosen to be with Mya, and now that he was trying to move on with his life, she seemed to miss what she had.

As he drove, Maurice decided that he was going to let the chips fall where they may. If Kenya didn't want to believe him, then he wasn't going to force the issue. He was tired of fighting with her and trying to convince her that his love was for her and her alone. Nothing he did or said made a difference.

Maurice knew, however, that if things didn't work out, he wouldn't be fortunate enough to find another woman like Kenya, and if he couldn't have her, then he wouldn't spend his life looking for a replacement.

As he pulled up to her complex, he prayed that she'd be ready to listen to reason and give their love another try, one last try, because nothing was going to come between them again. That is if Kenya believed him. He got out of the car, dashed upstairs to her place, and knocked softly on the door, hoping not to have a replay of last night's drama.

When the door opened and he saw James standing there, his blood boiled. "What the hell? Did you spend the night?" Maurice snapped.

"I did, but it isn't what you think," James explained. "Kenya needed—"

Maurice, unable to control his rage, punched his brother in the face, forcing him backward. "You've been planning this all along!" he hissed.

Kenya ran into the living room when she heard the loud crash. Since she'd just stepped out of the shower, she only had on a short terry-cloth robe. Maurice's eyes stretched, owing to incredulity.

"Are you two sleeping together?" Maurice demanded.

James rose to his feet and stood toe to toe with his brother. "You're an idiot. I spent the night here telling Kenya how much you two needed to work things out, and you come here accusing me of sleeping with her?"

"Besides," Kenya snapped, "you're the one with the sex tape."

Before Maurice could reply, James punched his brother, nearly breaking his nose. "That's just for being stupid," he said.

Holding his nose, Maurice fought the urge to retaliate. "Is there something that you two need to tell me?"

Kenya walked into the kitchen and grabbed a dish towel. "Mo, we need to talk." She handed him the towel so that he could wipe his bloody nose.

James looked from Kenya to Maurice, then headed out the front door.

"Maurice," Kenya said, "you have a lot of nerve."

"I have proof that this DVD is a fake. All you have to do is have an open mind about it. There's no way that I'd sleep with Lauryn again when I have you. You're the woman that I want, Kenya. I just can't keep trying to prove myself to you over and over again. I need you to trust me."

"How can I? Trust is a two-way street, and the barbaric way you acted when you came in here shows me that you don't trust me, either," she said, then abruptly stopped talking. "Then again, maybe seeing your brother in here this morning made you feel an eighth of what I've been dealing with."

"But I haven't given you any reason not to trust me," he said. "Since we found our way back to each other, I've been bending over backward to prove to you that I'm not the same selfish bastard I was in college. But at every turn, you've distrusted me." He took her hands into his. "Do you want to fight for us?"

Looking away from him, she didn't know what to say. All night she'd thought about the answer to that question. "I wanted to hurt you back," she said, her voice barely above a whisper. "When I saw that DVD, I felt like I had been transported back in time, and I was standing in your dorm room all over again. I thought I had learned something, y'know. I knew this time that things were going to be different because I thought you were different. But that DVD said that you weren't and I was a fool again."

He gently squeezed her hands. "That DVD is a fake. I went to the videographer. He has the old videos that Lauryn brought in for him to splice together. But I don't want to prove that this is a lie and then, in a few weeks or a few days, Lauryn pulls another trick, and we're at this point again."

Sliding her hands out of his grasp, Kenya rose to her feet and walked over to the window. "Maurice, maybe we aren't meant to be," she said. "Right now, all I want is to see you suffer the way I have. That's why I tried to seduce your brother."

"What?" he snapped. Maurice rose to his feet, dropping the towel from his nose. "I can't believe you. I have to go." He headed for the door, not looking back at her.

Kenya closed the gap between them, grabbing his shoulder. "Nothing happened," she said. "It wouldn't have changed anything or made me hurt any less."

"Why would you do that?"

"I wanted you to hurt," she repeated. "I didn't want James. I just wanted you to know how this feels. This is what I've been dealing with for years. That lurch in your heart is what I've felt every time I have seen you with Lauryn. . . ."

"I don't want Lauryn. I've never tried to do anything to purposely hurt you, Kenya. I thought you were different, but it seems like you and Lauryn are two sides of the same coin." Maurice pulled the engagement ring from his pocket and placed it in her hand. "I don't want this. Sell it or whatever."

"No, it's your ring. You keep it," she said as she pressed the ring back into his hand. "Let's just let this be good-bye."

Maurice dropped the ring, then rushed out of the apartment and slammed the door. Kenya placed her hand on the knob, wanting to open the door and tell Maurice that she was wrong. Instead, she reached down and picked up the ring, then headed into her bedroom.

On the other side of the door, Maurice stood, with his hand poised to knock on the door. He wanted to take back their good-bye and forgive her for what she'd done. But his pride wouldn't let him. She had embarrassed him, just like Lauryn had when she'd bolted from the altar. Kenya was the last person he'd ever thought would do something like try to sleep with his brother. But James wasn't innocent in all of this. Maurice ran to his car and headed for his brother's place. James had some explaining to do.

Kenya sat on the sofa, tears running down her cheeks. She couldn't explain her actions; she couldn't explain why she wanted to ruin her chance at happiness with Maurice. Looking at the ring, she wondered what would've happened if she had taken his word and not sought revenge. They'd be planning a wedding and looking for a nice island to honeymoon on. When the phone rang, she hoped it was Maurice.

"Mo," she said.

"No, it's Imani," her friend replied. "I heard from your mom the other day, and she said you're getting married. I thought we were friends. Why didn't you tell me?"

Rubbing her forehead, Kenya sighed. "There's not

going to be any marriage. You and my mother can rest easy. Maurice and I are done."

"So, that's why you were expecting him to call?" Imani questioned. "You don't have to lie to me about your intentions with Maurice. I just hope that for your sake, he has changed."

"Imani, I don't feel like this right now. You and Angela can go have another conversation about my life and send me a transcript," Kenya snapped.

"Whoa, Kenya," Imani said. "I'm on your side. I was actually calling to let you know that I'm coming to Charlotte today."

"Why are you coming here? You can say I told you so over the phone," Kenya snapped.

"You have such a low opinion of me. Smith is having an alumni reunion in a few months, and I'm on the planning committee. Today is the general meeting, which the alumni association presidents have to attend."

"Uh-huh," Kenya said.

"Really. I'm calling to see if you are going to be free for dinner," Imani said. "And it's your treat, since you're the big-time attorney, and gas costs a grip."

Kenya's spirits were starting to brighten slightly. Hanging out with Imani would take her mind away from thoughts of Maurice. "I guess I can buy you dinner. But the drinks are on you. When are you getting here?"

"Well, I'm in Spartanburg right now," Imani said. "I'll call you when the meeting is over."

After hanging up with her friend, Kenya started cleaning her place. All of the nervous energy she had helped her whip her place into tip-top shape in no time flat. As she headed into her bedroom, she decided to organize her closet. When she opened the door, her suitcase fell from the top shelf, and an orchid petal floated down to the floor. As she picked it up, her mind wandered to the time she and Maurice had spent together in the Bahamas. If things weren't so complicated, they could be together and be happy.

I was a fool to think that Maurice and I could rewrite history and have a happy ending when I haven't forgiven him for what he did, she thought. *Why can't I get past this thing with Lauryn?* Kenya didn't realize that she was crying until her tears hit the petal, making it look transparent. She tossed the petal toward the trash can, but it landed on the floor. *Pull yourself together,* she told herself as she wiped her eyes with the back of her hand. *You got what you wanted. Maurice is out of your life.*

But Kenya knew that losing Maurice was the last thing that she really wanted. She couldn't keep lying to herself. She wanted to be with Maurice, but after what had happened last night and her confession to him, there was no way he'd ever forgive her.

"Sit down and listen to me, for a change," James snapped. "Kenya and I didn't do anything. I wouldn't betray you in that way. Whatever twisted relationship that you two have, it's not for me to come in between."

"I do love her, and you did betray me," Maurice snapped, refusing to sit down. "You kissed her, didn't you?"

"Yes, I did, but that was all it was. She admitted that the only reason she wanted to have sex with me was to hurt you," James said. "I'm not going to be a pawn between you and her. I won't apologize for being her friend."

Running his hand across his face, Maurice shook his head. "I don't know what to do. Maybe I should just throw in the towel."

"No, you shouldn't, stupid. Kenya loves you, and you love her. Why would you stop fighting for her?" James asked.

"She doesn't want to be with me anymore. If she did, she wouldn't have tried to seduce you, she would've listened to me about that DVD, and every day wouldn't be a struggle between us. This is for the best," Maurice said, though his words were hollow, and he didn't believe them.

"Lauryn wins again," James said.

"No."

"That's what it sounds like to me."

"What were you doing at Kenya's place this morning? Why did you go back?" Maurice demanded.

"I wanted to make sure we still had a friendship, despite what had gone down. And when I saw that DVD, I realized it was a fake, so I was trying to convince Kenya of that most of the night, until she tuned me out. Then you came over this morning, playing Rambo. Maybe you scared her off. Maybe she saw a side of you that she doesn't want to deal with, or maybe she just needs some reassurance."

"And are you supposed to give that to her?" Maurice questioned.

"I'm done. I'm out of your relationship with Kenya, and if you two are going to get together, it's going to be without my help," James said. "I'm tired of cleaning up after you."

"That's what you think?" Maurice asked.

James nodded furiously. "The first time you and Kenya broke up, I had to sit there and tell her you were a good guy, just misguided. When Lauryn left you at the altar, I had to dig you out of your self-imposed hermitism. I'm tired. So, go out and do whatever you have to do to get her back and send me an invitation to the wedding."

"All right," Maurice said. "I know what I have to do. I've got to get ready for training camp, and everything else is just going to have to be secondary."

James shook his head but didn't say anything. If Maurice wanted to be a fool, then he was going to let him deal with it.

Kenya and Imani walked to the patio of the Rock Bottom Bar and Grill. The evening weather was beautiful, and they'd decided to dine outdoors. Holding two cocktails, they sat at a table closest to the sidewalk so that they could watch people walk by.

"Charlotte really reminds me of Atlanta," Imani said. "Just with much better traffic."

Kenya laughed and took a sip of her drink. "Much better traffic. How was your meeting?"

Imani shrugged. "Interesting. I saw a lot of people I hadn't seen in years. And some people I hadn't wanted to see ever again in my life."

"Give me the dish," Kenya said, wiping a leaf from the table. Inadvertently, she thought about the orchid petal in her house. *Stop it,* she thought and tried to focus on what Imani was saying.

"And Yvette Mason was there. God, I'd forgotten how annoying she could be. She's a writer with the *Charlotte Business Journal.* Guess what she's working on this week? Hello, Kenya? Are you listening?"

"Yeah, yeah, annoying Yvette," Kenya said distractedly.

"She's working on a story about your law firm. She wanted me to give her your number, but I took her card instead." Imani handed it to Kenya. "Are you still thinking about Maurice?"

"No, not at all. As a matter of fact, I propose a toast. Here's to my life without Mo Goings," Kenya said more confidently than she felt.

Imani raised her glass. "I hear that." The women clanked their glasses, and Kenya fought the urge to cry.

Chapter 22

Maurice hadn't realized how hungry he was until his stomach started rumbling as he passed the Rock Bottom and smelled the grill smoke billowing from the restaurant. Since he'd just finished a three-hour workout and a pickup game of hoops with some guys at the University City YMCA, he felt as if he deserved a juicy steak and a fresh green salad.

His workout hadn't taken his mind off Kenya, as he'd hoped that it would. While he'd been lifting weights, a woman with a striking resemblance to Kenya had walked in, and Maurice had nearly dropped the 350-pound barbell on his chest.

As she'd gotten closer to him, he'd realized that it wasn't Kenya. She'd smiled at Maurice, mistaking his stare for interest. When he'd moved over to a machine to work on his quads, he'd seen another woman who reminded him of Kenya. As she'd squatted on the machine, he'd called out Kenya's name.

"Sorry," she said. "I'm Lola."

Maurice had mumbled his apologies, then attacked the machine for the next hour. All the while, thoughts of Kenya had danced in his head. He knew that he wasn't over her, and there was nothing he could do about it.

Parking his car across from the restaurant, Maurice dashed across the street and came face-to-face with Kenya. *God, she's beautiful*, he thought as he watched her take a sip from her glass. She smiled at the waiter as he set her dinner in front of her. His heart told him to leap over the green railing, pull her into his arms, and kiss her senseless. But he walked into the restaurant, avoiding a confrontation with Kenya. Suddenly, Charlotte felt like a small town. Maurice knew he was going to be running into Kenya, because they liked most of the same restaurants and went to the same shows and movies. He took solace in the fact that he would be heading to minicamp in a couple of weeks, and he'd be too tired to think about Kenya or anything else, other than learning the new offense.

While he waited to place his take-out order, Kenya walked into the restaurant from the patio and bumped into him.

"Excuse me," she said, then looked up at him. "Maurice."

"Kenya."

"I was just . . . excuse me," she said, then dashed away.

He had wanted to grab her arm and stop her, but when he saw that she was headed to the restroom, he was glad that he hadn't.

"Sir," the waiter asked, "are you ready to order?"

"You know what? I think I want a table outside, next to that woman who just walked in."

The waiter raised an eyebrow, then led him to the empty table next to where Imani was sitting. When she took a look at the man who'd taken a seat at the table beside her, Imani waved for the check, even though she and Kenya weren't finished with dinner.

"Imani," Maurice said, "why are you tripping?"

"Because when Kenya comes back over here, you're the last person that she needs to see."

"It's good to see you, too, Imani," Maurice said sarcastically. "You look great."

Imani shook her head. "Haven't you done enough? You haven't changed at all, have you?"

"Is this your business? You have no idea what's going on," Maurice snapped.

"I know that you're an asshole. You hurt her in college, she forgave you and gave you another chance, and you blew it again. What's wrong with you? Don't you realize that Kenya is the best thing that ever happened in your sorry little life?" Imani's voice had risen with anger, causing a few patrons to turn around and look at them.

Maurice shook his head. "Still the same old Imani. Always sticking your nose where it doesn't belong."

Imani looked toward the door and saw Kenya heading their way. "Mo, why don't you just leave? We've already toasted you out of her life."

"Are you done?" Maurice asked when he saw Kenya approaching the table. "Because I'm pretty sure that Kenya doesn't need you to speak for her."

"What's going on over here?" Kenya asked as she took her seat.

"Are you ready to go?" Imani asked.

Kenya looked over at Maurice and knew that she should've left. But she couldn't leave. There was so much she wanted to say to him, so much she needed to get off her chest. She needed closure, because she knew that they'd run into each other from time to time. Smiling at Imani, she said, "I'll meet you at the car."

"Kenya," Imani said.

"Imani, I can handle this. Meet me at the car. I'll take care of the check."

Placing her hands on her hips, Imani shook her head at her friend, as if she was silently telling her that she was making a mistake. Kenya nodded as she sat down. Turning to Maurice, she asked, "Was all of that noise about me?"

"Your friend needs to mind her business," he said.

"Imani's just looking out for me, and I'm not going to be mad at her for it."

Maurice rolled his eyes as he turned around and faced Kenya. "And I'm the bad guy here? I'm the one who tried to seduce your sister to prove a point?"

"No, you just had sex on DVD for me and the world to see," she countered.

"How many times do I have to tell you that DVD was fake? Even James tried to tell you, or were you too busy sticking your tongue down his throat to hear him out?"

Kenya reached for her purse, pulled out enough money to cover dinner, then rose quickly to her feet. "Go to hell, Maurice."

Standing, he reached out and touched her arm, willing her to stay. "Wait. I don't want to argue with you," he said. "We run in the same circles, and we're going to run into each other. Does it have to turn into a fight every time we say hello?"

"I guess we have no choice since my firm represents your realty company," Kenya said begrudgingly.

"Good thing you assigned us another attorney," he said flippantly.

She jerked away from him. "Then that means my office is off-limits. If I have anything at your place, burn it. The only thing left between us is business." Kenya stomped off.

Imani was waiting at the car, with baited breath. She could imagine Kenya telling her that she and Maurice were going to give it another try. But when she saw the look on her friend's face, she knew that was not what she was about to hear.

"I don't know why I even talked to him. What was I thinking? I must like this. I must like letting him trample over my feelings," Kenya said, her voice peppered with anger.

"What happened?"

"We argued, as usual," she said. "Maurice and I should've just ignored each other in the Bahamas. Why can't I get that man out of my system?"

Imani shrugged her shoulders. "For whatever reason, you love him. But Maurice is selfish, and the only person he cares about is himself. Look at what he's done to you again. You've never done anything but love him, and he hurts you at every turn."

Looking at her friend, Kenya thought about what she'd done with James so that she could hurt Maurice. She wasn't innocent, and she couldn't pretend that she was. She'd made the choice to seek revenge, and the consequences were losing Maurice. But she'd never felt as if she had him, anyway. Kenya had been constantly looking over her shoulder for Lauryn. And the old adage had proved to be true: when you look for trouble, you find it.

"Let's get out of here. The House of Jazz is hosting Mike Phillips tonight. Do you want to go?" Kenya asked.

"Sure. But can we head to your place and change first? I'm going to show you guys how we get down in Atlanta. And I need to call my husband."

Kenya smiled weakly. Maurice was supposed to be her husband. They should've been making wedding plans instead of breaking up again. "How's Roland?"

Imani waved her hand and laughed. "He's Roland. He and my mother are teaming up against me to try and force me to have a baby. I want children, but I'm just not ready right now.

That's one of the reasons I came up here this weekend. I swear that man's sneaking Viagra behind my back."

Kenya laughed thinking that Roland was acting like a dog in heat, trying to hump Imani at every turn. "You might as well have a baby. You're not getting any younger."

"Now you sound like my mother." Imani's face grew serious, and Kenya knew where she was about to go. "Did you ever tell Maurice what happened in Atlanta?"

"Yeah."

"Did he jump up and down and thank God?" Imani rolled her eyes as she spoke. "I'm sure he was all too glad to know that he didn't have the respons—"

"Give it a rest, Imani. Maurice was very upset when I told him about the miscarriage, because he wants to be a father," said Kenya. *Why am I defending him?* she thought.

Imani eyed Kenya quizzically. "Really?"

"He's not as bad as you think."

"I know that Maurice has never seemed to care for you as much as you care for him. I'm surprised he even graduated after you left," Imani ranted. "You wrote his papers, helped him with his math and everything else. You should get a cut of that huge contract he signed."

Kenya slapped her thighs. "Just stop, Imani, please. This isn't all Maurice's fault. I did something that I shouldn't have done, and he has a right to be angry at me."

"What did you do?"

Kenya unlocked the doors to her car, looking Imani in the eye. "Well, when I found out about him and Lauryn and the DVD, I wanted him to hurt like I was hurting. So, I tried to seduce James."

"James? As in his brother? Oh my God, Kenya! Have you lost your mind?"

Rolling her eyes at Imani, Kenya opened the driver's

door. "I know that I was wrong. Nothing happened, really. James and I kissed, but he knew what I was doing."

"And Maurice? He knows, too?"

Kenya nodded solemnly. "He's never going to forgive me. I mean, Lauryn isn't my sister, they were engaged to be married, and Maurice swears that the DVD is a fake."

Chewing her bottom lip, Imani shook her head from side to side. "It could be, not that it would make a difference. You and Maurice aren't good for each other. If it's not Lauryn, I'm sure he has a staple of groupies that follow him to every NFL city."

"I know you don't like him, but when things are good between me and Maurice, they're good. I love him, and I wish I could stop."

"You two are like a soap opera couple, just a lot of drama. Is that how you want to live your life?" Imani asked as she got into the car. "I've seen the good and the bad times with you two. The bad times almost killed you."

But it isn't always drama. It's just that I keep waiting for something from the past to wreck our future, Kenya thought as she got into the car.

The weekend flew by. Kenya and Imani shopped, partied, and avoided talking about Maurice. As Sunday began to wind down, Kenya tried to prepare for the week ahead, but Maurice invaded her thoughts. Sitting on the sofa, she remembered times that they'd sat in that same spot, kissing, eating popcorn, and watching movies. She couldn't even walk into her bedroom without thinking about the times they'd made love in her bed. Earlier that day, while she'd been cleaning up, she'd found one of his T-shirts, with a faint smell of his cologne on it. As soon as she'd got a whiff of it, she'd wanted to call him and tell him that she was wrong, that she was sorry that she'd used James to get back at him, and that she desperately wanted to believe that he didn't want to be with Lauryn. She hadn't, though. And now the silence in her place was too loud, the memories of the two of them too strong. She finally admitted to herself that she had allowed her insecurities to wreck her relationship with Maurice.

Kenya knew that on the outside she seemed to have everything together, but she couldn't help but remember the cruel taunts that had haunted her from childhood, when she was a chubby little girl and stout teenager. Maurice had seen through that for a while, but as soon as cheerleader Lauryn had come along, and it was bye-bye, Kenya.

Once again, she decided against calling. If their relationship was over, then so be it. But hadn't she done everything to please him? Kenya had the overwhelming urge to watch the DVD, despite the fact that she was going to have to come face-to-face with seeing the man she loved making love to another woman. After walking over to the DVD player and pressing PLAY, she watched with bated breath as Lauryn's image filled the screen. Leaning in to get a closer look, Kenya began to see that Maurice might be right. The drapes in his bedroom were different from the ones on the DVD. As she looked at the man on top of Lauryn, she realized that it wasn't Maurice. The man had the same body shape as Maurice, but taking a closer look at his face, she saw he didn't look a thing like Maurice.

Kenya shut the DVD off and dropped her head in her hands. "What have I done?"

Chapter 23

Sunday morning workouts usually took some getting used to for Maurice, but not today. He ran circles around the other wide receivers in the battery of drills that the new receiver's coach had drawn up. Unlike most of the other players, he wasn't bothered at all by the first day of mini-camp, which was a tune-up for the month-long training camp in Spartanburg. They didn't normally start on Sundays, but Maurice was glad that he wasn't in his penthouse, with the blinds drawn, lying in bed and thinking of Kenya.

"Damn, Mo, you are acting like you're auditioning for your spot," Homer said as they took a water break. "You're Super Bowl MVP."

"The Super Bowl's over," Maurice said, panting as he spoke. "I'm just trying to make sure we repeat."

"Sure you're not trying to get over that chick?"

"Man, whatever," Maurice said as he poured water over his head to cool himself.

"That was something, her leaving you at the altar, and for Mya. I was wondering why she wasn't giving me the panties. I was using all my moves on her. Guess we both wanted the same thing. A woman."

"Lauryn's out of my life and my mind. That b . . . I should've never gotten involved with her to begin with."

"Y'all were together for a long time," Homer said.

"A waste of time. She was a gold digger and a liar. I was too blind to see what was really going on." Maurice grabbed another cup of water and drank it quickly. Then he turned to his friend. "What's the gossip about me been?"

Homer shrugged his shoulders. "I don't listen to these dudes. You know how they are."

Maurice looked over at a group of guys huddled at one end of the field who were looking at him and Homer, with grins on their faces. "I'll bet."

"There was the occasional *Brokeback Mountain* joke. Smitty said he'd watch that movie if it starred Lauryn and her friend. Tell me that they at least let you watch."

Crushing the paper cup in his hand, Maurice fought the urge to deck his friend. "Are you insane? Why would I want to see that crap? Lauryn was going to be my wife, and whether it was a man or a woman, she cheated on me."

"And you did your dirt, too," Homer said. "Remember the Miami Dolphins game and the two women in our hotel room three years ago?"

"So?"

"From the way you're acting, I know that you're fighting feelings for somebody," Homer said.

"It's not Lauryn," Maurice said, his voice low. "When I was in college, I had the right woman in my life, and I let Lauryn come between us. Kenya and I had been dating since we were in high school, and when we got to college, I became a star, and girls started throwing themselves at me. Up until the moment I met Lauryn, I was faithful, tempted but faithful. Kenya caught us together, and that was the end of us. She went back to Atlanta, and I started this relationship with Lauryn. All the while, Lauryn was screwing her roommate. She was spending my money on Mya like she was the man or something. I was such a fool."

"Whatever happened to Kenya?" Homer asked.

Maurice picked up another cup of water. This was the part of the story that he didn't want to get into. Kenya was just around the corner, and neither of them had sense enough to work out their problems and be happy together. He knew that he had to atone for the past, but how long was she going to punish him, and why couldn't she see through Lauryn's deception? *Did she even watch the DVD to see that it wasn't me?* he thought.

"Hello," Homer said, waving his hand in front of Maurice's face. "Are you having heat stroke?"

"Nah. Kenya's back in Charlotte. We were seeing each other these last few months. When I found out that I couldn't get my money back for the honeymoon deposit, James and I went to the Bahamas, and Kenya was there." Maurice smiled as he thought about the moment he saw her in that red bathing suit.

"Wow, and you talked her into moving back to Charlotte?"

Maurice shook his head. "She was coming back, anyway. Her law firm opened a new office here, and she's heading it up."

"Then why aren't you two together?" Homer asked.

"Long story, and I got laps to run," Maurice said, then jogged off.

"Yo, Homer," Smitty called out. "What's up with your boy? He's making us all look bad."

Homer flipped Smitty off and headed over to the offensive coordinator's huddle.

Kenya punched in the first three digits of Maurice's telephone number; then she hung up the phone. She'd already called him three times, only to get his voice mail. *I can't keep doing this to myself. If it's over, then it's over,* she thought. *I shouldn't try to change things. It's obvious that he doesn't want to talk to me.* Kenya tossed her cordless phone across the room and turned the television to ESPN.

"The Super Bowl champion Carolina Panthers opened up their minicamp today," the announcer said. "From the looks of things, these cats are looking to repeat."

The camera cut to Maurice running a route to catch a pass from quarterback Jake Delhomme. "Mo Goings, last year's Super Bowl MVP, looks to be in mid-season form. The Panthers are going to need stellar play from Delhomme and Goings if they're going to have a chance to repeat, because the Atlanta Falcons . . ."

Kenya shut off the television, happy to know that Maurice wasn't avoiding her. But with the start of football season around the corner, Kenya couldn't help but wonder if he was going to fall back on his old groupie-chasing ways. She picked up the phone and dialed his number again, silently praying that he would answer.

"Hello," he said.

"Maurice, it's me. Kenya," she said.

"I know. Caller ID. How are you?"

"I need to talk to you, see you, if possible," she said.

"I'm kind of tired, and I don't want to argue with you today."

"I'm not looking for an argument. As a matter of fact, I want to apologize to you. I've been a fool, and I should've believed you when you said that Lauryn was making trouble for us. It doesn't make sense, but I'm still intimidated by your feelings for her. When you chose her over me, I never got over it, and I keep thinking that you're going to wake up one day and realize that I'm not the woman you want."

"Kenya," he said, his voice low and husky. "I made a mistake when I let my crotch think for me. I've learned from that, and you're the only woman that I've ever loved with my entire heart and soul. But you don't trust me, and I don't want you to feel like you have to keep looking over your shoulder, thinking that I'm going to leave you for Lauryn or anyone else."

"Maybe it's best that we just be friends," she said but didn't mean it.

"I don't want to be just your friend, Kenya. I want it all, your love and trust. Can you give me that?"

"Yes," she said timidly.

"Do you mean it, Kenya? Because I'm not trying to lose you again. But I won't deal with accusations at every turn. We're probably going to run into Lauryn again, and you're just going to have to know that you're the woman I love, need, and want."

"I can do that," she said, "because I do love you."

"Well, if you really love me, open the door."

"What?"

"Open your door," he repeated.

She dashed to the door, not caring that she was wearing a pair of grey sweatpants and a midriff-baring tank top, with her hair pulled back in a crude ponytail. When Kenya opened the door and saw Maurice standing on the other side of the threshold, she flung herself into his arms, dropping her cordless phone to the floor.

Hungrily, Maurice captured Kenya's lips, kissing her as if he'd been away at war. They stumbled inside, and Maurice shut the door with his foot. She savored the taste of his tongue as they fell backward over an arm of the sofa. With Maurice on top of her, she felt every throbbing muscle pressing against her. Unable to contain her wanton desire for him, she tugged at the waistband of his shorts until Maurice caught on and removed them in one quick motion.

His erection nearly spilled from his boxer shorts, and Kenya reached between his legs and stroked his manhood, making him moan in delight.

"You have on too many clothes," he said, his lips against her ear. He slipped a hand inside her sweatpants, then used his finger to push aside the satin material of her panties. She was hot and wet, and Maurice couldn't wait to taste her essence on his tongue. When he pressed his finger inside her, Kenya groaned and arched her body against his. Her breasts swelled against his chest as he used his finger to brand her from the inside. Maurice pulled back from Kenya, then scooped her up in his arms. "I'm going need more space than this sofa," he said as he headed for the bedroom.

So many thoughts ran through Kenya's mind as she wrapped her arms around his neck. Would their relationship last this time? Could she really put all her trust in Maurice and not get hurt again? What about James? How would their relationship change? Would he welcome Kenya into the family, knowing what she'd tried to do? Did Maurice still want to marry her?

He looked down at her, noting her silence, and asked, "Are you all right?"

"I'm fine," she replied, pushing her negative thoughts aside.

Laying her on the bed, Maurice eased in beside her. "If you have something you want to say, go ahead and say it." Gently, he stroked her cheek.

She reached up, took his hand in hers, and brought it to her lips, kissing it gently. "I want you," she said.

It didn't take long or much effort for Maurice to ease Kenya's clothes off and toss them aside. "I can't wait until we can do this every night," he said, then took one of her breasts in his mouth, darting his tongue across her nipple until it harden like a brown diamond. Kenya grasped the sheets as he alternated from her right to her left breast. Her body was on fire, and she could feel her desire building between her legs and spilling onto her thighs. Maurice felt it, too, as he slipped his hand between her thighs and traveled into her moist valley.

With her eyes closed, Kenya let passion take her nearly to the brink under Maurice's touch, and when he replaced his finger with his tongue, she nearly climaxed. "Oh yes, Mo," she moaned. "You feel so good."

He lifted her hips, pulled her deeper into his kiss. Kenya grabbed the back of his neck as her legs began to twitch. He moved his kiss up to her stomach, back to her breasts, and finally rested on her lips. Positioning himself between her legs, their sex organs touched, and she shivered, anticipating the moment when he'd enter her. Neither of them thought about protection as they became one. They had a slow and steady rhythm that gave Kenya multiple orgasms. Each touch, caress, and kiss he delivered made her hormones rage like an inferno in the desert.

Maurice wrapped his arms around Kenya's waist as he rolled over so that she could be on top of him. "Look at me, baby," he said. "Look at me, and tell me you love me."

Opening her eyes, she stared down at the man she loved while gyrating her hips against his pelvis. "I love you, Maurice. I love you," she repeated, like it was a mantra.

"I don't want nobody else but you, Kenya. You're all I'll ever need," he moaned.

His words were nearly enough to bring her to a climax, and when he gripped her hips and pulled her back and forth, she couldn't hold back. Neither could he, and they reached the crescendo of their lovemaking together. Kenya collapsed on his chest, and Maurice kissed her forehead as he wrapped his arms around her tightly.

"You know, I got a house full of boxes, living-room

furniture that's not set up, and a big bed, which I've been sleeping in alone," he said, referring to their shopping trip.

Lifting herself up on one elbow, she smirked. "You could have sent it back."

"And have to go shopping all over again? Nah, that's all right. You can come over and fix it," he said.

"Are we jumping back into things too fast?" she asked.

Maurice frowned. "We wasted nine years and the last few months fighting, breaking up, getting back together, and fighting some more, and I'm sick of it. If I wasn't a fool in college, we'd be married and probably working on Maurice Lamont Goings III. So, no, we're not moving too fast, and I'm not going to let you talk yourself out of our life together."

Smiling, she leaned in and kissed him softly on the lips. "You're right. But there is no way I'm having three Maurices running around my house."

"All right, then," he said, tugging at her hair. "I guess I can ask the man upstairs for a daughter or two."

"You're serious about having kids, huh?" she said. Kenya couldn't help but think about her miscarriage. Immediately, she wondered what her relationship with Maurice would have been like if she'd had that child.

"You can have more children, can't you?" he asked. "Do you want children?"

"Yes, I do, and I'm medically clear to have children. I don't think that when we were in college, either of us was ready to be parents, and God knew that, too."

"Wouldn't it be something if we made our son or *daughter* tonight? That means we have to get married right away so when people start counting the months, it'll add up."

Kenya's face lit up and a smile touched her lips as Maurice reached for the engagement ring on her nightstand. "Let's put this back where it belongs," he said as he reached for her left hand. "And it's not coming off again."

"No, it isn't."

Maurice kissed her finger, then took it in his mouth, sucking it seductively. It didn't take long for the duo to start making love again.

The next morning, Maurice was up at dawn, watching Kenya as she slept. Her face looked angelic, and her body looked heavenly. He wanted to make love to her until sunset, but he had to get across town and make it to mini-camp, and he knew Kenya had to go into the office. Still, he didn't wake her; he simply stroked her arm with his index finger. This felt so right, though he knew her friends and family were going to question her decision to give him another chance and to accept his proposal. It didn't matter, because he was never going to do anything to hurt her again, and he wasn't going to let Lauryn interfere anymore. Maurice decided that after today's training session, he was going to get a restraining order against Lauryn.

He leaned down and kissed Kenya's full lips. "Wake up, babe," he said.

She tossed her head away from his. "Too early."

"No it's not. Wake up, sleeping beauty." Maurice slipped his hand underneath the sheet and stroked her bare bottom.

Moaning and rolling over to face him, she opened her eyes. "You should've done that to begin with."

"And as much as I want to spend all day in bed with you, you have to go to work, and I have to go to work," he said, then slipped out of the bed, pulling all the covers off Kenya.

She sat up in the bed, glaring at Maurice. "You don't play fair," she said as she begrudgingly rose from the bed and headed into the bathroom.

"How about I buy you breakfast to make up for it?" he asked as he heard the shower start.

"That's a start, but you know I'm not a morning person, so consider yourself in my debt," she called out.

Chapter 24

Maurice drove Kenya to her office after they finished breakfast at the Coffee Cup restaurant, which was across the street from Bank of America Stadium. Hopefully, today wouldn't be a long one, and he could plan a special evening for Kenya, with roses, candlelight, and lovemaking. He was going to need his strength. As he approached the gate to the practice field, Homer met him.

"What happened to you last night? Smitty had a slamming party. He's going to take your party king crown if you don't watch it," Homer said, closing his hand on Maurice's shoulder.

"I had my own party last night, and I have a wedding to get ready for," Maurice said, with a wide smile.

Homer stepped back from Maurice and looked at him as if he were speaking in a foreign tongue. "Wedding? You took the les—"

"Kenya, the woman that I should've married years ago," Maurice said. "Last night we kissed and made up and kissed some more. We decided that we'd wasted enough time and we need each other."

"So, this is the honey from the islands?"

"Yeah, and the only woman I've ever truly loved." Maurice couldn't have stopped smiling if he'd wanted to.

Homer slapped Maurice on the back as they headed into the facility. "I hope this one works out for you, bro."

"Oh, it will, because this is true love," Maurice said.

Kenya sat at her desk, noticing for the first time that she could see the Panthers practicing from her window. Her lips spread into a smile as she thought about Maurice on the field. Her fiancé. Now, how was she going to tell her mother and Imani that she and Maurice were back together?

"This is my life, and he's the man that I love. They're going to have to accept it," she said aloud.

"Miss Taylor, did you say something?" Talisha asked from the doorway.

"Thinking aloud. Is everything all right?"

"Mr. James Goings is here to see you."

Inwardly, Kenya shuddered. She wasn't sure what she was supposed to say to James, and she really wasn't ready to see him right now. But she had no choice.

"Send him in, and can you get us some coffee?" Kenya said.

Her assistant nodded and showed James in. Kenya smiled weakly at her future brother-in-law.

"Good morning," she said.

"Morning," he said, then closed the door. "We need to clear the air."

Placing her hands flat on the desk, she sighed. "I know, and I've been wanting to call and say something. I just didn't know what."

"I was struggling with that as well," he said. "But somebody has to say something. With that said, you and Maurice belong together, and I hope that you don't think kissing me makes him love you any less."

She dropped her head to hide her smile. "I know," she said. "Maurice and I got back together last night." Lifting her head, she looked James in the eye. "But I'm concerned about us. I don't want there to be any tension between us. You've always been a good friend to me, and I don't want my stupidity to change that."

"I've always wondered what you see in Maurice. He can be selfish. He can be arrogant and inconsiderate," James said. "But he's my brother, and I love him. That's why I tried to always look at you as Maurice's girlfriend, especially when you came back to Atlanta all those years ago. I was glad that you even spoke to me after what he did. I know Maurice loves you, and for some reason, you two belong together. You make him responsible. Maurice doesn't want to do anything to hurt you, and God help the next person that tries to come between you two."

Kenya rose from her seat, walked over to James, and gave him a sisterly hug. "Thanks for being understanding and not holding what I did against me."

"You didn't do it alone. I'm just glad we didn't go any further," James said when they released each other. "I've got to go. The city sent the contracts, and I have to get moving on our project before Mo heads to training camp and football becomes his life."

As he left, Kenya prayed that when she talked to her family and friends, things would go as smoothly.

Biting the bullet, she picked up the phone and called her mother.

"This is Angela Johnson-Taylor. I can't take your call at this time. Please leave a detailed message, or to reach the newsroom, press zero," her voice mail played back.

For a split second, Kenya thought about leaving a message

on her mother's voice mail, telling her that she and Maurice were getting married, but she knew that wasn't the right thing to do. As a matter of fact, she needed to face her parents head-on, with Maurice by her side. *We need to take a trip to Atlanta,* she thought as she hung up the phone.

"Talisha," Kenya said over the intercom, "will you bring me my calendar for the week?"

"Yes, ma'am," Talisha said.

Talisha walked into Kenya's office, with her appointment book and a bouquet of red and white roses. "These just came for you." She set the roses and the book in the middle of Kenya's desk.

"Thank you," Kenya said as she plucked the card from the flowers, though there was no doubt that Maurice had sent them.

> *Your love is like a song that I can't stop singing and a poem that I can't stop reciting. Thank you for coming back into my life and giving us another try.*
> *—Love Maurice.*

Kenya held the card to her chest. If other people didn't accept her love for Maurice, then it would be their problem. She refused to allow outside forces to tear them apart again.

"Good news, gentlemen," head coach Stephen Ford said to his team as they huddled. "I like what I've seen these last two days. I'm confident that none of you have the proverbial Super Bowl hangover. Training camp starts in three weeks. If we have any hopes of winning it all again, then we're going to have to give it our all in camp. No personal distractions, no front-office talk on the field. I just want hard work. I don't know about y'all, but I want to be on top of the mountain again. We got the talent. I just need the commitment."

The team cheered, and everyone was pumped up, as if the big game were tomorrow.

"With that said, consider minicamp over," said the coach.

Maurice was happy to hear those words leave the coach's lips. Homer leaned over and whispered, "God must have heard my prayers, because they were killing us out here."

"I know," Maurice said.

Once the coach told everyone to head to the locker room, Maurice darted off the field and was the first one inside.

"Yo, Mo," Smitty called out. "Sorry to hear about your wedding. I guess if I had gotten left for another woman, I would've gone into hiding, too."

Maurice turned around and looked at the former star wide receiver and smirked. "Damn, you still play here?"

Growling, Smitty jumped in his face. "You think you're hot shit or something? You might be the man on the field, but you're obviously not in the bedroom, or that hottie would be your wife."

Folding his arms across his chest, Maurice leaned on his locker. "That's all you got, Smit? Let's see. I took your job. Rumor has it that you might be going to Arizona so we can get a real receiver, and all you can do is throw old news in my face?"

Thinking that things were going to get ugly, Homer stepped between the two men. "Hey, we're all teammates, and minicamp has been cut short. Chill out."

Smitty walked away, glaring at Maurice. When he was out of earshot, Homer said, "I'm surprised you didn't take a swing at him."

"I don't have time for that. I have a life. Smitty doesn't," Maurice said as he grabbed his towel and headed for the shower. He looked over his shoulder to make sure Smitty wasn't behind him, ready to sucker punch him, the way he'd done to a rookie defensive back three years ago, after he'd questioned his heart on the field. Smitty's reputation of being a hothead was legendary in the league. But Coach Ford had a policy on fighting. He would bench anybody, star or not, for fighting, and Maurice hadn't ridden a bench since his days in Dallas.

He made it through the shower without another confrontation with Smitty. Then he was free to go take care of his business with Lauryn and plan a night for Kenya. As he drove to the courthouse to get the restraining order against Lauryn, he thought about waking up with Kenya and how they'd wasted too much time looking over their shoulders for Lauryn. This restraining order was going to keep her away, but was it going to be enough to prove to Kenya that he didn't want Lauryn anymore? *She knows that. That's why we reconciled last night. This order is about our sanity and keeping Lauryn from pulling any more of her tricks,* he thought as he headed into the building.

Lauryn stood outside of Maurice's building and glared at the doorman. "What do you mean you can't let me in? I have business with Mr. Goings. We were going to get married."

"I have my orders," the doorman said, not allowing her to enter.

"How much do I have to pay you to let me in?"

"You don't have enough money to cost me my job," the doorman said. "Now leave, or I'll be forced to call the police."

Lauryn folded her arms across her ample chest. "I'm standing on a public sidewalk. What are they going to do? Arrest me for standing?"

Someone tapped her on her shoulder, and she turned

around and looked at Mya's face. "So, you're stalking me now?" she demanded.

"No, but you can't play with people's lives," Mya said, then threw an unlableled DVD in Lauryn's face. "Maurice knows what you did because I told him. You chose me, but since we've been together, all you've done is try to worm your way back into his life. If you didn't want me, you should've told me instead of pretending to love me."

"This is neither the time nor the place," Lauryn said.

Mya grabbed her arm. "Oh, it is, because you're not welcome in my house anymore. Your things will be packed and on the doorstep. If you get them, fine. If not, oh well!" Then Mya slapped Lauryn as hard as she could. "I hate you, and I wish to God that I'd never fallen in love with you."

Neither of them noticed Maurice walking up the sidewalk. "Lauryn, I'm glad you're here," Maurice said sarcastically when he reached them.

Lauryn smiled brightly. "Really?"

He looked from Lauryn to Mya, then reached into his gym bag. "Here you go," he said as he handed Lauryn the restraining order. "According to this paper, you're in violation of this restraining order."

Mya began laughing hysterically. "How does it feel, Lauryn? After all of your scheming, you're alone. I don't want you, and neither does Maurice."

Maurice turned to the doorman. "If she's not gone in five seconds, call the police."

"I bet when Kenya sees that DVD, you're going to be alone, too," Lauryn snapped.

"Kenya's seen it, Lauryn, and guess what? We're still getting married. See, I let you use your body to keep me away from the woman I loved all of those years ago, but what Kenya and I have is real. You can't come between us again.

I was stupid before, but I've learned my lesson." Maurice walked into the building, leaving Lauryn standing in the middle of the sidewalk, with a bewildered look on her face. Mya had already gotten into her car and driven off.

As Kenya headed down to the parking lot, she remembered that Maurice had driven her to work. Reaching into her purse, she pulled out her cell phone and called him.

"Hey, babe," he said when he answered.

"I was wondering if you were going to pick me up, or do I have to walk home?" Kenya asked.

"You think I'd leave you stranded like that? I'm right out front, and I have a surprise for you," he said.

"I have a surprise for you, too," she said as she started for the entrance of the building. When she arrived there, she found Maurice sitting on the hood of a cherry red 2008 Mustang convertible, with a vanity plate that said HERS.

"What is this?" she asked excitedly.

"Just what it says. Yours," he said as he extended the keys to her.

"This is too much," Kenya said as she took the keys from him. "I can't believe you did this. When did you have time to do all of this?"

"I did this after I saw you admiring my car, and I told myself, 'When we get married, she's going to need a pony of her own,'" he said.

Kenya wrapped her arms around his neck and kissed him on his earlobe. "Thank you so much," she said.

"This is just the beginning," he said. "Let's go."

Kenya slipped in the driver's seat and gripped the steering wheel, smiling because she was just as much of a Mustang freak as Maurice, though she had never had the nerve to buy one herself. She turned to him and asked, "When is minicamp over?"

"Ended today," he replied. "Coach said we were all giving maximum effort, and since training camp is coming up soon, he gave us time off."

"Good," she said as she pressed the gas pedal to the floor, "because we're going to Atlanta."

Maurice shot his eyebrows up. "Atlanta? When?"

"Tomorrow, I guess. I can't just call my family and tell them that you and I are getting married, and you need to face them with me."

He gripped the seat as she took a sharp turn a little faster than she should've. "Do you think that's a good idea?"

"Well, I've already made the plans. We're going to meet at Houston's so that my father can't get his hand on his gun, and we're going to tell them. Why don't you invite your mother?"

Maurice shook his head. "I don't think so. I'm not sure that I want her to hear what your people are going to say about me. Turn left up here," he said.

"Where are we going?" Kenya asked.

"You'll see when we get there." He laughed, then said, "Make a right."

Kenya followed his directions, and they ended up at Fourth Ward Park. "What are we doing here?" she asked as she pulled into a parking spot near the fountain.

"You'll see," he said as he hopped out of the car. Maurice led Kenya to the picnic area, where there was a gourmet meal waiting for them. "You like?"

Kenya surveyed the scene: the red roses in the center of the table, two tapered candles burning at the end of the table, and expensive champagne chilling in a bucket of ice. Dinner consisted of slow-roasted salmon over wild rice, a green salad, and chocolate mint mousse for dessert.

"I love it," she said.

Maurice motioned for her to sit down. "So, tell me about this Atlanta trip?"

She placed her napkin in her lap and looked up at him. "I think we've had enough conflict to last a lifetime, so I want to make it clear to everyone that you're the man I love and the man I'm going to marry. It would be nice if they stood beside me on this," she said.

"I feel you on that," he said. "But what if they don't?"

Kenya shrugged her shoulders. "Can we cross that bridge when we get to it?"

"And let's not think about that tonight," he said as he leaned over the table, with a forkful of salmon.

After dinner, Maurice and Kenya took a moonlit stroll around the park. She looked over at him, smiling and silently hoping that when her family looked at him they'd see how much he loved her.

Chapter 25

Kenya and Maurice didn't make it to Atlanta until two days after their romantic dinner in the park. Though they were supposed to leave the previous day, they took advantage of not having to go to work and spent the day in bed, making love.

Driving to Atlanta in her Mustang, with the top down and the man she loved by her side, should've been fun for Kenya, but the closer they got to the Georgia state line the more nervous she became.

"You're quiet," Maurice said. "Is everything all right?"

"I'm fine," she lied. "I just want everything to go well." Tightening her grip on the steering wheel, she had a flash of her mother chasing Maurice out of the house, wielding a meat cleaver as she ran after him.

Maurice placed his hand on her knee and smiled. "It will. Think positive."

Kenya shot him a sidelong glance before looking ahead at the road. "My father hates you. You do know that, don't you? And my mother doesn't like you, either."

"Mr. Taylor is going to be fine," Maurice said confidently.

Kenya and her father, Henry, didn't have an extremely

close father and daughter relationship. But when it came to keeping his little girl safe, Henry would do anything to protect her. Angela and Henry had made it clear that they thought Maurice was toxic, and that they wanted nothing more than to banish him from Kenya's life permanently.

"Yeah," she said, though she didn't believe it. Instead of feeling like a confident adult, she felt as if she were a teenager bringing home the neighborhood bad boy for dinner.

"What happens if your family doesn't stand by us?"

"Nothing changes. We're still going to be together," she said. "I love you, and no one is going to change how I feel. I couldn't even change that, and I tried hard."

"I can't blame you," he said. "I didn't give you a reason to love me. I can't blame your family for thinking that we're a mistake."

"But we're not," she said.

"No, we're not. I've made all of my mistakes, and they're called Lauryn Michaels."

"Please, don't bring her up," Kenya said, wrinkling her nose. "I'm surprised she hasn't reared her ugly head lately."

"She doesn't want to go to jail," Maurice said.

"What do you mean?"

"I took out a restraining order against her, because I don't want her anywhere near us."

"When did you do that?" Kenya asked.

"A few days ago. Lauryn wants to cause problems for us because she thinks that somehow she can creep back into my pocket. Her girlfriend even dumped her."

"How do you know that?"

"They were outside of my building the other day, when I went home after practice," Maurice said. "If Lauryn shows up again, she's going directly to jail without passing Go."

"This isn't a game," Kenya said. "A piece of paper probably isn't going to keep her from causing trouble."

"She can only cause trouble if we let her," Maurice said. "I don't plan to allow that."

Kenya sighed and didn't answer. Why was she still letting Lauryn's ghost affect her? *Maurice is with me and not her. So, I'm going to have to stop letting her name bother me,* she thought.

By the time they made it to Atlanta, Kenya wasn't thinking about Lauryn; she was worried about facing her parents. "Before we head to my parents' house, can we stop for a drink?" she asked.

"No. You're driving, and alcohol isn't the answer," he joked.

"Whatever," she said as she pulled into the parking lot of Justin's, a restaurant and bar on Peachtree Street. "I know my parents."

Getting out of the car, Maurice couldn't help smiling. "You act as if we're teenagers," he said. "You're a grown woman, and what can they do? You're not a trust-fund baby who's going to have all of her money taken away. I think you're overreacting."

"Maybe you're right. We'll see, won't we?" She sprinted to the entrance of the restaurant.

Maurice and Kenya took a seat at the bar once they made it inside. "How about we just have some coffee," he whispered before the bartender walked over to them. "If you go to your parents' smelling like liquor, just imagine how that's going to make me look?"

She waved for the bartender and turned to Maurice. "You got jokes," Kenya said before ordering a gin and tonic. "I'm just worried, Mo. And I know the only thing this drink is doing is putting off the inevitable."

"Then let's go." Maurice slammed a twenty on the bar.

"There's no need to fear anything. If we could find each other after all of these years, anything is possible."

Though Maurice was saying all the right things to calm Kenya down, he was just as nervous as she was, if not more. He knew that if he were Kenya's father, he wouldn't want to see Maurice in his house, on his daughter's arm.

When she pulled into her parents' driveway, he didn't think about the times they'd played hide-and-seek in the backyard; nor did he think about the first time they'd made love in the toolshed. The only thing that flashed through his mind now was getting punched in the face by Henry Taylor or getting told off by sharp-tongued Angela Taylor. The punch was looking more and more inviting by the minute.

"Ready?" Kenya asked as she turned off the ignition.

"I should be asking you." Maurice stepped out of the car, smoothing his khaki shorts and green golf shirt.

Kenya knocked on the door, then reached out for Maurice's hand.

"Kenya, what's he doing here?" Angela said when she opened the door.

"Ma, before you say anything, can we come inside?" Kenya said.

Angela stood aside, allowing Maurice and Kenya to enter. "Where's Daddy?" Kenya asked.

"In Covington, with Jimmy. They went fishing. I told him you wanted to have dinner at Houston's, but that man said we're having a fish fry."

"He's catching dinner?" asked Kenya.

Angela shook her head. "He's going to say that he did. But, anyway, enough of the small talk. What the hell is Maurice doing here, and what did you mean by a big announcement? And it had better not be what I think it is."

"It's nice to see you, too, Mrs. Taylor," Maurice said.

Angela rolled her eyes at him. "Uh-huh. Kenya. Kitchen. Now."

Kenya smiled at Maurice as her mother nearly dragged her by the arm into the kitchen. Maurice was too afraid to sit down but felt like a fool standing in the middle of the living room, like a brother who was about to be carted off to jail. Just as he was about to sit down, the front door opened.

"Angie! We came across a mess of . . . What in the hell are you doing here?" Henry said, his voice booming like thunder.

Kenya ran into the living room. "Daddy," she said as she wrapped her arms around his neck.

Henry hugged his daughter loosely. "Kenya, I'm glad you're home, but why is he here?"

Maurice looked from Kenya to Henry as Kenya walked over to him and grabbed his hand.

"Dad, Mom," Kenya said as Angela walked into the living room. "Maurice and I are getting married."

"What?" the Taylors said collectively. Henry stormed onto the front porch, muttering profanities that made Maurice blush.

Despite his misgivings, Maurice followed Henry onto the porch. "Mr. Taylor?"

"Boy, I don't want to talk to you," Henry said angrily. "Haven't you done enough to hurt my daughter? Now you come here and claim you want to marry her? I've seen Kenya cry over you too many nights, and I won't watch it happen again."

Maurice folded his hands underneath his chin. "There's nothing I can say to change the past."

"You're damned right!" Henry grabbed Maurice by his collar and pushed him against the door. "The best thing for you to do is to walk away. You'll never be welcomed into this family." Henry dropped his hands and stepped back from Maurice.

"What about what Kenya wants? I love her, and I know I've made mistakes, but she's forgiven me," Maurice said, rubbing his neck.

"Then my child's a fool," Henry said before rushing into the house.

Maurice shook his head, thinking, *That went well.*

Kenya rushed to her father when he walked in the door. "Daddy."

"What are you thinking, Kenya? Just what the hell are you thinking?" Henry asked.

Angela nodded in agreement.

"I love him, and we're getting married," Kenya said.

"Why?" Angela asked. "You know that Maurice is an arrogant, selfish bastard. What about that DVD of him and that woman?"

"It was a fake," Kenya said.

"DVD?" Henry questioned.

"Wait, wait," Kenya said, waving her hands. "Neither of you have to live with Maurice. I just wanted some peace, and I wanted us to sit down and be able to talk like adults."

Henry walked out of the living room, grumbling about the mistake that Kenya was making and how she was on her own. Angela turned to her daughter.

"Is this about money?" she asked.

"What?" Kenya slapped her hand against her forehead in frustration. "Mother, you know I don't need Mo's money. This is about me loving him and wanting him. I never got over him, and who am I to turn down a second chance with him?"

"He should be thanking God for you, and not the other

way around," Angela said. "I don't like this, but you're an adult. Just don't expect me to support this union."

"Then I guess there's nothing left to say," Kenya said as she grabbed her car keys from the coffee table.

"Wait. I don't want you to leave here angry. If something happened to you, I wouldn't forgive myself," said Angela. "Henry!"

Kenya's father walked into the living room. "What?"

"They came too far for us to let them leave without feeding them. So, get the fish ready," Angela said. "Tell *him* that he doesn't have to stay on the porch."

Kenya walked outside and looked at Maurice. "Are you okay?" she said, then sat on the step, beside him.

"I'm sorry," said Maurice.

"What are you apologizing for?"

"Everything that I've caused, this domino effect that I've had on your life," he said. "I didn't know that my actions had had such an adverse effect on your—"

Kenya placed her finger to his lips. "It's going to take some time to win them over, but we got the rest of our lives to do that."

"Sounds like a Vegas wedding to me."

Kenya kissed him on his nose. "Nope, because you're going to go in there and win them over. I don't know how, but you're going to."

Maurice sighed. "All right. I mean, I understand where they're coming from. If you were my daughter, I wouldn't want some jerk coming back into your life, either."

"You're no jerk."

Maurice turned around and saw Henry frowning at him. "Yeah, if you say so," he said as he and Kenya rose to their feet.

Kenya walked in ahead of Maurice; then Henry blocked

Maurice's entrance. "I heard what you said out here talking to Kenya," he said. "You mean that?"

"Yes, sir, I do. I love Kenya, and I've always loved her."

"Humph. You had a hell of a way of showing it. Imagine listening to your daughter crying her eyes out when she thinks no one's around. There's nothing a father can do to heal a broken heart. If it happens again, you're going to have a short career, because I just might kill you. And I ain't going to a tawdry Las Vegas chapel to watch my only child get married."

Maurice held his hand out to Henry. "Sir, I wouldn't dream of it. Kenya can have the wedding that she wants."

Henry shook his hand. "And you're paying for it. Come on in so we can clean and cook this fish."

One down and one to go, Maurice thought as he followed Henry inside.

Kenya and Angela sat on the back porch, silently sipping iced tea. Kenya turned to her mother. "Will you say what's on your mind?" She leaned back in her chair and set her glass on the wrought-iron table, ready to hear everything that her mother had to say.

"I think you're making a huge mistake with this boy. Sure, he's charming and attractive, but he's not loyal. You know that."

"All in the past, Ma. If I can forgive Maurice, why can't you?"

Angela reached out and took her daughter's hand in hers. "Because he hurt you, and don't think that I don't know what happened in college."

"Because I told you," Kenya said. "He cheated on me. I was—"

"At Clark Atlanta. The baby."

Kenya fell silent, chewing her bottom lip and fighting back the tears. Angela patted Kenya's hand and continued talking.

"I waited for you to tell me. Then I thought about some of the things I'd said before you went off to college. I didn't make it easy for you to talk me. I had such high hopes for you, and I thought being tough on you was the way to make sure you achieved your goals. When you were going through so much, I was powerless to help you, and he was off the hook in Charlotte, living it up. I watched you cover up your heartache with schoolwork and then your career, and there he was on *SportsCenter,* celebrating in the end zone and the Super Bowl. I hated him. Hated what he did to you and hated the fact that you never got over him."

"How did you know all of this stuff?" Kenya asked.

"Because I'm no fool, and not much goes on at Clark Atlanta that I don't know about. Besides, you're my daughter, and you were on my insurance at the time," Angela said. "I didn't know how to comfort you."

Kenya stared off into the lush woods in front of her. She wished that she'd shared her pain with her mother, but she'd been afraid. "I wanted to tell you. I just didn't want to disappoint you."

"You wouldn't have disappointed me. You couldn't have," Angela said, then wrapped her arms around Kenya. With tears in her eyes, Angela held Kenya and rocked back and forth. "I've always been proud of you. I always knew that you were destined for great things, and look at you. I don't want to see you go through that ever again. This marriage may be opening you up to more pain and heartache. You know how these athletes live. Michael Vick got sued for giving a woman herpes, Rae Carruth was convicted in connection with the death of his son's mother, and do I need to mention O. J. Simpson?"

"But Maurice isn't like that. We've talked about this. I know he has a past, but that's just what it is."

Angela dropped her hands to her sides. "And how long will it be before he falls back on his bad habits? The groupies and parties, and you'll be left alone, maybe with a family to raise."

Angela's words fed into Kenya's quiet insecurities, watering the seeds of doubt that she'd unsuccessfully tried to bury. "I believe Maurice when he says that I'm the only woman he wants. He didn't have to . . . Mom, you married your first love. Why don't you want the same for me?" she said.

"If he wasn't Maurice Goings, the man who hurt you as deeply as he did in the past, then I wouldn't have a problem with it."

"He's changed."

"Can you be sure of that?"

Kenya chewed on her bottom lip before she said, "Yes, I'm sure. All I want is your love and support."

Before Angela could answer, there was a crash in the kitchen, which drew the women inside. Fish were scattered across the floor, and Maurice was laughing with Henry.

"Boy, you ain't that far removed from the country. The fish is out of water. It's dead," Henry said through his laughter.

"I've never handled fish that wasn't completely dead," Maurice said.

Angela placed her hands on her slender hips as she surveyed the scene. "What's going on in here?"

"Cleaning fish," Henry said matter-of-factly. "You two were outside yapping, so we had to do something to get dinner started if we wanted to eat tonight."

Angela looked from Henry to Maurice as if they were two imposters. "You're in here with all of these knives, and there's no blood?"

"Ma," Kenya said, shooting her mother a cautionary look.

"Well," Angela said as she walked over to the refrigerator and pulled out a bag of cornmeal, "I guess I'd better help, or I'm going to have fish guts all over the place."

Kenya smiled as she watched her family cutting and gutting fish together. *This can work,* she thought. *She'll come around.*

Chapter 26

To say that there was tension at the Taylor dinner table would be the understatement of the year. Kenya's eyes darted from her mother to Maurice every time a knife clanked against a plate. Each time she wondered if Angela was going to throw a utensil at him. Though Henry seemed a bit more accepting of having Maurice sit next to his daughter, he was uncharacteristically quiet: he did not even tell stories about fishing at the creek in Covington.

"Well, this fish is good, Daddy," Kenya said, breaking the uncomfortable silence.

Angela nodded. "Yeah. Doesn't taste like freshwater fish at all."

Henry rolled his eyes at his wife as he dove into his meal. "It's the Old Bay seasoning that makes the difference."

Kenya sighed. When were these people going to speak their minds? If everything was out in the open, then they could move on, and she and Maurice could go about planning their lives. Maurice reached under the table and rested his hand against her thigh.

Angela noticed his movement and dropped her fork. "Okay, I can't take this. Maurice, I don't want you to marry my daughter, I don't want you touching my daughter, and I don't want you in my family."

"Mrs. Taylor—"

"Boy, shut up! Shut up! You have inflicted more pain on my daughter than I care to think about, and she's just going to let you waltz back into her life and give you a chance to do it again. You've always been selfish, from the time you and James were little boys. Just because you can play football doesn't mean that you have the right to treat people like dirt. That's how you treated my baby, and I don't know why or how Kenya can forgive you. I know I can't." Angela pushed back from the table, sending her chair crashing to the floor. "Kenya, you're an adult, and you can do what you want to do. I just wish you wouldn't do this."

Angela stormed out of the kitchen. Henry excused himself from the table and followed his wife down the hall.

"Okay. Your mother hates me," Maurice said. "That's real good."

"She knows," Kenya said. "About the baby and all."

He dropped his head. "You told her?" he said.

"No. I was on her insurance, and she's known for years. She thought that I would come to her and talk about it. I just never thought that I could," Kenya said. "She's going to have a hard time getting past that."

Maurice stood and glanced sidelong down the hallway. "You think I should go talk to her?"

Kenya shook her head furiously. "She's not going to listen to you," she said.

"I can't just stand here and do nothing," Maurice said, then took off down the hall.

As he walked away, Kenya prayed that her mother didn't have access to any sharp objects.

* * *

Maurice stood in the doorway of Angela and Henry's bedroom, not meaning to eavesdrop but unable to say a word.

"Kenya's an adult, Angie. She's capable of making her own choices. She's not a little girl anymore," Henry said.

"So what? She'll always be my little girl, and if I see her walk into a fire, I'm going to try and stop her. How can you just give him a free pass, knowing that . . . I just don't believe it. I know you men stick together on things, but this is your daughter."

"Maurice is a genuine good guy who made a mistake. You didn't hear him talking to her. I think he loves her, and he knows if he hurts her again that I'll kill him," Henry said.

"I want to kill him now," Angela said as she made eye contact with Maurice. "What do you want?"

"Mrs. Taylor, you have every right to hate me. I know that there's nothing I can say to make you change your mind about me, but what about Kenya?" Maurice walked into the room and stood against the wall.

Henry slipped out of the room, because he knew Angela and Maurice needed to talk alone. Angela rose from the bed and stood toe to toe with Maurice. He looked down at her, since he towered over her by a foot. Kenya definitely got her feistiness from her mother.

"You're a sorry excuse of a man," Angela said through clenched teeth. "All of these years Kenya was dying inside. She lost you, her child, and she gave up her dreams, because they all seemed to include you."

"She told me about the baby, and I can't tell you how guilty I felt, and I know that there's nothing I can do to take her pain away or change what I did. But I was young and messed up big-time, but I promise you that I will never do anything to hurt Kenya again," Maurice said.

"You say all the right things, Maurice. Your silver tongue

has always been your secret weapon, but I'm not one of your little fans. You're a liar, and you will always be one in my book."

Unable to control his frustrations, Maurice blew up. "But this isn't about you, Mrs. Taylor. Kenya has made her choice, and you can hate me all you want, but do you want to lose your daughter in the process? We're getting married, and we don't need your damned permission."

Henry stormed into the room. "All right, you won't talk to my wife in that tone. Now, you can't expect that either one of us would be jumping for joy because you're engaged to our daughter!"

Maurice ran his hand across his face. "I'm sorry. I was out of line for raising my voice, but I meant what I said. Kenya and I are getting married, I love her, and I'm going to do right by her."

"Stop all of this right now!" Kenya cried from the door. "This isn't the way I'm going to live my life. Constantly choosing between Maurice and you guys. No one's asking you to fall in love with Maurice. All that matters is that I love him."

Angela threw her hands up. "Fine, Kenya. It's your life. I'm going to clean up my kitchen." She pushed past Maurice and bolted out of the room.

Henry shook his head and followed his wife.

Once they were alone, Maurice drew Kenya into his arms. "That went well," he said sarcastically.

"Oh, that's one way of looking at it," she said. "Let's get out of here."

Kenya and Maurice left her parents' house quietly. There were no hugs good-bye and no other confrontations or loud arguments. Instead of driving back to Charlotte, the couple decided to stop at the downtown Hilton.

Inside the room, Kenya curled up on the bed, wishing that things had gone better with her parents. Maurice eased in bed, beside her, wrapping his arms around her shoulders.

"Honey," he said, his lips close to her ear. "I know things didn't turn out the way that you wanted them to, but your parents know where we're coming from."

"I know," she said as she turned around and faced him. Kenya stroked his cheek and smiled weakly. "I guess I hoped they'd see you the way I do."

"Maybe one day they will, but that's my problem. I have to win their trust. There's nothing you can do to change their opinion of me. I have to prove to them that I am worthy of your love."

Kenya leaned in and kissed him on the nose. "I already know that you're worthy."

"They're just looking out for their baby girl," Maurice said. "I can't blame them."

"Even though I wanted my parents to stand behind us, I'm not going to let them change my mind about marrying you," Kenya said.

"But are they going to show up? Do we want to have a—"

Kenya brought her finger to Maurice's lips. "Our wedding is about us and not them."

Kissing her finger, he nodded in agreement. "So, when are we going to do this?"

Kenya shrugged. "I don't know, but the sooner the better."

"You're not going to change your mind on me, are you?"

Kenya rolled her eyes, biting back a comment about her name being Kenya and not Lauryn. "I'm not changing my mind," she said and then leaned against his chest. "I love you, and there's nothing anyone can say or do to make me change my mind."

Maurice kissed Kenya tenderly on the back of her neck. "I thank God for every day that you're in my life. Your mother's right, though. I'm selfish. When we get married, I'm going to want you all to myself. And I do have a silver tongue, and talking ain't the only thing I do with it." He ran his tongue down her neck and across her shoulder before flipping her over and lifting her tank top to expose her breasts. Kenya melted as he took her rock-hard nipple into his mouth, flicking his tongue across it before devouring it as if she were a piece of sweet candy. She felt dizzy with yearning. Thoughts of her parents were pushed from her mind, and she was filled with the untold pleasure that was about to come as he eased down her body, using his teeth and fingers to pull her panties off. Desire pooled between her legs, and she was so wet that Kenya thought she had a river flowing between her thighs.

Maurice spread her legs and kissed her inner thighs before moving to her tender folds of flesh. Kenya moaned in delight and dug her nails into his shoulder as he flicked his tongue across her throbbing clitoris. Her legs shook, and her juices flowed like an ocean. She grasped the blanket as he deepened his kiss, touching every sensitive spot. Kenya arched her back, pushing her body closer to his mouth, because she wanted to feel more of him, wanted him to make her scream.

Maurice reached up, sensuously massaging her breasts and making her body hotter than an inferno. Ready to feel his manhood deep inside her valley, Kenya tugged at Maurice's ear, whispering, "I want you. Inside me."

He didn't need any more coaxing as he spread her legs and lifted her hips to his and slipped inside her. She heard wedding bells and thought of babies and sitting on the porch, holding his hand. Opening her eyes, she saw that the man she loved was staring at her as well. Their hearts seemed to have one beat; they seemed to breathe the same air as they shared their love. Their union was complete when they climaxed together and fell asleep in each other's arms. Finally, Kenya felt secure with him, felt as if they had a future, and nothing, not even her parents' disdain, would change that.

The next morning, Kenya and Maurice didn't want to pull themselves out of bed. But with a four-hour ride back to Charlotte, they were forced to climb out of bed, shower, and hit the road.

"Are you sure you don't want to stop by your parents' place before we go?" Maurice asked as they got into the car.

"No. My mother's probably at work, and knowing my dad, he's in Covington with my uncle. They had their say last night, and I don't think I want to hear anything else right now."

"I do have one request. I'd like to go see my mother before we leave. She should be at the bakery, and we can get a free meal."

"Okay. In all of this, I hadn't even thought about the fact that we didn't tell your mother about us."

Maurice laughed. "I'm sure James has filled her in. But I should tell her myself. And don't worry. My mother has always loved you."

Kenya pinched him on the shoulder. "Funny."

They headed for Auburn Avenue, in the heart of the Sweet Auburn Historic District. Maurice's mother had worked off and on for years in a bakery that locals loved and tourist couldn't get enough of. When the owner died two years ago, his family asked Maryann to take over the day-to-day running of the bakery. Though she didn't have to work, because Maurice took care of her bills and anything else she needed,

Maryann agreed because she wasn't the type of woman to sit at home. Besides, she loved cooking and meeting new people. Maurice would've been happier if his mother had stayed home or moved to Charlotte and had relaxed after the hell she'd endured when he was growing up, but he has happy because she was.

"Does the bakery still have those sticky buns your mom used to bring us in the summer?" Kenya asked.

"They sure do. But I can't have any. I'm in training," Maurice said sadly. He loved those five-hundred-calorie buns, and he could never eat just one. But with training camp coming up, he needed to keep his weight down. The last thing he wanted was for some rookie to come into camp and take his place.

"Well, we'll split one, because I don't want all of those buns sticking to my hips."

"No, I've got something a lot better for those hips," he said in a seductive growl.

Kenya slapped him on the shoulder as he opened the door to the bakery.

"You ever think about moving back here?" he asked.

Kenya stopped in the doorway. "Are you getting traded to the Falcons?"

Maurice shook his head. "I'd better not be. But there is life after football."

"I know, but I like Charlotte, and moving right now wouldn't be a good thing for me being that my job just transferred me from Atlanta. Moving back isn't an option."

"You don't have to work, Kenya. I make—"

"You really don't expect me to quit my job and become one of those stereotypical NFL wives," she said, with her hands on her hips. "That has never been my goal."

"I know that," he said. "But if you wanted to move back to Atlanta, we could."

Kenya kissed him on the nose. "You and James have your business in Charlotte, and you're becoming sort of an icon in the city."

"And I don't want our kids to grow up with the Holly-weird syndrome, either, thinking that the world is theirs because of who I am."

"Trust me, they won't," Kenya said, "I'm not going to have any of that. When we have children, I'll keep them firmly grounded in reality, no matter how many Super Bowl rings their daddy has."

They headed for the counter, and when Maryann saw them, she bolted from behind it, ignoring the line of customers, and enveloped Maurice and Kenya in a big bear hug.

"I'm so happy to see you two, *together*," she said. "I thought James was pulling my leg."

"It's true," Maurice said through his smile.

Maryann looked at her grumbling customers, then ushered Kenya and Maurice to an empty table in a corner. "I'll be right back with sticky buns and coffee. Let me clear this line."

"Why don't you have anyone working with you?" Maurice asked.

"I'm glad you volunteered," said Maryann. "Kenya, you don't mind if I take him for a few?"

"Not at all, Mrs. Goings," Kenya said.

Maryann waved her hand. "You know we aren't that formal. You can call me Maryann. We're about to be family."

As Maurice and his mother walked away, Kenya couldn't help but wish that her family had welcomed Maurice the way Maryann had welcomed her.

The customers, who'd previously been grumbling about standing in line so long to wait for their morning sweets, were excited to be served by Atlanta's favorite son—even if he did get their coffee orders wrong.

Kenya smiled as she watched him interact with the customers. Even when some of the ladies, both young and old, flirted with him, it didn't bother her, because she knew who he was going home with and where his heart belonged. Kenya no longer had to question Maurice's love or loyalty. He was totally hers.

The bakery cleared as quickly as it had filled. Maryann put a sign that read BACK IN FIFTEEN MINUTES on the door, locked it, and took a seat with Kenya and Maurice. "All right," Maryann said as she set coffee and sticky buns in front of them. "How did this reunion happen? James told me bits and pieces, but I want to hear the whole story."

Maurice pinched off one of the buns and smiled at Kenya. "The first thing she did when she saw me was slap me."

Maryann laughed. "And I'm sure you deserved it," she said.

"Maurice, tell the truth," Kenya said. "You were eyeing me like I was a piece of meat on a grill."

Maryann popped Maurice on the hand as he picked up another piece of the bun. "You're in training. Anyway, after you guys met on the island, Kenya, you just decided to move back to Charlotte?"

Kenya shook her head as she took a slow sip of coffee. "I was already moving to Charlotte, and your son was the last person that I wanted to see. So, imagine how surprised I was when he was one of the first people that I ran into in the Bahamas."

Maryann shook her head as if she was reliving bad memories from Maurice's involvement with Lauryn. "I can't blame you for not wanting to see him. After all, he was supposed to marry that heifer." She paused to bite into a bun. "I'm not sorry that they didn't make it past the 'I dos,' but I was hurting that it was so public."

Maurice picked up his coffee. "I messed up, but that's

behind me, and who cares about her anymore?" He looked pointedly at Kenya.

"That's right," Kenya said.

"I'm glad that you've forgiven my son, but I'm sure Angela doesn't feel the same way," Maryann said as she poured more coffee into Kenya's cup.

Kenya shook her head. "It doesn't matter, though. Maurice and I aren't children, and we don't need my parents' permission to get married."

"I know that, and I also know how close you and your mother are. But she'll accept this marriage when she sees how happy you are. Just look at that smile on your face. The two of you have been grinning and smiling since you walked through the door."

Kenya touched her own cheek, unaware of the fact that she was smiling. However, she did know that Maurice made her feel like nothing else in the world mattered.

"Ma, not everybody thinks your son walks on water, like you do."

Maryann sucked her teeth. "Boy, don't make me slap you. So, how long are you two going to be in town?"

"We're on our way back to Charlotte," Maurice said.

Maryann nodded. "I'm glad you stopped by. Should I assume that things didn't go so well with your parents, Kenya?"

"Not exactly, but my dad seemed a little more accepting than my mother," Kenya said.

"Then he'll work on bringing your mother around. That's the good thing about having a real marriage. You work things out as a team," Maryann said as she rose to her feet and held her arms open to Kenya. "My son has always loved you."

Kenya hugged her future mother-in-law tightly. "I know."

Maurice looked down at his watch. "We'd better get going," he said. "Ma, I'll call you when we get home."

Maryann kissed her son and ushered the couple out the door. "Drive safely, and no speeding," she admonished.

"Yes, ma'am," Kenya and Maurice said as they headed out the door.

The drive back to Charlotte seemed to go by quicker because there wasn't that much traffic since most of Atlanta was at work. Obviously, someone was smiling on them, Kenya thought as she drove down the nearly empty interstate. She cast a sidelong glance at Maurice.

"Your mother's so sweet," she said.

"When she wants to be. She loves you, though. Always has. She didn't take to kindly to me bringing Lauryn home that first Thanksgiving," Maurice said.

"I don't blame her, there was enough turkey there already. I saw you two that day," Kenya said.

"Really? I-I . . ."

"I wanted to throw up when I saw her in that micromini skirt, hanging on you like a cheap suit. I was thinking that maybe it was love because your mother was going to eat her alive." Kenya laughed. "But everything happens for a reason. I was never happier that we were going to Covington for Thanksgiving dinner."

"Believe it or not, it took everything in me not to go over there to see how you were doing," he said.

"I believe it—not!" she said.

"I had to wait until Lauryn went to sleep, and then there was the chance that your dad, your mom, or you would have shot me."

Kenya shook her head. "I never thought I'd look back on this and laugh," she said. "That was the most hurtful period in my life."

"I'm sorry," he said.

"You don't have to keep apologizing. I realize that I needed that pain to grow and realize who I was. For too long, I allowed you to define me, and I tried to do everything that I thought would make you happy. If it hadn't been Lauryn who broke us up, it would've been something else, because we were growing in different directions, yet we didn't want to admit it."

"Why do you think we found our way back to each other?"

"You grew up."

All Maurice could do was laugh.

Chapter 27

Two weeks after Kenya had returned from Atlanta, she still hadn't spoken to her mother. It was as if the women were locked in a battle of wills to see who would call whom first.

Kenya and Maurice were planning a simple and low-key wedding, and they were going to get married after the month-long training camp ended in late July. There would be no cameras; there would be no ESPN news flashes about this wedding. Kenya wanted the day to be about her and Maurice.

"Miss Taylor," Talisha said over the intercom, "you have a visitor in the lobby."

"Who is it?" asked Kenya.

"Angela Taylor."

Hearing her mother's name shocked her. What was she doing here? Was she going to throw her support behind her union with Maurice, or was she here to restate her objections?

"I'll go down and meet her," Kenya said, suddenly feeling a sense of dread wash over her. She rose to her feet and smoothed her cream slacks and tugged at her pink tunic. Maybe she should've worn a designer suit instead. Kenya shook those thoughts out of her mind. Her mother had never cared about how her daughter looked, and they had rarely argued. So, maybe her mother's visit wasn't going to be another argument.

By the time she reached the lobby, Kenya had gone over in her mind every reason why her mother was there, from the absurd to the benign. Coming face-to-face with Angela, she returned the warm smile her mother greeted her with. "Mom, what a surprise."

"Yes, well, I would've called but I wasn't sure if you'd answer," Angela said. "I went to an editorial conference here at the *Charlotte Observer,* and I couldn't come to this city without coming to see you."

Kenya hugged her mother tightly. "Thanks for coming. Let me take you to my office."

"Yes, let's see how the other half lives. This is a nice building," Angela said. "And I see it's right across from the football stadium."

"I was wondering how long it was going to take . . ."

Angela shook her head as they stepped on the elevator. "I'm not here for an argument," she said. "I still think you're making a mistake, but this isn't about me."

"What?"

"I don't like this decision of yours, but it *is* your decision. How can I respect you as an adult if I don't respect your choices? You're a smart woman, and obviously, there is something you see in Maurice that I never will."

"So, are you coming to my wedding?" Kenya asked.

"You think I would miss it? And, no, I'm not going to object."

The elevator doors opened, and the ladies stepped off and then walked into Kenya's office. Angela nodded in wonderment as she looked around her daughter's space. "Impressive."

Kenya offered her mother a cup of coffee. "So, what accounts for your change of heart?" she asked Angela.

"Because when you left a few weeks ago, I thought I'd pushed you away. That's something I never want to do. We've always had a great relationship. When your friends were driving their parents crazy as teenagers, you were a little angel. We never had that mother-daughter drama. Sure, you and Maurice were doing whatever teenagers do, but you did what I asked of you. Never broke curfew, came to me with your problems, and you never lied to me. The older you got, the more I came to respect you and realize that your father and I did a great job of raising you.

"The whole thing with Maurice hurt me because it hurt you so badly, and I tried to stay out of it. I even stopped speaking to Maryann, even though it wasn't her fault. I didn't even get my sticky buns for Saturday morning breakfast for a long time, because seeing you in so much pain made me angry. Your father told me to let you work through it, and when I was about to let it all go, I found out that you'd lost Maurice's baby."

"We've gone over this," Kenya said.

"I know, but the point I'm trying to make is, your life is your life, and I'm going to have to support your decision, even if I don't agree with it," Angela said. "Besides, I don't want to become my mother."

"What does Grandma have to do with this?" Kenya asked, furrowing her brows in confusion.

As a little girl, Kenya didn't see her maternal grandmother often, and when Louise Johnson died, Kenya felt like she didn't know her grandmother enough to be really sad about it.

"There's a reason why my mother didn't come over for family dinners and during the holidays. It wasn't because she was jet-setting around the globe, either. She never liked your father. She thought Henry was too country, not sophisticated enough to be a part of our family."

"Why would she think something silly like that? It's not like Atlanta has always been some big metropolis," Kenya said. "Besides, Daddy has always been a good provider and . . ."

"That didn't matter to her. It was always about appearances and what made her and our family look good or bad. With her, it wasn't about what I wanted. It was what she wanted," Angela said, with a far-off look in her eye. "I hate that our relationship was destroyed because I loved your father. I love Henry, and I loved my mother. She wanted me to choose, and I did. That's a position that I never want to put you in. I felt like that's just what I was doing. When we had our argument, I had a flashback to that night my mother disowned me."

Kenya touched her mother on the shoulder. "Mom, I love you, and I don't think that we're going to end up like you and Grandma."

"I'm not going to let it happen," Angela said. "Even if that means I have to be Maurice Goings's mother-in-law."

Kenya hugged her mother tightly. "If you get to know him and let go of the past, you'll see what I see."

Angela wiped the tear that slid down her cheek. "I doubt I'll ever see him as you do, but I'm going to try."

Maurice stood in the Brothers Reality office, waiting for his brother to come in. It had been months since he'd checked on their projects or visited the work space. But the rift between him and his brother was his main concern as he sat down at James's desk. Maurice realized that he'd taken advantage of his brother over the years. He had allowed James to be his cleanup man; he had allowed him to step in and take the hits that he, Maurice, should have taken. He owed James an apology, and he was going to give him one.

Angela's words rang in his head as he waited for James. *You say all the right things, Maurice. Your silver tongue has always been your secret weapon, but I'm not one of your little fans. You're a liar, and you will always be one in my book.*

"What are you doing here?" James asked when he walked into the office and dropped his briefcase on his desk.

"I came to talk to you," Maurice said. "How's business?"

"You should know. You own the place. Mind if I get my seat, or are you here to take over?"

Maurice rose to his feet and walked away from his brother's chair. "I'm here because I want to apologize to you for all of this stuff that's been going on and how I've been treating you. Even when we were kids, I used you to get me out of trouble. I know it was wrong."

"What? You must need a blood donation or something," James said as he started up the computer.

"No, I don't. I've taken advantage of you, I made you take the heat for some things that I should've been a man about and stood up to, and I accused you trying to be with Kenya when I knew that you two were just friends," Maurice said as he sat on the edge of the desk. "I don't want us to have any bad blood between us. We're brothers, and that means more to me than anything else."

James folded his arms across his chest and looked at his brother. "Yeah, all right," he said.

"Come on, man. I'm pouring my heart out here."

"And I've heard this song and dance before, too," James said. "Do you mean it this time?"

"This time?" Maurice asked.

"Yes, Mo, this time. I've heard you apologize to me so

many times over the years that I've lost count. 'James, I'm sorry I don't spend more time with the business,' or 'James, I'm sorry I asked you to sneak that freak out of the house for me.' I'm sick of being your wingman, and I don't appreciate how you accused me of trying to move in on Kenya when I spent the night with her, trying to convince her to give you another shot."

Maurice nodded. "And I . . ." James cut him off.

"How do you thank me? By being an asshole. You're my brother, and I love you, but it's going to take more than words. Maybe you need to start pulling your weight around here so I can have a life that doesn't involve cleaning up your messes."

Maurice looked at his brother thoughtfully. "Is it really that bad? I mean, I've done some things, and I've asked you to do some things for me that I shouldn't have, but we're brothers."

James folded his arms across his chest and leaned back in his chair, then laughed. "It hasn't been that bad, but it's been bad enough."

"The only thing I need you to do for me is to be my best man," Maurice said.

James rose to his feet and crossed over to his brother. "You think you're going to actually make it through the ceremony this time?"

"Aw, I see. You got jokes," Maurice said as he pulled his brother into his arms and hugged him. "I should've never gone down the aisle with anyone other than Kenya."

"That's the smartest thing I've heard you say in years." James stepped back from Maurice. "Come on and buy me breakfast."

They headed to the Coffee Cup, and once they sat down, the tension between them floated away like butterflies in the summer sun. They laughed about Maurice's upcoming

wedding and how different it would be from the media
circus Lauryn had planned.

"You know Momma was thrilled when I told her that
you and Kenya were getting back together. I could see her
smile all the way from Atlanta."

"I wish Kenya's mother was just as happy," Maurice said.

"She doesn't look too sad to me." James nodded toward
the door.

Maurice turned and saw Kenya and Angela walking into
the restaurant, smiling and laughing. Kenya's eyes met his;
then she tapped her mother on the shoulder. Angela glanced
over at Maurice and James, then smiled thinly.

Maurice, against his better judgment, motioned for them
to join him and his brother. *Lord, please don't let this
woman come over here tripping today,* he told himself.

James and Angela embraced when she reached the table.
"Look at you, little James Goings. You look great. So tall.
I remember when you were just knee high."

"Thank you, Mrs. Taylor," said James. He pulled a chair
out for Angela as Maurice and Kenya kissed.

"I didn't expect to see you here this morning," Kenya
said. "Hi, James."

"Hey, Kenya," James said, flashing her a big smile.

Angela looked around the quaint restaurant, surprised
to see such a diverse crowd of business people in fancy
suits; construction workers in dusty jeans, holding hard
hats and safety glasses; and a few people with ear, nose,
and eye piercings and tattoos, who were not workers in the
corporate world.

"This is an interesting place," Angela said. "It reminds
me of some of the greasy spoons in Atlanta."

Kenya and James nodded, while Maurice looked down
at the dog-eared menu. He didn't know what to say to
Angela or what she was going to say to him.

"What's good here?" Angela asked, looking pointedly at Maurice.

"Just about everything. I like the cheese omelet and a side of bacon," Maurice said as he looked up at Angela.

Angela drummed her fingers on the table. "All right, let's cut the bull," she said. "For my daughter's sake, I'm going to try and be nicer to you. It's going to be hard, because I still think this marriage is a—"

"Mom," Kenya warned, raising her eyebrows.

"Listen," Angela said. "I'll never see you through the same eyes that my daughter does. But I'll respect her decision, and if being your wife is what she wants, then I'll have to live with it. One day, maybe you and I will be friends."

Maurice smiled at Angela. "Thank you, Mrs. Taylor. I know that I did some things in the past that . . ."

Angela waved her hand. "The past is the past, and I want to believe that you've learned your lesson. I won't make the same mistake that my parents made. I don't have to live with you, and I promise, I won't carve you instead of the turkey at Thanksgiving."

Everyone at the table laughed, and Maurice felt like he and Angela would get along one day, though he wasn't ready to reach across the table and hug her just yet.

"All right," James said. "This is all touching and what not, but I'm hungry. Hand me that menu, and somebody get the waitress."

Kenya hugged her mother, and they proceeded to order a down-home breakfast.

Chapter 28

Kenya and her mother decided to take a walk after stuffing themselves with fried eggs, bacon, and homemade biscuits. "That was a really nice thing you did in there," Kenya said after they'd walked a few blocks in silence.

"I meant it, in case you were wondering," Angela replied.

"I know."

"Have you two set a date?"

"We're going to get married soon, before training camp starts."

"That's not too far away. How are you going to plan a wedding in that short amount of time?"

Kenya smiled. "With your help. I can't do this without you and Daddy."

"Your father stands behind you, too. He came around a lot quicker than I had expected. That's probably because he doesn't know about the baby, and I'm not going to tell him."

"Thanks, Mom."

"I guess you and Maurice have the right idea, starting over and letting the past go. People talk about doing that all the time, but you're living it. Maybe I can learn from you," Angela said.

"Learn what?"

"How to be a better person. I've never been a very forgiving person. Your father and I split up when I was pregnant with you because I thought that he was cheating on me."

Kenya's eyes stretched to the size of quarters. "What?"

"He wasn't, but I thought he was. That's what men do, or at least that's what I thought."

"Do I really need to hear this?" Kenya said. The last thing she wanted to know was that her parents were human and had dealt with some of the same issues that she'd faced.

"Just listen. I went home to my parents for a few months, and your grandmother was too happy. She was ready to pay for my divorce, and she was introducing me to men that she thought were socially acceptable, and I hadn't even decided that I was done with my marriage. She made my life a living hell, so I had to face my problems on my own and save my family. It took a lot for me to go back to my husband and forgive him. But in the end, I had to ask him for forgiveness, because I'd been wrong, not him. All the time I thought Henry was cheating on me, you know what he was doing?"

Kenya shook her head.

"Planning a baby shower for me with the help of one of the secretaries who worked with him," Angela said. "That's why he'd hang up the phone when I'd come in the room. That's why he'd go out to lunch with her and not tell me about it. I'd ruined my own surprise because I got in my own way. You would think that I had learned my lesson. But here I am, doing it again, passing judgment and not knowing all the facts."

"Mom," Kenya said, fumbling for the right words to say.

"I'm sorry," Angela said. "I shouldn't have been so adamant about your relationship with Maurice. This is your business, and there's no reason for me to stand between you and true love. But I'll be watching him, and if he hurts you again, there'll be hell to pay."

"You won't have to worry about that. Maurice loves me, and he wouldn't do anything to hurt me again."

Angela smiled. "He'd better not."

Maurice was stunned at how well breakfast had gone with Angela and Kenya. As he sat in his condo, he wondered if Angela was telling the truth, and if she'd really give him a chance.

The phone rang, breaking into his thoughts. "Hello?" he said.

"Maurice, it's Lauryn."

He hung up the phone. Seconds later it rang again.

"What the hell do you want?" he demanded.

"I want to say I'm sorry," Lauryn said. "Listen, I know that I've done a lot of things that I shouldn't have, and the first thing I should've done before we planned our wedding was told you that I was having a relationship with Mya."

"So. What do you want now? And don't tell me that it's a second chance, because that's not going to happen."

"I know that you and Kenya are getting married. I guess I just need some help. You know I haven't worked in a while, and I want to start over, outside of Charlotte. So, if you could find it in your heart to—"

"You're calling me to ask for money? I can't believe you have the gall."

"I'm trying to do this the nice way, but if I have to go to the tabloids about you, then I will."

"Do what you have to do, but no one will believe anything you have to say. You've already proven yourself to be a liar. So, why don't you find a buck and buy a clue?" Maurice slammed the phone down and threw the handset across the room. The last thing he needed was for Lauryn to rear her head again when everything was going so well. She reminded him of a fungus: every time you thought you'd killed it, it came back.

He stood and paced back and forth. If he gave Lauryn money, he'd be opening a Pandora's box that he might never be able to close. But he didn't want Kenya to pick up a newspaper and read Lauryn's lies, or whatever she was going to say to reporters. *I'm not going to worry about her,* Maurice thought.

He decided that he needed to cut Lauryn off at the pass, and he didn't need to hide it from Kenya, either. But going to Kenya right now, when everything was going so well between them, just didn't seem like a good idea. He knew she still had doubts, and he didn't want to add to them. However, giving in to Lauryn was not an option.

Sitting down and stretching his legs across the coffee table, Maurice thought, *Lauryn isn't crazy, and this is going to blow over, and I hope it's sooner rather than later.*

The phone rang again, and Maurice ignored it at first, figuring it was Lauryn. But he answered it when the ringing became annoying. "Yeah?"

"Mo, check out the E! channel," James said. "Lauryn is on there."

"You've got to be kidding me. She just called me, trying to extort money. I guess this was part of her plan," he said as he flipped on the television.

"The ex-fiancée of Super Bowl MVP Maurice Goings said she's going to write a book about her experiences with the superstar and disclose the real reason why they didn't make it to the altar," said E! News host Ryan Seacrest. The camera cut to Lauryn, sitting in a studio. A female interviewer was sitting with her. "We're here with Lauryn Michaels, who has inked a six-figure deal with a New York publisher to write her tell-all memoirs about her life as an almost NFL wife and why she walked away."

"Hi," Lauryn said, then smiled as she looked into the camera. Maurice felt as if her eyes were boring into his soul. Silently, he prayed that Kenya was nowhere near a television.

"A few months ago you were living a dream, with fancy clothes, trips, and money. Not to mention you were engaged to one of the hottest football players out there," said the interviewer. "You gave it all up. Why did you do it?"

"Well, not every pretty picture is what it seems," Lauryn said. "My relationship with Maurice Goings was just that, a one-dimensional picture."

The interviewer leaned in. "How so?"

Lauryn crossed her long legs, exposing a sliver of her thigh. "Maurice may be the man on the field, but he certainly isn't off it. I'm not saying that he's gay, because he's never come out to me. But he didn't have a problem with my relationship with another woman. Mo would drive me to her house and finance our weekends away. And while I was gone, he was always surrounded by other men."

"You mean his teammates?" asked the interviewer.

Lauryn shook her head and looked into the camera. "Nope. That I could understand, but he spent a lot of time at a local gay and lesbian club, and I never understood why a straight man would hang around so many gay people."

"Are you gay?" the interviewer asked.

Lauryn shook her head and laughed. "No, I'm not. I was confused and experimenting. I love men," she said.

"That lying . . ." Maurice shut the television off. "Do you believe her?"

"You should sue her," James said. Maurice could still hear the interview in the background.

Maurice's phone gave a call-waiting beep. "Hold on," he said. "Hello."

"Maurice," Kenya said. "What the hell is Lauryn talking about? What can we do to stop her?"

"She called me and asked for money. Then James called to inform me about her interview."

"You know what? We're going to have to put a stop to this," Kenya said, her voice filled with fire and rage. "I'm not going to have her sullying your reputation or casting her dark cloud over our wedding. Talisha, close the door, and I need you to bring me all that you have on slander and libel."

"Baby, calm down," Maurice said.

"Did she think that she could just go on television and spread these lies and not deal with any repercussions? Did she even think about what this could do to your career?" Maurice heard a loud thud in the background, and he assumed that it was a law book landing in the middle of Kenya's desk. "And I'm going after that publisher if they publish that trash. She's a lying little—"

"You know what?" Maurice said, smiling despite himself. "You haven't asked me once if what she said was true."

"I don't need to ask you if it's true or not. I trust you, and I don't believe a word coming out of that lying tramp's mouth." He could hear the flames in Kenya's voice, and that frightened him. She was more than angry; she was furious. "I'm sick of Lauryn and her mess, and I'm not going to take it anymore. I have to go."

After she slammed the phone down in his ear, Maurice grabbed his jacket and headed for Kenya's office. He had a bad feeling about what was going to happen next.

* * *

"Talisha, stay here, and keep looking up libel and slander law. I have to take care of something," Kenya said as she printed Lauryn's address from the Internet. She didn't care how long she was going to have to wait for Lauryn; this was ending today. Kenya blew out of the office and headed down to the parking lot. She wasn't surprised that Lauryn had been living in a poorer part of Charlotte since the breakup with Maurice. Kenya knew that this was about money and revenge. If Lauryn thought that she was going to lord it over them and pop up with lies and trouble anytime she felt like it, she had another thing coming.

Kenya pulled up to the Royal Orleans apartment complex and waited. She didn't know if Lauryn's interview had been pretaped or if it was live. All she knew was it didn't matter how long she had to wait to see that evil witch; she was going to sit right there. Her cell phone rang, and she saw that it was Maurice. Kenya decided not to answer it, because she didn't need to hear the voice of reason. This thing between her and Lauryn wasn't just about him: it was about Kenya facing the demon that had plagued her for nearly a decade.

The phone continued to ring. Just as Kenya reached for it, she saw Lauryn exiting a cab. "Sorry, Mo, but you're going to have to wait." Kenya pulled her jacket off and hopped out of the car. "Lauryn!"

Lauryn turned around and glared at Kenya. "What the hell do you want?"

Quickly, Kenya closed the space between them, standing toe to toe with her nemesis. Looking at Lauryn, Kenya could easily admit that she was a beautiful woman, but she had no soul, no substance, and that was why things hadn't worked between her and Maurice. He might have fallen for her face and her body when they were in college, but Kenya knew that Maurice wanted more than that, and that was why they'd found their way back to each other.

"You need to stop this little vendetta of yours, because Maurice and I are going to be together. Learn to live with it," Kenya snarled.

Lauryn laughed and pointed her finger in Kenya's face. "You think this is about you? I don't give a damn about you. Never have. You were the one who let me inside your head. You let me run you out of town. This has always been about Maurice, and he had a chance to squash all of this. I could've called E! News and had them kill the story if he had just given me what I asked for. He brought this on himself. You're nothing but the one thing that he knew he could fall back on. If you want to call it love, then go ahead, but you were a contingency plan and nothing more. So what if you two fucked in high school. The moment I smiled at him and flashed him a little skin, you were an afterthought."

Propelled by nine years of aggression, anger, and frustration, Kenya slapped Lauryn and pushed her down to the ground. "I'm sick of you," she hissed as she stood over Lauryn, who was holding her cheek. "You think Maurice is a prize that can be won and lost. But he's a man with a heart and a soul, things you don't have."

Lauryn rose to her feet and pushed Kenya, causing her to stumble backward. She didn't lose her footing, though, and grabbed Lauryn's collar. "You're the one who thinks that she's won something. So what if he's in your life again," Lauryn said. "How long do you think this is going to last? When he goes on the road and sees all of those other women, do you think he's going to care about how much you two love each other?"

"Maurice is different now, but you wouldn't know that, because you're still the same gold-digging tramp that you were in college." Kenya released Lauryn's shirt and gave her a little shove. "If you publish this book or spread any more lies about Maurice or anything else, you're going to be slapped with a lawsuit. Consider this your first and final warning."

"Am I supposed to be afraid of you?" Lauryn snapped. "I'm not. You and Maurice can kiss my ass."

Kenya wanted to pummel her but decided that she wasn't worth it. "Fine, Lauryn. If you want to find your-self in court for the next few years, then keep spreading your lies about Maurice. But you and I both know that the only person who's confused about their sexuality is you."

"You'd like to believe that, but you don't know for sure, do you?" Lauryn smiled sardonically. "The next time he leaves you, it might just be for a man."

Kenya shook her head and started for her car. "Go to hell, Lauryn."

Lauryn flipped Kenya off as she drove away, and Kenya fumed inwardly. She wanted Lauryn to disappear, not only from her life, but from the earth. *Coming here was a mistake. All I did was make myself even angrier*, Kenya thought as she sped down Beatties Ford Road, praying that she didn't get stopped by a police officer. As she reached a stoplight, her cell phone rang again. Knowing it was Maurice, she decided to answer this time.

"Hello," she said.

"I'm at your office. Where are you?" Maurice asked, his voice peppered with concern.

"I'll be there in a little bit."

"Kenya, you didn't do anything crazy, did you?"

"If you're asking if I talked to Lauryn, the answer is yes."

"What happened?"

Kenya snorted. "A little pushing and shoving, that's all. I told her that if she writes this book, she'll be tied up in legal red tape for years."

"Baby, I can't have you fighting my battles."

"This is our battle. What she says and does affects you, but it affects me, too, and I don't like living on standby wondering what that crazy heifer is going to do next. We're not in college anymore, and she put your life in danger."

"I know, but I don't need you going after her," he said. "There's no telling what Lauryn might do if she thinks that she's cornered."

"What did you ever see in her?" Kenya asked as she slowed her car down. "Has she ever been stable?"

"I was young, and I didn't know that things were going to turn out this way. I always thought that I'd get married once and that you'd be underneath the veil."

"Don't try to be slick with me right now. Was it just the sex? You can't honestly tell me that you loved her in any way, shape, or form."

"Do we have to do this? Kenya, Lauryn isn't going to be a threat to us unless you let her be. The guys in the locker room know me and what kind of guy I am. The media is going to run with this story for five seconds and then move on to Angelina Jolie and Brad Pitt."

"So are you saying we should ignore this?"

"No, I'm saying you need to get to your office so we can concentrate on us and nothing else."

It's not that simple, Kenya thought as she snapped her phone shut.

Chapter 29

Maurice paced back and forth in Kenya's office as he waited for her to arrive. Something about their phone conversation didn't set well with him. Her voice didn't sound right, and he was worried that she would do something crazy. She'd gone after Lauryn once. What if she did it again?

He stuck his head out the door and looked at Talisha. "Has Miss Taylor called?"

"No, sir," Talisha replied exasperatedly.

"I'm sorry," he said, realizing that he'd been asking her the same question every five minutes since he'd hung up with Kenya twenty minutes ago.

Seconds after he walked back into Kenya's office and sat down, Kenya walked through the door. Maurice stood and drew her into his arms. "I was worried about you," he said.

She pushed out of his embrace. "I was serious about what I asked you on the phone. What did you ever see in Lauryn, and what does that say about the kind of man that you are?"

"You're kidding, right?" Maurice asked, flabbergasted that she was turning a nonissue into an argument.

Kenya threw her jacket across the room and glared at him. "I'm serious." She dropped her head in her hands. "I'm sorry. It's just that this situation with Lauryn isn't going to go away, and I'm already sick of it."

"What do you want me to do? I can't just pay her off, and you can't go out and beat the hell out of her."

"I know, but if this book becomes a reality, then you're going to be answering a lot of questions that . . ."

"Maybe we need to fight fire with fire. I called a reporter friend of mine from the *Charlotte Observer,* and he's coming over so that we can talk about Lauryn's book and our wedding."

"You think that's a good idea?" she asked. "I thought we were keeping the media out of our relationship."

"I'm not going to hide from Lauryn's lies, and I'm not going to let her sully my reputation."

"Having dueling stories in the media isn't going to help. Let's just sue her," Kenya said as she walked over to her desk. "I printed this stuff after I saw her on TV and talked to you." She handed Maurice a folder filled with information.

"It would cost more to sue her than to feed a story to a friend."

"Are you forgetting that I'm an attorney? I could represent you, and Lauryn needs to pay for what she's trying to do."

Maurice shook his head. "I don't want to take this to court."

"Is there something you're afraid I'm going to find out?"

"Do you really think Lauryn is going to get on the stand and tell the truth? There would be more outlandish lies, and I don't want to put you through that. Look how crazy it's already making you. We should be talking about wedding plans. We have your mother on our side and everything. I'm tired of fighting."

"Then maybe we shouldn't even get married. This is too much work."

"You mean that?"

She turned her back to him. "Yes."

He quickly closed the space between them and grabbed her shoulder, forcing her to face him. "We haven't gone through all of this to let Lauryn come between us again."

"She's always been between us."

"It doesn't have to be that way."

Kenya shook her head; her eyes filled with tears. "But it is that way. It's been that way since you chose her all of those years ago. This is too much and . . ."

"Miss Taylor, there's a reporter from the *Observer* here for you and Mr. Goings," Talisha said over the intercom.

"Give me a minute," Kenya said.

"Do you want to do this, or do I send him away?" Maurice asked.

"Fine. Send him in," Kenya said to him and Talisha.

A lanky journalist, dressed in wrinkled tan slacks and a collarless shirt, walked in the office. "Mo, what's up?" he said.

"My man Ross," Maurice said as he and the reporter shook hands. "What's up?"

"You tell me. Swanky place. Is this your attorney?" Ross asked, nodding toward Kenya.

Maurice smiled. "No, this is the love of my life. Kenya Taylor, this is Ross Mackins, one of the few reporters that can be trusted in this town."

Kenya extended her hand and gave Ross a weak handshake. "I'm here just to observe," she said.

"That's cool with me," Ross said, then turned to Maurice. "So, what's the deal with your former fiancée?"

"She's trying to extort money from me," said Maurice. "I think she's crazy. I'm not gay, and I've never felt that I was gay. Don't get me wrong. I don't have anything against gay people, but . . ."

"What he's trying to say is Lauryn is crazy, and she knows that in the testosterone-driven NFL, the best way to discredit a man is to call his sexuality into question," Kenya said, leaning over Maurice. "Make sure you write that Lauryn is crazy."

Ross and Maurice laughed until tears streamed down their faces. "And that's why I love her," Maurice said through the laughter. "Seriously, Lauryn's the only one who has a question about her sexuality, being that she left me at the altar for her best friend, who's a woman."

"So is that why you were missing in action all spring?" Ross asked.

Although he was talking to Ross, Maurice looked at Kenya. "That, and I had to convince the one I let get away to come back." He went into the story about how he had seen Kenya on vacation and she'd wanted nothing to do with him.

"You can't blame me," Kenya said. "Your so-called wedding was all over TV, even on ESPN."

"You must not watch Leno or Letterman," Maurice said. "I was the butt of jokes for weeks, and as I sat uptown, living with pizza boxes and on the verge of breeding roaches, I realized that I made a mistake nine years ago, when I let this woman walk out of my life."

Kenya smiled despite herself and listened as Maurice talked about getting over his relationship with Lauryn and the surprise of finding Kenya again.

"Getting to the meat of the matter, the readers and possibly your teammates are going to want to know how you didn't know that your woman was sleeping with another woman," Ross said.

"I really didn't care. I figured she was cheating, because Lauryn was the stereotypical NFL girlfriend. Very flirty. Always in the club. By the time that we were about to get married, I just wanted to get through the wedding. I had an ironclad prenup, and I wasn't worried. Then the wedding didn't happen, and I was looking like a fool. I tried to ignore it, but it hasn't gone away."

"So, Kenya," Ross said, "how are you dealing with suddenly having your relationship in the spotlight?"

"I'm not," Kenya said as she rose to her feet. "I don't understand why people want to know what goes on in his life off the field. It's not terribly exciting."

"Ouch," Ross said as he scribbled on his notepad.

Maurice pinched Kenya's arm playfully. "She's right, though," he said. "We're just a normal couple that's going through an extraordinary mess."

After an hour of telling the reporter their side of the story, Maurice and Kenya were tired and ready to head home. Maurice could still sense that everything wasn't okay, despite Kenya's smiles and laughter during the interview. As they walked down to the parking lot, Kenya was silent.

"What's wrong?" Maurice asked.

"I'm not going to do this every time there's a paternity claim or some other woman decides that she wants to get rich off you," Kenya snapped. "I just . . . God, is this how our life is going to be?"

"What are you talking about? You watch too much TV, and you know that after all of this with Lauryn, you're the only woman that I'm going to touch, and when you get pregnant, there will be no question that I'm the father. An hour ago you wanted to fight. Now you're throwing in the towel?"

She sped up, walking three steps in front of him, and then she stopped and turned around to face him. "Mo, I'm scared. Why do you even want to marry me in the first place? Is this about love or redemption?"

He slapped his hand across his forehead. "I thought we'd gotten past this! I thought we had finally decided that we were letting the past go."

"How can I let it go when, every five minutes, it's in my face again? If I have to tell one more person how we reconnected, I'm going to vomit. You're famous. I'm not, and nor do I care to be."

"You want me to quit the league and move to some small town where they've never heard of me so we can live the simple life and act like we haven't made mistakes?"

She raised her eyebrows as if to say, "We?"

Maurice nodded his head before she spoke, "Yes, Kenya, we. You act as if I'm the only person who messed up. You kept your pregnancy a secret, and more recently, you tried to seduce my brother. Do you see me throwing it up in your face every time things get hard?"

"I'm going home. I need some time alone," she snapped, then stomped off.

As Maurice watched her get into her car and speed away, he thought, *Am I ever going to make it to the altar?*

What is wrong with me? Kenya thought as she slowed her car. *I've let Lauryn get to me again, and I'm pushing this man away. I know Maurice loves me, but why can't I get past this thing with him and Lauryn? I guess I got this from my mother. Can I really live like this? Questioning Maurice at every turn and believing the worst about him.*

Kenya pulled over at a Chinese restaurant and sat in her car. She wasn't hungry, but going home was not an option. She knew that when she got into her apartment, the only thing she would think about doing was calling Maurice.

This marriage isn't going to work, she thought as she started her car again. *I'm going to have to end this.*

Chapter 30

Hours had passed since Maurice had heard from Kenya, and that wasn't like her. Even when they had their quarrels, they still talked on the phone at night. *She doesn't think that I'm going to let her go this easily,* he thought as he grabbed his car keys and headed for the door.

Hopping into his car, he sped to Kenya's place, ignoring every posted speed-limit sign and not giving a damn about the possibility that a police officer would pull him over. Luckily, he made it without inspiring the ire of the Charlotte-Mecklenburg Police Department. When he spotted Kenya's Mustang in the parking lot, he released a sigh of relief. At least she was at home. Now it was on to the hard part. Taking the stairs two at a time, he ran to her door and banged on it as if he were mad.

"What?" Kenya snapped when she opened the door. "Maurice, is there some sort of emergency?"

"Yeah, there is," he said, stepping inside without being invited. "See, I've got the feeling that you think we're over or that we're going to have some sort of drama every day of our lives."

She shook her head. "I don't want to do this. I just want to curl up with some files and then go to sleep."

"Why not curl up with me and go to sleep? Kenya, I can't let you walk out of my life, and I'm not about to let you throw our relationship away."

"All we do is move from one crisis to another. If it isn't Lauryn, then it's my parents. And now I have to deal with Lauryn's book and this media blitz that you're going to have to do to convince your teammates that you're not gay." Kenya slapped her hand against her forehead. "It's tiring. Once all of this dies down, I think we should quietly go our separate ways."

Maurice shook his head and stood so close to her that their lips nearly touched. "Nope, because we tried that nine years ago, and look how that worked out. The next time I head to an island for a vacation, I want to know you're there, because you're going to be by my side."

Kenya's eyes became glossy with unshed tears as she took a step back from him. Maurice could feel her defenses breaking down. "I can't get over what happened in the past, and that means we don't have any type of future," she said.

"You won't give us a chance," he said, nearly pleading with her. "Kenya, I love you too much to let you walk away from me again. I was a fool back then. I let my libido take over when I should've listened to my heart." He drew her into his arms and spoke against her ear. "You tell me that you don't love me and I'll walk out that door and never come back. I won't call, and I won't bother you ever again." He pulled her closer to him and felt her heart beating overtime against her breastbone. Maurice knew that he wasn't leaving her apartment, because as much as she tried to deny it, she loved him too much to throw away what they had.

Kenya pushed away from him. "I hate it when you do

this," she said, turning her back to him. "You say the right things, and I want to believe you, but . . ."

Touching her shoulder, he said, "No buts, Kenya. Nothing matters but me and you and how we feel about each other. I love you, and, damn it, you know you love me. Hell, your mother is going to give me a chance. How can you just deny what we have and tell me that these last few months didn't mean anything? Or that being together is too hard and you don't want to try?"

Kenya turned around and shook her head. "Please stop it!" she exclaimed. "Do I love you? Yes, and I've never stopped loving you, but love isn't enough."

"How do you know? Have we even tried? You're making a snap judgment because of what happened nearly a decade ago, when I was an immature punk. You've grown, I've grown, and . . ."

"Lauryn is still out there," she said. Kenya pointed to her head. "And she's in here. I can't get the image of you and her out of my head."

Maurice led Kenya over to the sofa and took her hands in his. "Please tell me that you're not going to let her win. Kenya, I want you and no one else. What do I have to do to prove that to you?"

"Kiss me," she whispered.

Maurice didn't have to be told twice. As he pulled Kenya into his arms and gently kissed her, hoping to ease all of her doubts and eliminate her fears. Soon his kiss turned fiery and passionate. She melted against his body, and Maurice took the opportunity to slip his hands underneath her thin tank top and cup her breasts, massaging them until her nipples perked up underneath his fingertips. A soft moan escaped her throat as one of his hands slipped between her thighs, pushing her cotton boxer shorts aside. He felt the wetness of her arousal as he slipped his finger between the folds of her skin, stroking her mound of sensuality until her legs shivered.

Kenya leaned forward and wrapped her arms around his neck as she ground against his finger, imagining that his manhood was buried deep inside her. Her lips grazed his neck as she felt herself about to climax. Maurice removed his finger and pulled her shorts off.

"I want to taste you," he murmured as he leaned back on the sofa and lifted her hips to his lips. "You're mine, and you're going to know it by the time we're done."

Words failed her as his tongue took the place of his finger and he lapped her sexual juices, making her dizzy with delight. Kenya cried out as Maurice deepened his kiss, sucking her pleasure point until she lost all control. Pulling back, Maurice rose to his feet, then lifted Kenya and took her to her bedroom so that he could make love to her with the fervor she deserved.

Once in the bedroom, Kenya pulled her shirt off and lay on the bed, totally naked. Maurice stared at her flawless body, smiling because she was going to be his wife and this would be what he'd come home to every night. After a hard practice, he'd be able to unwind with her. After she tried a tough case, he'd massage her tension away and feed her dinner that he'd order from her favorite restaurant. When he looked at Kenya, he saw a bright future, which he'd never give up.

"I love you so much," he said.

"I love you, too. And I do want to be with you forever," she said. "I'm scared."

He joined her on the bed, wrapped his arms around her, and buried his lips in her neck. "You don't have to be. The only thing that can stop me from being with you is death. No other woman can even compare to you."

Maurice kissed her reply out of her mouth before she

could speak. She was sweeter than sugar, more addictive than any drug sold on the street. With shaky hands, she pulled at his clothes, stripping him until they were both naked.

"Don't let me run from you again," she whispered as she wrapped her legs around his waist.

"You're not going anywhere but down the aisle," he said, slipping his erection into her. She was hot and tight and felt damned good. Maurice didn't even care that he hadn't bothered to pull the condom out of his pants pocket. He wouldn't mind making a baby with her. It would be his redemption for allowing her to suffer through the loss of their child so many years ago. Maurice had so much to make up for; so many mistakes that he'd made had caused Kenya a lifetime of pain.

"I'm sorry," he said as he felt his climax creeping up on him.

"Sorry?" she asked breathlessly.

"For everything that I've ever done to hurt you." He collapsed against her breasts, kissing each one gently. "Marry me."

"I've already answered that question."

"But how many times have you changed your mind?"

Kenya thumped him on the top of his head. "Shut up."

The next morning, Kenya and Maurice woke up wrapped in each other's arms. Smiling at Maurice, Kenya reached out and stroked his smooth cheek. He opened his eyes and smiled at his future wife.

"You're just going to lie here when we have a wedding to plan?" she quipped.

"I don't see you moving, either," he said, grabbing her hand and kissing it.

"Let's just get married in bed and stay here."

Maurice flipped her over and straddled her body. "Don't give me any ideas. As much as I hate to get up, I do have to head over to my office. I told James that I was going to give him as much help as I could on this project."

"You're actually going to do some work?" Kenya said, then kissed him gently on the lips. "I think I'm impressed."

Maurice smirked at her. "Want to go have breakfast before I go in to be bossed around by my brother?"

"Sure. As long as you join me in the shower," she said as he rolled over onto his side. Maurice didn't have to be told twice as he followed Kenya into the bathroom.

Following their shower and a quick romp in the bathroom, on the counter, they headed to the Coffee Cup. Kenya stopped at a newspaper box and purchased a copy of the *Charlotte Observer.* She knew that Maurice's story was in the paper, and she hoped that this would shut the town and everyone else up.

"I'd almost forgotten about our story," he said as they took a seat in the crowded restaurant.

"I still say we should sue the—"

"Maurice Goings," Smitty said, then slammed a copy of the paper on the table, in front of Maurice. "You stay in the news, don't you?"

"Get out of my face, dude," Maurice growled. His face was a knot of anger.

Smitty threw his hands up. "I'm not here to fight with you. I know how you feel. Some women will say anything and not give a damn about how it will affect you."

Maurice raised his eyebrows at his teammate, not knowing what to make of his support. The two had never been friends, and when Maurice took his starting spot as wide receiver for the Panthers, the animosity between them could have been cut with a knife.

"Thanks, man," Maurice said.

"Stuff like this is enough to take a man out of his game," Smitty said.

Maurice nodded. This was the antagonistic bastard that he was used to. "Don't worry. Your spot on the bench is secure."

Smitty laughed. "Whatever." Then he walked away.

"Nice guy," Kenya said. "He's not coming to the wedding, is he?"

Maurice shook his head and laughed. "He's a jealous jerk," he said as he waved for a waitress.

Kenya opened the paper and turned to the sports section. The story about Maurice was on the front page of the section, underneath the headline SCORNED EX SLINGS MUD.

"What the?" Kenya read part of the story aloud. "In a case of he said/she said, Carolina Panthers wide receiver Maurice Goings and his ex-fiancée, Lauryn Michaels, exchange verbal jabs in the media. She says that he's gay and that he encouraged her bisexuality, and she is planning to write a tell-all book about her years with the football star. He says that she's a liar and a gold digger, who has tried to extort money from him as he plans a new life with a Charlotte attorney." She tossed the paper aside. "I thought you said that this guy was your friend."

Maurice picked up the paper and continued reading the story. "Goings, who was rejected at the altar by Michaels, said the only person confused about their sexuality is Michaels. 'She was having an affair with a woman and using me because she wanted to get rich.' Michaels, on the other hand, said Goings is the one having a sexual identity crisis. 'I can't say that I saw him in bed with another man, but the signs were there.' When asked what those signs were, Michaels said to read her book. So, who's telling the truth? The new fiancée, Kenya Taylor, who has known Goings and Michaels for years, said that she knows Goings isn't gay. 'Lauryn is crazy, and she knows that in the testosterone-driven NFL, the best way to discredit a man is to call his sexuality into question.' Goings and Taylor were high-school sweethearts, and both attended historically black Johnson C. Smith University. Then Michaels came into the picture."

Kenya threw her hand up. "Please spare me," she said. "I've heard enough."

"It isn't that bad," Maurice said as he scanned the rest of the article. "All I want is for people to know that Lauryn is a liar and I finally got the right one."

Kenya leaned over the table and kissed Maurice on the forehead. "Do you think this is going to shut her up?"

He shrugged his shoulders. "I hope so, but it doesn't matter," he said. Before Maurice said anything else, the waitress walked over to take their orders. As Kenya rattled off her request for the breakfast special, Maurice looked at his watch.

"I'll have what she's having, but make mine to go," he said.

"You're leaving so soon?" Kenya asked once the waitress walked away.

"James is already going to kill me because I'm late," Maurice said. "He'll just have to get over it."

"That doesn't sound like a brother who's willing to work," Kenya teased.

"Yeah, whatever you say," he said. "I'm going to sit in on some meeting and get up to speed on our housing project. Your attorney is coming to meet with us in about twenty minutes." As he rose to his feet, the waitress came over with his boxed-up breakfast and Kenya's plate. As Kenya dug into her breakfast, she waved good-bye to Maurice, who then dashed out the door.

After finishing her breakfast, Kenya headed to her office, much happier than she had been when she'd left the previous day. "Good morning, Talisha," she sang as she walked into her office.

"Miss Taylor, there's someone here to see you. A Lauryn Michaels."

Kenya's smile was quickly erased. "Where is she?"

"In your office. I tried to stop her."

Kenya held up her hand. "I'll handle this, but keep security on standby." She walked into her office and found Lauryn sitting on the edge of her desk. "What in the hell are you doing here?"

"Swanky digs, Kenya. Who knew that you would turn out this way? Nice little article that you two have in the paper today."

"If you don't tell me what you want, I'll have security escort you out," Kenya said forcefully.

"Fifty thousand dollars. That will make me and my book disappear. Mo isn't going to do this unless you convince him to do so." She twirled a lock of her hair around her finger. "If you don't help me, then it's going to be on your head when some defensive lineman tries to take Maurice's head off because he thinks Maurice was looking at his package."

Kenya grabbed Lauryn's shoulder and yanked her off the desk. "You extortionist! You're not getting your grubby little hands on a dime from me or Maurice, and if you write that book, it will never see the light of day. Now get out of here."

"You don't get it, do you? It doesn't matter if my book is the truth or a lie. Maurice's reputation will be ruined, and you're going to spend your entire marriage wondering and fighting rumors. Is he on the down low? Are those nights out with the boys sex parties? When is my HIV test going to be positive?"

"You're a fool," Kenya said. "Are you sure you gradu- ated from college? You're not going to profit from lies, and

I will personally file a lawsuit to stop you and will spend every waking hour of my day trying to bury you."

"And what's going to happen to Maurice as you fight to bring me down? He's going to be so busy proving his manhood by sleeping with every woman that looks his way, and once again, you'll be crying and running away."

Kenya had had enough of Lauryn's mouth, and before she knew it, she punched her in the face, knocking her down. Then she was on top of her, like a cat pouncing on a mouse, and banging her head on the floor. Screaming profanities, Kenya unleashed a *Dynasty*-style beating on her. The women tussled on the floor, knocking over chairs and Kenya's bookshelf. The loud crashing noises prompted Talisha to make a frantic call to security.

Lauryn kicked Kenya off her. "You stupid b . . ."

Again, Kenya pounced and pushed Lauryn against the wall. "I've never hated anyone as much as I hate you. Ever since you set your sights on Maurice, all you have wanted is his money and the title of NFL wife. You never loved him, never cared about him, never knew him."

Lauryn pushed Kenya out of her face. "So what? If you think Maurice or any other man will love you, then you're a bigger fool than I ever thought you were. He's going to hurt you again, and I hope that—"

"Is everything all right in here?" the security officer asked as he burst through the door.

"Get her out of here," Kenya exclaimed, pointing at Lauryn.

The officer looked at Lauryn's bloody nose and split lip. "Do I need to call for a doctor?"

"Out! Get her out of here, and if she needs a doctor, let her get one herself," said Kenya, who was nearly shrieking. Once she was alone in her office, Kenya walked into her bathroom and took a look at her reflection. Her hair stood on top of her head as if she were Don King, her jacket had a faint blood stain, and one of the sleeves was ripped. She snatched her jacket off and turned the water on to wash her face.

There was no way she'd get any work done. Walking out of the bathroom, she looked around her office and saw that it looked as if a bomb had exploded.

"Talisha, please cancel all of my appointments today," Kenya said through the door.

"I've already done that Miss Taylor," replied Talisha as she rose to her feet and walked to the doorway of Kenya's office. "Is everything all right? That woman made some threats as she walked out of here."

"I'm not worried about her. She makes threats all the time," Kenya said dismissively. "Can you call the maintenance staff and get them to clean up this mess? Once you're done with that, take the day off on me."

"Thank you, Miss Taylor." Talisha rushed back to her desk and picked up the phone.

Closing her door, Kenya gathered her things, flung her ripped jacket over her shoulder, and wished she'd had a minibar installed in the office, because she needed a drink, despite the fact that it wasn't even noon yet. Grabbing her keys, she took the service elevator to the parking lot and dashed to her car, hoping that none of her employees saw her leaving in such haste. She unlocked her car door, and as she was about to slide into the driver's seat, a shot rang out, shattering the back window of the SUV. Everything went black.

As Maurice sat in a meeting with James and Juan Peters, their attorney, the strangest feeling washed over him. It was as if someone had poured ice water down his spine.

He stared out the window, nodding at the sounds of the voices, although he was unable to follow the words.

"Mo," James said, nudging his brother. "Are you with us?"

Maurice focused his eyes on his brother. "Yes."

"Did you hear Juan?" James asked.

"No. If you could repeat the question," Maurice said.

"I asked when you and boss lady are getting married," said Juan as he closed the file in front of him. "She's a good lady. A little tough, but fair."

Maurice smiled tersely. "We don't have a date yet, but before training camp," he said as he rose from his chair. He shivered again; the ice water was back. "Excuse me, guys, I need to go make a phone call."

James and Juan looked at each other and shrugged their shoulders. Maurice had been acting strange all morning. James thought his brother was just bored.

As soon as Maurice got into the hallway, he whipped out his cell and called Kenya's office. The phone rang and rang, which he found to be odd. Talisha wasn't at her desk, and that girl normally stood guard over Kenya as if she was the CIA and the FBI all rolled up into one package. Again, he felt chills. Dashing out of the building, Maurice raced to his car and drove over to Kenya's office. Three blocks from his destination, Maurice was stopped by a roadblock. He rolled his window down and motioned to the police officers. "What happened here?" he asked one of the officers.

"There was a shooting, and the perimeter has been sealed off. Aren't you Mo Goings?" said the officer.

Maurice nodded, not in the mood for small talk or answering questions about the upcoming season. "Do you know who was shot?"

The officer shrugged and pulled out his ticket book. "I'm just directing traffic, but can I have your autograph?"

Though part of Maurice wanted to tell the man hell no, he signed the book. "Listen," Maurice said, "my fiancée works in this building, and I need to check on her."

"I can't let you drive through here, but you can park over there," the officer said, pointing to a parking meter a few feet away. "Then you can just walk over to the building."

"Thanks," Maurice said, glad that his signature had paid off. He parked the car and ran toward the building as if it was Sunday afternoon and Jake had thrown a bomb pass to him. Yellow tape greeted him, along with detectives, who were combing the area for clues. Most of the attorneys from Kenya's firm stood outside; their eyes were red and their cheeks tearstained. Maurice scanned the crowd, searching for Kenya. He didn't find her, but he saw Talisha in deep conversation with a police officer. He didn't like where his mind was taking him. *Kenya, where are you? Please be inside, talking to some policeman or something.* With long steps, Maurice rushed over to Talisha. She turned to him, with a pained look in her eyes.

"What's going on?" Maurice asked.

Talisha looked up at the officer, and then her gaze fell again on Maurice. "I'm sorry," she said.

"Sorry for what? Tell me what's going on," said Maurice.

Talisha stroked her hair and silently cried. "Miss Taylor was shot in the parking deck."

Maurice's knees buckled, and his heart leapt to his throat. "No," he groaned. "That can't be right. Who would want to shoot her? She's a contract attorney. She makes people money." His throat burned with rage and anger. "Where is she?"

"They took her to Carolinas Medical Center and . . . ," said Talisha, her voice trailing off.

"Was she?" Maurice stopped before the word *dead* could leave his mouth. He thought about the nine years he'd wasted and about how he and Kenya could've had a life together if he hadn't been such a fool. He had spent years with a woman who didn't love him and who wanted nothing more than his money. "Do the cops know anything?"

Talisha shook her head. "I told them about the woman who was here earlier, but they think it may have been a robbery or something."

"What woman was here earlier?"

"Lauryn Michaels. She and Miss Taylor had a heated argument."

Without saying another word, Maurice tore away from the building. If Lauryn had anything to do with Kenya's shooting, she was going to pay dearly.

Chapter 31

"Grandma," Kenya said as her father's mother appeared before her. She looked beautiful in her snow-white dress, and her wavy hair was just as white. Her smile was warm and tender.

"Do you miss my shortbread cookies that much?"

"Grandma, where am I?" asked Kenya.

"Almost home, but I don't think it's your time," she said as she placed her arm around Kenya's shoulders. "You're too young, and you have a man who loves you so much that he'd never be the same if you left him now."

"I'm tired, Grandma," said Kenya.

"You're not old enough to be tired. You don't know what tired is. Have you thought about how my Henry will feel if you just give up? Have you ever given up on anything? Wake up, baby."

Kenya opened her eyes and stared at the paramedic who was working to bring her around.

"We got a pulse," the woman paramedic said. "Miss Taylor, can you hear me?"

In her mind, Kenya said yes. Obviously, it didn't translate.

"Patient is still unresponsive," the paramedic said.

"She's lost a lot of blood. Make sure they have a few bags ready in the ER. She's going to need surgery."

"I'm fine," Kenya said in her head. "My back is just a little sore. What happened, anyway?"

The paramedic monitored her vital signs and noted an improvement. "She coming around. Her heartbeat is stronger."

"She must have been in shock," another paramedic said.

The woman paramedic closest to Kenya looked up at him and said, "Getting shot in the back will do that to you."

Shot? Somebody shot me? In her mind's eye, Kenya replayed the last few hours. First, there was the fight with Lauryn, her office was in a mess, and she and Talisha were going home. Then the blackness. She didn't remember seeing a shooter or even hearing the gunshot.

"Maurice," Kenya moaned.

The woman paramedic looked down at Kenya. "Miss Taylor, can you hear me?"

"Shot. Maurice. Help," cried Kenya.

"Yes, you were shot. Did this Maurice person shoot you?" asked the woman paramedic.

Kenya thought she said no and that she was shaking her head. "Help. Shot. Maurice." She closed her eyes. The little bit of energy she'd had was gone.

When the ambulance arrived at the emergency room, a few camera crews were there. The news of Kenya's shooting was spreading like wildfire. The woman paramedic realized that Kenya Taylor was Maurice Goings's fiancée. Quickly, she ran over to a police officer.

"I think we have another Rae Carruth situation," she whispered to him. "She said Maurice shot her."

The news of Maurice's possible involvement in Kenya's shooting spread almost as quickly as the initial news of the shooting. Memories of former Carolina Panthers wide receiver Rae Carruth, who was serving a prison sentence for the murder of his pregnant girlfriend and the attempted murder of their son, were conjured as soon as detectives told the media that they were not ruling anyone out as a suspect.

But what the paramedics and police didn't understand was that Kenya was worried that the shooter would shoot Maurice, too. She hadn't seen Lauryn pull the trigger, but she knew that Lauryn was the person who'd tried to kill her. Kenya just couldn't tell anyone. She was doped up on pain medication as the doctors waited for the swelling in her spine to go down before attempting to remove the bullet. She didn't know that as soon as her parents were contacted by the Charlotte-Mecklenburg police, they had hopped in their car and had sped to Charlotte so fast that they had gotten speeding violations in three states.

Angela held Kenya's hand, stroking it gently. "Who did this to you, and why? I don't want to believe that Maurice had anything to do with it."

"He couldn't have," Henry said. "Not the way he loves Kenya."

Angela rolled her eyes. "Maybe she came to her senses and told him that she wasn't going to marry him."

"Stop it," Henry said. "You told her that you supported this relationship. Do you want her to treat you the way you treated your mother?"

Angela dropped Kenya's hand. "But if he shot her, I will personally take care of him with my bare hands."

"You can't listen to the news, and if you would've listened carefully, you would know that the only thing they said was the police aren't ruling anyone out as a suspect."

"These professional athletes think they can get away with murder and anything else under the sun. Kenya is not . . ."

"Mom," a weak voice said.

Henry and Angela turned to the bed and saw that Kenya

had opened her eyes. "Baby girl," Henry said before kissing Kenya on the forehead. "Thank you, Jesus."

"Kenya, don't try to talk too much," Angela said. "Thank God you woke up. We were so worried."

"Maurice," whispered Kenya.

"What about him? He hasn't even been here," Angela said, not hiding her disgust.

"Is he safe?" Kenya asked.

"Why wouldn't he be?" Angela asked, biting her tongue, because she wanted to say so much more.

"She's crazy," Kenya said, then began to cough.

"Who are you talking about?" Angela asked.

"Lauryn did this to me," Kenya said.

Henry rushed out of the room, in search of a nurse.

Maurice sat in the nondescript sedan, staring at Lauryn as she packed her sports car, the car that he'd bought for her. Did she really think that she was going to get away with this? She had tried to kill the woman he loved, and now she was going to try and slink out of town like the bottom-feeder that she was. He wanted to shoot her or grab her and choke the life out of her. But he knew the right thing for him to do was to get her to turn herself in to the police. Slowly, he emerged from the sedan and stealthily crossed the parking lot.

Lauryn closed her trunk, then turned around, coming face-to-face with Maurice. She jumped back, slamming herself against the car's bumper. "What are you doing here?"

"Going somewhere?" Maurice said. His voice was menacing and low. "I know what you did, and you're not going to get away with it."

"What did I do?" Lauryn said.

Maurice grabbed her shoulders. "Don't play with me.

You shot Kenya, and you're going to turn yourself in to the police."

"Let me go!" Lauryn screamed.

"As soon as we get to the police station," Maurice snapped as he pushed her toward his car.

Lauryn jerked away from Maurice and reached into her waistband, pulling out a gun. "I could kill you right now! It's a shame that Kenya didn't die. Look at my face," she said, pointing to her black eye and bruised nose. "Look what she did to me. That doesn't matter to you. The only thing you care about is your precious little Kenya. It's always been like that. I knew you always thought about her, and all those years when you claimed to love me, you were pining for Kenya. That's why I was with Mya. She loved me without conditions."

"And you used her," growled Maurice.

"Shut up!" Lauryn pointed the gun at Maurice's chest and rested her finger on the trigger. "I knew I came in second to her, and that's why it was so easy to put you second. I'm going to get in this car and drive away, and you're going to join Kenya in a hospital bed."

With catlike reflexes and the force of an inside lineman, Maurice tackled Lauryn at the knees, forcing her backward. The gun went off, sending a bullet soaring into the air. Maurice wrested the gun from Lauryn's hand and then kicked it away. Lauryn tried to claw his face as she rolled on top of him while they wrestled.

"You never put me first. It was always something other than me," Lauryn hissed. "Kenya, football, your family. No one has ever put me first." Tears dropped from her eyes, but Maurice wasn't moved.

"You've always been selfish, and if no one else put you first, you did," Maurice snapped. He held her wrists with one hand and called 911 from his cell with the other. "Why did you do it?" he asked after hanging up with the 911 operator. "Why didn't you just leave me alone? When you left me at the altar, I let you keep everything. I let you keep the car. I even finished paying the lease on your place, which, I know, was Mya's apartment. But you kept being greedy, kept trying to bleed me for more money, and now you have tried to kill the *only* woman that I've ever loved."

Lauryn spat in his face. "I hope the bitch dies."

Maurice felt every nerve of his body burn like it had been set afire. He wanted to stuff those words down her throat. But he didn't. Instead, he waited for the police.

Angela paced back and forth outside of Kenya's room. Maybe her daughter was confused about who'd shot her. Maybe Kenya just didn't want to believe that Maurice had done this to her. Something didn't set well with Angela. Why hadn't Maurice been to the hospital to check on his fiancée? If he loved Kenya as much as he claimed, then why hadn't she heard from him?

Just as Angela was about to walk into Kenya's room, she heard footsteps behind her. "Mrs. Taylor," a detective said. "We've apprehended a suspect in the shooting of your daughter."

Angela held on to the doorknob. "Was it . . . ," she asked, her voice trailing off.

"Lauryn Michaels has been charged with the attempted murder of your daughter," said the detective.

Angela looked over the detective's shoulder and saw Maurice nearly running down the hall. When Maurice reached her, Angela opened her arms to him, hugging him tightly. "She's been worried about you," she whispered.

"How-how is she?" asked Maurice.

Letting him go, Angela said, "Step inside and see for yourself."

One of the hardest things that Maurice had ever had to do was walk into Kenya's hospital room. Just the thought of losing her when they had been given another chance was more than he could stomach. The shooting was his fault, because he had been the one who'd brought Lauryn into their lives. Taking a deep breath, he walked through the door and found Kenya awake and alert.

"Mo," Kenya said, her voice a little hoarse.

Crossing over to her bed, he kissed her lips sweetly. "I've been so worried about you, and I know it's taken me—"

"Lauryn. You have to call the police about her, because she's . . ."

"In jail. I'm sorry that I brought all of this madness into our lives. If I had lost you . . ."

Kenya brought her finger to his lips. "But you didn't. I'm going to be fine."

Maurice noticed that her legs weren't moving. He placed his hand on her thigh, and she didn't flinch. He moved his hand away quickly so that she wouldn't see that he knew that she was paralyzed. "I know you will," he forced himself to say.

Later, when Kenya had drifted off to sleep, Maurice and Angela stood outside her room to talk about her condition.

"I guess this is the part where the real Maurice shines through," Angela said after telling him of Kenya's spinal-cord injury. "As long as she is walking and fits your NFL image, you want to marry her, but—"

"You have such a low opinion of me. Do you really think that I would walk out on her now?" said Maurice, struggling to keep his voice down and his anger in check. "I put my life on the line to find the woman who tried to kill her. I don't care how hard it's going to be or what I have to do. Kenya's going to walk down the aisle and into my arms."

Angela folded her arms across her chest and leaned against the wall. "I hope that you prove me wrong. But I just don't see that happening."

Maurice stomped away from Angela for fear that he'd say the wrong thing out of anger and make a tense situation even worse.

Henry, who'd seen the exchange between Maurice and his wife, stopped Maurice at the end of the hall. "Son, let me talk to you, and if you tell anyone we had this conversation, I'm going to say you're a liar," Henry said as he closed his big hand on his future son-in-law's shoulder. "Step outside with me."

"Mr. Taylor, I really don't want to argue with you or your wife any more today. I just had a gun pointed at my chest, got my face scratched up, and was accused of attempted murder."

"Boy, I know that, and I said, 'Let's talk.' I've got to school you on something. If you're going to marry Kenya, then you need to know this about Angela. She thinks she's the boss. But she's not. You need to be in there with my daughter, and Angela needs to go sit down somewhere else. I've lived this already. My in-laws, neither of them liked me, and I only had the best of intentions toward my wife. I thought I was doing her a favor by just being passive and backing away from her family. But I wasn't. All I needed to do was to stand up for myself and let them know that my family was my business. You're going to have to do that with Angela. There's no other way around it. This attitude must have been passed to her through her DNA."

Maurice's eyebrows knotted in confusion. "What?"

"I'm not giving you the green light to disrespect my wife, because I'll hurt you," Henry said. "But Kenya is going to be your wife. You need to establish that fact with her mother. And you do that right now, before you look up and twenty years have passed."

Maurice nodded and turned back down the hall. Angela was sitting beside Kenya's bed as the doctor stood at the foot of the bed. Slowly, Maurice opened the door.

"Doctor, what's going on?" Maurice asked.

"Maurice Goings?" the doctor said excitedly.

Angela cleared her throat. "Maybe you should leave, Maurice."

"No," Maurice said forcefully. "I need to hear what's going on with my *future wife*."

Kenya nodded. "I want him to stay," she said.

Angela rolled her eyes and shook her head. "Fine."

"Well," the doctor said, "as I was saying, the swelling of the spinal cord has decreased significantly. However, Ms. Taylor doesn't have any movement below her waist right now. Once the bullet is removed and with extensive rehabilitation, there's no reason why she won't regain full mobility."

"When will you know for sure?" Maurice asked.

"If the decrease in swelling continues and the drugs that we've given Ms. Taylor work, then we should be able to operate in a few days. Provided that there are no other complications," explained the doctor.

Angela clutched her chest. "What kind of complications?"

Maurice stroked the back of Kenya's hand, silently re-assuring her that everything was going to be just fine.

"Infections and things of that nature. I don't anticipate that, but you never can be too careful," said the doctor.

"I want the best neurosurgeons working on this case," Maurice said. "Money is no object."

Angela rolled her eyes. "Money can't buy everything," she mumbled.

Maurice ignored her. "Because I'm going to need my bride ready for a December wedding."

Kenya smiled up at him. "I love you so much," she whispered.

Maurice kissed the back of her hand gently and said, "I love you more than you'll ever know."

Epilogue

"And the Carolina Panthers are headed back to the NFC championship game," the announcer said. "Bring on the Dallas Cowboys!"

Kenya, who was sitting in the luxury box with the other team wives and girlfriends, leapt to her feet and cheered wildly. The fact that she could stand was nothing short of miraculous. It had taken one six-hour surgery to remove the bullet from her spine, six months of rehabilitation to learn to walk again, and physical therapy to rebuild lost muscle. And at her side the entire time had been her soon-to-be-husband. Kenya had no idea how he'd been able to stay by her side with the grueling schedule of training camp in Spartanburg. But every night, he'd been right by her side, helping her with her exercises and giving her encouragement when she wanted to give up.

Kenya had even told him to leave her alone. One night, after she'd had a rough day, she'd refused to see Maurice when he arrived at the rehabilitation center. But Maurice wouldn't be deterred. He'd forced his way into her room. "What's going on?" he'd asked.

"I said I didn't want to see you," she'd snapped, then turned her back to him.

"I know what the nurse said, but I'm here and I'm not leaving," he'd replied.

"Will you stop treating me like a charity case? What if I never walk again?"

He'd sat on the edge of the bed and placed his hand on her back. "That's the pain talking. I know this is hard . . ."

"You don't know a damned thing. You're walking. You didn't get shot in the back. I did. What happens when you want a woman who can walk, dance, and make love to you without pain? I'm not going to wait for you to—"

"You think I'm going to leave you? Kenya, you can't believe that. You can't think that I'm going to leave you when you need me the most."

She'd gingerly turned on her side and looked at him. Tears had shone in her eyes and had threatened to spill over. "There's no way you can say that. We don't know the future, and if I'm in a wheelchair for the rest of my life, you're going to tire of me having to depend on you. You're going to grow to resent me."

"Stop pitying yourself. You're going to walk again, and I'll never resent you. Damn it, I love you, and nothing can change that." Maurice had lifted Kenya from the bed, gently placing her on the floor. "You can do this, babe. You can and will walk again."

He'd held her hands, and they'd taken baby steps. "You'll be dancing in my arms in December."

Kenya hadn't believed it at the time, but now she was standing and ready to dance at her wedding, which was just one week away.

After the game, Kenya stood outside of Bank of America Stadium, among the fans waiting for Maurice. It had taken her awhile to be able to stand in a crowd without looking over her shoulder. Lauryn was locked away in the Mecklenburg County Detention Center, having been charged with aggravated assault and attempted murder. Kenya and Maurice had pleaded with the judge to deny Lauryn's bail, and their wish had been granted. The trial was scheduled for early next year, but Kenya wasn't worried about that. Right now all she could think about was her New Year's Eve nuptials.

The crowd roared as Maurice was the first man through the tunnel. He pumped his fist in the air and scanned the fans for Kenya's smiling face. Finding her, he hopped the barrier and pulled her into his arms.

"You were so good, baby!" she exclaimed.

"I know. But all I could think about was doing this," he said, then kissed Kenya with a fiery passion that made both of them shudder.

The fans around the couple cheered and whistled at them.

"Ready to go?" Maurice asked when their lips parted.

"Oh yes. I'm ready to go and ready to be yours forever," said Kenya.

He scooped Kenya up as if she were a bride to be carried over the threshold. "I like the sound of that."

And then they were off to begin their lives together, putting the past where it belonged—behind them.

Check Out These Other
Dafina Novels

Look For These Other
Dafina Novels

Available Wherever Books Are Sold!

Check out our website at www.kensingtonbooks.com.